JOHN COLVILLE

The author was born in 1915. Educated at Harrow and Trinity College, Cambridge, where he won a Senior Scholarship and first class Honours in history, he passed the Diplomatic Service exam at an unusually early age. He was a close friend and associate of Churchill, whose trustee and executor he became. He served as a fighter pilot in the R.A.F. and took part in the D-day operation. As Private Secretary to the Queen when she was Princess Elizabeth, he married one of her ladies-in-waiting, Lady Margaret Egerton, and has two sons and a daughter.

He is at present chairman of the Ottoman Bank and an honorary fellow of Churchill College, Cambridge, where his diaries are lodged.

Sir John Colville is the author of eight previous books including FOOTSTEPS IN TIME and THE CHURCHILLIANS.

VOLUME ONE: 1939–OCTOBER 1941 is also published by Sceptre.

'Fascinating, witty and (in wartime) illegal . . . sharper than any memoirs, it includes outspoken biographical notes'

Richard Mayne, Encounter

'Valuable, authoritative, entertaining. This is by far the best picture of Churchill that exists'

David Hunt, The Times

'Honest, trenchant and compulsive reading'

Time Out

'Riveting . . . (has the) outstanding merit of personal honesty . . . As interesting and varied a life as could be conceived'

Elizabeth Longford, Literary Review

'Sir John has shrewd observations and revealing stories about other great figures of the war – Eisenhower, Montgomery, Bomber Harris on the military side and Roosevelt, Eden, Attlee and Stalin on the political side. His descriptions of London under German bombing are terse, accurate and vivid . . . There is no better portrait of Churchill at the height of his powers'

Drew Middleton, New York Times

'A thousand gleams of humour and humanity, of the unexpected and the bizarre'
Kenneth Rose, Sunday Telegraph

'The daily journal of an acute observer can give "the flavour of the time" . . . if he is indiscreet, clever, candid and percipient. In all these respects Sir John Colville is an undoubted success'
Robert Blake, Financial Times

'Conveys that sense of being in a grandstand seat in those perilous times'
Russell Lewis, Daily Mail

'Valuable and immensely readable'
Douglas Johnson, New Society

'His diary will take its place in our historical literature'
John Grigg, The Listener

'Peppered with fresh anecdotes . . . A portrait of Churchill that is incomparably intimate and vivid'
Alistair Cooke, The New Yorker

'This great work will last, will be read and re-read . . . ranks not merely as a diary but as a work of art'
James Downey, Irish Times

John Colville

THE FRINGES OF POWER
Downing Street Diaries 1939–1955

Volume Two: October 1941–1955

Copyright © 1985, 1987 Hodder and Stoughton Ltd.

First published in Great Britain in 1985 by Hodder and Stoughton Ltd. in one volume (including part one *1939–October 1941*)

Sceptre edition 1987

Sceptre is an imprint of Hodder and Stoughton Paperbacks, a division of Hodder and Stoughton Ltd.

British Library C.I.P.

Colville, John, *1915–*
   The fringes of power: Downing Street diaries 1939–1955.
   Vol. 2, October 1941–1955
   1. Colville, John, *1915–*
   2. Private secretaries – Great Britain – Biography
   3. Diplomats – Great Britain – Biography
   I. Title
   941.082′092′4   DA585.C64

   ISBN 0-340-40336-5

Printed and bound in Great Britain for Hodder and Stoughton Paperbacks, a division of Hodder and Stoughton Ltd., Mill Road, Dunton Green, Sevenoaks, Kent (Editorial Office: 47 Bedford Square, London, WC1 3DP) by Richard Clay Ltd., Bungay, Suffolk. Photoset by Rowland Phototypesetting Ltd., Bury St Edmunds, Suffolk.

ACKNOWLEDGMENTS

I am indebted to the executors of the estate of the late Miss Helen Waddell for the reproduction of her verse on p. 156.

Miss Sheila Legat kindly typed the many thousand words of my manuscript diaries twenty-five years ago and I am grateful to her, as I am to Miss Joyce Macleod who with unfaltering accuracy retyped them for publication together with the narrative and the notes included in this volume. I am also much indebted to Mr Hilary Rubinstein of A. P. Watt & Co., to Mr Thomas C. Wallace of W. W. Norton & Co. and by no means least to Mr Ion Trewin of Hodder and Stoughton whom I have discovered to be the eighth Pillar of Wisdom.

CONTENTS

Preface 11

PART TWO: October 1941–August 1945

 1. The Other Ranks   October 1941–January 1942 15
 2. The Troop Decks   January–February 1942 21
 3. Training in South Africa   February–
    December 1942 43
 4. Marking Time   January 1943–Summer 1943 63
 5. Back to the Fold   September 1943–January 1944 71
 6. Anzio and the Blitz Renewed   February–
    March 1944 89
 7. Count-down to OVERLORD   April–May 1944 103
 8. Operational Interlude   May 20th–August 2nd, 1944 115
 9. Second Quebec Conference   August–September
    1944 129
10. Victory Deferred   October–November 1944 153
11. Drama in Athens   December 1944 165
12. Build-up to Yalta   January 1945 185
13. Appeasing Stalin   February 1945 197
14. Across the Rhine   March 1945 207
15. Victory and Chaos   April 1945 225
16. Party Politics Renewed   May–June 1945 241
17. End of War Coalition 257

PART THREE: October 1945–October 1951

18. Pastures New   October 1945–October 1951 267

PART FOUR: October 1951–April 1955

19. "Churchill is Back"   283
20. New York and Washington   January 1953   315
21. The Prime Minister's Stroke   327
22. The Bermuda Conference   345
23. Visit to the U.S.A. and Canada   June 1954   357
24. The Prime Minister's Resignation   373

APPENDICES

Appendix 1. The Coronation of Queen Elizabeth II   383
Appendix 2. The Suez Crisis 1956–7   389
Appendix 3. Postscript to Suez   395

Biographical Notes   401
Glossary   435
Index   437

PREFACE

As a Third Secretary in the Diplomatic Service, aged twenty-four, I was seconded to 10 Downing Street shortly after the outbreak of the Second World War to be an Assistant Private Secretary to Neville Chamberlain, the Prime Minister. I kept a diary in which I chronicled the hopes and plans (mostly disastrous in the event) to which I listened during that gloomy and, except at sea, inactive winter of 1939–40.

When the Government changed, in May 1940, I found myself serving a new master, Winston Churchill. My experiences during the stormy and dramatic summer of 1940 and the first tense nine months of 1941 were recorded day by day and recently published in Volume One of the paperback edition of this book.

I found it intolerable to bask too long in comparative safety and comfort when most of my friends and contemporaries were in uniform. Having two brothers, one in the navy and the other in the army, I thought that joining the air force would be at once symmetrical and exciting. Moreover, as Churchill, himself a former Hussar, had told me that the R.A.F. was "the cavalry of modern war", seeking to enlist in it seemed my best chance of escaping from the sometimes stifling atmosphere of Whitehall. As physically fit as could be desired, I was a little too short-sighted to qualify as a pilot, though I did not need spectacles (and still do not). So I hit on the bright idea of having contact lenses, then a fairly new device, fitted at my own expense and offering myself to the R.A.F. as an experimental guinea-pig. The R.A.F. fell for the bait and so, with the powerful and persuasive advocacy of Clementine Churchill, did the Prime Minister.

This second volume of my diaries begins by describing the sharp and in many ways wholesome shock which I received from the contrast between my life as a somewhat pampered member of the Prime Minister's staff and as an Aircraftsman 2nd Class in the mess-decks of an overcrowded troop-ship. The latter was not described in detail in the hard-back edition of the book and is now published for the first time.

After two years in the R.A.F. I was recalled to 10 Downing Street and thenceforward, apart from an exciting interlude in 1944, flying fighter planes in Operation OVERLORD, I was at various times in the next twelve years close to the centre of power and not always just on the fringes. Thus this second volume of my diaries is partly a record of contrasts and partly an unpremeditated tribute to the greatest statesman Europe, perhaps indeed the world, produced in the twentieth century. It was my good fortune that he treated me for some twenty-five years as a close friend and confidant, attaching no significance to a forty-year age gap. He said to me: "One day you must write about all these things we have seen together." This excuses, I hope, the occasionally critical accounts I had written many years before. Since many of those mentioned in these pages, well-known names at the time, are liable to be unfamiliar to later generations, I have included biographical notes at the end of this volume, as I did in Volume One, and have marked those concerned with asterisks in the text *.

PART TWO

OCTOBER 1941– AUGUST 1945

ONE

THE OTHER RANKS
OCTOBER 1941–JANUARY 1942

"How old are you?" asked Winston Churchill when I was about to leave 10 Downing Street.

"Twenty-six," I replied.

"At twenty-six Napoleon commanded the armies of Italy."

"Pitt was Prime Minister at twenty-four."

"On that round you win," admitted the sixty-six-year-old Prime Minister.

It was a rare triumph to score against him by repartee.

The shock I experienced in change of life-style was volcanic. At one moment I was living in luxury, at least by war-time standards, and basking in the Prime Minister's favour. A few days later I was sleeping on the floor of an unfurnished flat off Regent's Park, an Aircraftsman 2nd Class at the Aircrew Receiving Centre known in the R.A.F., not at all affectionately, as Arsy-Tarsy. We were fed, by no means lavishly, in the Zoo. The pay was two shillings a day,[1] but the Treasury, with surprising generosity, decided to make up the balance of the £400 a year I had been earning at 10 Downing Street.

After a fortnight of injections, kitting out in uniform and total boredom I was drafted with a group of fellow-aspirants for flying duties to an Initial Training Wing at Cambridge. On arrival in those familiar surroundings, I was sitting patiently in one of the courts at Magdalene College, with my heavy white kit-bag beside

---

[1] Raised to 2/6d when I was promoted to Leading Aircraftsman.

me, when I saw approaching two ancient Fellows wearing long gowns, top-hats and high starched collars. One I recognised as that paladin of good English, Sir Arthur Quiller-Couch. The other, sporting an Old Etonian bow-tie, was the erudite Foreign Office Librarian, Sir Stephen Gaselee. I rose and greeted him. He looked at me in my aircraftsman's uniform and shuddered. "What," he exclaimed, "has the Diplomatic Service come to?" Quiller-Couch nodded mournfully and they passed on.

Eight weeks of drill, gymnastics and rugger on "the Backs", coupled with elementary lessons in navigation and signals, passed without great tribulation, even though we slept on palliasses, four in a room, in the neo-Gothic extension of St John's College and spent tedious hours during the night as sentries on the Bridge of Sighs. I never discovered what we were protecting and against whom. I passed one or two guard-duties learning, by moonlight, several of Shakespeare's sonnets from a small volume given to me by Gay Margesson and easily pushed into a tunic pocket on the approach of an officer or N.C.O. When not on guard I could escape to dine with friendly dons at Trinity and other colleges, though there were those who looked askance at anything so common as an A.C.2 at the High Table.

I set that right on discovering that Bachelors of Arts in the armed forces could be admitted to the degree of Master of Arts for a fee of £1. When I duly presented myself in the Senate House, the Vice Chancellor announced in Latin (using the old pronunciation) that I was the first man ever to be admitted to that degree in the uniform of the Other Ranks of His Majesty's forces. So I acquired the right to dine at the Trinity High Table free of charge four times a year and presumably still can.

That afternoon I had arranged to play squash with a fellow airman in a court belonging to St John's College. It was the afternoon in the week when the College reserved the courts for its R.A.F. infiltrators. When we arrived at the court we had booked, two undergraduates were occupying it. We pointed out politely that it was reserved for us. One of the usurpers replied rudely, using several four letter words, that he had no intention of being ousted by common airmen whose presence in St John's was in any case unwelcome to him and his friends. With all the pomposity I could muster, I said: "You are addressing in this uncivilised manner a Master of Arts of this University, and unless you leave the court at once, I shall inform the President of your College of your disgraceful manners and indiscipline." They left. The £1 my M.A. had cost me seemed money well-spent.

After a short Christmas leave with my family at Helperby in Yorkshire, regaled by my Uncle Clive Coates' 1870 and even 1848 pre-phylloxera port, I was sent in the freezing days of an exceptionally cold January to a bleak embarkation camp at Padgate, near Warrington in Lancashire. Although disinclined to believe, at that stage in my career, that the pen was mightier than the sword, I recorded my subsequent experiences in a new diary for 1942.

Thursday, January 1st–Monday, January 5th
On December 31st I left Cambridge, with mixed feelings of elation and regret, for Padgate, a vast and dreary camp near Warrington, Lancashire.

I have now been there nearly a week, living in a wooden hut in acute discomfort and spending most of the time in long queues at the Naafi. Most nights I have been to Manchester, to dine and read Robert Graves' *I, Claudius* at a hotel, and on Saturday I managed to get thirty-six hours' leave and so proceeded to Madeley,[1] where I stayed the night with Aunt Nancy and Hugh. Nevertheless I hope never to be in a drearier or more depressing camp than Padgate, nor to be quartered with more obscene and utterly uninteresting companions. They mostly came from the I.T.W.s[2] at Torquay and at Scarborough. There is one nice observer from Cambridge, with whom I have made friends.

This introduction is much less entertaining than the one I planned in the train last night; but then that was after dinner.

Tuesday, January 6th
We do nothing at Padgate and there is no discipline. This morning it was proposed we should do P.T., but half the occupants of

[1] A house in Staffordshire belonging to my grandfather, which my father and mother shared for most of the war with my mother's elder sister, Lady Annabel Dodds* and her husband.
[2] Initial Training Wings.

my hut did not parade at all, and of those who did a fair proportion, including myself, absconded at the door of the gymnasium, "browned off" with the cold and the waiting, and adjourned to the Naafi where we fought in a queue for half an hour.

I had lunch in the camp for the first time. I dislike having to bring my own knife, fork and spoon, but I was rewarded by finding beef-steak pudding.

I got out of the camp at 4.00, half an hour earlier than is permitted, by walking in the middle of a group of Sergeant Pilots. Peggy[1] had told me that Ruth Wood[2] was at Knowsley and so I rang up and was invited to dine. I was given a lift by a passing Wing Commander almost to the door.

Knowsley is a large Victorian house standing in an immense park and, though not beautiful, is less repulsive than many houses of its date. I had tea with Lady Derby[3] who is stone deaf, speaks with a guttural accent and has a disconcerting habit of understanding one to say the exact opposite of what one has said. Ruth was also there and Lord Derby hobbled in on a stick later. The conversation was a little difficult, e.g.:

Lady D.:   Perhaps you would like to have a bath before dinner.
Self: There is nothing I should like more; there are none at Padgate.
Lady D.:   Ach, you are very lucky then.
Lord D.:   He says there are *not* any, my dear.
Lady D.:   So he will not want one.

Ruth led me away to another room where we gossiped, largely about Mary Roxburghe[4] and Zara[5] (our only friends in common)

---

[1] Margaret, Marchioness of Crewe.
[2] Ruth Primrose, granddaughter of Lord Derby and of the former Liberal Prime Minister, Lord Rosebery. Married to Charles Wood, later 2nd Earl of Halifax.
[3] Daughter of the Hanoverian "Double Duchess", well known in late Victorian times, who first married the 7th Duke of Manchester (Lady Derby's father) and then the prominent politician, "Harty-Tarty", 8th Duke of Devonshire.
[4] My mother's half sister, married to 9th Duke of Roxburghe.
[5] Mrs Ronald Strutt, later Mrs Peter Cazalet.

till dinner-time. I had a luxurious bath and then dined alone with Ruth, since Lord D. has been unwell and wanted to feed alone. We talked of the P.M. and Lord Halifax.*

After dinner Lady Derby summoned Ruth and me into the presence and we talked politics for half an hour until Lord Derby signified his wish to go to bed. In a moment of aphasia and under the influence of the very excellent champagne with which I had been regaled, I made the worst gaffe of my life. I quoted P. J. Grigg* as saying that David Margesson,* whom Lord Derby had been praising, was the only Secretary of State for War since Haldane who had been any good at all. The words were hardly out of my mouth before I remembered Oliver Stanley,* and I recovered lamely by saying that P. J. was of course thinking of Hore-Belisha* and Eden.[1] Ruth afterwards said she did not think Lord Derby had taken it in. I trust that she was right.[2]

I went by taxi, for which Lord Derby insisted on paying, to Liverpool and caught the last train to Padgate.

Wednesday, January 7th

Today the almost unbroken bright weather which has character-ised this autumn and winter gave way to fog. We were disturbed at 9.00 a.m. by an irate Corporal who wanted to know if we thought we were living in a hotel. This had no effect, but the report of a hut inspection did, and we crawled reluctantly from beneath our heaps of blankets. We had an F.F.I. (Free From Infection) inspection, intended to ensure that no one had contrac-ted V.D. in the last week and a certain sign that our departure is imminent.

At 2.30 we stacked our kit-bags for removal and I did a little voluntary hard labour in loading them on to sixty-foot lorries. There are 600 pilots and observers going in this draft and each has two kit-bags, full of flying kit, etc. which will not be wanted on the voyage. A third we shall carry in addition to our packs.

---

[1] Later Lord Avon.*
[2] Lord Derby himself had been Secretary of State for War from 1916 to 1918, and his son, Oliver Stanley, held the post between January and May 1940.

I went to Warrington after 4.00 p.m., did some successful shopping and then caught a train to Manchester where I spent the evening in comfort at the Queen's Hotel.

TWO

THE TROOP DECKS
JANUARY–FEBRUARY 1942

Thursday, January 8th
We paraded at 9.00 in full marching dress. During a long wait on the platform the Padgate band played to us, jazz at first and then, as we entrained and steamed away, "Auld Lang Syne".

We went to Liverpool and lorries took us from the station to the docks. Together with numerous ground staff and several thousand soldiers, the six hundred of us went on board the Orient liner *Otranto* (20,000 tons), painted grey and carrying a Bofors gun in the bows. Our quarters are, at first sight, horrifying; we live between decks, messing eighteen at the tables which might hold twelve comfortably and slinging our hammocks over the tables. There are not enough hammocks and so some of us will have to sleep on mattresses on the floor. There is very little room to move or to stow one's belongings.

After a preliminary and somewhat daunting inspection, I went up on deck hoping devoutly that the sea would be smooth and seasickness rare. It is a lot to hope in January. We are told that we shall be from six to eight weeks at sea and so should have time to get used to these conditions, but the seamen say this is an exaggeration.

I found a saloon aft and was sitting there when seized by a Warrant Officer to be one of the guards on the gangway tonight. After tea in our pig-sty, with the added disadvantage of having to wash up our utensils in a tub on deck (where I could see

nothing) I put on the arm band of an S.P.[1], strapped on a revolver
and put in a number of turns of duty on the gangway, interspersed
with occasional visits to the big, badly lighted saloon. On guard
from 2.00 a.m. until 4.00 a.m. as well as from 8.00 to 10.00
p.m. I think I shall take to drink.

Friday, January 9th

During my guard I had political arguments with a foreman of
stevedores and my fellow guard, a Welsh R.A.F. electrician. I
slept in the saloon, spreading my hammock over a number of
hard chairs.

Yes, the prospect is gloomy. Our space between decks is
unnaturally overcrowded and the ceiling is very low. A large
cage rails off one of the holds which is covered above by a
tarpaulin. The whole scene resembles very closely the living
quarters in the *Victory*.

This is the first time that I have known real discomfort without
any escape which money or influence or friends can provide.
There is nothing to be done but to accept the situation and I
really feel quite cheerful, considerably more so than most of my
companions. But I never expected to experience worse than
Padgate; and Padgate was luxury in comparison.

We had lunch at 12.00 hours. It was edible, if not particularly
appetising: a tasteless soup drunk out of our mess tins, boiled
beef with potatoes and multi-coloured, bullet-like peas, and sago
pudding.

The ship left the dock, together with several others, presumably intended for the same convoy, and anchored in the Mersey
ready to sail. It was piercingly cold, but bright and sunny.

I have found two observers who, more lucky than most of us,
have a cabin on an upper deck with a wash basin. They have
agreed to let me shave there, which is as well since below there
are only twelve basins for about four hundred of us.

It is interesting to note how often one hears it said, here and
everywhere, that Russia has turned the scales in this war and
has saved us. It is also noticeable what a trend there seems to

[1] Service Police

be towards the Left, coupled with an almost universal faith in Winston. We were blamed for cold-shouldering Russia before. How short the public memory is!

Saturday, January 10th
I have got a hammock and it is quite comfortable, though cold. Unfortunately they are slung in such close proximity that one is continually bumped and when seasickness starts it will be revolting. Generally speaking the survival of the fittest seems the only possibility.

I feel a constant temptation to dwell on memories of the times when I lived in luxury and had room to move; but this is disastrous as the subsequent awakening to reality is thoroughly disagreeable. It is better to remember that I have never known such squalor and dejection and am never likely to know it again. Also, once we sail the days of blue skies and moderate seas will not be far distant and the intervening period has just got to be survived!

I have not seen any weevils yet, but cockroaches abound.

I am thinking of spreading an alarm that I have seen several rats leaving. As a matter of fact no self-respecting rat would stay.

We got under way at 1.00 p.m., steaming very slowly out of the Mersey into a silvery sea with scarcely a ripple.

Chief sensation this afternoon is boredom. The after-saloon is crowded and noisy; the deck (we are not allowed on the top two decks) is cold in spite of the sun; someone is asleep in my corner in our cattle-truck below, so I am sitting on deck, well muffled up, reading George Meredith's *Richard Feverel* and enjoying it despite frozen feet.

We seem to be heading a slow convoy, escorted by a submarine chaser, and are presumably bound for the Clyde to pick up our real convoy.

The queues at the canteens are so long as to make entrance impossible, though there appears to be an unlimited supply of chocolate, etc. for those who can bear to wait long enough. We had an orange for tea, the first I have seen for many months.

Four of my companions have contrived to get a cabin by

collusion with – and payment to – a number of merchant seamen, of whom about a hundred are on board travelling to the Cape to pick up ships. I could have been "in on it" but decided that life in a hammock, though cramped and in many ways distasteful, is not an experience to be missed. I shall probably regret my decision before long. Slept well, but cold in spite of a hot salt-water bath.

Sunday, January 11th

After breakfast, which is at 7.00, walked round the deck with an eighteen-year-old airman called Potts, who messes opposite me and wants to be a farmer (on a big and scientific scale!) after the war. As dawn broke we saw land and before long discovered that we were entering Belfast Lough. We anchored there, surrounded by men of war and merchantmen.

Went to a voluntary church parade at 9.00. It was held in a room too dark to see and was not very well or inspiringly conducted.

So I went to the R.C. Mass at 10.15, which was a very different matter; well and reverently done in the after-saloon and containing an address well suited to the occasion. Emphasis was laid on the fact that today is the festival of the Holy Family and this theme was used simply and tellingly as a comfort to those who are leaving their homes and families.

I then was impressed to act as escort to two airmen on a charge for smoking on deck last night after the black-out. They each got seven days' detention. We – that is the escort – conducted them to the cells which struck me as more comfortable than our normal quarters.

Books are a wonderful refuge. When I open *Richard Feverel* I soon lose myself in Meredith's ornate prose. He has a great capacity for kindling the imagination.

Chocolate and cigarettes are sold in abundance, a consolation to many for the other mortifications of the flesh. They have mostly overeaten grossly of the former and I fear the worst if the sea is rough; but we show no signs of leaving Belfast tonight.

It is boring that the whole R.A.F. should have but one

adjective at their disposal. Sexual relations are ascribed to the most unlikely objects with wearisome frequency.

Monday, January 12th
Now we really are off. We moved in the early hours of this morning and when I came on deck I could see Ireland to port and Scotland to starboard. The sea was still smooth except for a gentle swell, but as the day wore on the northerly wind freshened and the sea roughened considerably. We lost sight of land but appear to be proceeding almost due north.

Seasickness is widespread but practised with discretion, I am glad to say. Personally I feel aggressively well so far and am enjoying the rising sea and the strong breeze.

Owing to the number sick I am on guard again. From my post on the lowest deck I can see fifteen ships of the convoy, painted grey, cutting their way through the seas. There seem to be about twenty in all, mostly big ships but slow (the speed of the convoy is only eleven knots, I gather from one of the crew), and we are escorted by about four destroyers and a light cruiser. These ships are a fine sight, and were especially so this morning when the sky was blue and the clouds reddened by the rising sun. Tonight, as the weather deteriorates, mist is enveloping us. Soon it will be dark.

These guards are a nuisance. I have been on from 1.00 to 3.00 p.m. and I am on again from 7.00 to 9.00 p.m., from 1.00 to 3.00 a.m. and from 7.00 to 9.00 a.m. Also the people in whose cabin I shave have been deprived of it, to make way for the crews of the Bofors and other guns on board, so that my one ease has been removed. Heavy roll developing.

Tuesday, January 13th
Quite a big sea was running during the night and this ship rolls and pitches abominably (whence the poor quality of this handwriting). This morning the force has gone out of the wind, leaving a clear sky, a pleasant if cold breeze and a heavy swell. Seasickness continues unabated, and on the whole my watches on the after-deck last night showed me that the army are more

revolting than the R.A.F. Personally I feel extremely well so
far, but constipated.

The overcrowding is being made worse by the continual
putting out of bounds to troops of further lavatories, bathrooms,
etc. This is causing discontent as it is felt that the officers,
W.A.A.F.s, etc. have two whole decks to themselves, with
lounges and dining-rooms, while we are living in impossibly
cramped spaces. An opinion I have heard many times is that the
prisoners in the *Altmark*[1] were lucky in comparison!

I spent nearly all day on deck, where it grew increasingly
cold, but was one of the few who felt well enough for meals.

I noticed last night, by the Pole Star, that we had changed
our course to the westward and today we seem to be going
slightly south of west – a welcome surprise.

Our curtain of destroyers remains, spread round the convoy
at some distance from it; all our guns are manned (and each ship
in the convoy seems well armed: we have a Bofors, a 4.5-inch
in the stern and a good many Lewis guns); but so far we have
seen no periscopes or Focke-Wulfs. *Absint!* Life on a raft is the
only existence I can imagine more abject than our present state.

After a hot salt-water bath, I climbed into my hammock about
7.30 and dreamt beautiful dreams.

Wednesday, January 14th
(As I was writing this the raft on which I was sitting broke adrift
and threw me on to the deck.)

This morning we were so crowded that it was difficult to get
up: hammocks slung so close that they almost touch, in front
and behind as well as at the side; someone asleep on the
mess-table beneath, somebody else on the floor nearby. We all
have to sleep in our clothes in case of emergency and one can't
help feeling filthy, being always dressed in the same increasingly
soiled garments.

I watched the sun rise out of the sea on a cloudless horizon.

---

[1] German ship from which British prisoners, taken from ships sunk by the
Graf von Spee and confined in holds below the water-mark, were rescued in
1940 by a daring raid into a Norwegian fjord.

We are now steaming due south, which is an unexpected pleasure. Wind S.W., moderate; sea quiet with a slight swell. Speed about thirteen knots.

At 10.00 every morning we muster on deck at our boat stations, wearing life belts. Nausea has been so vanquished that everybody is singing this morning. Sentimental songs, such as "Home, Sweet Home" seem to be thought appropriate, also the usual "I, I, Ippy", "My eyes are dim, I cannot see", "Rolling home", and the thing, of which I don't know the name, about getting "no promotion this side of the ocean".

There are 3,500 troops and airmen on board, apart from merchant seamen passengers (on their way to pick up a ship at Durban) and the crew. I am told this ship usually carries 1,000 troops. Nasty night in prospect.

Thursday, January 15th
We rolled a lot during the night; my kit-bag fell with a resounding crash; all the hammocks seemed to foul each other; I have the symptoms of a heavy cold, which is not surprising considering the confined space and the numbers infected. Long, moaning hoots on the siren about midnight showed something was amiss.

Apparently our steering went wrong. Awoke to find we were on our own, having drawn away from the convoy to avoid collision. Gradually more ships appeared and by 11.00 we seemed to be rejoining the rest of the herd. The destroyers were careering about like sheepdogs. Wind S.W., moderate. Squally.

During the afternoon the escort performed strange contortions, destroyers chasing each other round in circles while the convoy remained almost stationary. No explanation. Finished *Richard Feverel.* Wind freshening.

Friday, January 16th
We must be about the latitude of Bordeaux. It is much warmer and the sun shines spasmodically.

This morning we had a little excitement. I was sitting aft reading George Eliot's *The Mill on the Floss* when an aircraft was sighted and we were told to take cover. I managed to do so in such a way that I could see. The aircraft, presumably a

Focke-Wulf Condor, came nearer, we fired several shots at it, and it sheered off. However it has seen the convoy and we may be attacked later. *(11.45 a.m.)*

5.15 p.m.: This incident has had tiresome consequences. The convoy has turned west instead of proceeding south, which will, I suppose, delay our progress. Secondly, we have all been kept below decks this afternoon, while the crew are at action stations, except for fifteen minutes' airing under cover on one of the lower decks. Our mess tables are uncomfortable for long periods at a stretch.

Saturday, January 17th
We have got a battleship with us this morning. She seems to be of the Queen Elizabeth.[1] class. Our course is now about S.S.W.; cloudy, sea moderate.

The day's routine for me is usually as follows:

6.00 a.m.:   Lights turned on.
6.30 a.m.:   Get out of hammock, fold same, put on trousers and jacket.
7.00 a.m.:   Breakfast. Wash utensils in salt water on deck. Leave fetid atmosphere below and go on deck.
9.45 a.m.:   Muster at boat stations. Inspected. Hang about till 11.00, falling in and out periodically.
12.00:   Lunch. Spend afternoon on deck.
4.30 p.m.:   Shave. Fresh water is only available twice a day and crowd is excessive in morning.
6.00 p.m.:   Tea. Washing up precarious in dark.
9.30 p.m.:   Lights out.

Although I in no sense regret the course I have taken, I already begin to feel the absence of companions with whom I can really talk. The majority of the prospective air-crew on this ship, though amiable and always ready to be helpful, are poorly educated and lacking in experience. There are some, whom I

[1] She was, however, H.M.S. *Resolution* of the Royal Sovereign Class.

have not yet got to know well, whose standard of education is higher – indeed I have found one reading the second part of Goethe's *Faust*. Probably this is more noticeable to me in the confined space of a ship where there are so few activities and so little, beside discomfort, that we share in common. I found enough people to make a game of poker and gambled happily from tea till lights out.

Sunday, January 18th

Much warmer. Presumably we are somewhere in the latitude of the coast of Portugal. Went to the R.C. service at 10.00 in the Recreation Room (as the stuffy after-saloon is called).

The rumours have to be heard to be believed; where we are, where we are going, etc.; mostly as ridiculous as they are unfounded.

It is difficult to ensure the safety and cleanliness of my contact lenses in these conditions and they are a constant nuisance.

Poker again tonight, but the players were mostly very indifferent and the game palled.

Somebody stole my hammock and so I had to steal somebody else's (immoral but inevitable in this nest of jackdaws) and it was a singularly ill-shaped one.

Monday, January 19th

Course south. Sea smooth. Very warm and raining. Overcoats to be left off. Where we can stow them I can't think.

The rain cleared enough to enable us to do P.T. on the upper deck for about half an hour. The exercise was sorely needed.

In the afternoon I found a young man whose family had been in the Indian Army for generations. I talked to him for long and thought that if he represented the British in India that genus has been much misrepresented.

After playing poker, I thought the atmosphere so repellent that I went up on deck to sleep, slinging my hammock on some convenient hooks. Much groping in the dark.

Tuesday, January 20th
Woke up at 6.00 to see the beginnings of a truly glorious sunrise.
   It is hot now and the water is deep blue like the Bay of Naples.
I suppose we are approaching the tropics.
   Finished *The Mill on the Floss*, which has fine passages but
some "longueurs".
   We are evidently going to do P.T. every morning now, which
is a good thing. A series of lectures is also being arranged.
   Am struggling with *Faust (Erster Teil)* which I have borrowed
from an ex-undergraduate of Cardiff University, called Coles.
   Slung my hammock on deck again, but after midnight we were
all turned out as the C.O. thinks the hammocks would be in
the way in case of an emergency. Unlike most people, I was
weak-minded enough to obey and go below.

Wednesday, January 21st
We are in the tropics now and lime juice is being issued.
   Am reading Negley Farson's *Behind God's Back*, a vivid, if
slightly John Guntheresque, description of Africa. It contains a
useful essay on South African politics. I wish I could meet Smuts,
but fear there can be no chance. Together with Roosevelt,
Winston and Chiang Kai-Shek, he is one of the four great men
alive today. The Führer, etc., may be clever; but they can't be
great because they are bad.
   Though the sun shines warmly, there is a pleasant breeze and
the heat is no greater than that of an English summer.
   Slept for'ard, on one of the lower uncovered decks, so as to
look up at the stars. As I came up on deck late, after playing
poker, most of the best places had been taken and I had to make
shift as best I could in a confined space between some rafts and
a coil of rope. Though cold, it was worth it to escape the
atmosphere below.

Thursday, January 22nd
Everybody is busy preparing their tropical kit as we are to
parade in it tomorrow. Nearly everybody was in khaki this
afternoon, in spite of the fresh breeze. I sewed red propellers
on to my khaki tunic; I should not have made a good seamstress.

Those immediately surrounding me are: the would-be gentle-man farmer (Potts), two prospective chemists (one with a very pronounced cockney accent of the ugliest type), an apprentice to a butcher, the son of a doctor, a commercial traveller (our Corporal in charge of this mess table) and a clerk from the Westminster Bank at Runcorn, who laments leaving his bank.

Friday, January 23rd

We are all in tropical kit today, wearing topis. I got up from my very hard bed on the deck before 6.00 and then had a hot salt-water bath so as to be reasonably clean before putting on clean clothes – the first for weeks. I hope never again to be so consistently dirty for so long.

But topis or no topis, it can apparently be cold in the tropics and today I thought it was bitter.

I have now taken to sleeping on the deck every day after lunch. This afternoon I had a long conversation with two amiable balloon barrage men on their way to the Middle East. They want to know what will happen if Russia invades and occupies Germany! Such is optimism.

Shoals of flying fish are scuttling away from the ship.

We only get fragments of news occasionally by wireless. This afternoon I heard that Walter Sickert and the Duke of Connaught were dead. The latter was a striking link with the past – godson of the Iron Duke.

Saturday, January 24th

The muggy atmosphere has given me a splitting headache which persisted with greater or lesser intensity throughout the day. I finished Farson's *Behind God's Back*, which is the most ungrammatical writing I have ever come across. It is an irritating method of seeking for effect.

We expect to reach Freetown tomorrow. This evening we have all been issued with quinine; and, in case the entrances to the harbour should be mined, the paravanes have been dropped overboard.

Have started *Nicholas Nickleby*.

Sunday, January 25th

We arrived at Freetown in the early afternoon, thirteen days out from Belfast. It is terribly hot and I feel drowsy and headachy – in fact quite unable to appreciate the niggers[1] diving overboard for coins.

Finally, at 5.00, went to see the Medical Orderly, found I had a temperature, and so reported "special sick" to the Orderly Room (the normal time for reporting sick being 7.00 a.m.) The Orderly Room was full of people being put on charges for buying fruit from natives.

However, in spite of the temperature, the M.O. was not greatly perturbed and my hopes of spending a (comparatively) comfortable night in the sick ward were dashed.

I slept below, the first time for some days – in deference to the thermometer and in fear of mosquitos. We have all been given more quinine: after all, Sierra Leone is "the white man's grave". The coarse and unutterably dull conversation of the members of my mess deck seated immediately below my hammock (a) kept me awake and (b) made me feel quite Curzonian about the masses. There were no mosquitos – and no black-out.

Monday, January 26th

Heat damnable but tempered by a faint breeze. Spent nearly two hours in a queue to see the M.O. More or less recovered. Lay on the hard deck – and it *is* hard – all day, dividing the time between fitful dozing, *Nicholas Nickleby* and idly watching niggers, whose command of English swearing is remarkable, diving for sixpences (they spurn pennies) in the intervals of singing "I, I, Ippy" in hoarse, unmusical voices.

Discontent is growing. The latest ground for it is the difficulty in procuring drinking water, which keeps on running dry and tastes foul even when procured. The inadequacy of the food is also resented, especially as the officers feed plentifully and well. The merchant seamen, on their way to man the *Aquitania* at

[1] Forty years on the word 'nigger' is offensive. It was not considered so in 1942 and I have refrained from tampering with the original text in order to satisfy the better taste of the 1980s.

Durban, almost organised a mutiny because one of their number, found on a deck from which he was excluded, was set upon and severely manhandled by a party of Marines on the orders of the ship's universally abominated Flight Sergeant.

Tonight there was a concert, under an awning aft, drawing on the talent of the ship's company, which might well have been buried. It was stifling on deck and difficult to sleep.

Tuesday, January 27th
P.T. at 8.40, the first for some days.

We lay all day in Freetown. The convoy is taking some time to get oil and water owing to its size. Sierra Leone is more like the Highlands than my idea of Africa: there is a range of wooded hills and we are too far off to see the tropical growth. But it exuded a steamy mist all day despite the fact that this must be the coolest time of year.

Night is the pleasantest time. This evening I played poker, winning £1 for a change, and then, stripped to the waist, strolled on deck and listened for a while to another ship's concert.

The canteen is very poor. It is sold out of everything desirable such as tinned fruit, and today I waited in a long queue for nothing more appetising than some packets of peppermints.

Wednesday, January 28th
For some reason, perhaps in honour of my twenty-seventh birthday, Sierra Leone was more gracious in its climate this morning and an almost cool breeze blew until the heat of the forenoon choked it.

It was still dark when I fell out of my hammock at 6.15 a.m. Breakfast consisted of some nasty fish, strange-tasting tea and the usual hunks of thinly-buttered bread. I read *Nicholas Nickleby* on deck until the ship's muster – when we are inspected at our boat stations – which is now at 10.30. I am a confirmed Dickens lover now: his satirical power and sense of the ridiculous are unsurpassed, though perhaps this book is less enjoyable than some.

There was a water-bottle inspection at 2.00 p.m., to ensure

that we had not allowed the works to get rusty, and I played poker after that till 4.00.

As the lack of space on deck, and the hardness of the planks, is particularly trying in the long afternoons, I have come to an arrangement with a merchant seaman called Luke whereby, in return for 25 shillings, I am to have the use of his bunk each day after lunch. As there is also a wash basin in his cabin (which is a two-berth one), my cleansing difficulties may be a little eased.

I was on guard this evening, but for twelve hours instead of the usual twenty-four. My first duty, from 7.00 to 9.00 p.m., passed agreeably enough as I was posted on "A" deck and had the best possible view of a film (Joe E. Brown in *A Natural Born Salesman*) being shown to the officers. After being relieved I fetched some tea from the galley – hot tea is very cooling in this climate – and drank it with some forthcoming L.A.C. clerks in the Orderly Room.

Then I was on again from 1.00 to 3.00 a.m. and sat talking to Tony Potts on "A" deck.

Thursday, January 29th

After getting some more tea from the galley, and stealing some rolls, I went to sleep on "B" deck and managed to close my eyes for two and a half hours before being disturbed by reveille.

Finished *Nicholas Nickleby*, rejoicing in the fate of Mr Squeers, delighting in the Cheeryble brothers, but somewhat antagonised by the hero's primness.

I went to Luke's bunk after lunch and slept. It is not too clean and its owner, in defiance of all the regulations and ship's orders, has bought a monkey from one of the nigger bum boats. I suspect he will prove a smelly, if not a germ-carrying companion. Luke is proposing "to get him organised" for sale at Durban. Apparently he bought him for a pair of trousers.

We sailed from Freetown shortly after 3.00 p.m. We steamed out of the harbour into our position, passing the fast ex-French *Louis Pasteur* (with only one funnel completed), the decrepit *Viceroy of India* and the three-funnel *Strathnaver* to starboard. and the *Stirling Castle* and *Britannic* to port. The remainder seem to be ahead of us, but the convoy is now smaller, some of the slower ships having proceeded elsewhere, and I hope faster. The rumour is that we go straight to Durban without touching the Cape.

Lovely fresh breeze on deck. What a contrast to that fetid harbour!

After our usual game of poker I sat on deck for'ard in the moonlight. A man played the harmonium while the hundreds of troops sprawled about the deck sang. It was a much more enjoyable entertainment than the organised concerts at Free-town.

Friday, January 30th

Started the day badly by getting out of my hammock clumsily and cutting myself in an embarrassing place. The Orderly in the hospital, when asked for first aid, said none of the books prescribed bandages for such a wound; however he contrived something.

As a diversion I started reading R. H. Tawney's *Religion and the Rise of Capitalism.*

The convoy is sailing S.S.E. There are less ships than before, but the *Resolution* is back (she nearly ran into us tonight) and we must be making twelve knots or more.

Luke's monkey, though engaging, is too energetic for comfort and I suspect his cleanliness.

Saturday, January 31st

I am reading *Quentin Durward* pari passu with Tawney's book, the latter being too heavy-going to read without respite. The only advantage of this voyage is the gap it is filling in my literary education.

We crossed the equator this afternoon without any ceremony or celebration. It is surprisingly cool, almost chilly.

Sunday, February 1st

Last night the convoy looked magnificent in the light of the full moon. I leant over the rail talking to Coles about Charles I and

Strafford and watching the dozen or so silent ships to port of us.

This morning I went first of all to the R.C. Mass and then, by way of contrast and to exercise my voice in loud singing, to the amorphous C. of E. service.

Today, Luke's monkey, bent on an amorous excursion to the cabin next door, where another monkey resides, climbed out of the porthole and, losing its way, emerged on the deck above. It was captured by a steward who refused to surrender it to its owner and ran off with it to the authorities, by whom it was mercilessly destroyed. Luke, who has Irish blood, hung about all day in search of the wisely elusive steward and ended by knocking down, and severely damaging, the wrong steward. Result: Luke is in the cells (from which he has temporarily broken gaol). Joe, who shares Luke's cabin, secretly agrees with me in welcoming the monkey's disappearance, though we are sorry for Luke. He himself is merely biding his time till we reach Durban and he can take vengeance on the right steward.

Monday, February 2nd
The cloudy equatorial weather has now retreated before clear skies, a refreshing breeze and a sea of Mediterranean blue. Flying fish, glinting silver in the sunlight, rise in shoals or in pairs and skim the waves like partridges rising from a field of turnips.

It is 4.30 as I write and I have been sleeping for two hours in Luke's vacated bunk. At the end of our mess table four hungry youths are devouring tinned pears. It is a constant complaint that we do not get enough to eat (though personally I can well live on what we do get, though its quality is poor) and that the deficiency has to be made up by purchases of tinned fruit from the canteen on the few days that such purchases are possible. Joe brings me up some tea at 4.00 from the merchant seamen's mess.

Our nightly games of poker now attract six players. We sit at the end of one of the long narrow tables, using a blanket as a tablecloth, the table decked with bottles of beer which we drink from the bottle. The play is good-tempered and not unduly high (maximum raise of 1 shilling). I have taught them nearly all, but am not by any means a big winner. Indeed it would embarrass me if I were. We finish the evening with two rounds of jackpots about 9.00 and I am on deck in my hammock by 9.30.

Tuesday, February 3rd
Re-read and greatly enjoyed *Vile Bodies*. Evelyn Waugh is a good antidote to Sir Walter Scott.

One man in our cattle-truck – though fortunately on the other side to me – has been taken suddenly ill. It is thought to be a cerebro-spinal meningitis – in other words the dreaded spotted fever. We are not allowed below except for meals and we are to sleep on "A" deck (the officers' deck). The maddening thing is that we shall presumably be kept in quarantine and not allowed shore-leave at Durban.

Our Corporal I/C No. 50 Mess Table and I slept down below to keep a watch on people's belongings and guard against the rapacity of wandering merchant seamen. An officer assured us that this meningitis is of the non-contagious variety. Nevertheless everybody else was obliged to sleep on deck.

Wednesday, February 4th
We were awoken early and told to parade in the foyer ("foierr", it is pronounced) at the foot of the main staircase. The sight of the Padre, in surplice and hood, gave me the first indication of why we were there. Soon there appeared six of the crew, bearing on their shoulders a flat board covered with the Union Jack. A human figure was outlined beneath the flag. The sufferer from meningitis had died during the night. He was only nineteen.

The Padre read the funeral service, and at the sentence of committing his body unto the deep, the board was tilted and the weighted corpse slid into the sea. Three airmen fainted, one on top of me, whether from the stuffiness of the atmosphere or from horror I do not know.

The scene left a macabre impression. Sorrow for the poor wretch's unsuspecting parents was the sentiment most generally expressed.

There is a good deal of political talk on this ship. It is all Left wing, partly stimulated by envy at the comparative spaciousness and luxury in which the officers are living, but largely, I think, indicative of a general tendency in England today. The success of Russian arms, and a belief that Conservative policy has wilfully antagonised the U.S.S.R. in the past, is partly responsible. There is a good deal of misconception, and a good deal of genuine egalitarian feeling which augurs ill for "the old school tie" and the powers that be – whom nobody seems to accept as being ordained of God.

Tonight I won 30 shillings at poker, which is more than I can do with a good conscience.

Thursday, February 5th
The Trade Winds blow cold and it was disagreeably chilly in my hammock during the night, especially as hammocks do not lend themselves to the sagacious arrangement of blankets in the dark.

One of the oldest of the merchant seamen passengers – he served in troopships in the last war – tells me that of the many ships in which he has sailed this is incomparably the worst. He says all the merchant seamen are unanimous on this point – and they live in very much greater comfort than do we.

The latest grievance is the drinking water which has become contaminated with salt water and is all but undrinkable. Tea made with it is a strange beverage.

Today they are selling oranges at the canteen (luxuries unobtainable in England except by babies) and a dozen of these does much to supplement my diet which mainly consists of thick slabs of bread and margarine; though, in fairness, I must admit we had edible mutton chops for breakfast this morning.

I won another 15 shillings at poker in spite of rash play and mad bluffing.

Friday, February 6th
I slung my hammock below last night as I wanted to wake up early and have a hot salt-water bath, and below the lights automatically wake one up at 6.00. On deck, they say, it was freezing.

Today, except for brief interludes of sunshine, we might be back in the North Atlantic. Grey skies, a rough sea and brief rain squalls combine with a piercing wind to dissipate all idea of the tropics (the Trade Winds, I suppose).

I finished *Quentin Durward* which I should probably not have had the patience to read ashore. I ended by enjoying it, but cannot pretend that Scott's romantic style retains its charms for me, and his wilful perversions of history are trying. Began Trollope's *Vicar of Bullhampton*, a book of which I had never heard.

I still continue to win indecent sums at poker.

It was very cold and rough on deck, despite a greatcoat and a thick pullover.

Saturday, February 7th

The sea has risen a lot and the wind is strong, so that it is assumed we are approaching the Cape of Good Hope. But it is always difficult to find out where we are or when we arrive and any true information is swamped in rumours.

The cold wind grows colder and we are all – except the officers – inadequately clothed in this flimsy khaki tropical kit.

I managed to lose at poker tonight and then braved the elements on deck. But the ordeal of finding – and still more arranging – one's hammock in the black-out is considerable.

Sunday, February 8th

Went to the C. of E. service, which was very vocal but not badly conducted in spite of a limp sermon about Joshua, the son of Nun, and Caleb and a land flowing with milk and honey.

The change back to the heat of summer is startling, though in the wind it is still cold enough for men to lie about swathed in blankets. The main subject of debate is whether we shall land at Durban in khaki or air-force blue; indeed subjects of greater interest are hard to find and the B.B.C. news is (a) dull (b) depressing. As a result one easily falls into semi-sentimental reveries. Today I was sitting on one of the huge cases on deck, gazing at the sea in a gap between two lifeboats, and I began thinking of the many joys, delicious smells, careless ease and secure family happiness, so readily taken for granted. Suddenly, as if to remind me of the grimmer present, the bows of H.M.S. *Resolution*, and then her whole length, surged forward into the space between the lifeboats as she moved forward to take up some new position. That grey camouflaged hull and the 15-inch guns represent a wide gulf in my life, and in the English way of living, between those days of quiet plenty, sight-seeing expeditions, bad bridge and racing pockets, when change was so gradual and small personal problems, such as the vagaries of point-to-point favourites, were the main complications of life, and when a chocolate soufflé seemed the just and natural culmination of a well-spent April day.

Today we have been better fed than before. Indeed there was enough to eat. This may be the result of persistent complaints but is more probably due to our nearing our destination so that food reserves can be used.

Monday, February 9th

We are presumed to be about to round the Cape and part of the convoy is preparing to leave us for Cape Town. Apparently the rough and cold weather we experienced the other day was due to the Trade Winds and not to the Cape.

Am living chiefly on bread and butter and oranges, but thriving and less inclined to dwell on the prospect of beef-steak than most of my fellows.

This morning the M.O. gave us a lecture on V.D., with especial relation to its dangers at Durban, and including a historic résumé. It appears that syphilis was discovered, and brought to Europe, by Christopher Columbus!

Tuesday, February 10th

This morning I finished *The Vicar of Bullhampton*. Though there are novels with more attractive characters, Trollope's are strikingly realistic. They act and react as normal human beings rather than romantic heroes and heroines. The book deserves inclusion among his better-known works.

This morning I saw an albatross. A Squadron Leader spoke to us on the prevalence of enemy spies in South Africa and on the racial animosity of Afrikaaner and Englishman. A very wise precaution as obviously most airmen know nothing of South Africa and Herzog and Malan are not even names to them.

This evening it is just like a summer twilight on the Solent and, sitting on one of the few seats on deck, I am reminded of those evening sails home from Bembridge with a fair reaching wind and a gentle ruffled sea. That, I fear, is a joy of the irredeemable past.

Our Flight Lieutenant says the Padre, who acts as censor, is grieved by the tone of most of the letters written home. So are all the officers; but then they have not experienced the conditions.

Wednesday, February 11th
On guard – I hope for the last time in my life. My post was in the Sergeants' mess from which a companion ascends to the galley. The heat therefore was staggering.

When trailing round with the Corporal of the guard, while other sentries were being posted, I penetrated into some of the living quarters of the troops on "H" deck aft, and I was forced to the conclusion that even though our quarters on "G" deck would be condemned by the R.S.P.C.A. for cattle, theirs were worse. No wonder morale is low.

I watched the Sergeants eating their meals and at night I hung about in the galley exacting scraps of food from reluctant chefs. As I was on duty eight hours out of the twenty-four, I had plenty of time to occupy and devoted part of it to learning two from the small book of Shakespeare's sonnets given me by Gay. They were those beginning: "They that have power to hurt and will do none" and "When to the sessions of sweet silent thought".

Thursday, February 12th
This morning my guard in the Sergeants' mess was diverting. First of all one of the mess orderlies fell down the companion with a tray of fried liver. Then every time he tried to get up in the slippery mess, he fell flat on his face again and Sergeants and other mess orderlies following in his wake added further Falstaffian touches to the scene. Then the Orderly Officer took

a strong line with the Sergeants who arrived late for breakfast and turned numbers of those august personages away, to the great delight of humbler creatures in the vicinity. Altogether my time for relief at 8.00 a.m. seemed to come with unusual speed.

We have today been five weeks on board the *Otranto* and this is our last day at sea. Altogether we shall have been steaming for just over twenty-eight days when we reach Durban tomorrow.

In spite of our imminent arrival and immunity, at this point, from enemy attack, it was only to be expected that we should have boat drill and air-raid alarms this morning. Such is the military mind. The great debate is whether we are to go ashore in blue or in tropical khaki. The latter is in a repulsive state after weeks of wear without respite and the heavy, damp heat of today makes it, and its wearers, still more unsavoury.

THREE

TRAINING IN SOUTH AFRICA
FEBRUARY–DECEMBER 1942

Friday, February 13th
From my hammock I could see land when I awoke. It was distant, like a bank of clouds, but it became rapidly more distinct and we docked in Durban shortly after 7.00. After some havering, and many unnecessary parades in full packs and webbing, we were eventually allowed ashore at about 3.30 p.m. Never since the break-up of Dotheboys Hall have there been such scenes of jubilation, displayed on this occasion by much whistling out of tune and a great deal of boasting of "the number of beers I am going to put away", etc.

Nobody who has not lived in a pig-sty for five weeks can realise what intense joy can be derived from a haircut and shampoo, especially when the weather is unbearably hot; and it is necessary to live on garbage for the same length of time before duly appreciating steak and fried eggs, even when indifferently cooked in a large popular café. And, *pour combler le tout*, the cigarette shops were stocked with Chesterfields, which are as extinct as the brontosaurus in England.

Durban is a spacious town which contains more vile municipal buildings of neo-gothic design and unsightly material than any town I have ever contemplated. But its spaciousness compensates for much and, above all, the blaze of lights and headlamps after dark is medicine to eyes accustomed for over two years to the Stygian darkness and painful hazards of a black-out.

After my preliminary steak I took a bus – free to the troops

– and, sitting next to a Zulu lady suckling her child, I went to
Point Road, near the docks, and entered the office of Mr T. B.
Davis, King of South African Stevedores. That remarkable
personage was away in Mombasa, attending to business and
recovering from the death of his frail and adored wife. His
brother, a shorter edition of T.B. but stone deaf, was there and
so was his son, Glenham. Their office is a poky little place,
giving but small indication of the wide interests they control.

Glenham took me to his home, a cool villa on a hill overlooking
the city. From a wide veranda I feasted my eyes on the unwonted
sight of a town ablaze with lights and the ships in the harbour
beyond. I had a bath – oh! rapture – and many a cool drink.
Glenham has two daughters, of whom the younger is the image
of her maternal grandmother and very pretty in a pre-Raphaelite
way. They were all extremely friendly and almost embarrassing
in their hospitality.

We dined and then went to a magnificent air-conditioned
cinema to see Myrna Loy and William Powell in *The Thin Man*,
afterwards returning to the villa and more food. Finally, Glenham
drove me, cool and refreshed, back to the ship which was a
revolting mass of turgid, drunk humanity. As a result of too
many iced Coca-Colas, I lay in my hammock perspiring more
than I should have believed possible.

Saturday, February 14th

We entrained for Lyttelton at 12.00 with hoots of joy which
were accentuated by a good lunch served by real waiters on
plates which we did not have to wash up ourselves.

The train climbed several thousand feet in Natal, with rocky
gorges, plateaux and waterfalls, and then proceeded through
green fertile country, much of it very like England. The violent
heat gave way to the cool of an English summer's day. Only a
number of black men and occasional kraals reminded us we were
in Africa. Every now and then the train stopped and we all, with
the engine driver in the van, rushed out to pick apricots from
trees by the side of the track. An *ungeheuer* thunderstorm
almost blew the train away and all night the landscape was
illuminated by a display of lightning.

There were six of us in a carriage with green leather seats and at either end of each coach were balconies on which to breathe the high air and admire the scenery. I liked my travelling companions. They included a fellow who speaks German well and hails from near Rowlands Castle and a charming farmer from Wiltshire.

I had a drink late at night and sat next to the Squadron Leader in charge, whom I pumped for information. My heart sank when I heard of the delays we are likely to experience.

Sunday, February 15th

We awoke on the high veld, nearing Pretoria. At about 7.30 we reached Lyttelton, detrained and went to the camp in lorries. It is a conglomeration of red brick huts, with iron bedsteads and mattresses. We were issued with pillows and blankets. We had an excellent breakfast; hot ground rice, fried eggs, mutton chops, brown bread (the South African standard loaf) and apricot jam. The food is obviously first class.

The South African pupil pilots tell us horrifying stories of the outrages committed in this district by the nationalist Ossewa Brandwag.[1] Several air-force men, including the Adjutant, have been set upon and seriously damaged. It is inadvisable to go about alone after dark.

150 of us are to go tomorrow to an A.T.W. [Advanced Training Wing] and I am one of the lucky ones. In South Africa they have an extra course of ground work after I.T.W. [Initial Training Wing] is finished, and this will take six weeks. Then, if we pass our exams, we go to E.F.T.S. [Elementary Flying Training School]. All this is at the expense of the wretched South African pupil pilots who are being held back to let us go forward.

We were allowed out at 4.00 p.m. and I sallied forth for Pretoria with two companions. We easily secured a lift from a passing car, which contained a fair-haired, bespectacled young Afrikaner with his wife and two small children. They were very friendly and, in spite of the newly-introduced petrol rationing,

[1] Member of the extremist pro-Nazi Afrikaaners Group.

insisted on taking us to see the Fountains Valley and then driving us round Pretoria. We sat on the back of the dickey and revelled in the soft green scenery.

The first thing they showed us in Pretoria, at my request, was the school in which Winston was held prisoner and from which he made his escape. Then they took us uphill to the great Union Building, like a Renaissance palace, with its glorious flower garden and its view of the whole town and surrounding hills.

When this kind man, of Huguenot descent, dropped us, we met several of our friends and dined hugely (eleven courses for 2/6d.) at the Hellenica Hotel, where several of the party drank more than was good for them. I ended the evening pleasantly and plutocratically with a glass of brandy and a good cigar.

Outside, in Church Street, I heard a familiar voice coming from the wireless in a small café. It was Winston announcing the fall of Singapore. The nature of his words, and the unaccustomed speed and emotion with which he spoke, convinced me that he was sorely pressed by critics and opponents at home. All the majesty of his oratory was there, but with a new note of appeal, lacking the usual confidence of support. Probably the breakaway of the *Scharnhorst* and *Gneisenau* from Brest has contributed to the volume of criticism with which he is faced. Even greater than the loss of Singapore, with all its strategic significance, I felt the poignancy of the Prime Minister's position; and the fact that I was here in Pretoria, so closely associated with his early notoriety, made me feel it all the stronger. Perhaps distance and the fact of being out of it make me imagine things blacker than they are; but there was something about his voice and delivery which made me shiver, and dissipated the pleasure of a happy evening.

Monday, February 16th

I nearly missed the posting, but took the necessary steps just in time and marched with the others to the A.T.W. camp which adjoins the other. We were greeted in a most friendly way by the Officer Commanding and the South African N.C.O.s who are to be in charge of us. We divided up into three flights and settled into red brick huts, with twenty-five beds per hut. We have no sheets, but blankets, pillows and mattresses.

Our course, which includes many subjects done at E.F.T.S. in England, ends on March 26th, and there is a neatly typed programme posted in the hut to show what we do each day.

We got down to work at once, starting with one and a half hours of signals procedure (call signs, etc.), then proceeding to lunch, which was not quite as lavish or good as in the camp we left this morning. The afternoon and evening are devoted to work, but we have three hours free between 4.00 and 7.00. We dine at 5.30.

Negro servants come and undertake to do one's washing for a consideration. This is a boon, as one of my three kit-bags is crammed with it.

We were photographed in groups of twenty-five – for post-mortem purposes! And we had the usual lecture on V.D., beginning with gramophone records and ending with "Under the Spreading Chestnut Tree".

Tuesday, February 17th
Rose at 5.30. It is necessary to do so in order to shave before parading for roll call at 6.15. Then there is breakfast, followed by the Adjutant's parade, which includes an inspection and twenty minutes' drill at 7.30, and lectures consecutively from 8.00 till 12.30. We were all dropping with sleep, probably owing to the new experience of living at 5,000 feet. Subjects include: navigation, meteorology, engines, theory of flight, Morse procedure and the Browning gun.

After lunch we parade at 1.40 for courses from 2.00 till 4.00, and then again from 7.00 to 8.30. One day a week we have games in the afternoon and one day a free evening. On other evenings one of the periods is study, during which one may work at what one wishes.

We had a good lecture by an Information Officer on political and economic conditions in South Africa. This is a very sensible form of lecture, provided throughout the South African forces, with the intention of keeping the men informed and interested.

At 4.00, when we should have been free, we were paraded

with the rest of the camp and set to scavenge. This was considered the height of ignominy, and one of our pupil pilots, a Sergeant with several years' service, complained to me that it was degrading to one who had held warrant rank. It is strange how many of these people stand on their dignity. It was on the tip of my tongue to reply that I held the King's Commission[1] and therefore had better reason to grumble!

Wednesday, February 18th

The day is a long one and we are going to be very hard worked, besides which there is plenty of bull shit! Nevertheless, when work ended at 8.30, the judicious assistance of a little beer worked wonders and we sang raucously; "Aunt Eliza"[2] had a great success.

Thursday, February 19th

Plotting courses on graph paper with rulers and protractors is very primitive and unsatisfactory.

Engines are child's play to most pilots under training, but to me, who have owned a car for years and hardly ever looked inside its bonnet, the subject presents problems.[3]

Theory of flight is useful and should be interesting but seems to be poorly taught.

Having a free evening, I went into Pretoria alone, intending to visit the High Commissioner's Secretariat. Tony Bevir had written to Lord Harlech* about me, and Liesching, of the Dominions Office, had written to various members of Lord Harlech's Secretariat. A long pilgrimage to their headquarters at Bryntirion was in vain as a nigger there informed me they were all at the Cape until April. Pretoria is winter H.Q. So I dined alone and in state at Polly's, the best hotel, and returned early to Lyttelton by train with a young South African air gunner

---

[1] As a Third Secretary in H.M. Diplomatic Service.

[2] An obscene ditty sung to the tune of the German National Anthem.

[3] Strangely enough, I later scored eighty-seven per cent in the examination, beating two out of the three former R.A.F. "fitters" on our course, which shows that I was a better examinee than engineer.

from Durban. He seemed afraid of the Ossewa Brandwag as we walked along the dark empty road.

Friday, February 20th

The various forms of ground corn, differing in colour, which they give us for breakfast *vice* porridge are very good.

In the afternoon we had P.T. in the boiling sun, followed by a hilarious if unruly game of "German Handball", and then an hour devoted to brightening the bungalow and our possessions for an inspection tomorrow. Thank heavens I wasn't born a window cleaner. I complicated things by cleaning them with a rag soaked in paraffin.

We are to go to E.F.T.S. on March 28th, if we pass the course here. Morse at ten words a minute seems the most problematical test to me, though the Browning gun, engines and theory of flight have their difficulties.

I see Winston has been forced to change and contract his Cabinet. Stafford Cripps* is in it, an appointment which I remember David Margesson suggesting a long time ago, and an opportunity to dispense with Greenwood has at last arisen. Finally, Beaverbrook* will probably be less exasperating in the U.S. than at home.

Saturday, February 21st

The hut inspection passed off with much bull shit, even including the polishing of mess tins which we don't use. Then came a blow. Seventy-five per cent are allowed out for the weekend. The remainder, of whom I was one, have to be in for the night but may normally go out for Saturday afternoon and during Sunday. Today, owing to an Ossewa Brandwag scare, this has been stopped and we were told we must spend the weekend in camp.

However by bullying the Orderly Officer and straining our powers of imaginative lying, a friend and I got passes after lunch and went up to Roberts Heights, some four miles away, where there is a magnificent swimming bath. While there, I talked politics with two South African Sergeants from Natal, very pro-British. They were in favour, unlike the majority of Afrikaaners, of a liberal and educational policy towards the natives. Like everybody else, their admiration of Smuts is without reserve.

Roberts Heights, with its avenues of blue-gum trees, is an idyllic spot. There is also a well-appointed Y.M.C.A. at which to drink orangeade. Towards evening we caught a bus to Pretoria and dined cheaply in that lifeless town. A young South African Corporal, so English that he was *plus royaliste que le roi*, insisted on standing us drinks, and giving vent to his patriotic feelings; and then we returned by train to Kloofzicht, walking back across the veld to the camp and shuddering at the thought of puff-adders.

Monday, February 23rd

Am Bungalow Orderly. This entails sitting in the bungalow all day, missing parades and classes, acting as custodian of the others' belongings, and cleaning and sweeping the bungalow. If all else fails, I can qualify as a housemaid after the war.

It rained comparatively steadily all day which made it seem quite like home. But I gather the rainy season is very short here and consists chiefly of thunderstorms.

Tom Daniel, a wild, good-looking young athlete from Bedford School, and I went to dine at the I.T.W. where we heard the food was better. It wasn't. It had deteriorated all round.

I see from the papers that P. J. Grigg is the new Secretary of State for War and David Margesson in the wilderness. I am sorry for David. Winston has the greatest admiration for P. J.; he had intended him as successor to Horace Wilson.[1] I suppose David was sacrificed to popular anti-Guilty-men clamour.

Tuesday, February 24th

Everybody is short of money and, perhaps injudiciously, I have lent a good deal to various sharers of my bungalow. "The gang", as they call themselves, to whom I have affixed myself, includes Tom Daniel, and a tall, deliberate Scot with a sense of humour and no respecter of persons, called Jock Ferguson.

---

[1] Close adviser to Neville Chamberlain, retained by Winston Churchill as Secretary to the Treasury.

The rains continued with violence this afternoon. The nightly noise, fighting and horseplay in the bungalow is an indication of the youth of its inhabitants, whose average age is only about twenty.

Wednesday, February 25th
Today was our day for "Recreational Training", which means that we play instead of working from 2.00 till 4.00 p.m. With a number of others I was transported by lorry to Roberts Heights where I swam.

The R.A.F. are not behaving too well, particularly those who arrived in the immediately preceding convoy, about a month before us. They are noisy, tactless and spend their lives complaining of the conditions. This is particularly shaming when so many South Africans are being held back in their courses to make room for the R.A.F.; and when the Orderly Officer comes round at meal-times it is embarrassing to see some twenty or more of the R.A.F. rise from their places to complain of the food while not a South African moves. And people talk of the desirability of democratising the Diplomatic Service!

Thursday, February 26th
I don't think the R.A.F. and the S.A.A.F. mix very well. Tonight in the canteen I noticed all the R.A.F. sitting together at one group of tables, drinking beer and singing noisily, while the S.A.A.F. sat in another part of the room, singing equally raucously – English patriotic songs for the most part.

Friday, February 27th
In spite of much shouting the discipline is very poor. Members of my flight even smoke on parade – as I remember seeing the *Gardes mobiles* do outside the Embassy in Paris during the ceremonial parade on New Year's Day – and they all talk on the march. There will probably be trouble soon unless they mend their ways.

This afternoon we had an illuminating lecture on South African industry, with especial reference to Johannesburg and gold. The South Africans seem quite confident about the future of that industry; personally I wonder whether gold will retain its value in the post-war economic reconstruction. If it does not, South Africa's largest and most prosperous city will become a depressed area.

I played tennis on the very hard courts. I am discovering some quite interesting personalities in my course: a civil servant, clerical grade, who hails from the Air Ministry and is one of the notorious Mr Brown's [Civil Servants' Trade Union Leader] henchmen; and a young Corporal who comes from the regular air force and compares it very favourably with the army.

Saturday, February 28th

Went to Johannesburg for the weekend after the morning's work had ended. It is a modern city of square blocks basking in the prosperity of the gold boom, producing forty per cent of the world's gold and called, out here, the Golden City. Though characterless, like most planned towns of this century, it is not displeasing and some of its lofty buildings are quite fine architecturally. Its shops are excellent and – as is seldom the case anywhere in these days – anything can be bought that is wanted. Seventy years ago it was just veld.

After sending some parcels of food home, I went to an air-conditioned cinema and saw Tyrone Power in *A Yank in the R.A.F.* As in Durban, the pro-British sentiment of this audience, shown in the cheers they gave and the songs they sang, was striking.

I noticed today, as I have noticed everywhere else, that the white people seem to go out of their way to be offensive and snubbing to the natives. Since I have been in South Africa I have heard no word addressed to a black man except in anger.

Stayed at the Carlton, the best hotel in Johannesburg.

As the remainder of my 1942 diary is largely concerned with the details of flying training I have selected a few entries less parochial than the remainder and largely related to weekend visits to Lord and Lady Harlech in Pretoria and Judge Schreiner in Johannesburg.

Sunday, May 10th

I spent the whole morning talking to Lord Harlech on subjects ranging from Italian art and Portuguese architecture to English politics and the R.A.F.

He told me he had broken with Chamberlain through protesting at Lady Chamberlain's ill advised dabbling in Italian politics in the spring of 1938. He was absorbingly interesting about such varying subjects as rubber plantations, T. E. Lawrence, the Palestine imbroglio, the native problem in South Africa (he feeling, as I do, that the South Africans treat the natives shamefully, and Lady H. feeling still more strongly), General Smuts, and our whole Colonial policy in Africa. In return I was able to tell him some interesting facts about recent political events in England and I launched into an indictment, possibly overdrawn, of R.A.F. training out here. I found that he knew and agreed with many of my chief complaints and he promised to talk to the Air Commodore about the remainder.

On the 1.00 news I heard the best public inanity of the war: Princess Juliana's declaration of "the invincible certainty of the impending end". What a horrible warning against the search for adjectival embellishments!

After lunch we played tennis. Two Rand journalists were among the players and their summing up of African political questions was interesting. They said that in the last analysis the Government of South Africa is in the hands of the farmers.

Lord Harlech told me that Smuts had been hurt by the P.M.'s failure to consult him about Casey's appointment as Minister of State.[1] Smuts believes this to be the critical year of the war and the crux of the matter to be whether Russia can withstand the German summer onslaught.

After dinner Lord Harlech himself drove me to the station and insisted on waiting more than half an hour in the cold until the overdue Witbank train came in. Clutching my scanty luggage (for packing which the butler contemptuously refused a tip!) and

---

[1] The Australian Richard Casey (later Lord Casey and Governor General of Australia) had been appointed Resident Minister in Cairo in succession to Oliver Lyttelton (later Viscount Chandos*).

Harold Butler's *The Lost Peace* which Lady Harlech lent me, I returned drowsily to Witbank, much refreshed for this brief contact with the intelligent outside world.

Sunday, June 21st

Mid-winter, but v. warm and sunny here in Pretoria. Lady H. gets electric shocks from everything she touches.

Went to the early service, in a packed church at Arcadia, with my hostess and her son, John.

After breakfast I went to the office and had a long talk with Price, the Deputy High Commissioner, an exceedingly delightful little man. Ran down the R.A.F. training out here and the maladministration and the behaviour of the R.A.F., as I never cease doing to Lord and Lady H., Brigadier Salisbury Jones, etc. Met Admiral Willis, C. in C. of the naval forces out here.

There was more tennis, with admirals and generals (who are v. formidable to a L.A.C.), after lunch. Tom Fraser, who was a Cambridge Cricket Blue, and I were quite unable to vanquish General Lock and his A.D.C.

I had dinner on a tray in the drawing-room, before Lord H. drove me to the station to catch the 7.40 train to Standerton. A terrible gloom was cast on us all by the German announcement that Tobruk has fallen – captured after a twenty-four-hour assault when it formerly held out so many months. Lord H. told me that Smuts considered the German success owed much to their new 88 mm. anti-tank gun.

Reached Standerton at 1.30 a.m. after a surprisingly comfortable journey.

Friday, July 3rd

Caught the 12.50 train to Johannesburg to stay with Mr Justice Schreiner, a South African judge, son of a former Prime Minister of the Cape, and a Fellow of Trinity. The judge, his wife and children were most welcoming and agreeable. His house possesses a well-stocked library which is a rarity in South Africa and his conversation, on matters South African and European, is well informed and interesting.

Sunday, July 5th

Spent the morning indoors, browsing in Lin Yutang's *My Country and My People*, Gibbon's *Decline and Fall* and *Mein Kampf* by Adolf Hitler. The latter makes one think that all Germans should be exterminated – though in reality I deplore the Vansittartism[1] which is not uncommon in these days, especially in the armed forces.

The judge is trying a special treason case (sabotage is fairly widespread out here and death is the penalty) so that the house is guarded by police.

News from "up north" is better. The 8th Army seems to be making a successful stand against Rommel's drive into the Valley of the Nile. The effect of Tobruk's fall has been deep in South Africa, with scarcely a family that has not one of its members or connections a prisoner. Smuts has launched a great recruiting drive and there is a movement to restrict amusement and concentrate on winning the war.

Saturday, August 29th

Went to Pretoria to see Cecil Syers* who has just arrived in South Africa as Deputy High Commissioner. Lunched with him at the Pretoria Club and spent the afternoon and evening with him and his wife at Bryntirion. Cecil told me two noteworthy things: (1) That my appointment at No. 10 was recommended by Alec Cadogan* (2) That Horace Wilson had never wished nor expected to accompany Chamberlain to Berchtesgaden. He, Cecil, had dined with H. J. at the Travellers several days before the Munich crisis began, and H. J. had then told Cecil of the projected meeting with Hitler but had shaken his head when Cecil's face lit up at the prospect of going with Mr C. and had said that only F.O. officials could or should accompany the P.M. It was Chamberlain's own insistence, supported by the emphatic advice of Sir John Simon,[2] that had been responsible for Horace Wilson going.

[1] Sir Robert Vansittart, Formerly Permanent Under Secretary at the F.O., was notorious for his anti-German sentiments.

[2] Sir John Simon was Chancellor of the Exchequer at the outbreak of war, and was Lord Chancellor in Churchill's Coalition Government.

Friday, September 11th

Took off for an hour's solo. After some aerobatics and a practice forced landing, did a glide approach and perfect three-point landing on the Uitkyk auxiliary landing ground – omitting to lower my undercarriage! Sat for an hour disconsolately on the wing, listening to the warning horn blowing ironically in my ear, and answering caustically the questions of inquisitive pilots who landed round me like flies round a jam-pot.

Finally a Flight Lieutenant from the Maintenance Squadron came out by car to inspect the damage – air-screw and reduction gear damaged, flaps broken, centre section cracked, pitot head broken – and to take me back twenty miles to the aerodrome. On the way the careless native driver involved us in a smash which might have proved very serious, but in which we were miraculously unscathed.

Two crashes in one morning are a bit much! Received at the aerodrome with a mixture of amusement, reproach and sympathy.

Left by the midnight train for Johannesburg, *en route* for Pretoria to stay with the Harlechs.

Saturday, September 12th

Lord Harlech knew about my crash. Frew, the A.O.C.,[1] had rung him up to say his week-end guest was undamaged! How Frew knew (a) I was staying with Lord H. (b) had had a crash, I cannot imagine.

Played tennis with the Stuttafords. He is Minister of Commerce. Dr Colin Steyn, the Minister of Justice, was there.

Amongst other interesting things, Lord H. told me Aneurin Bevan was in Lord Beaverbrook's pay! And Lord B. is still flattering and fluttering round the P.M.

Sunday, September 13th

To the early service with Lady H. and John Ormsby-Gore.

Walked in the gardens at Government House, where Lady Duncan's floral efforts are admirable and the green grass is reminiscent of England.

[1] Air Vice Marshal Frew, Senior R.A.F. Officer in South Africa.

An Australian diplomat, Mr Keith Officer, who came to lunch, has just returned from confinement in Tokyo. He thinks the Japanese, whose part in the war bears no relation to their feelings towards the other Axis powers, will take from nine months to a year to crush after Germany has collapsed. And he suspects that Russia will remain neutral, being glad to see England and America occupied for a time! He says all the Diplomatic prisoners were v. well treated by the Japanese.

Monday, September 14th
Charged with all ceremony before Wing Commander Snelling with "conduct prejudicial to discipline and good order" (Section 40 of the Air Force Act). The Wing Commander, who could not see that failure to lower an undercarriage was either, dismissed the charge, not without many sharp words and a promise of wrath to come (which didn't materialise). Not quite sure that this choice of a wholly irrelevant section of the Act for the charge wasn't something of a ramp – if so, shameful, though a relief.

As there had been a considerable number of landings with undercarriages retracted, the authorities in Pretoria had, only a few days previously, ordained that in future the punishment was to be twenty-eight days' detention. Another R.A.F. pupil pilot committed the same offence as I did on the same day. He, too, was discharged on some trumped-up excuse, no doubt because our C.O. was not prepared to see any of us consigned to a South African "Glass-House".

Saturday, October 24th
It is jacaranda time, and Pretoria is adorned with these trees, with their wealth of blue flower. The whole city is dressed in blue.
  Played tennis at the Pretoria Country Club, which has a fine view but is less luxurious than that at Johannesburg.
  Lord H. tells me that the sinking of ships homeward bound from the Cape has been alarming, but the Admiralty refuse permission to publish losses. One submarine was located on the surface, but the South African Ventura which took off to attack

discovered, on reaching the target, that no bombs had been loaded!

General Alexander* attacked the Germans "up north" – the beginning, I hope and think, of the Allied offensive. The war should be over next year.

Sunday, October 25th

Went to the early service with Lady H. and John. It was packed as usual.

Mrs van der Byl, very pretty and overdressed, came at 11.00 a.m. with Miss Lucy Bean (the South African Lady Reading[1]) to see me and talk about Cowes. Lady H. had tea and cakes provided, the best South African tradition, in deference to Miss Bean.

Mrs van der Byl is a snob and affected, but she has, they say, a kind heart. She asked me to stay at the Cape and also promised to take me to see Smuts (at present in London), who is a great friend of hers, next time I go to Pretoria. Her husband is one of the favourites for the Governor-Generalship, which may fall vacant any moment now. Apparently Judge Schreiner is another possibility.

Tennis with Lord H., the Adjutant General and the First Secretary of the American Legation.

Lord H. tells me that Ludlow-Hewitt, Inspector General of the R.A.F., who has just finished visiting all the South African training stations, was favourably impressed on the whole, but reached the same conclusions about the teaching of ground subject as had I. This is a relief, because I was somewhat appalled to find he had in London seen all my letters on the subjects to Louis Greig!

Am reading Evelyn Waugh's *Put out more Flags* lent me by Lady H., the absorbing *Screwtape Letters* by C. S. Lewis sent me by mother, and Charlotte Brontë's *Shirley* borrowed from Judge Schreiner. Have just finished Negley Farson's *Way of a Transgressor*.

---

[1] Stella, Marchioness of Reading, was the founder and head of the Women's Voluntary Services in Britain.

Friday, October 26th

Long week-end in Jo'burg. Spent it quietly with the Schreiners. The judge is in process of trying a melodramatic treason case, centring round one Leibrandt. The actively seditious element in this country seems to be quite strong.

Finished Balzac's *Père Goriot*.

The war is going v. well on all fronts – Tunis, Libya, Russia and the Far East – except Standerton where the accident rate, including several fatal crashes, is alarmingly high of late. About four planes are being "written off" every week.

Friday, December 11th

General Smuts visited Standerton, his constituency, and also made a speech at the air school in one of the hangars. He stood about five yards from me, and spoke both in English and Afrikaans. He was halting, but his informality and his mannerisms were charming. He said he dreaded to think what 1943 would bring about in the air and nothing would make him accept an invitation to any German or Italian city. The whole of Africa would shortly be ours.

He spoke of his recent visit to London and said that Mr Churchill slept when he was working and worked when he wanted to be sleeping, a remark which rang very true! I noticed a Churchillian influence on his oratory as a result of the five weeks' visit – e.g. constant use of the word "tremendous" and the phrase that N. Africa would be a "spring-board" for Allied attacks. But he didn't say anything was sombre or mortal!

Friday, December 19th

Went to High Commission House for the week-end. Took the wrong luggage by mistake and arrived, clutching a toothbrush and some Phillips Dental Magnesia, at the end of a large cocktail party. Just missed Smuts, but ran into Frew who introduced me to his wife as "the man I am most anxious to get out of Africa". The reason is that the P.M. and/or Louis Greig have been sending numerous telegrams about me with kind but excessive zeal on my behalf. A flippant allusion, in a letter to John Peck* or somebody,[1] to the fact that at Witbank I was not considered reliable, dashing or intelligent enough for a commission apparently produced a sally from the P.M. *in the Cabinet* – at least so Cecil Syers alleges – and a consequent letter from Archie Sinclair[2] to Lord Harlech. This is all rather silly and very embarrassing.

Lord Harlech was interesting as ever. Amongst other things he told me: (1) An example of Chamberlain's lack of tact. Lord H. returned from his father's funeral to the Colonial Office to be told that his seals of office had been sent for to the Palace. N.C. never even wrote asking him to relinquish office and never saw him in person. (2) Sir John Simon's technique at the Cabinet when Foreign Secretary. He would produce a paper setting out all the pros and cons of a question but reaching no conclusion. He would look to his colleagues for a decision. When a point of view was expressed, and then only, he would bring into play his brilliant powers of criticism – but in a purely destructive way. Thus he had a hopelessly "negative mind". (3) Palestine. A federation of Arab states was hopeless since Ibn Saud alone could head it and he was too old. The only solution was to govern Palestine as a Crown colony.

Sunday, December 21st

Lady Harlech returned from the Cape where she had been seeing John Ormsby-Gore off to England. She read aloud an amusing letter from Tommy Lascelles[3] describing Winston, on the night the British offensive in Egypt opened, walking down the corridors of Buckingham Palace, where he was attending a dinner in honour of Mrs Roosevelt, and singing "Roll out the Barrel" at the astounded royal pages and footmen.

Lord H. obviously thinks he should be taking a more important part in the war – as do I – and I gather he would like me to say a few words in the right quarter when I get home, at any rate as regards the desirability of his returning to England for a few

---

[1] It was in fact a letter to my mother (see page 64).
[2] Later 1st Viscount Thurso.*
[3] Sir Alan Lascelles, Private Secretary to the King.

months next summer. He says Attlee is rotten at the Dominions Office and the appointment of Oliver Stanley, *vice* Lord Cranborne,[1] at the Colonial Office makes things worse. Neither S. of S. now knows the least thing about Dominions or Colonies. Smuts was furious when he heard of the change.

Incidentally it appears that Smuts was responsible for Cripps leaving the War Cabinet and going to M.A.P.[2] The idea is that Cripps, alone of Ministers, is capable of dealing with the scientists and inventors, especially with regard to anti-submarine measures. Shipping losses are now v. serious and a lot of ships homeward bound from the Cape have been sunk.

Dan Pienaar, South African General and popular hero – a possible Smuts of the future – has been killed in an air crash.

[1] Later 5th Marquess of Salisbury.*
[2] Ministry of Aircraft Production.

FOUR

MARKING TIME
JANUARY 1943–SUMMER 1943

Training to be a pilot in South Africa had been a slow process, for there was a constant shortage of spare parts for the Tiger Moths and Miles Masters in which I was taught to fight as well as to fly. The contrast between life in a South African Air Force flying school and week-ends in Johannesburg or Pretoria was striking. S.A.A.F. discipline was stern. The food and accommodation were good, but the rules imposed were severely old-fashioned and pack-drill, wearing an overcoat, two full packs and carrying a rifle with fixed bayonet in the blazing mid-day sun, was not an uncommon punishment. By contrast we had to parade for half an hour at 5.30 a.m. every day, wearing in the early morning cold of the High Veld nothing but a khaki shirt, with the sleeves rolled up above the elbows, a black tie, shorts, khaki woollen stockings and brightly polished black shoes.

Although the R.A.F. air-crew under training were widely known as the Blue Peril, the hospitality and friendship offered us once we were outside the barbed wire was boundless. As we walked in uniform through the streets of Johannesburg, total strangers would tap us on the shoulder, ask if we had anywhere to spend the week-end and invite us to stay, providing every luxury and entertainment they could afford. If we sought a lift, it was rare for the very first car not to stop.

Due to a strange sequence of events I had one disturbing experience. At the Elementary Flying Training School to which I was first posted, the Chief Ground Instructor was a Flight

Lieutenant who had been a schoolmaster in civilian life. We were all far too keen to get our wings to be excessively ill-behaved; but he treated us as recalcitrant schoolboys. I protested and fell foul of him. Our instructor in navigation was also an unimaginative martinet. Thus at the end of this initial course, although I received a good report for flying, the Chief Ground Instructor marked me as below average for such qualities as intelligence, endurance, leadership and dash. The higher grades were Exceptional, Very Good and Good, but I received no such distinction in any of the eight qualities listed. He also pronounced that I was definitely not recommended for a commission.

I was not particularly distressed. Indeed, I thought it would be romantic to become a Sergeant Pilot; and I wrote a cheerful letter to my mother[1], informing her that I was shaping reasonably well as a pilot but was considered unworthy of a commission as being below average for intelligence.

My mother was, amongst many other things, a co-opted member of the Shoreditch Borough Council. The members were all socialists, except for a sprinkling of Communists; but they were devoted to my mother, peer's daughter though she might be, because she had for over thirty years worked assiduously for the people of Shoreditch. At a council meeting complaints were voiced that commissions in the armed forces were only given to public schoolboys. My mother intervened to say this could not be quite true, for her youngest son who had been at a public school was thought unsuitable for a commission. As she had quite often invited Borough Councillors to our house and I had from time to time accompanied her to Shoreditch, I was not entirely unknown to them. They changed tack. "What," they cried. "Lady Cynthia's son not to be given a commission! Monstrous, unthinkable!"

One of the Councillors told this story to a great social worker, Sir Basil Henriques, with whom my mother sat as a J.P. in an East End Juvenile Court. A few days later Sir Basil lunched with Anthony de Rothschild at the office of N. M. Rothschild and Son. There was another guest whose name he did not catch.

[1] Lady Cynthia Colville.*

He told Anthony de Rothschild about me. The other guest twirled his moustache and expressed surprise. Sir Basil discovered, after this third party had left, that he was Jack Churchill, the Prime Minister's brother, who, not surprisingly, recounted what he had heard, doubtless with a few picturesque additions, at 10 Downing Street.

On the following morning the Cabinet had before them Anthony Eden's proposals for the reform of the Foreign Service, the amalgamation of the Diplomatic and Consular Services and an improvement in pay and allowances. Foreign Service officers were, Eden told the Cabinet, a body of exceptional ability who were most inadequately rewarded.

The members of the Cabinet approved the Foreign Secretary's proposals, but to everybody's astonishment the Prime Minister (with his tongue deeply in his cheek) said he could not agree. He had had, as one of his private secretaries, a young man from the Foreign Office who had indeed met *his* requirements, but whom, he said, glaring ferociously at Sir Archibald Sinclair, the Secretary of State for Air had pronounced below average for intelligence. If that was what men of discernment like Sir Archibald felt, clearly the Foreign Secretary's high praise of the Diplomatic Service must be discounted. This is the account given to me two years later by Sir Archibald.

The penny dropped and the Cabinet saw that the Prime Minister was not intending to be taken seriously. However, that did not prevent telegrams speeding to Pretoria. Sir Archibald Sinclair and the Dominions Secretary telegraphed to Lord Harlech. With a face of thunder he asked me what I had been up to. Having two months previously moved to an advanced flying school, where I was happy as a sandboy and had forgotten all about the hostile Chief Ground Instructor, I asked in all innocence what Lord Harlech meant. He explained and I was mortified.

Worse was to follow. Churchill telegraphed to General Smuts. The Chief of the Air Staff telegraphed to Air Vice Marshal Frew, the principal R.A.F. Officer in South Africa. Descending from a solo flight in a Miles Master, I was ordered to go straight to Pretoria, a staff car and driver being most surprisingly provided.

I was subjected to an intelligence test and, since it was one obviously intended for backward schoolchildren, I deserved no great credit for scoring one hundred per cent. The High Commissioner and the Secretaries of State for the Dominions and for Air were duly reassured; and the Prime Minister was assuaged. For me it was the most embarrassing episode in my career and an extreme example of how the smallest mole-hill can attain mountainous proportions.

The African population with whom we came into contact were always smiling and friendly, so much so that I got into trouble for travelling, at the invitation of a few garrulous Africans (with whom I fell into conversation at the Johannesburg railway station) in a native train back to the E.F.T.S. at Witbank. I had missed the last "white" train which would have got me back to camp by 23.59 hours. However, it was against the law and I was subjected to dire threats by the Sergeant Major on the following morning.

When I was at Standerton, every day a squad of Basutos, in immaculate uniforms, drilled with assegais instead of rifles (they were not allowed to carry fire-arms) on the square in front of our quarters. They did so with evident pride and with the precision of the Brigade of Guards. We were not encouraged to talk to them. The only places in which black and white mixed freely, other than as servant and master, were the Anglican Churches, and kneeling at the altar rail of Johannesburg Cathedral on Easter Day I was wedged between two devout Africans. The white Dean told me he had received a letter from one of his black flock who had been sent with a labour battalion to minister to the British army in Egypt. It read: "The Imperial troops are kind and friendly: they have white faces but they have black hearts."

One Friday evening I was trying to hitchhike from Johannesburg to Pretoria to stay at High Commission House with the Harlechs. For once the passing cars seemed disinclined to stop, but eventually a blue Plymouth drew up. Its sole occupant was a black driver. "Does the baas want a lift?" he asked with diffidence. The baas said that nothing would please him more and got in. During the drive to Pretoria the driver told me he had been educated at an Anglican Mission, that he had four children and, on enquiry by me, that he earned ten shillings a week. He was intelligent and thoroughly likeable.

I asked him to drop me in the central square in Pretoria, but a short walk from the High Commissioner's house. I tried to give him half-a-crown, which was less than one day's pay for a Leading Aircraftsman like me; but he insisted it had been an honour to drive one of the King's soldiers and a tip would destroy his pleasure. What about using it to buy a present for his children? While we were amiably arguing, a look of terror came into his eyes and he hastily let in the clutch. A heavy hand fell on my shoulder. I turned round and saw two huge granite-faced Sergeants of the Military Police.

"Is it usual in the R.A.F. to take lifts from niggers?" one of them asked in a heavy Afrikaans accent.

"I don't think so, Sergeant," I said. "We don't have many in England."

"It is lucky for you, Airman, that you are not in the Union Forces, or you would be in for a lot of trouble – and unless you want a real good beating, you 'ad better not do that again."

Meekness was essential, for I knew that I had infringed Union Defence Forces regulations which we in the R.A.F. had been ordered to respect. I was allowed to go; but I was uneasy. I told Lord Harlech what had happened. He said it did not surprise him, but no such thing would be tolerated in the three British High Commission territories of Bechuanaland, Swaziland and Basutoland which he, and not the South African Government, controlled.

On December 30th I wrote in my diary: "We celebrated the completion of our long and wearisome training with much hilarity and beer – the R.A.F. and S.A.A.F. being at last on good terms – and the pouring of many buckets of firewater over other revellers."

Friday, January 8th
The Wings Parade at long last. It was hot, but not unbearable. The ceremonial went off without a hitch. Wings were presented by a South African Air Force Colonel in the presence of many spectators. He made a not very eloquent speech in which he

said that most of us would probably be dead within a year, but it didn't matter if we died for our country – not tactful I thought, in the presence of aged parents, wives, sweethearts, etc. Then we marched off to the strain of "Auld Lang Syne".

I then endured a forty-eight-hour train journey from Johannesburg to Cape Town, through the Karoo in midsummer heat, in a second-class compartment with no sleeping accommodation and food and drink only available at occasional wayside stations. This was followed by three compensating weeks of leisure and unexpected entertainment in Cape Province. The Harlechs provided their usual hospitality, and Mrs van der Byl took me to see General Smuts and then to hear him and Dr Malan slang each other in Parliament.

At the end of January 1943, I sailed for home in the liner *Orion*. The convoy was a small one: four large liners or merchantmen proceeding at twelve knots in company with H.M.S. *Valiant,* a battleship repaired after a limpet-mine attack at Alexandria, and her four escorting destroyers. This was fortunate because enemy submarines were rampant, especially off the coast of South-west Africa. It was a more comfortable journey than on the way out, but owing to my remonstrance about conditions on board the *Otranto,* officers and Sergeant Pilots were a great deal less luxuriously catered for than previously. The voyage from Cape Town to the Clyde lasted four weeks, and the sea, unusually for February, was as still as a lake. There were fifty French *matelots* on board, bound for Britain from Madagascar to rally to de Gaulle.* Not one of them spoke a word of English and I volunteered to teach them. So every morning I sat with them on deck, laboriously declining the verbs "to be" and "to have", making them repeat after me the simplest nouns and adjectives, refusing to tell them the English translation of *merde* and other comparable words and generally discovering the problems of the teaching profession. As we sailed into a sunlit Clyde on February 28th, one of my pupils, a hulking seaman with a beard, gratified me by saying: "Thou art good *professeur."* But I realised that in my lessons I had doubtless placed too much emphasis on the second person singular. The trendier clergy now go too far the other way in addressing the Almighty.

We went to Harrogate where there were separate Personnel Receiving Centres for Air-crew Officers and Sergeant Pilots. A few days later, while drilling with the other Sergeants, I was subjected to yet another embarrassment. A Corporal from the Orderly Room came rapidly across the parade-ground and spoke to the officer who was drilling us. We were called to a halt and the officer announced that Sergeant Colville was to report at once to the Commanding Officer. Though my conscience was reasonably clear, I was alarmed: it was like being summoned to the Headmaster's study.

I saluted and stood to attention.

"Sergeant Colville," said the C.O., "I am instructed to commission you immediately as a Pilot Officer."

"But, Sir, I like being a Sergeant Pilot."

"Don't argue. Do as you are told. This is an order from the Air Ministry; and I am instructed to say that if you are short of money to buy a uniform, I am to advance you a loan."

I thought of protesting further, but I did want to join one of the Tactical Reconnaissance Squadrons, flying Mustangs, and for some obscure reason they would only accept officers. So after hasty reflexion I decided to profit from this unexpected stroke of fortune. I simply said "Sir", which was the accepted way of signifying obedience to an order, saluted once again and went into the town, without the proffered loan. I bought off-the-peg an officer's uniform that miraculously fitted. Together with the requisite cap, shirts and insignia it cost about £10 and required no clothing coupons.

I later discovered the reason for this curious development. The Prime Minister, having through some grapevine heard of my return, sent a telegram to the officers' mess at Harrogate, addressed to Pilot Officer Colville. It read: "Delighted you are safely back. Pray seek permission to come to Chequers for luncheon on Wednesday. Winston S. Churchill."

The telegram hung about in the officers' mess for forty-eight hours, until the Adjutant, having ascertained that no Pilot Officer Colville was expected, opened it. When he read the contents he was aghast, as he subsequently told me, and rang up the Air Ministry. Terror was struck there too and instructions were at once given that I must be commissioned at all costs. So, to the relief of the Air Ministry, I arrived at Chequers, where Churchill was recovering from pneumonia, wearing the uniform and wings of a Pilot Officer. It was a peculiar way of earning a commission, but the Prime Minister did not have the slightest idea of what he had done.

FIVE

BACK TO THE FOLD
SEPTEMBER 1943–JANUARY 1944

After two refresher courses and three weeks' operational training on Mustangs, I joined No. 268 Squadron of the Second Tactical Air Force, equipped with single-seater, four-cannon Mustangs, at the end of September 1943, a few days after my father died. We lived in tents at Funtington, almost at the gates of Stansted where I had spent so many hospitable week-ends earlier in the war. By the mere chance of standing in for an experienced pilot while he went to have tea, I had my first operational flight, involving an air-sea rescue off the coast of Cherbourg, within two days of joining the Squadron. I then developed the disgusting disease of impetigo as the result of sleeping in infected blankets. The hospitable Lady Bessborough, undeterred by my hideous sores, insisted on my moving into Stansted.

A few weeks later, out of the blue, my commanding officer, greatly puzzled (for he knew nothing of my previous career), informed me that I was to report to 10 Downing Street on the following morning at 11.00 a.m. sharp.

"It is time," said the Prime Minister, "that you came back here."

"But I have only done one operational flight."

"Well, you may do six. Then back to work."

I was posted to 168 Squadron and completed the six from Sawbridgeworth, without mishap, flying across the Channel at five feet above the waves to escape the enemy radar. One non-operational incident made a deep impression on me. I was on a practice cross-country flight over the eastern counties when my single Allison engine suddenly cut out. Looking anxiously down I saw an aerodrome with a long tarmac runway on which I contrived to make a glide approach and landing.

It was only a few miles from Cambridge and I asked if I might have transport to the railway station. The duty officers said yes, but I must await the take-off of that night's raid; for it was a bomber airfield, lined with Lancasters and Halifaxes due for inclusion in a gigantic assault on Berlin. So I stood outside a hangar and watched one three-ton lorry after another debouch a hundred or more young men, who walked silently and unsmiling to their allotted aircraft. Accustomed as I had already become to the gaiety and laughter of fighter pilots, I was distressed by the tense bearing and drawn faces of the bomber crews. At that time, late in November 1943, some eighty per cent were failing to complete unscathed their tours of thirty operations. Of courage they had plenty, but there was nothing but lip-biting gloom registered on those faces.

I returned to Sawbridgeworth much more thoughtful and disturbed than when I set out that morning. Yet when I flew the following day on an operational sortie over northern France, hoping to find some trains to riddle with cannon-shot, it was with contrasting enthusiasm and excitement that four of us taxied to the take-off. I had reason to be thankful that since I wore contact lenses and could only keep them in for some two hours, I had been allocated to a Fighter rather than to a Bomber or Coastal Command Squadron.

I said goodbye sadly, sure that I was going to miss the spirit of adventure, the friendliness of my brother officers and the exhilaration. I assumed that I should fly no more and felt that I had wasted time and effort in order to make six uneventful operational flights. Just as on several occasions when I thought I was leaving No. 10 for the last time, I was proved wrong.

On December 15th, 1943, while I was enjoying a few days' respite at Madeley, the Prime Minister having left for the Cairo and Teheran Conferences with Roosevelt and Stalin, I received an urgent summons to return to No. 10 in uniform. Though surprised by the latter requirement, I did so. I discovered that

Churchill was seriously, perhaps mortally, ill with pneumonia at Carthage and that I was to escort Mrs Churchill to his bedside.

Except for the weekends I was at Chequers, the entries in yet another new diary were shorter than those for 1940 and 1941 and more concerned with personal, family and social affairs. When abroad I either made notes which I amplified on returning to Downing Street or wrote fuller descriptions and later pasted them into my diary, but I have excluded those which I judge to be trivial. The following selected extracts begin when I was summoned back to London from Madeley in December 1943.

Thursday, December 16th
Went to the House of Commons to hear Attlee announce the P.M.'s illness which he did in very lugubrious tones. A "clamp" looked like preventing our departure, but finally we heard that we could take off in a Liberator from Lyneham. Mary accompanied Mrs Churchill, and I drove with Miss Hamblin – a seemingly endless journey in the mist and blackout. We dined at Lyneham, a rather sticky dinner in a special mess, but Mrs C. was calm and managed to seem cheerful. We took off at 11.30, Mrs C., Miss Hamblin and I on mattresses stretched on the floor of the Liberator, and spent most of the night sitting up, talking and drinking coffee as Mrs Churchill could not sleep and was rather alarmed. The weather, except for the take-off, was perfect and we had a calm flight at 5,000 feet.

Friday, December 17th
It was still dark when we landed at Gibraltar. We had breakfast at Government House, where we found General Ismay* on his way home, and took off again for Tunis at 9.30. We flew over Algeria and the Kasserine Gap. I took over the controls for a short time. We landed at 3.00 p.m., being met by a large party including Sarah, Tommy Thompson, John Martin* and Air Chief Marshal Tedder.[1] We drove to the White House at Carthage, where the P.M. was lying. He sent for me and I found instead of a recumbent invalid a cheerful figure with a large cigar and a whisky and soda in his hand.

[1] Air officer commanding the Desert Air Force.

I was billeted in a magnificent villa, with gaudy mosaic decoration, in the Arab village of Sidi Bou Said. It belongs to the d'Erlangers.

Saturday, December 18th
A fleet of American cars stood waiting before the doors of the White House, ready to take anyone anywhere. With John Martin I went into Tunis, stopping to look at a German cemetery at Carthage – very well kept in contrast with ours. Tunis is a dull town. It is quite unscathed by the bombing except for the docks which are flat.

The Coldstream are guarding us. Bill Harris[1] is Second in Command. Visited them in their mess.

Sunday, December 19th
Began to take an active part in the work of the Private Office. Strange after more than two years' absence; but though the P.M. was much better, there was little doing.

Bill Harris and I walked up to the Cathedral at Carthage where Louis IX died and is buried.

The party at the White House included Mrs Churchill, Sarah, Tommy, Joe Hollis,* John Martin, Francis Brown, Lord Moran* and three other doctors; also Randolph.* The Tedders were in and out all day.

Monday, December 20th
Bill Harris lunched and escorted some of us to Longstop Hill and Medjes el Bab. The signs of battle are few and the scene is a notable contrast to the French battlefields after the 1918 war.

Tuesday, December 21st
Accompanied Bedford and Pulvertaft (two of the doctors) on a tour of the native quarter of "Kasbah" in Tunis. Prices exorbitant.

---

[1] Married to my cousin Betty Coates. He and I were at the same preparatory school, in the same House at Harrow and in the same college at Cambridge. After the war he became a Q.C.

Randolph was very silly with the P.M., producing exaggerated accounts of the French arrests of Flandin, Boisson, etc. Winston almost had apoplexy and Lord Moran was seriously perturbed.

At tea-time the P.M. suddenly got up and walked into the large white hall in his dressing-gown.

Generals Neame and O'Connor and Air Vice Marshal Boyd, all in army battle dress, came to dinner. They have just escaped from prisoners' camps in Italy. I sat next to Tedder who was flippant but agreeable.

Wednesday, December 22nd
An expedition to Dougga. We found it with difficulty but it was well worth the long drive. The Roman remains, especially the theatre, are first class and the site of the whole ruin is superb.

Randolph is causing considerable strife in the family and entourage. But the P.M. likes playing bezique with him.

Friday, December 24th
Walked slowly down from Sidi Bou Said (where nearly all of us sleep) with General Alexander, whom I did not find an easy conversationalist, though he is pleasant.

There was a great influx of Generals and others to discuss Operation SHINGLE[1] and, in particular, the question of providing landing craft. Maitland Wilson (C. in C. elect),[2] Tedder, Air Vice Marshal Park (from Sicily), General Gale (Quartermaster General) and others were there. The P.M. rose from his sick bed to hold a conference in the dining-room.

After dinner I made a strange sortie with Randolph to call on some French people, whom we surprised in the middle of a large dinner party. We sat embarrassed on the sofa until they rose from the table. I was a bit ashamed of these shock tactics.

Christmas Day
General Alexander, Mrs C., Sarah, Lord Moran and I went to an early service arranged by the Coldstream in an ammunition

[1] The projected landing in Anzio, north of Naples.
[2] Field Marshal Lord Wilson. Commanded the British forces in Greece in 1941 and held numerous commands in the Middle East, becoming Supreme Allied Commander in the Mediterranean in 1944.

shed. There was a dramatic culmination when, as the Padre said the *Gloria in Excelsis*, the bells of Carthage Cathedral pealed loudly from the hill above and a white dove, which had been roosting on a beam in the shed, fluttered down in front of the congregation.

There was a great conference, which included five Commanders in Chief: Eisenhower,* Maitland Wilson, Alexander, Tedder and Admiral Sir John Cunningham.[1]

At luncheon the P.M. proposed everybody's health in turn. Harold Macmillan[2] and Desmond Morton arrived just before it.

In the evening there was a cocktail party to which many were bidden. The party, through the midst of which the P.M. walked as if in perfect health, merged into a cold stand-up dinner and everybody finished the day feeling the merrier for Christmas.

I thought Harold Macmillan, with whom I had a long talk, rather finicky and probably a little insincere.

Sunday, December 26th
The Generals and Randolph left.

I walked with Mrs C., Sarah and Lord Moran to look at the remains of Carthage docks. The old Punic town stretched along by the sea, just where we are living, but so thoroughly was *Carthago deleta* that the only remains date from a later Roman epoch.

The P.M. dined in the dining-room for the first time. After dinner I took a paper of Lord Cherwell's, about the new German reprisal weapon (the V.1), to show Tedder and found him, his wife and staff finishing dinner at his headquarters. I sat long talking to him, with brandy, champagne and cigars (Christmas celebrations presumably), and found him particularly agreeable, thoughtful and interesting.

Monday, December 27th
We flew to Marrakech. The P.M. went in his York. Joe Hollis and I went in a Liberator with all the W.A.A.F. cypherers and

---

[1] Commander in Chief, Mediterranean.
[2] British Resident Minister in North Africa. Later Earl of Stockton.*

had a very bumpy journey. One of the engines cut dead and a side panel blew in. The air was icy, the W.A.A.F.s shrieked and Joe and I had to hold the panel in place with all the strength we had until the flight engineer contrived to make temporary repairs.

On arrival we drove to the spacious and luxurious, if slightly vulgar, Villa Taylor where the P.M. had already arrived. Excellent food cooked by a French chef, formerly of the French Embassy in Moscow. I was sleeping at the villa; most of the rest of the staff were at the Hotel Mamounia.

The villa was lent by the Americans and Americans were both guarding us and organising our entertainment, a task they performed without counting the cost.

Tuesday, December 28th
Lord Beaverbrook arrived unannounced though expected. He was in high spirits. Max Aitken[1] came with him en route for Cairo.

John Martin and I penetrated into the back streets of the Medina, the genuine unspoilt and very beautiful native town, which is fortunately out of bounds to the American troops.

After dinner the P.M. decorated Max Aitken with the ribbon of the 1939–43[2] Star (hastily cut off my second tunic). "Little Max" has an imposing array of decorations. Then we played poker, unruly but amusing. I made the mistake of trying to call Lord Beaverbrook's bluff but ended by losing only £2.10.0. The P.M. was wildly rash but successful. He divided the gains and losses by 1,000, with Lord Beaverbrook's agreement, to suit my economic position. Otherwise I should have lost £2,500, which I certainly do not possess.

Wednesday, December 29th
After lunching at the villa we all motored into the foothills of the Atlas mountains and admired the glorious scenery. We returned

[1] Group Captain Max Aitken, D.S.O., D.F.C., a hero of the Battle of Britain. Succeeded his father as Chairman of Beaverbrook Newspapers until the company was sold to Trafalgar House. Renounced the Beaverbrook peerage because he thought people should know of only one Lord Beaverbrook.
[2] Later the 1939–45 Star war medal.

in time to entertain some of the W.A.A.F. cypherers to tea (they came in batches throughout the visit until all had been). The P.M. took them up the tower to look at the walled Medina and to watch the sunset.

At dinner the P.M. made the first apologia I have ever heard him make for the Baldwin Government: "The climate of public opinion on people is overpowering."

But he says this war will be known in history as the Unnecessary War.

Thursday, December 30th
We picnicked near a river in the Atlas foothills against a background of prickly pear. All of us except the P.M. and Lord B. walked up the valley, through a ramshackle Jewish village, and Mrs C. and I forded a stream on a donkey while the others, led by Lord Moran, preferred wading to the risk of verminous contact. But neither Mrs C. nor I suffered for our rashness.

The Beaver was greatly impressed by the antagonism of the Moorish and Jewish children who refused to play with one another. The Jews looked much less happy and self-confident than the Moors. We fed them with biscuits, cakes and oranges and gave a larger share to the Jews. Went to the great square in the Medina with Lord B., Mrs C. and Sarah.

Friday, December 31st
General Eisenhower came to dinner and General Montgomery* with his A.D.C., Noel Chavasse, came for the night. We saw the New Year in early so that General M. could go to bed. Punch was brewed, the P.M. made a little speech, the clerks, typists and some of the servants appeared, and we formed a circle to sing "Auld Lang Syne". I was linked arm in arm with General Montgomery and the American barman.

Mrs Churchill was the only person I knew who always succeeded in subduing General Montgomery, though she became fond of him. On this occasion when it was time to have a bath before dinner, she turned to the A.D.C., Noel Chavasse, and said she looked forward to seeing him in half an hour.

"My A.D.C.s don't dine with the Prime Minister," said Monty tartly.

Mrs Churchill gave him a withering look. "In my house, General Montgomery, I invite who I wish and I don't require your advice."

Noel Chavasse dined.

On another occasion, some years later, Monty announced on the croquet lawn at Chartwell that all politicians were dishonest. Mrs Churchill, with flashing eyes, said that if that was his view he should leave Chartwell at once. She would arrange to have his bags packed. He apologised profusely, and stayed.

She was equally forthright, though less withering, with General de Gaulle who, whatever his periodical differences with her husband, never ceased to respect and admire her.

Saturday, January 1st [Marrakech]

The whole party, including Montgomery, picnicked in an olive grove. Monty was talkative but not bombastic. He made two notable remarks in the presence of Lords Moran and Beaverbrook, though not in mine. They were that his chaplains were more important to him than his artillery, and that he thought the 8th Army would vote in an election as he told them to vote.

Monty left by air after dinner to take up his new Command in England.[1]

Sunday, January 2nd

Lord B. was going to take Sarah and me to Fez in the Liberator, but he changed his mind just as we were setting off.

I rode a white horse with a mouth of iron in company with Nairn,[2] the British Consul at Marrakech. We cantered through the orange groves and olive trees of the gardens belonging to the Sultan of Morocco's palace.

[1] The operational command of the Allied land forces for the re-entry into Northern Europe, Operation OVERLORD.

[2] Subsequently Consul at Bordeaux where the Churchills again made friends with him and his wife, an accomplished artist who accompanied Churchill on his painting expeditions during a holiday at Hendaye after the defeat of Germany.

At dinner the P.M. and the Beaver went over the whole course of the last war and of this. At one moment the P.M. turned and said to Commander Thompson, "But, Tommy, you will bear witness that I do not repeat my stories so often as my dear friend, the President of the United States."

Speaking of the Chiefs of Staff, he said, "They may say I lead them up the garden path, but at every stage of the garden they have found delectable fruit and wholesome vegetables."

Monday, January 3rd

There was a picnic followed by a beautiful but long drive above the snowline of the Atlas. We stopped many times to admire the scenery, in particular at a forester's house built in a sublime position. The forester's wife recognised the P.M. and was overcome.

The local French General and his wife (de Villate) dined and offered to arrange a wild boar hunt for us. It could and should have easily been arranged, had Tommy subsequently shown a little more initiative.

Tuesday, January 4th

President Beneš came to lunch. He is agreeable but specious and, perhaps, unduly optimistic. He told us (1) that Russian aid for Czechoslovakia would certainly have been forthcoming at the time of Munich; (2) that the famous Russian treason trials had been fully justified. Tuchachevsky, Kamenev, etc., had been plotting with Germany because, as sincere Trotskyists, they thought that German help in the overthrow of Stalin was morally justifiable and that they were acting in the true interests of Russia. The plot had been discovered by the Czechs; Beneš had thought that the Soviet Government were intriguing with Germany; he had protested to the Russian Minister at Prague who had been amazed at his unfounded accusations and had reported them to Moscow in complete bewilderment; these accusations had put the Soviet Government on the scent; (3) that he had discussed the Polish and Czech frontiers with Stalin (he was on his way back from Moscow), and had agreed to a common Russo-Czech frontier in the east. He discussed the new Russo-Polish frontier at length with the P.M. on the basis of the Curzon line.[1] Stalin is determined to have Lvov.

Beneš, Smutmy (one of B.'s ministers) and Lebedev, Soviet Ambassador to the Czechs – who spoke no word of English, French or German and had hair like a virtuoso – came to dine.

The P.M. talked of flying to Malta to discuss Operation SHINGLE further, but strong pressure was brought against his so doing. The Operation, scheduled for January 22nd (I am writing this on January 22nd, having decided to write no word of future operations in this diary, however securely I may keep it at No. 10) was showing signs of flagging owing to landing craft problems.

Wednesday, January 5th

Generals Bedell Smith (Eisenhower's Chief of Staff), Gale (Quartermaster General at Algiers), Gammell and Devers arrived for an hour or two on their way back from London. I went to meet them at the Mamounia (Tommy, the Flag Commander, was still in bed) and brought them up to the villa.

I did not go with the others on a picnic but had an agreeable lunch in the garden with Lord Beaverbrook, Lord Moran and Joe Hollis.

Beneš, whose aircraft went u/s last night, again came to dine. Talk was of when the war would end. The P.M. was cautious: "I wouldn't guarantee it won't end in 1944." Beneš was confident: "We must be ready for a German collapse any day after May 1st." The P.M. put it to the vote round the table whether Hitler would still be in power on September 3rd, 1944. There voted:

Yes – the P.M., Lord Beaverbrook, Captain Sanderson (Grenadier Guards) and I.

No – Beneš, Smutmy, Lord Moran, Tommy, John Martin, Sarah, Joe Hollis.

Thursday, January 6th

A small picnic: P.M., Mrs C., Tommy, self. We went back to the scene of our first picnic, a stream running over multi-coloured

---

[1] The frontier proposed after the First World War but extended eastwards after Poland's defeat of the Red Army in 1920.

pebbles between hills on which stood a Jewish village to the right and to the left the house of the local Caid and an old French fort. The P.M. had painted the scene when last he was at Marrakech and the picture hangs in the passage at the Annexe.

The Glaoui of Marrakech, a dignified chieftain in white robes, came to tea. The P.M. thrilled him by showing him the strategic layout in the map-room (which had just been established in the room next to the P.M.'s bedroom by Captain Pim and staff, who had flown out for that purpose).

Again visited the Medina with Lord B., Mrs C. and Sarah. We saw the dancers, the snake charmers and the eloquent story tellers who stand surrounded by a crowd of squatting listeners. The Beaver, watching their gesticulations, said that oratory was the same the whole world over.

Friday, January 7th
First came General Maitland Wilson, and after lunch Alexander, Sir J. Cunningham (C. in C., Med.), Devers, Bedell Smith, Gale and a host of others for a great SHINGLE conference. I dined with the Generals' satellites at the Mamounia hotel. Fitzroy Maclean,* Brigadier accredited to Marshal Tito, and Randolph arrived. Maclean and R. are to parachute into Yugoslavia, taking with them a letter from the P.M. to Tito. Next to SHINGLE and landing craft, the Yugoslav problem, with its intricacies about abandoning Mihailovitch[1] and reconciling King Peter* to Tito, has been our chief interest out here.

Saturday, January 8th
There was a further vast conference in the dining-room, and then the tumult and the shouting died as the military departed leaving Maclean and Randolph behind.

[1] Royalist Yugoslav General who was the first to organise resistance to the German invaders, but soon resolved that the Communist partisans, led by Tito, were an even greater evil. Some of his followers therefore collaborated with the Italians, and even in a few cases with the Germans. He was, all the same, a true patriot. After the war, declining to flee from Yugoslavia, he was tried by Tito and, most disgracefully, hanged. His last words at his trial were: "I have been blown away by the gale of the world."

After dinner the P.M. and Randolph had a bickering match over the qualities of the Foreign Secretary and, in spite of Lord Beaverbrook's efforts, Randolph, having drunk too much whisky, could not be stopped. Fitzroy Maclean says, however, that all will be well in Yugoslavia owing to the absence of whisky and a diet of cabbage soup. Moreover Randolph will be a subordinate officer under his command.

Monday, January 10th

Lord Beaverbrook took Joe and me on a shopping expedition in the Medina. Joe and I had meant to go alone, buying cheap goods for our relatives, but the Beaver led us at breakneck speed from shop to shop in search of dress materials for Joe's family. He finally bought yards of very expensive but quite useless gauze and presented it to Joe. Then he took us through by-ways to an antique shop off the beaten track where we were received by a patriarchal old Moor who gave us mint tea and revoltingly scented quince jam which the Beaver refused for himself but, to our disgust, accepted for Joe and me.

On returning to the villa Lord B. rushed inside to greet Duff Cooper[1] and Lady Diana, who had just arrived by air from Algiers (where Duff Cooper is the newly appointed Ambassador to the Free French) and then dragged me off in a car to the French quarter of the town. There he bought me a magnificent white leather bag to give to whomsoever I wished.

At dinner Lady Diana made a dead set at the P.M. and fascinated him. "There," Lord Moran whispered to me, "you have the historic spectacle of a professional siren vamping an elder statesman." And it certainly was.

Tuesday, January 11th

After dinner all except the P.M. and the Beaver went to a reception given by General de Villate in honour of M. Puaux, the Resident General of Morocco. There was Berber music and Berber dancing in the garden and much French conversation in the house.

[1] Viscount Norwich.*

De Gaulle was due tomorrow. He was to lunch with the P.M. and it was hoped that a prolonged coolness between them would be terminated. But there was nearly a disaster. General de Lattre de Tassigny had, on the advice of Mr Macmillan (Resident Minister in Algiers) been invited to dine and stay the night on Thursday. A message from Algiers, given to me over the telephone by Duff Cooper's Counsellor (Kingsley Rucker), said that General de L. de T. had felt he should ask de Gaulle's permission. De Gaulle had said it would be "most inopportune" for him to accept at present.

The P.M. was furious and said in that case he would not see de Gaulle. Duff Cooper with difficulty pacified him, and the conversation merely became a heated discussion between Mrs C. (very anti-French), the P.M. (temporarily anti-French) and the Duff Coopers arguing the other way.

Wednesday, January 12th

At 8.00 a.m. Sawyers, the P.M.'s butler (slightly swollen headed since Stalin drank his health at Teheran) said the P.M. wanted to see me. I went in my dressing-gown, was asked to repeat the message about de Lattre de Tassigny and was told that a message should be sent to the airfield to tell de Gaulle, on arrival, that the P.M. did not wish to waste his valuable time. Duff, summoned in haste from the Mamounia, managed to pacify the P.M. once more.

De Gaulle arrived for lunch, at which I was not present, and spent the afternoon in conversation with the P.M. who told him, in a firm but friendly way, just where he got off and remonstrated about the recent arrests of Flandin, Boisson, etc., at Algiers.

After dinner, in an expansive moment, the P.M. promised I could rejoin my Squadron for OVERLORD. I got Lord Moran to bear witness to this and went jubilant to bed.[1]

---

[1] "You seem to think," Churchill said to me, "that this war is being fought for your personal amusement." There was a pause. "However, if I were your age I should feel the same, and so you may have two months' fighting leave. But no more holidays this year."

Thursday, January 13th

There was a review of French troops at which the P.M., in his Air Commodore's uniform, and de Gaulle stood side by side at the saluting base. The rest of us, with French and Moorish dignitaries, were in the stand behind. I was particularly impressed by the Spahis and the Zouaves – less so by the formation "shoot-ups" undertaken by the local French Flying Training School.

We had a picnic in glorious country at a place called the Pont Naturel. There was a deep gorge through which a stream ran, falling from rock to rock into limpid blue pools. Lady Diana gave one look at it and said Alph![1] The P.M. insisted on being carried down and scrambling over the rocks.

Sarah gave a cocktail party for the myriad hangers-on – American officers, W.A.A.F. cypherers, the crew of the York, etc. There were Berber dances. Harold Macmillan arrived.

Friday, January 14th

The party flew, in four aeroplanes, to Gibraltar. We made a detour to fly over Casablanca and lunched admirably en route.

At Gib. there was a further SHINGLE conference while Mrs C., Sarah, John Martin and I were taken up to the top of the rock and through some of the tunnels. Embarked on H.M.S. *King George V* for home. Very comfortable cabins, the officers having turned out of theirs for us. The P.M. slept in the Admiral's sea cabin and there was a "High Table Mess" in the Petty Officers' quiet room.

Saturday, January 15th

At sea. Sunshine and gentle breezes as we steamed westwards towards the Azores. Paced the quarter deck and explored the ship, which is an exceedingly overheated one. All the arrange-

---

[1] In Xanadu did Kubla Khan
 A stately pleasure-dome decree;
 Where Alph, the sacred river, ran
 Through caverns measureless to man
 Down to a sunless sea.
　　　　　Coleridge.

ments were admirably conceived and nothing was left undone –
even Marines to precede and escort us down the passages.

There was ear-splitting battle practice – including the 14-inch
guns – after lunch with our escorting cruiser, *Mauritius*. Each
ship fired at the other at an angle off. In the evening we all dined
excellently at a mess dinner in the Ward Room.

Sunday, January 16th

Divine service, very well conducted, in the Ward Room. All
present except the P.M. and the Beaver. Sea still calm, but we
had turned north and the skies were grey.

Monday, January 17th

The P.M. went all Harrovian after lunch and said that the lines
"God give us bases to guard and beleaguer, etc." had always
inspired him greatly, despite the fact that he detested football.
He spent an hour or more in the gun-room answering questions
from the delighted Subs and Midshipmen.

We landed at Plymouth at 11.00 p.m. and boarded the train.
Found many letters awaiting me, including the news that Terence O'Neill* was engaged to Jean Whitaker and that poor Dick
Bock, nicest of 168 Squadron, had been shot down in the sea
and died of exposure last Friday.

Tuesday, January 18th

At Paddington the Churchill family and the Cabinet awaited the
train and greeted us effusively.

The P.M. made a dramatic entry into the House of Commons
– the real reason for his hastening home – and was loudly
cheered. He answered his Questions and then held a Cabinet
meeting in his room at the House, leaving at 1.28 to lunch with
the King at 1.30! *Plus ça change, plus c'est la même chose*, I
observe.

After dinner I took some oranges and lemons (of which rare
luxuries I have brought back a large number) to Argyll House.
Mother and I spent half an hour with grandfather[1], who is in

[1] Robert Crewe-Milnes, 1st and last Marquess of Crewe.*

bed but looking well and cheerful in spite of having now gone all but stone blind. Peggy, returning from dinner at the Spanish Embassy, said she heard we had returned by sea – which shows how well that secret was kept!

Wednesday, January 19th
Put on civilian clothes; the first time I have done so for more than a few hours since 1941.

After returning from a meeting on Far Eastern Strategy in the C.W.R., the P.M. told me his heart was giving him trouble. He ascribed it to indigestion, but evidently he must now go warily.

Thursday, January 20th
The P.M. saw the Poles about frontiers. The problem is a hard one and the Soviet Government are ungracious bargainers. Negotiations proceeding on basis of the Curzon line.

Saturday, January 22nd
Operation SHINGLE – landings by Anglo-American force behind the enemy forces in Italy with the object of capturing Rome – has started well and General Alexander seems confident.

A good deal of work and kept up late with telegrams.

Tuesday, January 25th
Lunched with the P.M. and Mrs C. in the downstairs dining-room at No. 10. Other guests: Mrs Romilly,[1] Mrs Henley, Pamela Churchill, Lord Portal.* One of the worst phrases of the official jargon today is an "overall strategic concept". The P.M. said that he has an "underall strategic concept". The people of this country are becoming dangerously over-confident. There is, after all, a risk that we may suffer serious defeats this year, since the Hun is still very tough and his morale has not seriously

[1] Clementine Churchill's sister. Her elder son was one of the prisoners of war selected by Hitler as hostages in case things should go badly for him. Her younger son, Esmond, fought for the Spanish Republicans in the Civil War, joined the Communist Party, married Jessica Mitford and was killed in action in the R.A.F.

deteriorated. The P.M.'s "concept" is therefore to capture Rome, as a result of SHINGLE ("too many pebbles on the beach", John Peck says), and then while the cheering is still loud to make the most depressing speech of his career.

The Cabinet decided in favour of asking the King to make Princess Elizabeth Princess of Wales when she comes of age next April. The King did not favour the idea.[1]

Our policy with regard to Russo-Polish frontiers, about which the P.M. is going to telegraph to Stalin (with whom he now maintains a voluminous telegraphic correspondence), and also about Palestine and Greater Syria was thrashed out in Cabinet.

After dinner the operations in Italy monopolised attention.

Wednesday, January 26th
Italian operation going well; build-up ashore quicker than had been expected.

Thursday, January 27th
Lunched with Geoffrey Lloyd at Claridges; he wants a seat on a Ministerial Committee and thinks I can help.

Monday, January 31st
The P.M. was much disgruntled by a very ungracious telegram from Stalin about Russia's share in the Italian navy and said many harsh things about S., who is obviously less amenable on paper than in conversation.

---

[1] For accession purposes she came of age at eighteen, though everybody else still attained their majority at twenty-one. Presumably the Prime Minister put the suggestion to the King at his audience that evening.

SIX

ANZIO AND THE BLITZ RENEWED
FEBRUARY–MARCH 1944

Tuesday, February 1st

Went to the House with the P.M. whose replies to Questions, re-drafted by himself last night, were in a witty vein and delighted everybody.

A reply from Tito, very different in tone from Stalin's, arrived.

Lunched with David Margesson at Ciro's.

Dined with Gay in Baker Street and spent the rest of the evening at the Ritz with Diana Harvey and Zara Strutt (the latter in plaster of Paris). Talked to Zara in her bedroom (she pointed out that the plaster of Paris was a kind of *ceinture de chasteté*).

Friday, February 4th

Terence O'Neill's wedding to Jean Whitaker at the Guards' Chapel.

Left with the P.M. for Chequers. He went to bed for dinner and Tommy and I dined alone. The P.M. is suffering from indigestion and also very perturbed by SHINGLE's lack of success. It was strategically sound and it had a perfect beginning. He cannot understand the failure to push inland from the beach-head. While the battle still rages he is refraining from asking Alexander the questions to which the P.M. can find no answer, but his great faith in A., though not dissipated, is a little shaken.

Saturday, February 5th

General Donovan (U.S. Army), General Eastwood (to be vetted for Governorship of Gibraltar), and Mrs Churchill came in time for lunch. General Donovan, though straight from the SHINGLE area, can throw no light. (Operationally they have great courage; administratively none, said the P.M.)

Sunday, February 6th
The Polish Prime Minister (Mikolajczyk),[1] Foreign Secretary (Romer) and Ambassador (Raczynski) came to lunch. Also Mr Eden, Sir Owen O'Malley[2] (our Ambassador to the Polish Government), Lord Cherwell and Raymond Guest.[3] Except for the latter, all were present afterwards at a conference on Russo-Polish relations, at which I took notes and subsequently made a record. The Eastern frontier is the main difficulty, and the fact that the Poles do not believe in Stalin's good faith.

It was the first time I had sat all through a conference at which the P.M. was in the chair. He was certainly most effective as chairman.

O'Malley stayed to dine. He told me that the Balkan and East European countries still feel that Germany is their only hope of protection against Russia.

Monday, February 7th
Dined at the Savoy, in a private room, in a party given by Victor Rothschild to celebrate Judy Montagu's twenty-first birthday. There were present: the P. M., Mrs Churchill, Mary, Brendan Bracken*, Mr Harcourt Johnston, Mrs Montagu, Judy and Mrs Laycock (Angela Dudley Ward). Dinner was excellent and the wine, from the Tring cellars, included Pol Roger 1921, the Rothschild Château Yquem and a remarkable old brandy. There

---

[1] After General Sikorski's death he became Prime Minister of Poland. A man of high principle and determination, he was subjected to strong pressure by the British and Americans and finally deceived and cheated by Stalin and Molotov.

[2] British diplomat, married to the author Ann Bridge, he narrowly escaped involvement in the "Franc scandal" which shook the Foreign Office to its foundations in the 1920s. In consequence he lost seniority. Ended his career as a not very good Ambassador in Lisbon, but on Polish affairs he took a firm and praiseworthy stance.

[3] An American descendant of the 1st Viscount Wimborne and a cousin of Churchill.

was an extremely good conjuror who appeared at the end of dinner and whom the P.M. declared to be the best he had ever seen.

Wednesday, February 9th
Lunched at No. 10 with the P.M. and Mrs Churchill. The other guests were the Duchess of Buccleuch[1], the C.I.G.S. and Lady Brooke, James Stuart,[2] mother, Mr Irving Berlin (the American song writer and producer), and Juliet Henley. After lunch the P.M. forestalled Irving Berlin asking leading questions by himself addressing them to his potential interlocutor (e.g. "When do you think the war will end, Mr Berlin?"). This I thought was ingenious technique. Berlin said he thought Roosevelt would get in at the coming presidential election, and in this his name should help him because in all Republican systems human nature triumphed over constitutional principle and the hereditary system came into its own. This also applied to our own Labour Party in which the wife or son of a well known M.P. was always in demand as a parliamentary candidate.

It later transpired that the reason why Mr Irving Berlin had been bidden to lunch was a comic misunderstanding. There are sprightly, if somewhat over-vivid, political summaries telegraphed home every week from the Washington Embassy. The P.M., inquiring who wrote them, had been told by me, "Mr Isaiah Berlin, Fellow of All Souls and Tutor of New College." When Irving Berlin came over here to entertain the troops with his songs, the P.M. confused him with Isaiah and invited him to lunch – and conversed with him, to his embarrassment, as if he had been Isaiah.

The new Health Service is under discussion. Brendan and Lord Beaverbrook came round to persuade the P.M. against the decision taken in the Cabinet this evening which had been in favour of the Minister of Reconstruction's [Lord Woolton*] proposals. To bed at 2.40 a.m.

---

[1] Mary (Molly) Lascelles, well-known and widely admired wife of Walter, 8th Duke of Buccleuch.
[2] Viscount Stuart of Findhorn.

Thursday, February 10th
Submitted a letter to Stalin, thanking for the music of the new
Soviet anthem, and got it signed unamended. I think this is the
first letter the P.M. has ever written to S. (as opposed to
telegrams).

Gave Cynthia Keppel lunch at the Churchill Club,[1] in Dean's
Yard, of which I have just been made a member. A lovely building
and a good lunch.

Took Cynthia to the first night of Priestley's play *Desert
Highway*, which Mrs Churchill wanted vetted before she went
herself. It was a singularly bad play about soldiers in the
desert.

Friday, February 11th
It being my weekend off I went to North Weald, where No. 168
Squadron is, to fly. Arrived for dinner and slept in a room in the
mess.

Saturday, February 12th
168 today lost their Mustang I As to No. 2 Squadron and received
in exchange 2 Squadron's dreary Mustang Is. But I borrowed
one of the I As and flew for one and a half hours in the morning.
I tried to find Chequers, but the visibility was shocking and I
failed. Not realising there was wireless silence I demanded
a homing and an added stir was caused by the fact that I gave
my old call sign "Floral 51" – a number which no longer
exists. I was homed through a balloon barrage but arrived
safely.

Sunday, February 13th
Flew with Johnny Low,[2] an Australian. We did some close and
wide formation and a little air combat, during which I blacked

---

[1] A fine hall of Westminster School (evacuated from London) which was used
as a luncheon club for the higher echelons working in Whitehall.
[2] A man of sterling qualities and an excellent pilot. On returning to my
squadron in May 1944, I travelled to Odiham with him and the pretty
Australian W.A.A.F. to whom he was engaged. He was shot down and killed
three weeks later, one of those war-time tragedies which dented the callous
skin we had all temporarily grown.

out with surprising facility. Ended with a perfect three-point landing. Returned to London after lunch.

In a book I am reading Princess Lieven quotes Madame de Sevigné on sight-seeing: "What I see tires me, and what I don't see worries me". At the rate things are going in Italy I don't suppose there will remain much sight-seeing to be done after the war.

Monday, February 14th
The Polish question is coming to a head. Some people think that our attitude is a little reminiscent of Munich, but I am sure that the Poles' right course is to accept what they can get while still maintaining their right to fuller claims. O'Malley, our Ambassador, is evidently very much against selling out the Poles and points out that "What is morally indefensible is always politically inept".

Tuesday, February 15th
The Anzio bridgehead hangs fire, the Polish Government seems about to resign and Brendan says the home front is becoming seriously war-weary. Meanwhile we are approaching, in his view, one of "the most desperate military ventures in history" – about which too many people are far too confident. Cabinet approved new Health scheme. (Brendan opposing it violently.)

Wednesday, February 16th
To the House for Questions. The P.M. answered an inspired question about British casualties in Italy so as to give some ammunition for countering the American view that American troops are doing all the fighting. Actually it is the unenterprising behaviour of the American Command at Anzio that has lost us our great opportunity there.

We sent 900 bombers over Berlin last night and lost five per cent.

Friday, February 18th

Gave Gerry Fitzgerald's[1] Polish Jew friend, Flaisjer,[2] lunch at the Travellers. On saying goodbye he said: "You have not changed very much, Mr Colville, but you are, allow me to say, perhaps more majestic." I don't know whether this is a compliment or not, nor whether the reference is to increased physical majesty (due to the chef at Marrakech) or otherwise.

After lunch the results of the West Derbyshire by-election came through: Lord Hartington[3] lost to Mr White, the Independent, by 4,500 votes. This caused a pall of the blackest gloom to fall on the P.M. who is personally afflicted by this emphatic blow to the Government in view of the *verbosa et grandis epistola* which he wrote to Hartington, in which he lauded the political record of the Cavendish family. Moreover there was trouble at Brighton a fortnight ago when he wrote another long letter and, in the event, Teeling, the Government candidate, only scraped home in the safest of Tory seats.

Sitting in a chair in his study at the Annexe, the P.M. looked old, tired and very depressed and was even muttering about a General Election. Now, he said, with great events pending, was the time when national unity was essential: the question of annihilating great states had to be faced: it began to look as if democracy had not the persistence necessary to go through with it, however well it might have shown its capacity for defence. In sombre state he went off to Chequers.

---

[1] My mother's first cousin, cultured, insatiably thirsty for knowledge and a devout Roman Catholic bachelor with whom I often stayed in Cambridge. He failed by a few weeks to span two hundred years from his grandfather's birth to his own death, a record to which he was keenly looking forward.

[2] A brilliant Polish Jewish historian whom Fitzgerald housed as a non-paying guest throughout the war after his narrow escape from the Gestapo. Became a senior university professor in Israel.

[3] Eldest son of the 10th Duke of Devonshire. Married after a major religious controversy Kathleen Kennedy, daughter of Joseph P. Kennedy. She was viciously attacked for agreeing that any children of the marriage should be brought up as Anglicans. He was killed in action in 1944 and she died in an aircraft accident a few years later.

Sunday, February 20th
In the evening there was a short, sharp blitz. Incautiously I walked out of the Annexe to look at the rockets and flares, but a disturbance in the atmosphere immediately above my head warned me that something was amiss and, showing great speed, I reached the brick blast screen just as a stick of three bombs straddled the Horse Guards Parade. No. 10 was superficially damaged: all the windows and window frames were blown in and large pieces of plaster came down from the ceilings in the drawing-rooms, leaving gaping holes. Downing Street is carpeted with glass, a bomb at the corner of the Treasury (which killed several people in Whitehall) burst a large water main, and generally speaking the atmosphere is quite 1940-like. The glow of fires in the sky shows that the damage was widespread, though the Duty Group Captain tells me only sixty aircraft were over.

Monday, February 21st
The Ministry of Works and Buildings, under Lord Portal's personal supervision, cleared up the debris with amazing speed and boarded up all the windows (at No. 10).

Tuesday, February 22nd
The P.M. made a speech on the war situation in the H. of C. and it went very well.
   David Margesson dined with me in the mess and was afterwards invited to see the P.M., who is a bit worried about the Home Front and the future of the Tory party. The P.M. told me it was a great effort to him to make these speeches now.

Wednesday, February 23rd
Took Mary Churchill to see Terence Rattigan's new play [*While the Sun Shines*] and to dine at the Coq d'Or. Bombs fell in St James's Street and shook us in Stratton Street. The effort is small on the Luftwaffe's part but the results are considerable.

Thursday, February 24th
London seems disturbed by the raids and less ebullient than in 1940–41.

Tuesday, February 29th
Stalin has answered, unhelpfully, the proposals for a solution of
the Polish problem. If he had been willing to give a little he could
still have won for Russia the substance of everything he required,
and could have inspired new confidence and readiness to co-
operate in the U.S.A. and this country. When I look back at
Russian diplomacy during these last five years, it seems to me
sadly inept. A little courtesy and a little generosity could have
achieved much. As it is the establishment of really close relationships with the U.S.S.R. looks like being very hard to attain.

Thursday, March 2nd
Accompanied Mrs Churchill to see Bevin's "Back to Work"
Exhibition at Burlington House. It shows how disabled men can
be taught useful trades. I was impressed by the way in which
Mrs C. talked to all the men there and did the whole thing with
real thoroughness.

Friday, March 3rd
President Roosevelt's sudden announcement at a press conference of the recent negotiations with Stalin about Italian ships
came as a bombshell just before we left for Chequers, but the
P.M. finally reached the conclusion that this gaffe was due to a
blunder and not to malice aforethought. Still, he said some hard
things to Winant.*

Air Marshal Coningham[1] was at Chequers. In commenting on
the Anzio bridgehead the P.M. said, "I thought we should fling
a wild-cat ashore and all we got was an old stranded whale on
the beach."

Saturday, March 4th
The P.M. in benevolent but sombre mood. He is disturbed by
the attitude of Russia – Stalin refuses to be moderate about the

---

[1] "Mary" Coningham commanded the 2nd Tactical Air Force (in which I
served). A forceful and flamboyant New Zealander, he did not co-operate
wholeheartedly with the army and was a severe critic of Field Marshal
Montgomery's strategy and personality. Killed when a Tudor passenger
aircraft crashed in the Atlantic shortly after the war.

Poles – and many other matters, political and strategic. He said that he felt like telling the Russians, "Personally I fight tyranny whatever uniform it wears or slogans it utters."[1]

Late at night, after the inevitable film, the P.M. took his station in the Great Hall and began to smoke Turkish cigarettes – the first time I have ever seen him smoke one – saying that they were the only thing he got out of the Turks. He keeps on reverting to the point that he has not long to live and tonight, while the gramophone played the "Marseillaise" and "Sambre et Meuse", he told Coningham, Harold Macmillan, Pug, Tommy and me that this was his political testament for after the war: "Far more important than India or the Colonies or solvency is *the Air*. We live in a world of wolves – and *bears*." Then we had to listen to most of Gilbert and Sullivan on the gramophone, before retiring at 3.00 a.m.

Coningham is most obliging about promising me information about the future of 168 and 268 squadrons and today the P.M. renewed his promise that I might return to active service for the coming offensive.

Sunday, March 5th
After lunch, at which the shortcomings of General Maitland Wilson (Jumbo) were discussed with Harold Macmillan, the P.M. settled down to bezique with Pamela Churchill, and I went for a walk with the Prof.,[2] who talked like the gloomy dean. He foresees a crushing defeat for the Conservative Party at the next election and its possible collapse like the Liberals after the last war. He says that there is much annoyance in Government circles because Brendan and Lord B. attempt, by using their influence with the P.M., to sabotage measures such as the new health proposals about which they are hopelessly ignorant but which have been worked out by experts, with great pains and hard work, over a long period. Moreover he sees great danger in the efforts of Hudson, Amery, Lord B., etc., to sabotage

---

[1] A statement he embodied in a speech over a year later, on March 15th, 1945.
[2] Professor F. A. Lindemann (Lord Cherwell*).

agreement with the Americans over Article VII, which is intended to be an international measure to regulate the trade cycle. To oppose this in order to please the farmers, and thus retain the agricultural vote, would be wrong and perhaps politically disastrous too. Late in the day when the latter topic arose again the P.M., who is inclined to the Beaverbrook camp on this matter, quoted Bonar Law and applied the quotation to the Prof. "It is no use arguing with a prophet; you can only disbelieve him."

The P.M. has now taken to sitting in the Private Secretary's room in the evening for long periods. This makes it hard to work, unless feeding him with telegrams, and impossible to telephone. We got to bed about 2.00 a.m.

Monday, March 6th
Moved to 55 Chester Square where I am going to live, as a P.G., with Lady Ampthill.[1]

Charles Ritchie dined with me in the mess. He says that 14,000 members of the Canadian forces over here have married English wives.

Tuesday, March 7th
The P.M. says this world ("this dusty and lamentable ball") is now too beastly to live in. People act so revoltingly that they just don't deserve to survive.

Monday, March 13th
Brendan is very down on the President whom he suspects of being more interested in his own re-election than the common struggle.

[1] Tall and imposing, she was the daughter of the 6th Earl Beauchamp, a sister of Lady Maud Hoare (Sir Samuel's wife) and the mother of four tall, stalwart sons. She was a lady-in-waiting to Queen Mary and in both World Wars held the same position as head of the organisation for tracing British prisoners of war. She fought a stern, and expensive, rearguard action in the "Russell Baby" case, endeavouring to prove the illegitimacy of her eldest son's child. Another of her sons, Admiral Sir Guy Russell, commanded H.M.S. *Duke of York* when she sank the German battleship *Scharnhorst*.

There are signs of disquiet about the Atlantic Charter, to which the P.M. maintained in the House the other day Germany had no claim by right. I foresee that after the war is over the Germans will make the same play with alleged breaches of the Charter as they did after the last war with the repudiation of the Fourteen Points.

Tuesday, March 14th
Dined with the Hollonds[1] at Whitehall Court. We discussed the inaccuracy of history: every event appears different to different spectators and gains or loses colour and accuracy if described after the passage of time.

A violent raid. Bombs fell in Eaton Square and shook No. 55 Chester Square. Much impressed by the demeanour of Lady Ampthill's four old servants who showed great phlegm. I was really quite frightened.

Wednesday, March 15th
A problem is whether to go on supporting the King of Italy and Badoglio[2] or to accept the claims of the so-called "Six Parties" at Naples. The P.M. is adamant in support of the former policy, largely because he thinks any new régime would try to court favour from the Italian populace by standing up to the Allies. Roosevelt now seems to be veering in the opposite direction.

Tito is telegraphing most politely and shows every sign of wishing to be amenable.

Friday, March 17th
Montgomery lunched with the P.M.; his car is as ostentatious and covered with emblems as himself.

The P.M. did not go down to Chequers. I dined with Rosemary and Hinch at Boulestins. An air-raid warning sounded and the P.M. dashed off in his car to Hyde Park to see Mary's battery at work.

[1] H. A. Hollond, Dean and subsequent Vice Master of Trinity College, Cambridge.
[2] Marshal Badoglio, loyal subject of King Victor Emmanuel III, became head of the Italian Government when Italy sought an armistice in September 1943, and Mussolini was arrested.

Saturday, March 18th
The P.M. finally went off to Chequers at 5.30 p.m. after having King Peter* to lunch and cajoling him to do as we want in the Yugoslav imbroglio (but he won't take any action until after he has married Princess Alexandra of Greece on Monday). He also received a disagreeable note from U. J. [Stalin] about Poland. It is quite obvious that the Bear proposes to reach no agreement and accept no compromise and is fabricating all sorts of excuses to this end. His latest pretence is that there have been leakages (which are in any case almost certainly known to have come through the Soviet Embassy) about his correspondence with the P.M. and that therefore he cannot continue it. The P.M. took all this philosophically, but said that it was now obvious our efforts to forge a Soviet–Polish agreement had failed and that he would soon have to make a cold announcement in Parliament to this effect. It all seems to augur ill for the future of relations between this country and the U.S.S.R.

Tuesday, March 21st
This war would be much easier to conduct without Allies. I wonder if we shall ever reach a form of international organisation which will not be made a mockery by the fact that national policies are always self-interested and thus conflicting.

Wednesday, March 22nd
A debate in the House on the 1939–43 and Africa Stars. The P.M. spoke. M.P.s seem deeply interested in these trifling matters at a time when all the major issues of winning the war and the peace ought to be in their minds. Brendan tells me that the P.M. is seriously thinking of becoming Foreign Secretary himself, so that Eden may concentrate on the House of Commons and Home Affairs. The P.M. doesn't want Lord Cranborne as Foreign Secretary because he fears he might quarrel with him, Lord C. being obstinate.

Thursday, March 23rd
The P.M. did not go to the Cabinet this morning and, cause and effect, it completed its deliberations in half an hour. Instead he

went off by train with General Eisenhower to look at American troops.

Monday, March 27th
During the week-end the P.M. had a really rude telegram from Stalin and it seems that our efforts to promote a Russo-Polish understanding have failed.

Tuesday, March 28th
The Government were defeated in the H. of C. by one vote (Harvie-Watt was in his bath) over a clause of the Education Bill. Great political excitement; the P.M. welcomes this chance of hitting back hard at his critics and proposes to have the clause reinstated, making the matter a vote of confidence.

Wednesday, March 29th
Education Bill to the fore; P.M.'s box accumulating monstrous pile of urgent and unsettled matters.

Thursday, March 30th
Rode before breakfast, on General Eisenhower's horse, with Bridget and Jean [Greig]. Very refreshing.

The Government got its majority of over 400 and the P.M. was radiant. I thought it was cracking a nut with a sledgehammer.

At midnight we left King's Cross by train for Yorkshire. The party was the P.M., Jack Churchill, Tommy and self. The P.M. worked till 3.00 a.m.

Friday, March 31st
Left the train at Driffield. Inspected R.A.S.C. and corps troops, to whom the P.M. made a speech, and then the 5th Guards Armoured Division. Saw a tank display and the P.M. went for a ride in a Cromwell. General O'Connor (who was captured in N. Africa and escaped when Italy fell), Sir Harry Floyd[1] (B.G.S.) and Brigadier Mathews accompanied us everywhere. The Guards, with their Shermans, were very smart indeed. Before

[1] In civilian life Chairman of Christie's.

lunch we saw an exhibition of lorry driving through water at
Kirkham Abbey and there we met an old and very decrepit man,
Colonel Wormald, with whom the P.M. charged at Omdurman.

Rejoined the train at Malton, lunched on it and de-trained
at Harrogate where the population gave the P.M. a rousing
reception. Inspected the 15th Scottish Division and saw some
battle practice.

In the train, on the way back to Chequers, the P.M., who
had seen a note in the box referring to staff rearrangements
necessitated by my departure for the coming offensive, said I
couldn't go. This, however, is not the last word.

At dinner he spent most of the time repeating the *Lays of
Ancient Rome* and *Marmion*, which was a remarkable feat of
memory but rather boring. Brendan was at Chequers, a rare
event as he hates the place.

SEVEN

COUNT-DOWN TO OVERLORD
APRIL–MAY 1944

Saturday, April 1st
It was Mrs Churchill's birthday and the party was a family one, consisting of Duncan[1] and Diana, Sarah, Mary and Jack. I rallied first Mary and then Mrs C. in support of my plea to rejoin the R.A.F. in accordance with the P.M.'s promise. The clocks were advanced to double summer time and we sat up till 4.30 while the P.M. worked, Duncan read important papers not intended for him to see and I played Gilbert and Sullivan and old music-hall songs (which are the P.M.'s choice of music) on the gramophone.

Sunday, April 2nd
Monsieur Emanuel Astier de la Vigerie (a French Resistance leader) and Mr Garvin [former editor of the *Observer*] came to lunch with his wife. The P.M. came out with the supreme blasphemy that "every nation creates God in its own image". He gave Astier a bit of his mind about de Gaulle and the French National Committee (whose execution of Pucheu[2] has done them very great harm here and above all in the United States).

Mr and Mrs Attlee came to dinner. Cabinet changes are under discussion owing to Eden wanting to give up the Foreign Office as he doesn't feel he can manage it as well as the Leadership of

---

[1] Lord Duncan-Sandys.*
[2] Vichy Minister of the Interior 1941–42 and alleged to be responsible for the shooting of hostages by the Germans.

the House. At dinner the P.M. talked of the old order changing and said, "The pomp and vanity must go; the old world will have had the honour of leading the way into the new" – by which I daresay he meant a reference to himself. Even if he did not, it applies.

Monday, April 3rd
Up from Chequers in time to lunch with mother and Philip at the Guards Club. P.'s brigade look like being disbanded to provide reinforcements for the Guards division, though the P.M. has sent minutes to Montgomery and to P. J. Grigg protesting.

Tuesday, April 4th
On late duty. Cabinet reconstruction: Eden, James Stuart, Donald Somervell[1] and Edward Bridges present. Former proposals (Cranborne to F.O., Brendan to Dominions Office, Gwylym Lloyd George to Ministry of Information and Shinwell to Ministry of Fuel and Power) superseded by: Eden, Leader of H. of C. and Lord President of the Council; Cranborne, Foreign Secretary and Leader of House of Lords; Attlee, Deputy P.M. and S. of S. for Dominions. The Labour leaders were against Shinwell, who is a party rebel; and many people thought Brendan would be a disaster at the Dominions Office with the meeting of the Dominions Prime Ministers pending.

At 2.00 a.m. the P.M., having done a little work, said "I am now more dead than alive" and retired, very conversationally, to bed. The prospect of the Second Front worries him though he says he is "hardening to it".

Thursday, April 6th
P.M. very excited about financial scandal in Air Ministry connected with breeding pigs. Instigated by Lord Beaverbrook, of course. Lord B. stayed till 2.00 a.m.; we went to bed after 3.00.

---

[1] Attorney General. Briefly Home Secretary in 1945. Churchill always declared that his father was the master at Harrow who taught him to write good English.

Good Friday, April 7th
Spent the Easter weekend at Madeley, recovering from the effects of a very hectic ten days. I read part of *Paradise Lost* from the first edition there.

Tuesday, April 11th
The P.M. has saved Philip's brigade, which General Montgomery and the War Office wanted to disband and use as reinforcements for the Guards' Armoured Division. I sent him a minute on the subject after Montgomery's reply, saying that an officer of the brigade (i.e. Philip) had told me of the deplorable effect it would have on the men's morale and fighting spirit. The P.M. wrote: "Let me see this when the War Office reply comes in. We can then take them both on at once."

Wednesday, April 12th
Struck by how very tired and worn out the P.M. looks now.
     He marked my *cri de coeur* about rejoining my squadron: "C.A.S. What can be done?" This is most inappropriate, as it is purely a question of internal administration in this office.

Thursday, April 13th
The P.M. saw King Peter, whose chances of regaining his throne are visibly shrinking, and, it seems, persuaded him to dismiss his Government.
     We have been unnaturally busy for the last three weeks and the position is not improved by the P.M. assuming control of the F.O. while Eden is away on leave.

Friday, April 14th
The P.M. did not leave London for Chequers till nearly 8.00 p.m. and the afternoon at No. 10 was both hectic and annoying. Moreover I have let myself in for making all the arrangements for the visits of the Dominion Prime Ministers, and their entertainment, next month.
     Inoculated for T.A.B., typhus and tetanus. At dinner, Desmond Morton* was very gloomy. Everybody is nowadays. It all seems like the last act of a Greek tragedy. In the first act

one can stand Agamemnon being murdered in his bath; in the last, such an atmosphere of gloom and doom prevails that the audience sit in solemn dejection. Now, in the shadow of an impending struggle which may be history's most fatal, a restless and dissatisfied mood possesses many people in all circles and walks of life. And over everything hangs the uncertainty of Russia's future policy towards Europe and the world.

Thursday, April 20th

The P.M. has apparently now reconciled himself to my rejoining my squadron. After lunch he asked me what date I thought of going and then, in the copy of *My Early Life* which he was signing for the American, Mr McCloy,[1] he drew my attention to the passage on page 180 in which he describes his own difficulties in getting out to the Omdurman campaign.

Commiserating with the enemy on having their backs to the wall, the P.M. said to me, "I'd run like Hell to help Hitler, if I were a Hun!"

After dinner, reverting to the possibility of replacing Eden by Cranborne, the P.M. said that the trouble about the latter was that when he wasn't ill he would be obstinate. It would be a question of a fortnight's illness alternating with a fortnight's obstinacy.

Friday, April 21st

We spent the day at the House of Commons while the P.M. listened to the debate on Empire affairs and prepared his own speech. He re-wrote it in a last-minute feverish rush and wasn't even able to have his afternoon sleep in the bed which he had had specially installed in his room at the House. Nevertheless he made a good speech, showing more vigour than he has of late and presenting a fine apologia for the British Commonwealth and Empire. The House approved.

---

[1] American Under Secretary for War, later American High Commissioner in Germany and finally Chairman of the Chase Bank. Brother-in-law of Lewis Douglas who succeeded Winant as American Ambassador in London.

Monday, April 24th
Eden, looking scarlet with sunburn, stayed talking to the P.M. till 2.00 a.m. Anyhow the P.M. is no longer acting Foreign Secretary which is a merciful dispensation. To bed at 3.15 in spite of recent resolutions by the P.M. to make 1.30 his bedtime.

Tuesday, April 25th
The P.M. told me that I could have six weeks' operational flying and that he was feeling the same way himself. He would be among the first on the bridgehead, he said, if he possibly could – and what fun it would be to get there before Monty.

Wednesday, April 26th
The P.M. made a fiasco of Questions. He lost his place, answered the wrong question and forgot the name of the Maharajah of Kashmir. He announced a rise in service pay.

Thursday, April 27th
Question of bombing French targets, with consequent high civilian casualties, much to the fore. The P.M. and most of the Cabinet strongly against continuing.

Went in the car with Mrs Churchill to Regent's Park and walked across to Gloucester Gate discussing the war and admiring the cherry blossom.

Friday, April 28th
Motored down to Chequers with Mrs C. Field Marshal Smuts and his son, Jan, arrived shortly afterwards and we went for a walk with them up the hill, through flowering gorse bushes to the South African War Memorial. Smuts was very attentive to the wild flowers and the birds.

The P.M. arrived alone in his car, fast asleep with his black bandage over his eyes and remained asleep in the stationary car before the front door. At dinner Smuts said that order and discipline were the first essentials of a democracy; in these days too much was said of rights and too little of duties. There was a film, Smuts went to bed, and the P.M. worked till 1.30, when the combined efforts of the Prof., Tommy and myself got him to bed too.

Saturday, April 29th

The P.M. did not awake till 11.35, which was strange. After lunch Jan Smuts and I walked up Beacon Hill while the P.M. and the Field Marshal discussed the future world order in the orchard. The Prime Minister of New Zealand and Mrs Fraser and the First Sea Lord[1] and Lady Cunningham arrived at tea-time.

At dinner Smuts said, "You must speak the language of the Old Testament to describe what is happening in Europe today." There was another film, *Fanny by Gaslight*, after which all but the P.M. went to bed. I nearly put my foot in it by admitting that most of my operational activities in a Mustang would be photographic. The P.M. was indignant, said he understood my wanting to kill Huns, but really wouldn't let me go just to take photographs.

Sunday, April 30th

Colonel Hudson, just back from Yugoslavia where he was with Mihailovitch's people, swelled the party at luncheon. Mary also came and sat between Smuts and me. We had a three-cornered conversation. Smuts said Hitler was not a great man: he was utterly undistinguished though he had the capacity of spell-binding. It was a great disappointment to him to see how a civilised nation like the Germans could fall beneath that spell. It seemed to show that human nature was only capable of so much and no more; it must give beneath a certain strain. What the world needed was something more fundamental. We should all re-read the New Testament, not so much for the theology, which was out of date, but for the psychology. (I disagree.)

I sat in the sun in the orchard – it was almost too hot – talking to Jan Smuts who has the materialist outlook, the worship of science and progress which I found almost universal among young South Africans.

The Smuts and the Cunninghams left after tea. While the P.M. worked, I drove with Mrs C., Mr Fraser, Jack and Mary some way from Chequers and we walked home, in the most

---

[1] Admiral of the Fleet Sir Andrew Cunningham (Viscount Cunningham of Hyndhope).

perfect spring evening, pausing to see the tiny thirteenth-century church at Little Hampden, with its ancient frescoes, and to drink some draught cider at "The Rising Sun". There never was a more glorious evening: the beeches just bursting out in pale spring green, the sun slanting through the leaves in the woods and the bluebells coming out. I walked ahead with Mary who was a gay and sympathetic companion.

Mr Fraser told a number of boring stories about New Zealand at dinner, though he is really a nice enough old Scot with a good head on his shoulders. There was the usual film: excellent American fighter combat films and a weird ghost story called *Halfway House*. The evening was finally marred by the arrival of an offensive telegram from Molotov,* who quite unjustifiably claimed we were intriguing behind the back of the Russians in Roumania. This set the P.M. off on his gloomy forebodings about the future tendencies of Russia and, as he looked at his watch just before 2.00 a.m. and dated the last minute awaiting his signature, he said, "I have always not liked the month of May; this time I hope it may be all right." Curiously enough almost the first remark he ever made to me, four years ago exactly, was about the 1st of May.

Monday, May 1st
A mad rush to get to London by 12.00 noon in time for the opening of the meetings with the Dominion Prime Ministers at No. 10. The P.M. was late, of course, but the opening ceremony went off all right and afterwards there were the photographs in the garden.

Tuesday, May 2nd
A hectic day, mostly concerned with petty affairs. To add to the chaos caused by the presence of our Dominion guests, General Wilson, Fitzroy Maclean and Averell Harriman* have all arrived. I had a talk with Fitzroy who seems to find Tito congenial and says he has a sense of humour.

Thursday, May 4th
Afternoon party at No. 10 in honour of the Dominion P.M.s. Weather not suitable for the garden, as had been proposed, so

a vast concourse assembled in the rooms upstairs and it was all a great success. Archie Sinclair button-holed me about going back to the R.A.F. and said it was dangerous from the security angle. But I have the P.M.'s puissant support and he says he thinks Archie and the C.A.S. are being silly.

Friday, May 5th

More nonsense about my departure, Brendan and the C.I.G.S. lending a hand; but, with the P.M.'s support, I got my way.

Went to Odiham for a weekend's flying.

Sunday, May 7th

Flew over Chequers, rocking my wings, and then on a cross-country down to Cornwall.

Returned to London in time to go down to Cherkley for the night to stay with Lord Beaverbrook. Colonel Llewellyn[1] (Minister of Food) was there, Mr McCulloch (Canadian newspaper owner), Pamela Churchill and Mrs Richard Norton.[2] Excellent wines, accompanied by indifferent food, followed by a rather poor film, and spiced throughout by Lord B.'s very entertaining conversation.

Monday, May 8th

Lord B. wished us all farewell, gracefully, in his bedroom, talked about the decline of true Tory principles, told me I ought to stand for Rugby, and dismissed Llewellyn, McCulloch and me to London.

Gave lunch to the Archduke Robert[3] of Austria who wants to get a job in the R.A.F.

Friday, May 12th

The P.M. left on a tour of inspection with some of his Dominion colleagues. I visited the head of Air Ministry Intelligence, and

[1] Jay Llewellyn, Conservative Minister of dynamic ability who was later the first Governor General of the Rhodesian Federation.
[2] Daughter-in-law of Lord Grantley. Deeply cherished friend and mistress of Lord Beaverbrook.
[3] Younger son of the last Emperor, Karl, of Austria-Hungary and of the Empress Zita.

decided not to assume a false name when I go on Ops. (in spite of the fact that I have been photographed with the P.M. and in uniform): and had tea with Mrs Churchill to meet Monsieur Vienot, the Ambassador of the Free French.

Saturday, May 13th.
Reading the full reports of the Imperial Conferences (written by Sir Gilbert Laithwaite[1] almost verbatim), I am impressed (i) by the great tributes paid by the Dominion P.M.s to our own Prime Minister's leadership; (ii) the unanimity with which they praise our conduct of foreign policy during the last five years – in contrast to the prevalent criticism of it which one hears and reads in England.

Whatever the P.M.'s shortcomings may be, there is no doubt that he does provide guidance and purpose for the Chiefs of Staff and the F.O. on matters which, without him, would often be lost in the maze of inter-departmentalism or frittered away by caution and compromise. Moreover he has two qualities, imagination and resolution, which are conspicuously lacking among other Ministers and among the Chiefs of Staff. I hear him much criticised, often by people in close contact with him, but I think much of the criticism is due to the inability to see people and their actions in the right perspective when one examines them at quarters too close.

Sunday, May 14th
When I survey the vast amount of paper: Chiefs of Staff papers, Cabinet conclusions, memoranda circulated for various ministerial and inter-departmental committees, records of the European Advisory Commission, Foreign Office print, etc., etc. – papers full of interesting facts and suggestions among the inevitable verbiage – I pity the lot of the future historian. To summarise briefly what passed before my eyes every day would take pages of this diary.

[1] Eminent civil servant. Deputy Under Secretary at the India Office and Burma Office. Afterwards High Commissioner in Pakistan and Permanent Under Secretary at the Commonwealth Relations Office. Learned and wise.

Tuesday, May 16th

Went for the night to Mentmore, where grandfather and Peggy are living in the gaunt and almost deserted house, crammed with evacuated treasures from museums and galleries. Grandfather, racked with sciatica, was lying dressed in a chair. Though physically worn, he is still very much alert mentally and was full of political conversation.

Wednesday, May 17th

The last meeting of Dominion P.M.s took place yesterday and now the field is clear.

Dined with Mary Churchill, very pleasantly and well, at l'Ecu de France. Agreeable conversation is a far better entertainment than one which is ready made.

Thursday, May 18th

Lunched with Mrs Churchill alone at No. 10.

Presented the P.M. with a memorandum about this new book *Your M.P.*,[1] which is similar to *Guilty Men* in tone and may well have an equally wide effect. I feel that if we are returning to an age of politics by pamphleteers, the Right should show as much energy as the Left. The Conservatives have the funds at their disposal and they certainly have the material for an inquest into the past speeches and policy of their opponents. It should not be difficult to find publicists as clever – and as vituperative – as Cato, Cassius, Gracchus and Cassandra.

The P.M. was greatly interested in the book and had to be left to himself, fuming and muttering with rage, to read it after dinner in the dining-room.

Brendan came in with a declamation against the F.O., but seemed to have his facts muddled. The Italian offensive goes well.

---

[1] Sequel to Michael Foot's and Frank Owen's *Guilty Men*, written as Labour Party propaganda for the next General Election. Conveniently omitted all reference to the Labour Party's pre-war opposition to rearmament, conscription and the doubling of the Territorial Army.

Saturday, May 20th

Today I rejoin my squadron, which is at Odiham. Concerted efforts have been made to prevent my going, by people as various as the S. of S. for Air and Lord Cherwell. But the P.M. has held firm and, in order to meet the security point, it has been agreed that I am not to fly over enemy territory until D-day, after which my knowledge of the time and place of the Second Front would not be dangerous, should I be taken prisoner by the enemy.

The world is hushed and expectant. Nobody thinks of anything but the coming event – and I for my part am glad to have an opportunity of taking an active part in what may well be the most decisive of the decisive battles of the world.

EIGHT

OPERATIONAL INTERLUDE
MAY 20th–AUGUST 2ND, 1944

At Odiham 168 Squadron of the 2nd Tactical Air Force were living in tents near the perimeter of the airfield. When not flying we were given a great deal of exercise, including fifteen-mile route marches along peaceful Hampshire lanes where the beech trees were wreathed in those pale green leaves that are among the special pleasures of an English spring. In a remarkably short time all flabbiness had vanished and remembering how I had collapsed after racing Mary Churchill up Beacon Hill, I felt that now I could have run up and down twice without the smallest physical discomfort.

We were the sole R.A.F. unit in a four-squadron Canadian Mustang Wing, and our strength of twenty-eight pilots included a number of dashing, and without exception likeable, officers of the Royal Australian Air Force. They wore dark-blue battle dress and were locked in endless good-natured banter with their "Pommy" colleagues and our one rotund, gallant and consistently good-natured New Zealander. There was, I remember, little or no squabbling or back-biting, for human beings can live in harmony if they have one primary objective in common. It was so in war, at any rate in those sections of the R.A.F. I knew; but war is a heavy price to pay for harmony.

I was attracted by the individualist personalities of the Australians. Many of the Canadians, brave, friendly and resourceful though they were, seemed by contrast to have a rubber-stamped outlook and upbringing. Moreover, it was irritating to find that they regarded our French Canadian ground-staff, all volunteers since there was no conscription in French Canada, as second-class citizens. When it came to censoring the ground-staff's letters, their own officers were unable to perform the duty, for scarcely any of them could speak or even read French. A naturalised Czech, a Pole and I had to fill the gap. I found our ground-staff obliging and most anxious to serve us well, even though their peculiar French *patois* was a little difficult to understand. I had no doubt that the evident lack of sympathy between them and their English-speaking officers boded ill for the tranquillity of post-war Canada.

When I rejoined the squadron, on May 20th, 1944, they were operating vigorously, with many cross-Channel flights every day. Because I knew the place of the landings and the intended date, I was not allowed to venture beyond the British coastline until D-day; but on that memorable day I did take part in two reconnaissance flights deep into France, one over Falaise and one south of Bayeux. The Channel was bathed in sunshine, but there was thick cloud over northern France. We therefore flew low over the countryside, down the main streets of towns and villages (where the inhabitants waved ecstatically if there were no Germans about) searching far and wide, on that day fruitlessly, for signs of enemy troop movements.

It was thrilling as we crossed the Channel to look down on a sea boiling with ships of all kinds heading for the landing beaches. It was thrilling, too, to be part of a vast aerial armada, bombers and fighters thick as starlings at roosting-time, all flying southwards. Off the Normandy coast, where our troops and the Americans were forcing their way ashore, lay a semi-circle of grey battle-ships. Some, like *Rodney* and *Warspite*, were immediately recognisable, and as we flew over them at some 2,000 feet (for it was no longer necessary to skim the waves to outwit enemy radar) we could see their huge guns belching flame and smoke as they fired at targets inland. On a return flight that morning one popular member of our squadron, Flying Officer Barnard was, by a million to one chance, struck by a 15-inch shell from *Warspite*. He and his Mustang disintegrated.

The German fighters seldom appeared over the beaches, but

inland it was a different matter and though I never personally became involved in a dog-fight, it was soon a common event to meet Focke Wulf 190s or Messerschmitt 109s in squadron strength. On one occasion, near Lisieux, I was chased by nine of them. As our sorties consisted of only two or four aircraft, we found the tactics of Lord Thomas Howard as described by Tennyson in *The Revenge*, preferable to those of Sir Richard Grenville. This did not prevent our losing nearly a quarter of our pilots by the end of June.

I had three lucky escapes, two from German anti-aircraft fire and one from the Americans. On June 13th, over Carpiquet aerodrome, outside Caen, which was strongly held by the enemy, a shell blew a large circular hole in my port wing, missing both the vital aileron cable and the flap by a hair's breadth. Had the damage been half an inch further to one side or the other, my aircraft would undoubtedly have spun into the ground and as I was flying low I could not have baled out.

When I left Downing Street to rejoin my squadron, the Prime Minister had asked me to write and let him know how I fared. So on June 14th, shortly before the squadron moved to France, I sent him an account of my adventures on the previous day:

The weather had been unfavourable all day and when, in the afternoon, it cleared over here it was reported to be still poor over the operational area in Normandy. However at 4.30 p.m. there was a demand from the Ops. room for four pilots from 168 Squadron and we were told that photographs were urgently required of the road and stream southwest of Caen where the Germans are firmly ensconced and where an intense concentration had been encountered earlier in the day. F/O Stubbs, an Australian pilot, was to lead the formation and to take the photographs at the highest level permitted by cloud. Dickson and I, without cameras, were to provide support and fighter cover for the other two.

When we took off, just before 6.00 p.m., the English skies were clear except for broken cloud and there was a 40 m.p.h. westerly wind. We crossed the coast at Selsea Bill, climbed to 7,000 feet and flew over a cloudless channel in which I could see the usual stream of convoys and of small vessels, which, from the airman's point of view, have been the most impressive feature of the invasion. We made landfall at Ouistreham after about 20 minutes, but a bank of low cloud, not great in depth but obviously thick, made it necessary to dive to less than 2,000 feet over the beaches and the estuary of the Orne. I was on the extreme left as we turned to starboard round the southern outskirts of Caen, where the smoke of battle lay thick, and I had to open the throttle wide to keep up with the others. Then, as we approached the aerodrome south west of the town, the flak came up, concentrated, intense and accurate. Stubbs, who has long experience, says he has never seen it more accurate. We dived and writhed, slipped and skidded, but we could not shake the gunners' aim. White puffs of 20 mm., grey puffs of 40 mm. and the black puffs of heavy 88 mm. appeared above, below and on each side of my aircraft and the paths of tracer were too close to be comfortable. It was difficult to keep with the others: they were weaving, diving, climbing like things possessed; wispy low cloud came between us; and I had to take avoiding action myself besides keeping a weather eye open for enemy fighters. Suddenly there was a metallic sound and the aircraft shuddered. I was not quite sure whether I had been hit or whether the pace, the boost, and the high revs had been too much for the engine and something had given. Then I saw a gaping hole in the port wing where a 20 mm. shell had struck. Fortunately it was exactly between the aileron and the flap, damaging only the latter as far as I could see.

We finished the run just short of Villers Bocage and Stubbs circled southwards, returning to Caen to repeat the performance as he was by no means sure that the first run had been adequate. Flak followed us the whole way and I saw big black bursts above me. A tracer shell flashed past a few feet in front of the engine. But my aircraft was still flying smoothly in spite of periodic shocks which threw me out of my seat against the straps and were due either to atmospheric bumps or, more probably, to shells bursting immediately below me.

So I decided to press on and, opening the engine fully, I was level with the others when we approached Villers Bocage again and when Stubbs, observing noxious rockets ahead, turned sharp left to complete our task by means of a tactical reconnaissance of the roads south-eastwards to Thury Harcourt, Falaise and back to Caen. I was still on the left, a couple of hundred yards from Dickson, and we were flying through gaps in the cloud, the base of which was still low, climbing to a safer height.

The flak had stopped, but my wireless had failed and I could not communicate with the others. I saw them turn towards me, but a cloud separated us and when I emerged I could see no Mustangs. They were not far away, but the loss of lift in my port wing meant that the pace was a strain on the engine and I could not be sure whether the radiator and other vital parts were still intact. So I turned northwards, climbed to 7,000 feet (which is well above the light flak level) and set course for home. I crossed out between Bayeux, peaceful and apparently intact, and Courseulles and flew home at a good height in case I should have to bale out, scanning the skies behind for Focke-Wulfs most assiduously. Instead I ran head on into a formation of highly suspicious Typhoons.

The aircraft shewed no signs of lassitude, however, and the shadowy outline of the Cherbourg peninsula soon gave way to the familiar shape of the Isle of Wight. I crossed in at Selsea unmolested by friendly fighters (who have recently shown a conspicuous inability to distinguish friend from foe – at least so it appears to us) and, after "shooting up" the aerodrome control at Odiham to warn them that something might be amiss, I was relieved to find that my undercarriage and flaps both went down without trouble. I landed just as the other three, who thought I had come to grief, appeared in a faultless formation over the aerodrome.

After all this a technical failure in the camera, which seldom happens, made the photographs worthless. Moreover the intensity and width of the flak, combined with the necessity of constant evasive action and the speed with which it was expedient to pass through the area, had made it impracticable for any of us to empty our eight machine guns into an enemy gun position. I was sorely tempted to do so – it only meant diving 1,000 feet, but I was told later that to dive straight for an enemy gun position, with others bringing lateral fire to bear, is the surest method of suicide.

I had a responsive feeling this morning when the B.B.C. announced: "Yesterday evening many of our aircraft encountered unusually heavy anti-aircraft fire south-west of Caen."

I wrote again several times and received in Normandy a note from Churchill to the Private Office saying: "Good. Tell him how much interested I have been in reading his letters. W.S.C. 10.7.44." In sending me this message John Martin added: "We heard good news of you via Louis Greig and Archie [Sinclair], who had run into you during their visit to Normandy. As someone unkindly commented: It shows what a small part of France we have conquered so far."

On July 17th, sent to take line-overlap photographs of the railway running south-east from Caen, I had to fly straight and level to obtain results. A fragment of 88 millimetre shell penetrated my petrol-tank which fortunately did not explode. Thanks to the self-sealing device, it retained enough fuel for me to limp back home.

My third escape from injury came when, with three comrades, I was returning from a low-flying reconnaissance of Sees and Argentan and we passed over the Forêt de Cerisy in the American sector of the bridgehead. Failing to distinguish Mustangs from Messerschmitts, the Americans greeted us with a storm of machine-gun bullets. One passed through my tail-plane, two through a wing, but fortunately none through the cockpit. One of my companions, whose aircraft was alongside me, had bullets through both his feet but contrived to hold on long enough to make a landing. When our Group Captain telephoned to remonstrate, the American commanding officer said that he really must get round to having his gun-crews brush up their aircraft recognition.

It was, of course, easy to cast blame on the American gunners, but I fear that some of it attached to me. Our formation was off course, though since I was not leading it that was not my fault, and I did not realise we had entered friendly territory. A few minutes before, we had seen and attacked some German staff cars. When I noticed some more, which were in fact part of an American armoured division, I was flying on the right of our formation. I made a steep turn towards them for identification purposes. No doubt they should have recognised a Mustang which was, after all, an American aircraft, but my sharp turn in their direction must have seemed menacing and they had to make up their minds quickly as we were flying low.

It is not, in any case, for me to complain of poor aircraft recognition, for some days later I missed my only opportunity of shooting down a German fighter. I was returning alone to base having parted company with my companion in cloud, when I saw approaching, almost head-on, an American Thunderbolt. I waved cheerfully to the pilot as he passed and then, far too late for action, saw the black German cross on the fuselage. It was a Focke-Wulf 190 flying for dear life from some pursuing Spitfires. If I had made a sharp turn on to his tail he would have been easy prey. In retrospect, though certainly not at the time, I am glad I do not have his death on my conscience.

At the end of June we had moved to a landing strip in Normandy, a few miles north of Bayeux. Our tents were pitched in an orchard which despite a good deal of rain and low cloud was pleasant enough. There were dawn sorties, which at least for me had a romantic appeal; there were mid-day excursions to investigate or photograph something in which the Guards Armoured Division, whose servants we were, were interested; there were dusk sorties when the German flak seemed heaviest; and there were occasional treats when, usually contrary to orders, we would sweep down on German trucks, petrol bowsers or staff cars and riddle them with shot and shell. It was like an enjoyable day's rabbit shooting: nobody gave much thought to the human suffering we caused, for we had been at war for nearly five years and our sensitivities were dulled, at any rate in battle. It would have been hard to survive if they had not been. When it was all over we shed quicker than might have been expected the hard skin of callousness with which, quite naturally it seemed, most of us had so long covered our emotions.

The dawn patrol usually consisted of four aircraft flying to such towns as Lisieux, Argentan and Alençon and scouring the country as we went. We almost always came back over Villers Bocage and in the first hours of daylight I used to look down with delight on the elegant church and the little houses with red-tiled roofs, apparently still wrapped in sleep. It seemed to me to have a special charm. Then one morning, instead of the familiar quiet scene – for nobody ever shot at us from Villers Bocage – there was an ugly splurge of upturned clay and shattered walls. The small town, scene of a fierce tank battle the previous day, had been totally obliterated by Bomber Command during the night.

I was delighted to be back on French soil and in the evenings, when I was not flying, I often called on local farmers, bringing them chocolates, cigarettes and soap and being presented, in exchange, with Camembert cheeses and flagons of raw cider. The mayor of Magny, the nearest village, was welcoming and hospitable, but I was slightly pained by a white-haired lady who owned a small Louis XVI chateau and who told me that the Germans billeted on her had been *beaucoup plus correct* than the Allied soldiery. Doubtless she thought she had been tactless, because she then insisted on giving me a bottle of well matured Calvados, upon which I saluted smartly and said *Vive la France*.

Seeking a change from exclusively male society, we gave a dance in our large mess tent, importing a bevy of nurses from Bayeux. The nights could be unpleasant, for after dark German fighter-bombers usually raided the bridgehead. Our guns would open up and pieces of shell fragment would strike, though not penetrate, our thick canvas tent coverings. However, on the night of our dance all was quiet except for a Doodle Bug (V.1 pilotless aircraft), of which scores were already assailing London. Presumably due to the failure of its automatic compass it passed overhead on a semi-circular course and, to resounding cheers from all of us, sped southwards to the German lines.

The officers of our Wing outnumbered the girls who came to the dance by ten to one; and so I was lucky to engage the

attention of a pretty nurse during a full half-hour. Our conversation was not what it might have been in other places and at
other times, for in that Normandy orchard war was the only
topic that obsessed us all, male and female alike. My temporary
partner – I did not even ask her her name, nor she mine – had
been ministering that day to wounded young fanatics of an S.S.
Hitler Youth brigade which had been in the forefront of the
battle. She told me that one boy of about sixteen had torn off
the bandage with which she had dressed his serious wound,
shouting that he only wanted to die for the Führer. Another had
flung in her face the tray of food she brought him. She had
quelled a third by threatening, on sudden inspiration, to arrange
for him to have a blood transfusion of Jewish blood. "Rather
awful of me," she said, "but he at once became a whimpering
child and begged pitiably for mercy." It is remarkable in retrospect how many of those apparently incorrigible young demons
did, years later, evolve into decent, respectable German citizens; but probably the most fanatical sacrificed themselves on
an altar of Mars already dripping with blood, for dictators well
understand how to use and pervert the generous instincts of
youth.

   Leaving aside the besotted, and in reality tragic, Hitler Youth,
I think the victorious Allies have seldom paid adequate tribute
to the bravery and resilience of the German soldiers. They were
fighting for an iniquitous cause, to which many of them had at
one time or another been wrong-headed enough to offer faith
and enthusiasm. Now, however, in 1944, they were fighting for
their country's survival. They stood boldly against the combined
might of the whole British Empire, of the United States and of
the Soviet Union, with inferiority in the air and without the
invaluable foreknowledge which the decrypts of the German
ciphers from Bletchley gave to their enemies. Their population
was less than one seventh of the countries ranged against them,
all of which benefited from the unrivalled productive capacity of
the United States. It is no slur on the gallantry and toughness
of the British, American and Russian troops to assert that in
World War II, as indeed in World War I, the German soldiers
were the best in the world.

Once or twice I was given a lift into Bayeux, which was thronged with British soldiers, airmen and even sailors. One afternoon I watched an open lorry drive past, to the accompaniment of boos and cat-calls from the French populace, with a dozen miserable women in the back, every hair on their heads shaved off. They were in tears, hanging their heads in shame. Presumably they had not been sufficiently beastly to the Germans, although I have little doubt that some other citizens, far guiltier than those poor women, subsequently served the Republic in elevated spheres. While disgusted by this cruelty, I reflected that we British had known no invasion or occupation for some nine hundred years. So we were not the best judges of *résistance* emotionalism.

No doubt the unhappy occupants of the lorry would gladly have accepted the advances of the newly arrived liberators; but they and those of their sisters who escaped persecution did not reckon with General Montgomery, whose puritan zeal led him to decree that all the brothels should be closed. Military police were posted to ensure the order was obeyed. Undeterred and unabashed, several of the deprived ladies (though not, of course, the hairless ones) presented themselves in a field adjoining our orchard. Lines of airmen, including, I regret to say, the worthy Roman Catholic French Canadians, queued for their services, clutching such articles as tins of sardines for payment. We, the officers, watched this sordid display with a mixture of amusement and revulsion, but we took no deterrent steps for, after all, our lives depended on the goodwill of the ground crews; and it may perhaps be that through our daily flying duties we had temporarily sacrificed our own sexual energies to the god of war.

Constant operations were indeed tiring, mentally as well as physically, and so we were allowed an occasional day off. Strange though it may seem, our idea of a holiday was to go as close as we could to the front line. One evening a thousand guns battered three villages north-west of Caen, still held by the Germans weeks after the planned date of capture, as the preliminary to a raid by hundreds of Lancasters and Halifaxes of Bomber Command. Several of us set off along the road to Caen in our

Commanding Officer's jeep and from a vantage point well in front of our own guns watched an apocalyptic spectacle. While the guns thundered, waves of huge aircraft came in just as the sun was setting. We saw three or four Lancasters shot down, one quite close to where we sat, and the crash of falling bombs, added to the ceaseless boom of the guns behind us, was at once hellish and enthralling. It was only when several of our own shells, falling short, exploded uncomfortably near our small group of awe-struck pilots that we beat a retreat to safety.

On one "rest-day" I was even more foolhardy. I had a number of friends in the Guards' Armoured Division and 6th Guards' Tank Brigade with whom I used to go and dine when duty permitted; for after daylight operations the evening was often my own once I had censored a batch of French Canadian letters. With my cousin Terence O'Neill, many years later Prime Minister of Northern Ireland but at that time a Captain in the Irish Guards, I planned a day's sight-seeing. He borrowed his Brigadier's jeep and together with an Australian brother officer of mine, we set off for the front line.

We lunched off Camembert in a cornfield and then walked to Carpiquet airfield, where I had so nearly met my doom. Heavy shelling drove us into a front-line trench held by a Canadian unit. As we crouched there a whole squadron of Messerschmitts flew over our heads in a suicide raid on the Mulberry Harbour at Arromanches. With untypical accuracy our anti-aircraft gunners shot down three. Two parachuting pilots landed a few hundred yards from us, and I subsequently heard that not one of the remainder escaped the ravenous, watchful Spitfires.

It was a striking display of German courage. We thought the Canadian soldiers would fire on the parachuting pilots, because a few days earlier the German S.S. had killed several Canadian prisoners in cold blood and in vengeful fury their comrades had resolved to take no Germans prisoner. However, on this occasion, with praiseworthy restraint they held their fire. By contrast one of the pilots in my squadron was used for target practice as he parachuted down over a German S.S. Panzer division, who only had to await his landing in order to take him prisoner. He was dead long before he reached the ground.

After being unceremoniously ejected when we ventured into Caen, of which our troops only held half, we crossed the Orne at Benouville, were shelled again and were within a mile of the factory at Colombelles, still held by the enemy, when we all but stumbled into a minefield. We were saved in the nick of time from driving straight into the enemy lines by a soldier with a blackened face who leaped out in front of our jeep. Terence O'Neill, totally unperturbed, went into reverse and drove backwards to the Orne bridge singing, in his excellent tenor voice, "*Tout va très bien, Madame la Marquise.*"

After this foolish escapade we went back to dine at Terence's Brigade Headquarters, disguising from the Brigadier how nearly he had lost both his jeep and his Intelligence Officer. Accustomed to the dull and repetitive "compot" meals provided by the R.A.F., my Australian friend and I were astonished at the banquet Terence O'Neill offered us. In addition to his other duties he was a catering officer with a flair and had imported, as a useful addition to more war-like equipment, a poultry farm. It had crossed the Channel in the recesses of a L.S.T. (landing craft for tanks). The Brigade of Guards, as magnificent fighters as any in the world, saw no virtue in austerity on active service.

On the few occasions I was shelled on the ground, twice in France and once, later on, in Germany, I found it a great deal more alarming than being shelled in the air. Of course on the ground I was taking no part in the action, but was simply an inquisitive spectator. In the air I was involved personally and was intent on diving, climbing and twisting to confuse the gunners' aim. All the same the shuddering of the earth as shells burst on land did induce fear, at any rate in me, whereas the black but silent puff of an exploding anti-aircraft missile was an instant inducement to self-protective energy. Safety lay in the speed of my own reactions and I was too busy to be afraid. I think, too, that with no feet on the ground, and no sound from the exploding shells, I was in a strange way insulated from fear.

I therefore conclude, though doubtless many aircrew, and especially those who served in Bomber Command, would disagree profoundly, that it required greater courage to be a soldier than an airman. That only applies to being shelled from the ground: I was one of the few in my squadron who had no experience of aerial combat, exhilarating though that may have been for those who survived it.

Early in August my "two months' fighting leave" (extended from six weeks with Prime Ministerial consent) expired. I made my last operational sortie and was flown back to England in a Dakota which inadvertently flew over Havre, still in German hands, and was welcomed by a burst of mercifully inaccurate anti-aircraft fire. A fellow passenger was Lord Reith,[1] disguised as a captain R.N.V.R. Much better, he said, than being in Churchill's Government. How glad I must be to have got away from him. "On the contrary, Sir," I replied, "I am on my way back to him."

I had at least flown on more than forty operations and could tell myself that my training as a pilot had not been wasted. Back in London I went to see the Prime Minister, who gave me an affectionate welcome, and then found a comfortable spare bedroom on the top floor of the Travellers Club where I sank into such an exhausted sleep that I was unaware of the record number of Doodle Bugs which harassed London that night.

[1] Founding father and, indeed, Dictator of the B.B.C., he gave the impression of ruthless efficiency, but the efficiency seemed to desert him when he entered the Government, as Minister of Information and later Minister of Transport.

NINE

SECOND QUEBEC CONFERENCE
AUGUST–SEPTEMBER 1944

A few days after I came home, three more pilots in my squadron were casualties and two of my closest friends were killed when the 6th Guards' Tank Brigade went into action at Caumont. I had dined with the Grenadier battalion, of which my brother Philip was adjutant, on the night at the end of July when the brigade was ordered to move and had watched their Churchill tanks rumble off towards the scene of action.

August 8th–14th
I spent a week's leave at Madeley.

On the 11th came the sad news of Anthony Coates' death, broken to Aunt Celia in a letter from Philip. We were all plunged in gloom and mine was still further thickened by confirmation of a previous report, given me at Ardley by Bobby Rivers Buckley, that Sidney Cuthbert too had been killed. Both Sidney and Anthony had admirable qualities and no ordinary charm. So had a long list of my air force friends who have died in the last year. It is indeed uncanny how the best go. It is as if they had reached the standard set for us in this world, and need undergo no further trials, while the more imperfect live on, requiring more time and further chances. In no other way can I explain this constant decimation of the best; but how ill can we spare those qualities of unselfishness, common sense, good humour which would have been so valuable in a world and a generation devoured by rapacity and self-indulgence. It now begins to look as if the war will last but a few more weeks or months at the outside. If so the process may be halted in time. If not, it seems that the future is heavily weighted in favour of the cold, the calculating and the second best who have stayed behind the lines or have survived the risks of war.

Monday, August 14th

Returned to a sunbaked London from Madeley. The P.M. is in Italy, having Leslie Rowan and John Peck with him. John Martin and I are alone at No. 10 where hopes run high as Monty's trap seems to be closing on the Germans near Falaise and Argentan. Sleeping in the Central War Room as an insurance against Doodle Bugs.

Tuesday, August 15th

Operation DRAGOON (ex-ANVIL) took place this morning when American and French troops landed on the south coast of France. The Americans insisted on it; we were against it, considering that the troops could much better be employed by General Alexander in strengthening and hastening his drive northwards from Florence. The P.M., it seems, used all his powers against it; but the Americans were adamant. They shouldn't meet great opposition in view of the drain on the German strength in Normandy.

The weather remains hot and clear. It has been so for a fortnight now, atoning for June and July.

Long talks in the C.W.R., with Attlee and others. Attlee, though not impressive, is very pleasant when not being official.

Wednesday, August 16th

Saw Mary Churchill who has been shooting down Doodle Bugs at Hastings. She has grown much fatter, but looked gay and handsome. She is very distressed about Anthony. A patch discovered on the retina of one of my eyes.

Friday, August 18th

Dined at Mentmore. Saw grandfather, who now looks very frail and seems to have shrunk away but who still talks gaily of anything. I told him of my French experiences and he told me of past visits he had paid to Lisieux (in connection, I gathered, with racing stables rather than with St Thérèse). Peggy and I dined alone with a bottle of 1921 champagne and she confided to me that grandfather had not sciatica but cancer and could hardly live long. The Battle of Normandy is won.

Saturday, August 19th
Went to Chequers for the night. Mrs C., with whom I played much backgammon, Mrs Romilly, Jack Churchill with Johnny[1] and his wife, Mary, were there.

Sunday, August 20th
Spent the morning at Halton[2] and returned to Chequers for the afternoon – a long walk with Mrs C. in pouring rain – and the night.

Monday, August 21st
Returned to London from Halton for lunch and settled in at No. 10.

Read an interesting paper on Europe after the war in the form of a despatch (dated May 31st) from Duff Cooper. "Mortal hatred," he wrote, "now divides Russia from Germany, but human emotions, whether of love or hate, of gratitude or revenge, have seldom proved durable in politics and have played but a small part in the affairs of nations." In the margin the P.M. has written against this sentence: "*Gratitude* perhaps may fade but revenge does not. Cf. France 1870–1914, Germany 1918–1939."

Duff's thesis is that we can never allow one power to predominate in Europe, whence our wars against Philip II, Louis XIV, Napoleon, Kaiser Wilhelm and Hitler. In case Russia should take her place in the long line of states which have aspired to this role we should insure ourselves by creating a "Bund" of Western European States under our aegis and, it might well be, within

[1] Major Jack Churchill's elder son. A talented artist who painted the frescoes adorning the summer-house at Chartwell. Married at this time to Mary Cookson.
[2] R.A.F. hospital.

the framework of the British Empire which has so successfully contrived to combine federations and the retention of state sovereignty. It would be fatal to ally ourselves with the potential dominator because "the alliance of the wolf and the lamb is ever an uneasy partnership and the advantages accruing to the lamb are apt to prove temporary". In his reply Eden points out that to erect such a "Bund" would be to invite Russian animosity and a counter alliance in Eastern Europe. Frank co-operation and friendship with Russia is the proper course.

Against a reference by Duff to "the Prime Minister's proposal of a Union of England and France in 1940" ("Frangland", Michael Grant and I proposed to call it!) the P.M. wrote: "I had very little to do with this. It was a wave of Cabinet emotion."

Toulon has fallen, we are across the Seine, and in the Falaise pocket the carnage of Huns is said to be horrific.

Wednesday, August 23rd

An exciting day outside – Paris fell and Roumania capitulated – and a busy one in the Private Office where, John Martin going on leave and Tony being away, I was in sole charge. A message from the P.M. intended for the President of Brazil was sent (not by me) to President Roosevelt in error and President Roosevelt thanked for it. Much consternation.

Thursday, August 24th

In sole charge and very much snowed under. Talks with Eden, Brendan and the Prof. The last very much belittles the power and danger of V.2, the rocket. He says they will have a warhead of only a ton or so and will be less frequent or alarming than the Doodle Bug.

The Polish rising in Warsaw is a grim problem. They are fighting desperately against fearful odds. We and the Americans want to help in every way possible; in sending supplies we have been losing up to 30 per cent of our aircraft. The Russians are deaf to all pleas and determined to wash their hands of it all. They have even refused to let American bombers land and refuel on Russian airfields if their purpose is to help Warsaw. Explanations: (1) Pique at the fact that they were seriously checked at the gates of Warsaw, (2) According to Prof., a curious pride which makes them determined that other powers shall not do what they cannot do, (3) Fury at finding that the population of Warsaw and the underground movement are behind the Polish Government in London and do not support the puppet Moscow Polish National Liberation Committee.

Saturday, August 26th
England bathed in heat and sunshine and in consequence a pleasing absence of Doodle Bugs. Lay in the sun in the garden at No. 10 for an hour, admiring the very presentable flower border and a fine array of tortoiseshell butterflies. I shall always associate that garden in summer, the corner of the Treasury outlined against a china blue sky, with 1940 and the Battle of Britain.

Sunday, August 27th
Less busy. Alexander is attacking northwards against the Gothic line and the P.M. has prolonged his stay in Italy to be present in the initial stages. Meanwhile under the clear skies – I again made use of the garden at No. 10 – the Germans are reeling backwards in retreat across the Seine, making for the Somme, the Marne and the Jura.

Lord Beaverbrook asked me to Cherkley for the night, but there was too much doing for me to get away.

Monday, August 28th
Accompanied Mrs Churchill to a service in the crypt of St Paul's to celebrate the liberation of Paris. Cabinet and Chiefs of Staff attended as well as Diplomatic Corps. Rather embarrassed, therefore, to find myself in front row with Mrs C., the Edens and Sir John and Lady Anderson. Service simple but impressive, particularly when the band of the Irish Guards played the "Marseillaise" and none could prevent their cheeks going red with emotion. Yesterday General de Gaulle attended a Te Deum in Notre Dame and the occasion led to shooting actually inside the Cathedral. In St Paul's the emotion was less obvious, and the accompanying circumstances fortunately less dramatic, but

there was the same feeling that the end of a long, tragic period was symbolised in the fall of Paris. Perhaps it was a bit ironical that the service took place in front of the Duke of Wellington's tomb and ornate hearse.

Lunched alone with Mrs Churchill at the Annexe. Spent the afternoon in discussions about the plans for the coming conference at Quebec, difficult in view of the P.M.'s indecision whether he will travel by sea or air.

Tuesday, August 29th
Rose at 4.00 a.m. in order to meet the P.M. at Northolt; but his arrival was postponed owing to the weather and so Barker and I walked round Covent Garden instead.

The P.M. did arrive by York[1] at 6.00 p.m. and the Chiefs of Staff, Mrs C. and I were there to meet him. Lord Moran emerged from the aircraft looking agitated and we found that the P.M. had a temperature of 103 degrees, developed since luncheon. He was rushed home and put to bed, nurses and doctors appearing as if by magic. Small patch on lung.

Wednesday, August 30th
The P.M. was better and did a certain amount of work in bed. He also saw Eisenhower about the change in the scheme of command in Normandy.[2]

Thursday, August 31st
A very marked improvement and it was agreed that the arrangements for OCTAGON, the coming conference with the President, should be allowed to stand. The P.M. asked me if I wished to accompany him.

The King came for an hour and signed a submission creating Montgomery a Field Marshal. The P.M. intends this to show

---

[1] A four-engined high-wing passenger plane, one of which was at the P.M.'s disposal.
[2] By this arrangement General Bradley assumed command of the American armies in Normandy and Montgomery ceased to command all the land forces. Hitherto Bradley, whom Montgomery tended to denigrate, had commanded the American First Army.

that he is not being demoted by being made co-equal with General Bradley.

On looting: the P.M. told me that while at General Alexander's H.Q. in Italy he was given a caravan in which he observed two Louis XVI chairs. When he asked where they came from, he was told they had been "liberated".

Friday, September 1st

The P.M., with temperature normal, is in tearing form. He has entirely emptied his box. With regard to the progress of the war he says that he thinks the grand strategy will be highly approved, though there may be an undistinguished minority who proclaim we ought to have invaded in 1943. He told me it had been like a bullfight: TORCH, HUSKEY, etc., were like the preliminaries, the Picadors, the banderillas, etc. Then came OVERLORD, the Matador coming at the crucial moment to make the kill, waiting till the bull's head was down and his strength weakened. But DRAGOON, the landing in the South of France, has been a pure waste: it has not helped Eisenhower at all and, by weakening Alexander's armies, has enabled the Germans to withdraw troops from Italy to northern France.

Meanwhile our armies are racing to the Belgian frontier, faster by far than went the Panzers in 1940. There is a feeling of elation, expectancy and almost bewilderment and it may well be that the end is now very close.

Saturday, September 2nd

Took train to Slough at lunch-time and was there picked up by Sir Owen Morshead[1] who motored me to Badminton. We stopped for tea at Bristol with the Dean and Mrs Blackburne, a charming and most Christian pair. She was not, perhaps, so quick on the uptake as her husband and when, in discussing Buchmanism, I told her the limerick about the young man of Pretoria (whose confessions grew gorier and gorier, but by sharing and prayer, and some *savoir faire*, he arrived at the Waldorf Astoria) she said: "Oh, but I think it was Brown's hotel where they usually met."

[1] Librarian at Windsor Castle. Erudite, sensitive and delightful companion.

We arrived at Badminton in time for dinner. I sat between Queen Mary* and the Duke of Beaufort. The others in the party were the Duchess of Beaufort, Sir Owen Morshead, Miss Wyndham[1] and Major Wickham.[2] After dinner I went with the Queen to her sitting-room and had a long talk about politics and the war. For her seventy-seven years she is most uncommonly alert, quick and unbowed. Never have I seen a woman who carries so much jewellery so well.

Sunday, September 3rd

Said goodbye to the Queen at 9.00 and flew from Hullavington to Hendon in a Proctor piloted by a Dutchman, arriving at No. 10 before noon.

Lunched at the Churchill Club, where I found Hinch,[3] in a high state of indignation about the inadequacy of the morning service at Westminster Abbey today, a day of National Prayer. Leslie Rowan* and I went at 3.00 p.m. to Evensong and formed the same opinion. A small male choir of ten monopolised the singing and the character of the service was very unsuitable. The vast congregation took little part and can hardly have been inspired. Only the sermon, by Canon Don, was good.

Messages poured in to the P.M. on the fifth anniversary of the outbreak of war and I drafted rhetorical replies to Chiang Kai-Shek, the Dutch, the Belgians, etc., all of which were accepted. Meanwhile the P.M. was greatly upset by a telegram from our legation at the Holy See containing the text of a message from the women of Warsaw – which still holds out – to the Pope. It was truly pathetic and the P.M. drafted a telegram to the President containing it and suggesting that we might inform Stalin that in default of assistance to Warsaw we should take certain drastic action in respect of our own supplies to Russia.

[1] One of the nine children of the 2nd Lord Leconfield, and a niece of the Prime Minister Rosebery. Trenchant, assertive and often witty. Appointed lady-in-waiting after King George V died.

[2] Private Secretary to Queen Mary.

[3] Viscount Hinchingbrooke, M.P. for Dorset. Succeeded his father as 10th Earl of Sandwich, but later renounced his peerage in the hope of being re-elected to the House of Commons.

Monday, September 4th
Dreary drizzle, but that means nothing with the news of British troops in Brussels. People are expecting the armistice any day now (though the Huns show no signs of offering to sue) and there have been no flying bombs for four days. The Cabinet considered the problems of Warsaw, in connection with which much bitterness is arising against Russia, and sent a joint telegram to Molotov and to Roosevelt. It is a black cloud in an otherwise azure sky.

Tuesday, September 5th
Left Addison Road[1] at 9.40 for Greenock. Travelled in the P.M.'s train with him and Mrs Churchill, the three Chiefs of Staff, Lord Moran (plus wife and child), John Martin and Tommy. After a luxurious journey we reached Greenock at 7.00 p.m. and were transferred by tender to the *Queen Mary*. I found a large and spacious cabin and devoured an even larger and more spacious dinner (oysters, champagne, etc.) in the P.M.'s dining-room. There were just eight of us, the P.M., Mrs C., their immediate entourage, Lord Moran, Lord Leathers* and Lord Cherwell. Talking about a coming election the P.M. said that probably the Labour Party would try to stay in the Government (though the rank and file might not let them) until a year or so after the armistice so that they might profit from inevitable disillusionment at the non-appearance of an immediate millennium and might give time for the glamour to fade from a Government which had won the war. But if after that there was a great left-wing majority, let it be so: "What is good enough for the English people, is good enough for me."

After dinner I played three games of bezique with the P.M.

Wednesday, September 6th
A quiet day, the P.M. being still rather under the weather as a result of the substantial doses of M. & B.[2] he has been given during the last week. I lunched and dined with the P.M. and

[1] Now called Kensington Olympia Station.
[2] Antibiotic drug in its earliest form.

Mrs C., lunch being a small *en famille* affair, and General Ismay and Brigadier Whitby (the blood-transfusion expert) being invited to dinner. Both meals were gargantuan in scale and epicurean in quality; rather shamingly so.

The OCTAGON[1] party on board this ship is a vast one and its members fill a huge dining-room and more than the whole of the main deck. The Chiefs of Staff proceed with their normal deliberations, but as the P.M. did nothing today but read *Phineas Finn*, there is a certain air of tranquillity. I am trying to master the rudiments of the papers on finance in the post-war period which is one of the main subjects for discussion with the President.

The P.M. says that after all he will not "beat up" the Americans about DRAGOON. He will suggest that the controversy be left to history and add that he intends to be one of the historians. More talk about a coming election. If the Opposition tried to sling mud about the past, they would be warned that the other side, though preferring a truce to recrimination, had a full armoury of mud to sling back. The P.M. would not regret the loss of any of his Labour colleagues except Bevin,* the only one for whose character and capacity he had any real esteem. The others were mediocrities.[2]

On another subject, he said that of all the paper and the theories one reads it was wise to pick out certain firm principles (e.g. milk for babies!) and pursue them actively. One of his major tenets was this: we did not enter this war for any gain, but neither did we propose to lose anything through it.

Thursday, September 7th
Another quiet day, devoted by the P.M. to *Phineas Finn* and by me to walking about the deck and swopping "lines" with Liberator pilots on their way home. I also ploughed through the many files, political and economic, we have brought with us.

---

[1] Code-name for the Conference.
[2] Yet some years later he told me he thought Attlee his outstanding Labour colleague.

*One friendly American pilot, returning after an operational tour
of which he and his crew were among the few survivors, told me
he had much enjoyed his stay in England and thought it right
that his Government should have paid us the tribute of calling
this magnificent ship after one of our Queens.*

"But it's a British ship."

"No, no. It's the biggest and fastest in the world."

*"That doesn't alter the fact that it's British. If you lean over
the side – be careful not to fall overboard – you'll see the ensign
on the stern."*

He gasped, "You mean this really is British? And the Queen
Elizabeth *too?"*

"Yes, I do."

*"But they're the biggest in the world. How could our Govern-
ment have let themselves be out-smarted like that?"*

We are racing, at twenty-eight knots, through the mid-Atlantic
in the latitude of Cap Finisterre.

Lords Cherwell and Moran were invited to dine. The P.M.
produced many sombre verdicts about the future, saying that
old England was in for dark days ahead, that he no longer felt
he had a "message" to deliver, and that all that he could now do
was to finish the war, to get the soldiers home and to see that
they had houses to which to return. But materially and financially
the prospects were black and "the idea that you can vote yourself
into prosperity is one of the most ludicrous that ever was
entertained".

The menu for dinner was: Oysters, consommé, turbot, roast
turkey, ice with canteloupe melon, Stilton cheese and a great
variety of fruit, petit fours, etc.; the whole washed down by
champagne (Mumm 1929) and a very remarkable Liebfraumilch,
followed by some 1870 brandy: all of which made the conversation about a shortage of consumers' goods a shade unreal.

Friday, September 8th
We are in the Gulf Stream (to which our national debt has never
been sufficiently acknowledged) and the weather is very hot,
very sticky and cloudy like at the Equator. The P.M., who has

finished *Phineas Finn* and taken to *The Duke's Children,* which I myself read in Normandy, feels the heat acutely, says the ship has been abominably routed, and is definitely not his brightest and best.

I spent a good deal of time on deck, conversing agreeably with Antony Head,* various W.A.A.F.s and other representatives of the mixed bag which comprises this OCTAGON party.

Lords Leathers and Cherwell dined. The P.M. said he thought the Joint Planners, etc., were being too optimistic about an early victory. It was even money the Germans would still be fighting at Christmas and if they did collapse the reasons would be political rather than military.

Saturday, September 9th

The P.M., feeling more or less himself again, did a considerable amount of work, mostly connected with the strategic questions at the coming conference. He has not yet given his mind to the complicated problems connected with finance and the future of Lease-Lend, and Lord Cherwell is in despair.

The Gulf Stream heat, which the P.M. has found quite over-powering, persisted until midday when there was a sudden fall of about 20 degrees in temperature, accompanied by clear skies and a fresh breeze. I spent much time on deck and, going up to the bows, was greatly impressed by the sight of this great ship cleaving the waveless sea at some thirty m.p.h.

The P.M. had a slight temperature again and was highly irascible. Lord Moran does not think seriously of it – probably it is the heat – but he told me that he does not give him a long life and he thinks that when he goes it will be either a stroke or the heart trouble which first showed itself at Carthage last winter. May he at least live to see victory, complete and absolute, in both hemispheres and to receive his great share of the acclamations. Perhaps it would be as well that he should escape the aftermath.

I am reading Vita Sackville-West's *The Eagle and the Dove.*[1]

---

[1] The story of St Teresa of Avila (the Eagle) and St Thérèse of Lisieux (the Dove).

The descriptions of Lisieux evoke strong aerial recollections of that town, so familiar to me from 5,000 feet during June and July.

Perhaps foolishly, I took the P.M. a telegram from Attlee about the proposals for increasing service pay in the Japanese war. The P.M. thinks these proposals inadequate and ill-conceived and has said so. This telegram announced the War Cabinet's intention, notwithstanding, of publishing them before his return. He was livid, said Attlee was a rat and maintained there was an intrigue afoot. He dictated a violent reply (which was never sent) full of dire threats. Having no pencil or paper with me, I borrowed the P.M.'s red ink pen and scrawled it on the back of another telegram. To my horror he insisted on reading the production as it was and proceeded to correct what I thought was an illegible semi-shorthand with equal illegibility.

Sunday, September 10th

I had my first glimpse of the New World at about noon. After lunch we moored against the quay at Halifax and, amidst cheers from the troops on board, the party landed and walked to the train. Malcolm MacDonald and some Canadian dignitaries greeted us and the Mounties were there in full regalia. While the luggage was being put on the train the P.M. stood on the balcony at the rear of his "car" while the crowd sang patriotic songs, very well in tune. He made them a short speech.

The train was highly comfortable, the P.M.'s drawing-room car, in which I spent part of the evening, being particularly well appointed. Dinner was rather too much of a good thing – some ten courses. I sat next to Bob Laycock, the Chief of Combined Operations, who was very pleasant.

Monday, September 11th

We arrived at Wolfe's Cove, Quebec, at 10.00 a.m. The sun was shining brightly. The President and Mrs Roosevelt had arrived just before us and he was sitting in his car waiting to greet the P.M. Princess Alice[1] and Lord Athlone were also at the station.

We all drove across the Plains of Abraham to the Citadel, where we are staying. I have got a most comfortable room and we have a spacious office. The main body of the Staffs are at the Château Frontenac. I went up to the main drawing-room where the principal personages were assembled and talked to Lord Athlone, who strangely enough recognised me, but did not have a chance of being introduced to the President.

The Governor General and Princess Alice gave a large dinner party, but as there was no room for me I dined at the Château Frontenac with Buster Long[2] (née Marling), Mrs Hill and Barker.

The Russians have climbed down about Warsaw, but it may be too late.

Tuesday, September 12th

At 11.30 the Governor General and Princess Alice, the President and Mrs Roosevelt, the P.M. and Mrs Churchill faced a huge battery of photographers on the terrace outside the sun room.

At the end of a Chiefs of Staff meeting, over which the P.M. presided, I heard him say to Portal that he might discuss with the President this evening the vexed "Zones of Occupation" question. Knowing he had not read the briefs on the subject and that there was no time for him to do so before dinner, I volunteered to read them aloud to him in his bath. This bizarre procedure was accepted, but the difficulties were accentuated by his inclination to submerge himself entirely from time to time and thus become deaf to certain passages.

---

[1] Princess Alice of Albany, Queen Victoria's granddaughter, married to Queen Mary's younger brother Prince Alexander of Teck, created Earl of Athlone, who won the D.S.O. in the Boer War and was Governor General of both South Africa and Canada. Princess Alice was an energetic and stimulating person who lived frugally (usually travelling round London by bus) and was much loved by all and sundry for her natural simplicity and pleasant disposition.

[2] Daughter of Sir Charles Marling, former Minister at The Hague. She was in the A.T.S. and was working in the office of the Minister of Defence and Chiefs of Staff secretariat.

The P.M. told me he fears the President is now "very frail".

The original plan was for the British to occupy the south of Germany, the Americans the north and the Russians the east. For shipping and commercial reasons we were anxious to persuade the Americans to agree to a swap with us, since we wished to control Hamburg and other North German ports. We also thought it right that the French should have a zone, carved partly out of ours and partly out of the Americans'. Berlin was a separate problem which would have to be resolved later. We expected American opposition to our proposals, but in the event (and much to our surprise) they accepted them without demur, provided they had passage rights to the port at Bremen. At first they resisted the proposal for a French zone. This was only finally agreed, under British pressure, at Yalta the following February.

Wednesday, September 13th

The fine weather gave way to rain and cloud. There was a Plenary Session of the Conference at 11.30, before which the P.M. presented me to the President. As the Combined Chiefs of Staff were assembled when he did so, and as he included in the presentation a brief biographical sketch, I was acutely embarrassed.

As I had been away in the R.A.F. during Churchill's various visits to Washington, and had missed the Casablanca, Cairo and Teheran conferences, I was the only one of the Prime Minister's secretaries who had never met the President.

Seeking to remedy this, and because my R.A.F. adventures had endeared me to him, he insisted on making the presentation before a whole gallery of war leaders while I, disguised as a Flying Officer and feeling exceedingly foolish, stood first on one leg and then on the other.

When the P.M. had finished, the torture for all present was prolonged while the President addressed me for several minutes in flowery language as if I were a public meeting. Subsequent encounters with Roosevelt at the conference were more relaxed, but I heard him say nothing impressive or even memorable and his eyes seemed glazed.

We were fairly busy all the afternoon. We had a party in the Household dining-room at which Bob Laycock, Reggie Winn,[1] Antony Head, Charlesworth[2] and three American officers were present. Geoffrey Eastwood, the Governor General's Controller, who is the only member of H. E.'s staff left behind now that the Athlones have gone off on a tour, did the honours. The food here is quite unusually good.

After dinner the P.M. saw Pug, who is in trouble about strategic matters in S.E. Asia Command, and subsequently Dick Law, who arrived by train from Montreal.

Thursday, September 14th
Rain and mist again which made exercise difficult, though I did stroll up to the Heights of Abraham, and owing to the excessively good food I am feeling rather gross. Eden and Cadogan arrived during the afternoon and Mrs Roosevelt left. The Conference has been going exceedingly well from our point of view and the Americans are being amenable both strategically and financially.

After a vast Household dinner to which Admiral Leahy, deserting the Presidential fold, came, there was a shockingly bad film chosen by the President. The P.M. walked out halfway through which, on the merits of the film, was understandable, but which seemed bad manners to the President. At dinner Lord Moran gave me a dissertation on the poor use we have made of our great scientific brains and resources during this war; they have not been well co-ordinated or exploited. Though Moran is vain, egotistic and exceedingly indiscreet, his judgment of people is often shrewd, though by no means always. He has a low opinion of Anthony Eden, simply based on his handling of the Turks in Cairo, (and also of Pug). I cannot quite make up my mind whether he is right about Eden. He is certainly wrong about Pug.

[1] Hon. Reginald Winn, A.D.C. to Sir John Dill.
[2] Likeable A.D.C. to the C.I.G.S., Sir Alan Brooke, killed in the York aircraft which crashed on the way to the Yalta Conference (see footnotes p. 195).

While going to bed the P.M. told me some of the financial advantages the Americans had promised us. "Beyond the dreams of avarice," I said. "Beyond the dreams of justice," he replied.

Friday, September 15th
The day was taken up with the discussion of outstanding points and was crowned with further successes as far as our desiderata, political, financial and strategic go.

I shopped in Quebec in the afternoon, started a feverish cold, used the P.M.'s penicillin upon it, dined in a gargantuan way, talked to Admiral Wilson Brown (the President's Secretary) and went to bed early, leaving John Martin to cope with an after-dinner meeting about service pay.

Sat next to Eric Speed[1] at dinner. He is a very good conversationalist. He came the whole way out here with Eden in order to help set at rest the P.M.'s worries about this pay question. So did representatives of the Ministry of Labour and the Admiralty.

Saturday, September 16th
The Conference ended and the skies cleared for the occasion, hot sun burning down on the terrace and roof of the Citadel. There was a Plenary meeting at noon. After lunch the Chancellor of McGill University and the Senate arrived to confer honorary degrees on the President and the P.M. They, with the Athlones who today returned from their tour, assembled on the roof outside the sunroom for the ceremony. Both the P.M. and the President, the latter wheeled along in his chair by his black servant, were strange spectacles in their academic dress. They both made speeches. Lord Athlone said that both he and the P.M. had been educated "by Degrees".

Then, still on the sun roof, there followed a joint press conference. The battery of photographers and reporters was formidable indeed. The scene was as follows: in the background

---

[1] Private Secretary to David Margesson at the War Office and then Permanent Under Secretary. Quick-witted and always well-informed, he was later Chairman of Dalgety and Co.

rose the great bulk of the Château Frontenac; at the end of the parapet hung the flags of the three countries; below ran the St Lawrence, with a few white sails; and around clustered a great crowd, mostly journalists but, interspersed among them, the members of McGill Senate in their academic robes, the Athlones and their Household, Mrs Churchill, Mr Eden, Lord Leathers and the Prof. Facing the mob sat the President, the P.M. and Mackenzie King flanked by splendid mounties and leering G-men. The President spoke first, scarcely audible above the clicking cameras, and then the P.M. gave an impromptu talk which was truly remarkable for its force and eloquence. It was important that he should say nothing which the Republicans could construe as aid for Roosevelt in the forthcoming Presidential elections (they are already playing that tune) and I do not think he did.

The President left Quebec shortly afterwards, taking with him Admiral Leahy, to whom I had talked at lunch. Under a forbidding exterior the Admiral possesses an attractive personality. His pro-Vichy views were interesting if unacceptable.

The King sent a most cold message in reply to the P.M.'s requests for a fraternal greeting to the Duke of Windsor, whom the P.M. is to see at Hyde Park[1] on Monday. The P.M. dictated to me rather a crushing answer, but, as often, he subsequently had it destroyed and replaced by one more conciliatory.

Sunday, September 17th

Our luncheon party in the Household dining-room included Cruikshank, the P.M.'s press representative on this party who was formerly Editor of the *Star*, and also Nicholas Lawford. Upstairs the Archduke Otto,[2] intent on Legitimist intrigue, lunched with the P.M.

In the afternoon I walked round the Citadel ramparts which offer a magnificent series of views of the St Lawrence, the Île d'Orléans, Quebec and the Plains of Abraham. The P.M. suggested I should fly over Niagara tomorrow, but finding the

[1] President Roosevelt's family home in New York State.
[2] Eldest son of the former Emperor of Austria and King of Hungary.

distance great and the R.C.A.F. not altogether enthusiastic I finally cancelled the arrangements as I think the authorities would have thought it something of an imposition.

We all dined upstairs in the sunroom. Malcolm MacDonald was there and so was Mackenzie King, next to whom I sat. The P.M. launched a diatribe against de Gaulle. Mackenzie King told me that when a celebration of the capture of Quebec was held here the descendants of Wolfe and Montcalm were invited. They met in the Château Frontenac. They were in adjoining suites and the occasion of their meeting was in a dispute for the bathroom.

The P.M., Mrs C., John and Tommy left after dinner for Hyde Park. Lord Moran and I, remaining behind, had a long talk which rendered nugatory his preliminary dissertation on his own taciturnity.

Monday, September 18th
Quiet reigned at the Citadel. In the morning Geoffrey Eastwood and I went shopping. I bought a selection of books for the P.M. to read on the voyage, *Jane Eyre*, Lytton Strachey, etc., with some difficulty as most things in Quebec are French and as a prerequisite was large print.

After lunch Lord Moran, Geoffrey Eastwood and I drove through fine wooded hills, with the maple just beginning to turn red, to a fishing camp on the Valcartier river belonging to some people called Kernan. It was a lovely wild spot with adequate civilised comforts provided. Lord Moran and I put out in a canoe and fished for trout. We were both strangely inexpert.

Tuesday, September 19th
By train from Quebec to New York. I first set my foot on United States soil at a place appropriately called Whitehall. We passed, in a luxurious drawing-room car attached to a special train, through Montreal, Saratoga, Troy and so along the shores of Lake Champlain and the Hudson to New York. The so-called "dim-out" seems very unconvincing to English eyes accustomed to five years of Stygian blackness. Boarded the *Queen Mary* at 10.00 p.m.

Wednesday, September 20th

Sailed at 7.30. The New York skyline only just emerged from the mist through which a very sallow sun was struggling. This was disappointing. The P.M. and the Hyde Park party came aboard by tender from Staten Island, the P.M. looking far, far better – indeed, as John Peck would say, "in rude health".

Lord Leathers, Sir Andrew Cunningham and Pug were among those at lunch, the P.M. being in the best of humours and form. He only clouded over once, when he spoke of de Gaulle and said that of recent years "my illusions about the French have been greatly corroded".

It was again hot and cloudy, as on the voyage out. The P.M. slept for three hours in the afternoon, an all-time record, and I snoozed in a deckchair on the sports-deck. There are some 9,000 American troops on board, but the sun-deck is reserved for the OCTAGON party which has shrunk somewhat in size owing to the return of many of its members by air.

General Laycock, Antony Head and Lord Moran were invited to dinner, which as usual started with oysters and kept up to form. Antony Head was very good with the P.M. He argued and put his case well. Lord Moran (who is so critical that he runs down everybody in the party, especially the P.M., and so indiscreet that he does so indiscriminately) was obviously much put out by the course of the discussion on morale and courage, the P.M. being vicious in his attacks on the military psychoanalysts and declaring that it was more important to win victory by deploying the maximum number of men in the line than to waste thousands in rearward services for increasing the men's comfort.

Two noteworthy points which came out in discussion were (i) on the Russian front the Germans had to cover about twelve miles on a divisional front whereas in Normandy they had only had to cover four miles. Thus their effort against the Americans and ourselves was more concentrated than against the Russians; (ii) in Europe as a whole we had as many fighting men employed against the enemy as had the Americans. From the American papers one would scarcely suppose any British troops were fighting.

Thursday, September 21st

The usual round of alternating walks on deck and sessions in our rather stuffy office, together with periodic games of bezique and backgammon with Mrs Churchill. The First Sea Lord, Leathers and Whitby came to dinner, conversation ranging from a vivid picture of Edward VII receiving homage from a bishop the day before he died (the P.M. being Home Secretary then) to naval reminiscences which included personalities such as Fisher, Tug Wilson, Henry Oliver and Troubridge, and battles such as the Falkland Isles, Jutland and, in this war, Matapan. Cunningham gave an exciting account of Matapan and described how the only three Italian cruisers which had armour thick enough to withstand any of our cruisers ran straight into the 15-inch guns of the *Warspite*, etc. He also told us of the "limpet" bomb attacks on the *Queen Elizabeth* and the *Valiant* in Alexandria harbour, and said that he was himself thrown six feet into the air when that beneath the *Q.E.* exploded.

The P.M. finished the evening by challenging me to bezique and by insisting on continuing playing until 3.00 a.m. He says he will only ask for a six months' extension of Parliament's life in November so as to take the wind from the Labour sails.

Friday, September 22nd

After lunch I accompanied the P.M. and Mrs C. to a film, in Technicolor, about the life of President Wilson. He thought it very good; I thought it deplorably sentimental. Then we all went up on the bridge.

Just as last night I was required for bezique and played, with unvarying success, until 3.00 a.m.

Saturday, September 23rd

Proceeding at some thirty knots in a cool breeze and pleasant sunshine. Again accompanied the P.M. to the cinema, which was in the lounge, and afterwards lay in a deckchair on the sports deck between Buster Long and Joan Bright[1] with both

[1] Trusted personal assistant to General Ismay, who thought the world of her. Married Colonel Philip Astley.

of whom I had pleasant converse. At 6.30 General Ismay gave a cocktail party in his suite.

Sunday, September 24th
Went to church with Mrs C., the First Sea Lord, Lords Leathers and Moran, etc., at 10.30. The padre, an American, preached a most eloquent sermon about Amaziah and said that after this war we must be careful not to bring back with us, and worship, the gods of our enemy, as Amaziah did the gods of the Edomites. But he would refer to Amaziah as "the hero of our text".

Mrs Churchill gave a cocktail party at 6.30. It was quite beautifully executed by the ship's stewards. This was followed by a domestic dinner party, about which the chef took special trouble and at which the P.M. and Mrs C., Tommy, John and myself, Joe Hollis, Lord Moran and Brigadier Whitby were present. The P.M. regained some of his old spontaneous form and did not depend on reminiscences as much as he usually does now. He said that when he was Home Secretary his nerves were in a very bad state and he was assailed by worries in a way he never has been in the war. He then discovered that the best remedy was to write down on a piece of paper all the various matters which are troubling one; from which it will appear that some are purely trivial, some are irremediable, and there are thus only one or two on which one need concentrate one's energies.

Lord Moran said that when deterioration in a man set in the first things that went from him were those he had most recently learnt.

Played bezique with the P.M., who was in very mellow mood, till 2.30 a.m.

Monday, September 25th
We had hoped to land at Fishguard but the weather was against it and so we plodded on up the Irish Channel to the Clyde. This disappointed and annoyed the P.M., especially as his own most comfortable train awaited him at Fishguard.

We entered the Clyde in the afternoon and reached Greenock about 5.00. Mist and rain gave way to a glorious evening of sun-pierced cloud. David[1] came aboard with his C. in C. and after the P.M. had broadcast a brief address to the troops the party went ashore in a tender.

The First Airborne Division has been wiped out at Arnhem.

Wednesday, September 27th
Went down to the House with the P.M. who delivered the first half of his speech, on military matters, before lunch. He delivered it well and as it contained many new facts it was well received, though M.P.s, who are the worst mannered of men, began to troop out as lunch-time approached without waiting for the interval.

I lunched with John Martin at the Reform Club and returned to the House for the second, less acclaimed, part of the speech on foreign affairs. I then corrected the whole thing in the Official Reporters' Gallery.

Dined with Rosemary and Hinch in Great College Street. Alastair Forbes and Nicko Henderson* were there, also a woman novelist, and conversation was on a fairly high level.

Friday, September 29th – Sunday, October 1st
Spent the week-end at Stansted. It was hot and sunny, like June, and we sat out of doors. Marie Lou Rothschild[2] was there. On Sunday the Bishop of Chichester (notorious for his anti-bombing speeches in the House of Lords) and Mrs Bell, and Sir Richard Livingstone came over to tea. The last is Vice Chancellor of Oxford, a great educationalist, and I found him most agreeable. He thinks that every Secondary School should have teachers expressly for the purpose of inculcating some knowledge and appreciation of art and literature.

[1] My eldest brother.*
[2] Gentle and lovable French wife of Lionel de Rothschild.

TEN

VICTORY DEFERRED
OCTOBER–NOVEMBER 1944

Monday, October 2nd
Returned from Stansted. The P.M. was back from Chequers in time to have General Eisenhower to lunch.

A long Cabinet during which I talked to Colonel Llewellyn,[1] who is perturbed about our intention of winning favour from the Americans by refusing to take Argentine meat, just when we have landed a good contract.

The P.M. tells me he agrees with the Russian desideratum about future world organisation (which the F.O. oppose), namely that parties to a dispute should, if members of the Council and one of the Big Four powers, be allowed to vote in that dispute.

There is great trouble over recognition of the French Provisional Government, which the U.S.A. will not admit at any cost. De Gaulle has an excellent platform in demanding the restoration of France's position as a great power.

Tuesday, October 3rd
The toughening resistance of the Germans is damping unduly high spirits a little and, inevitably, reflecting on our future strategic designs.

Dined with Lady Ampthill. Guy, Leo and Phyllis Russell were there. Leo told me he had resigned from Monty's staff in France

---

[1] At this time Lord Woolton's successor as Minister of Food, having previously been President of the Board of Trade and Minister of Aircraft Production.

(a) because of the bombing of French towns, much of which he had reason to think unnecessary from the military standpoint, (b) because Monty allowed his own staff to loot and rejected Leo's protests, (c) because Monty was at heart "a fascist".

Wednesday, October 4th
While I was talking to the P.M. as he dressed after his afternoon sleep, preparatory to going to see *Richard III*, he quite seriously said that there ought to be some new hair brushes in the washing place below because those now there (which are in fact excellent) had black bristles which hid the dirt and because "in view of all the recent victories" the War Cabinet might really be entitled to have some new ones! Being a great man, his approach to trivial matters is often an unusual one.

Thursday, October 5th
In conversation with Eden the P.M. said that Bevin was "far the most distinguished man the Labour Party have thrown up in my time".

He made a statement, very insipidly, about the gallant but now, alas, overwhelmed insurrection in Warsaw. It lasted sixty-three days with scarcely any help. Mikolajczyk and Raczynski[1] came up to the P.M. in the lobby and thanked him for his words. The words, produced by the F.O., were good; the delivery, due to the P.M. being too long in his bath and having to rush, was poor.

Friday, October 6th
Having lunched with Buster Long at the Churchill Club, I was hoping for a reasonably quiet afternoon, but the Government got into difficulties over the Town and Country Planning Bill and the P.M. had to rush down to the House after lunch, hastily dictate a speech in the Foreign Secretary's House of Lords room and enter the lists. There followed two hours of Parliamentary knock-about to which I listened with enjoyment – Aneurin Bevan

---

[1] Polish Ambassador in London before and during the war. Still living there in 1987.

and the P.M. alternately bowing and biting, Buchanan[1] being interrupted constantly and accepting the fact with great wit and good humour, Pethick Lawrence[2] (for the respectable Opposition) being constructive, Lord Winterton declaiming that "Never in my forty years' experience of the House . . . etc.", and Sir Percy Harris's[3] rising being a signal for the House to empty. Hore-Belisha made a smooth speech in support of the Government, causing Gallacher[4] to congratulate him "on the assiduous way in which the Rt Hon. Member is working his passage home".

There followed a late night chiefly devoted to new ministerial appointments (Swinton* to Civil Aviation and Jowitt to Social Insurance), and to attempts to find a new Chairman of the Tory Party. David Margesson refused all blandishments to accept this and James Stuart failed in an intrigue to get Duncan Sandys appointed and thus clip his wings.

Saturday, October 7th

An exceedingly busy day, being almost single-handed. In the afternoon the P.M., while signing photographs (including one for Stalin) and books, began reading Vol. I of Marlborough aloud to me and continued about Sir Winston Churchill's home life and passion for heraldry for nearly an hour. At the end he said that as I had been subjected to this ordeal he would give me a copy for Christmas. He then worked till dinner, seeing various people and every now and then telling me I ought to read the leading article in today's *Manchester Guardian*.

At 11.30 p.m. the P.M., accompanied by John Martin, left for Northolt to enter the York and fly, via Naples and Cairo, to Moscow. At one moment he talked of taking me, but having had a very exhausting week I am not altogether sorry he did not.

---

[1] Labour M.P. for the Gorbals division of Glasgow. Originally a member of the left-wing I.L.P., he was a stalwart patriot.

[2] Ancient and stooping product of Eton and Trinity, ennobled and appointed Secretary of State for India in 1945.

[3] Stolid but dull leader of the Liberal Party in the House of Commons.

[4] The only Communist M.P. His son was killed in the war and he wrote a moving reply to Churchill's sympathetic letter of condolence. Churchill rather admired him.

Sunday, October 8th

Calm should have descended had not there been trouble about the drafting of guidance to the press in connection with the new Ministerial appointments. It being necessary to satisfy the opposing views of Archie Sinclair (who wants to be sure control of Civil Aviation is kept by the Air Ministry during the war) and Brendan (who wants to be sure it is not), I had to go and see Sinclair and telephone repeatedly to Brendan. Finally I produced a document which, like the second Prayer Book of Edward VI, satisfied both parties and was issued to the press.

The P.M.'s visit to Moscow, which is really very dangerous to his health, is, he assured me yesterday, entirely because he wants to discourage any idea that the U.K. and the U.S.A. are very close (as exemplified by the Quebec Conference) to the exclusion of Russia. His visit will make it quite clear that our counsels with Russia are close too, and that there is no tendency to leave her in the cold.

Miss Helen Waddell[1] has sent these verses to the P.M.:

> The Polish Eagle, nailed to the barn door,
> Torn wings outstretched, bedaubed with blood and turd;
> Beneath in German and in Russian script,
> "So perish all who trust in England's word".

She wrote it in 1939; she sent it now.

Monday, October 9th

On the way to bed I looked in as usual at the C.W.R. mess and talked to Edward Bridges* and Colonel John Bevan[2] (the Cover Plan Expert). We discussed the increasingly well authenticated

---

[1] Daughter of a presbyterian missionary in Japan. An eminent scholar, expert on medieval Latin lyrics and author of *Peter Abelard*, which was translated into nine languages.

[2] Head of the Cabinet Office section responsible for schemes to deceive the enemy. In private life senior partner of the stockbrokers Bevan Simpson and married to Field Marshal Alexander's sister-in-law, Lady Barbara Bingham (aunt of the missing Lord Lucan).

number of German atrocities against our soldiers (John Hussey[1] had told me of some of the results actually seen by members of 168 Squadron) by members of S.S. divisions. The question is whether or not some strong threat of retaliation should be made. Both Bevan and Bridges feared it would incite the Germans to yet worse. But we must exterminate the S.S. The next generation, tired of war reminiscences and probably as full of illusions as we were, is so likely to forget and, of course, those of our enemies who have the cunning to turn their coats in time will probably get away with it – at least in the lower ranks and especially if post-war Russian imbroglios lead some people to think Germany must be utilised as a buffer state. I become more and more persuaded that something drastic should be done about the youth, such as taking all children under eight from their parents and constructing vast state nurseries for them in South Germany. But who shall be responsible for their upbringing; who shall select their guardians; and *quis custodiet ipsos custodes?*

A disturbed night owing to demands from Moscow that the Polish Ministers shall at once fly there for conversations; and the Poles don't want to do so except on conditions.

Tuesday, October 10th
Things much quieter and nothing startling from Moscow. The P.M.'s daily post shows a strong body of feeling (a) demanding a war correspondent for the *Daily Worker* (refused by the Cabinet owing to its poor record in this war); (b) protesting against the release from internment of Captain Maule Ramsay, M.P.; (c) outraged because there is a shortage of housing and yet houses are being used to billet Italian prisoners of war.

Brendan says the Government will fall over housing and that Lord Portal [of Laverstoke] is in a state of hysteria, punctuated with frequent tears.

---

[1] Rotund and invariably affable New Zealand pilot in No. 168 Squadron. Correctly guessed in advance the date and place of the OVERLORD landing.

Wednesday, October 18th

The Moscow conversations seem to be going well and some progress has been made even on the vexed Polish problem, though there is a hitch about the definition of the Curzon line frontier.

Together with Mrs Churchill and Mary I went to Claridges to dine with the Bessboroughs in a private room there. Others present were Lord Linlithgow, Oliver Stanley, Tommy Lascelles (just back from visiting the front with the King; he agrees with Leo Russell that Monty is one of nature's fascists), Mrs Euan Wallace,[1] Lady Dorothy Charteris[2] and Rosemary,[3] Sammy Hood, etc. A good dinner, but the prevalent fashion of not dressing for dinner in London rather spoils the effect.

After dinner Mary and I joined a peculiar party at the Dorchester. It contained Sarah Oliver, Ann O'Neill, Pat Wilson (ex-Jersey) whose husband was only killed a few days ago, and several American officers; also Mrs William Randolph Hearst, Jnr., formerly of the Ziegfeld Follies. Many of them were drunk and Mrs Hearst paid for the champagne which flowed. Most of us then repaired to the Milroy, a new night club, from which Mary and I walked home at 2.00 a.m. Mary is being urged by Lord Beaverbrook to stand at the next election and is thinking seriously of so doing.

Thursday, October 19th

Represented the P.M. at a service at St Paul's in celebration of the liberation of Athens. A large throng headed by the King of Greece* was there and the service, partly in English and partly in Greek, was conducted by the Bishop of London jointly with the Archbishop Germanos, both in mitres and full regalia. I sat immediately behind King George who, poor man, is faced with great difficulties in regaining his throne. The Bishop of London

[1] Barbara, widow of Euan Wallace, former Minister of Transport.
[2] Daughter of the Earl of Kenmare, sister of the well-known columnist Lord Castlerosse and married to Sir Evan Charteris, K.C., who had been a prominent member of "The Souls".
[3] Pretty daughter of Lady Dorothy Charteris by her first marriage. Later married the Hon. George Dawnay.

preached a polished but dull sermon. Perhaps the most stirring thing was the singing, by the Greek choir, of their national anthem.

Friday, October 20th
Mrs C. has asked my advice on some papers sent by the Duchess of Atholl.[1] They show a horrible picture of the treatment of the Poles, especially the children, deported to Russia by the Soviet Government in 1939–40. If the Poles, taken thus for labour, were so abominably treated, what will be the fate of the Germans whom the victorious Russians will surely deport? But the more one hears of Teutonic atrocities, of which so many are well authenticated now, the less one can feel pity for the fate in store for them.

During dinner a V.2 rocket landed at South Norwood. It was the first I had heard. Its explosion was a long, rumbling roar.

Sunday, October 22nd
I went to Northolt to meet the P.M. on his return, via Cairo and Naples, from the very successful Muscovite conference. He arrived, well and cheerful, in the York and I accompanied him to Chequers, whither Duncan and Diana, Sarah, Brendan and Jack came. After dinner there was a film *The Hitler Gang*, in which the leading Nazis were represented in a most lifelike way. After it the P.M. cleared his box and then went into the Great Hall where Brendan and Duncan told him he ought to take more interest in the Home Front. There followed a violent discussion, though very good-natured, during which the P.M. said that if a majority of the Tories went into the Lobby against him during the coming debate on Town and Country Planning (the Tories oppose the Government plan for compensating owners of requisitioned land on the basis of 1939 prices), he would resign the leadership of the Conservative Party.

[1] Though a Conservative M.P., she was known as "Red Kitty" on account of her support of the Republican cause in the Spanish Civil War. She had a fine intellect, held honorary degrees from seven universities and was the aunt of Professor Sir James Butler of Trinity College, Cambridge.

Thursday, October 26th

Princess Beatrice[1] and the Archbishop of Canterbury[2] died. The latter's demise caused the P.M. no sorrow. In fact he was quite ribald about it. Nairn, from Marrakech, and Joe Hollis dined with me.

The P.M. gave up working on tomorrow's speech at 11.40 and went to bed at this record early hour.

Friday, October 27th – Monday, November 20th

I listened to the P.M.'s speech, about foreign affairs, corrected it for Hansard and then went off to Madeley with mother in order to collect some winter clothes. On Sunday I felt odd, took my temperature (102°) and retired to bed with chicken-pox, which was accompanied by a recurrence of last year's impetigo. I stayed in bed ten days and read *Mansfield Park* and *Dombey and Son*. While I was in bed Shane O'Neill[3] was killed in Italy, a tragedy which Aunt Nancy took with her usual philosophy. In the world outside, the P.M. visited Paris and had a triumphal reception,[4] Lord Moyne[5] was assassinated in Cairo, and the public were at last told about the V.2 rocket (of which everyone in England had long known unofficially).

When I could go out, I visited the Madeley P. of W. camp to look at the German prisoners. I also grew a moustache.

[1] Youngest of Queen Victoria's nine children and Governor of the Isle of Wight.

[2] William Temple, previously Bishop of Manchester and Archbishop of York. A scholar of distinction and profound philosopher. Churchill, who as far as clerics were concerned had a touch of King Henry II about him, disliked Temple's left-wing tendencies and outspoken political comments.

[3] Eldest son of my mother's sister Lady Annabel Dodds and first husband of Ann Charteris. He was second in command of the North Irish Horse and by a strange coincidence his commanding officer was Colonel David Dawnay. Their respective fathers had been killed in the First World War, standing side by side as first and second in command of the 2nd Life Guards. On this occasion Dawnay had only just moved a few yards away when a shell struck Shane.

[4] I had been going to accompany him, had not chicken-pox struck.

[5] Walter Guiness, 1st Lord Moyne, formerly Minister of Agriculture and Secretary of State for the Colonies, had been sent out to Cairo to succeed Oliver Lyttelton as Cabinet representative in the Middle East.

Tuesday, November 21st

At No. 10 I found Government changes in progress, Duncan Sandys replacing Wyndham Portal at the Ministry of Works. The Cabinet met at 6:00 and as they were already assembled in the Cabinet Room, the P.M. saw two M.P.s, Brabner and Wilmot, in our room in order to offer them Under Secretaryships. He turned us out and then, of course, the telephones began ringing. When I came back he said, "A lady with a foreign accent was asking for you." I replied, speciously, "Monsieur Massigli's secretary, I expect." Oddly enough it was.

Wednesday, November 22nd

Two long Cabinets took up most of the day. Reconstruction matters have now grown from a stream to a flood.

During the evening Duncan Sandys, who has in his great ambition been pressing for the Ministry of Works and Buildings, came to peruse with the P.M. the comments on his appointment in the early editions of tomorrow's newspapers. Brendan says that Duncan S. may do the job well because he is ruthless, but that unfortunately he is not good with subordinates and has adopted too much of the *Führerprinzip*. Certainly he is very unpopular. To bed after 3.00 a.m.

Thursday, November 23rd

The P.M. has taken exception to my moustache, which he told John and Leslie was "the worst thing that has happened since Randolph's beard"; so, in spite of the Atlantic Charter and the Four Freedoms, I suppose it will have to go.

In a minute about Spain (where the F.O. want to upset Franco's régime and to incite the U.S.A. thereunto) the P.M. says that his three cardinal tenets are (i) opposition to Communism; (ii) non-intervention in the internal affairs of other countries; (iii) prevention of one power dominating Western Europe by armed force, but reliance on a world organisation.

Friday, November 24th

Lunched at New Court with Tony Rothschild. General Sir Hubert Gough, Commander of the 5th Army in the First World War, and General Sir Clive Liddell were there.

To Chequers. Duncan Sandys came to dinner. We saw a French film called *Ignace* and the P.M. worked till 3.00 a.m.

Saturday, November 25th

Winant came with a letter containing a telegram from the President about civil aviation. It was pure blackmail, threatening that if we did not give way to certain unreasonable American demands, their attitude about Lease-Lend supplies would change. Winant was shame-faced about presenting it and didn't want to stay to lunch, but the P.M. said that even a declaration of war should not prevent them having a good lunch. The rest of the weekend was largely devoted to concerting, by telephone with Beaverbrook, a long reply. The Americans are also being tough, and even threatening, about a number of other things and the P.M. is disturbed at having to oppose them over so many issues. The President wanted to make a declaration to the Germans about our good intentions: it was a silly idea, ambrosia for Goebbels, and the P.M. turned it down flat. And there is a sharp wrangle about our imports of Argentine meat, the Americans being anxious to bring economic pressure on the Argentine.

Lord Woolton also came to lunch and talked about housing.

In the evening Mrs C. and Sarah came and we saw the film of *Henry V* in Technicolor, with Laurence Olivier. The P.M. went into ecstasies about it. To bed at 2.30.

Sunday, November 26th

Very busy all day with civil aviation and Argentine meat, while the P.M.'s box is hopelessly overcrowded with more or less urgent papers.

General Maitland Wilson, Lord Cherwell and General Ismay came for the night. Jumbo Wilson has little pig's eyes in his huge face. Saw *Left of the Line*, a film about the British and Canadian armies in OVERLORD. Not as good as *Desert Victory*, though the terrain was more familiar to me. To bed at 2.45 a.m.

Monday, November 27th

The P.M. had four meetings today, beginning with a Cabinet at 12.00 about his civil aviation telegram to the President. Lunched with Alexander Hood,[1] wrestled with some differences of opinion between the F.O. and the Defence Office (who always malign each other) and went to see Aunt Celia in hospital. She had a V.2 near her on Saturday. The same day one at Deptford fell on the local Woolworth's and killed over 150 people.

The P.M. said on Saturday that his election programme would be: free enterprise for the individual provided that (i) there were no big monopolies or cartels allowed (Lord Woolton cited as an iniquitous example the case of electric light bulbs, which he tried to assail by manufacturing and selling them for 1/- instead of 2/6); (ii) high taxation – though less high than at present – was retained.

Wednesday, November 29th

Rushed to the House at 2.00 and heard William Sidney[2] make his maiden speech in moving the Loyal Address which was seconded by a young Labour Scottish miner, Tom Fraser.[3] William spoke well and was loudly applauded for his eloquence as well as for his gallantry. The P.M. spoke later but I didn't wait for that.

Thursday, November 30th

The P.M.'s seventieth birthday brought such a spate of letters and telegrams as never was seen. Everybody, from the Shah of Persia to Harry Lauder, from Queen Mary to Rosa Lewis, sent their good wishes. With Leslie on leave, John Peck retiring early with a headache and Tony Bevir away I found the combination of ordinary work and the birthday almost unmanageable. Meanwhile the P.M.'s box is in a frightful state, with scores of urgent papers demanding a decision. He has frittered away his time in the last week and has seemed unable or unwilling or too tired

---

[1] One of my oldest friends. Served in the R.N.V.R. After the war a director of Schröder Wagg and Chairman of Tanganyika Concessions. Married Diana Lyttelton and succeeded his brother as 7th Viscount Hood.

[2] M.P. for Chelsea. Later Lord De L'Isle.*

[3] Labour M.P. for Lanarkshire. Joint Parliamentary Under Secretary for Scotland in the 1945 Labour Government.

to give his attention to complex matters. He has been reading the first paragraph or so and referring papers to people without seeing what is really required of him. Result: chaos.

ELEVEN

DRAMA IN ATHENS
DECEMBER 1944

Friday, December 1st
Another exhausting morning, the P.M. having many engagements and much untouched work awaiting him.

He went to Harrow for a school concert, accompanied by Mrs
Churchill, Jack, Donald Somervell, Amery, Geoffrey Lloyd, Paul
Emrys Evans[1] and McCorquodale.[2] The songs were good
except for the "school twelve" which was lamentable. A small
boy, with a magnificent treble, sang "Five Hundred Faces".
Afterwards there was a sherry party in the Headmaster's House,
where the P.M. talked long and charmingly to the school moni-
tors, such as he did to the midshipmen on the *K.G. V* last
January, enthralling but never patronising.

Saturday, December 2nd
Like an ostrich I dug my head in the pile of birthday greetings
and remained oblivious to telegrams to Tito, Stalin and the rest.
At Chequers great upheavals were going on as the P.M. delved
industriously into the accumulated masses of the last ten days.

There has been much excitement about the Duke of Suther-

---

[1] Conservative M.P. for South Derbyshire, friend of Anthony Eden and Lord
Cranborne. Formerly in the Foreign Office.
[2] Malcolm McCorquodale, M.P. for Epsom. Chairman of the well-known
printing firm. Chosen to be Chairman of the Conservative Party in 1952
when Lord Woolton was thought to be dying, but Woolton recovered and
so McCorquodale was given a peerage to compensate him.

land, whose matrimonial delinquencies made it necessary for him to resign the Lord Lieutenancy of Sutherland. He refused to do so and thus a notice was published in the Gazette "determining his appointment". This morning *The Times* and the *Daily Telegraph* decided this meant that the Duke had been *appointed* Lord Lieutenant and said so. Fur flies.

Sunday, December 3rd

After an industrious morning I went down to Trinity for the night, staying with Winstanley. I was present at a carol service in Trinity Chapel which was well attended and impressively conducted. All the bells of Cambridge ringing out struck me as a cheerful sound as I walked to Chapel with Winstanley across the Great Court; but he said that he always found church bells melancholy; they brought down upon him the burden of sorrows he had never felt and sins he had never committed.

Monday, December 4th

Lunched at No. 10 with the P.M. The other guests were M. Paul-Boncour,[1] Harold Macmillan and Harold Balfour,[2] who is going out to West Africa as Minister Resident, having just given up the Under Secretaryship of the Air Ministry. Paul-Boncour is described in the Foreign Office "Personalities Report" as assiduously cultivating the appearance of Robespierre, but, though perhaps Sea Green, certainly not incorruptible. I found him a crashing bore with his moans about the hard lot of the French people and his ceaseless reversion to the topic of arms for the French army. Also he spat while talking to an extent unusual even in France. The P.M. found him tedious too and spoke in French more execrable than usual, frequently calling upon me to translate and more frequently still turning to address Harold Macmillan in English, which Paul-Boncour cannot understand, about the iniquities of the Communists in Greece and of

---

[1] Constantly recurring Minister in the Third Republic. Prime Minister 1932–33. Foreign Minister 1932–34 and for one month in 1938.

[2] Won M.C. and bar as a pilot in the First World War. Conservative M.P. for the Isle of Thanet. A man of vigour and determination. Created Lord Balfour of Inchrye in 1945.

Sforza[1] in Italy. The P.M. becomes more and more vehement in his denunciation of Communism, and in particular of E.L.A.S. and E.A.M.[2] in Greece, so that before lunch today Mrs C. had to send him a note begging him to restrain his comments.

Crisis in Greece where E.L.A.S., the left-wing organisation, is getting out of hand. The P.M. stayed up till 4.00 a.m. dictating telegrams, and reading tomorrow's newspapers. Bob Dixon[3] came over from the F.O. and he and I remained with the P.M. while he dictated, but these late hours do not improve the quality of his work. ("Treat Athens as a conquered city", he wrote in his telegram to Scobie.[4])

As the Combined H.Q. at Caserta contained both British and American officers, we had a convention that telegrams we did not wish the Americans to read, because they were concerned with purely British matters, should be headed "Guard". Owing to the late hour at which the telegram to Scobie was being dictated, and the fact that at 4.00 a.m. the Prime Minister wanted it despatched immediately, I forgot to write the word "Guard" at the top. This had unfortunate results, because the Americans at Caserta telegraphed the text to Washington and the resulting leak to the press, from either the White House or the State Department, lent fuel to the explosive campaign against our Greek policy which was launched both in the American and British press. After this leakage I remember confessing my delinquency and Churchill saying kindly that it was his fault for keeping me up so late.

Tuesday, December 5th
In the House the P.M. made a statement about Greece and this was followed by clamorous demands from Aneurin Bevan,

[1] Italian politician of ancient descent and mushy liberal sentiment. Weak, vacillating and incompetent.
[2] The Greek guerilla organisation which had seized most of the country after the Germans left and was intent on imposing a Communist one-party régime.
[3] Pierson Dixon, Principal Private Secretary to Anthony Eden. Greek scholar. Wise, soft spoken and universally liked. Eventually Ambassador in Paris.
[4] Lieutenant General Sir Ronald Scobie, G.O.C., Malta, 1942 and Commander of the British Troops in Greece from 1944 to 1946.

Buchanan, Gallacher and Haden Guest[1] for an immediate adjournment and debate. The left wing see a heaven-sent opportunity for saying that we are supporting by our arms the forces of reaction in Italy and Greece.

Returned to the Annexe to find that the State Department in the U.S. had published a statement which could be interpreted as nothing but an attack on our Greek and Italian policies. Angry telegram from the P.M. to the President.

Thursday, December 7th

The chief topic is still the Greek crisis. The general public have no idea of the true nature of E.L.A.S., which they believe to be a heroic left-wing resistance movement.

Friday, December 8th

The P.M. spoke in the House of Commons, in reply to an amendment to the Gracious Speech about Greece and Italy. He was very telling and, as there was a good deal of interruption, had a good opportunity for showing his quickness in debate.

Evidently this Greek trouble is causing widespread criticism here and in America. I am sure the P.M. is in the right, and the inability of these Levantine bandits to postpone their internecine feuds until Germany is defeated is nauseating; but nevertheless there may be something in Desmond Morton's thesis that if the P.M. falls it will be over his handling of foreign policy. Moreover the belief, now current, that we support the monarchies of Europe as a matter of principle – whatever the will of the people – will not, in the long run, be to the good of the Crown in this country.

The P.M. did not go off to Chequers which upset everybody else's week-end arrangements.

Sunday, December 10th

The P. M. is at Chequers, swamped with papers which now fill three boxes, and still preoccupied with the military problems of Greece. Whatever their vices and their political asininity, the Greeks can certainly fight.

[1] Dr Haden Guest, Labour M.P. for Islington North.

Monday, December 11th

I think the P.M. and the Government are, quite unjustly, losing stock over Greece.

Tuesday, December 12th

The Isles of Greece, indeed. I shall never feel any sentiment towards them again. All the afternoon there were Cabinets on the subject, interspersed with visits from the King of Greece. He came three times altogether and proved very obstinate to the Cabinet's wish that he should appoint the Archbishop of Athens Regent. He told me that he was sure this rising was organised and inspired by the Germans.

At 6.00 the P.M. saw Eisenhower and Tedder. The former is having a disagreement with Monty about future strategy.

I dined at the Ritz with Lady Constance Milnes Gaskell.[1] The other guests were Mr and Mrs Douglas Woodruff,[2] Miss Freya Stark[3] (the Middle-Eastern expert), mother and an U.N.R.R.A.[4] expert called Rattigan. I thought Douglas Woodruff interesting, even though his political prejudices are very Roman. He said that the Church in Spain had suffered because the King had appointed the bishops and had taken care not to appoint anything but mediocrities. He also said that in 1934 the Left had revolted in Spain because Gil Robles and the Right won the elections and the democratic Left thought resort to force justified in order to prevent the Opposition getting into power.

Worked at No. 10 with the P.M. who was incensed, not unnaturally, at the discovery that one of his personal telegrams to General Scobie in Athens had been seen and published by the notorious anti-British American columnist, Drew Pearson.[5] It had reached the State Department without authorisation, through A.F.H.Q. Italy and somebody in the State Department

[1] Daughter of the Earl of Ranfurly and one of Queen Mary's ladies-in-waiting.
[2] Chairman and Editor of the Roman Catholic paper, *The Tablet*.
[3] Celebrated traveller and writer on Persian and Middle-Eastern affairs.
[4] The United Nations organisation for the relief of refugees.
[5] Journalist on the *Washington Post* with a source either in the White House or the State Department from whom he obtained secret or sensitive material. This was the telegram to Scobie mentioned on Dec. 4th.

had given it to Pearson. That such a thing could happen is incredible.[1]

Wednesday, December 13th
What with the leakage and the Greeks, no ordinary work is being done at all. And these Balkan monarchs do not make things easier; today it was Peter of Yugoslavia's turn.

I lunched with Flaisjer, a Polish Jew of no mean intelligence, at the Café Royal. He says that the guerilla freedom movements in Belgium, France, Yugoslavia, Greece, etc., which are giving so much trouble, are a legacy of fascism. They form themselves into a party and adopt the totalitarian thesis that the party has a right to dominate the State.

Thursday, December 14th
The King of Greece is being very obstinate, sincerely upholding what he believes to be the principles involved against the combined pressure of the War Cabinet and President Roosevelt to seek a solution of the Greek crisis by having the Archbishop of Athens appointed Regent.

The P.M. dictated part of his speech on Poland for tomorrow. He couldn't think of anything new to say on the subject and so inserted long quotations from his own earlier speeches and a certain amount of padding about the Sybilline Books and the *Liberum Veto*.[2] Then he was persuaded not to speak at all, but after dinner Anthony Eden came to No. 10, where the P.M. had returned from dinner with the Liberal Nationals at Claridges, and undid all the good work. This was mischievous as a speech is unnecessary and the P.M. is very tired.

Friday, December 15th
The P.M. made his speech – most of which he composed between 9.00 and 10.30 a.m. – at 11.00 and it went well in spite

[1] It was at this stage that the absence of the word "Guard" on the telegram was disclosed.
[2] In the Polish Diet, before the eighteenth-century partitions of the country, each member had a free right of veto so that legislation became a practical impossibility.

of his interposing an imaginary clause from the Atlantic Charter which led Kenneth Pickthorn[1] (who hates the P.M. because he has never been offered a job in the Government) to say that he doubted whether the P.M. had ever read the Atlantic Charter. The speech was a sensible lead towards a *via media*, though there now seems little hope of this.

Tuesday, December 19th

The P.M. apparently did badly over Questions in the House, especially about Greece. The Chief Whip says it is the first time he has seen the House really irritated and impatient with him. The P.M., who disagrees with Eden about Greece (Eden wants to overrule King George and get the Archbishop of Athens appointed Regent), said he would intervene tomorrow in the debate on the adjournment. The Foreign Office are terrified of what he may say and James Stuart, who thinks he has been speaking too much lately, did his utmost to dissuade him. But he insisted that he would make a short, gay and impromptu speech.

He stayed up till 3.00 a.m.

Wednesday, December 20th

To the House for Questions which were uneventful. The P.M. did not intervene about Greece. Another over-burdened afternoon – there is so much happening, Greece, Poland, a powerful German counter-attack on the Luxembourg frontier which has thrown the Americans some twenty miles back (Monty, who is suffering from personal pique as a result of a difference of opinion with Eisenhower about questions of command, is very gloomy about it all); and in addition to all this the usual mass of amorphous trivialities such as Honorary Fellowships of French institutions, the breaking up of battalions in which the P.M. has an interest (the Oxfordshire Hussars this time), etc., etc.

Thursday, December 21st

I met Alec Cadogan in the park. He said the P.M. was creating a deplorable impression in Cabinet now because he would not

[1] Fellow of Corpus Christi and one of the two Cambridge University M.P.s.

read his papers and would talk on and on. It is very distressing and unless he will delegate much of his work I see little hope of a change. Obviously he is hopelessly overtired and at seventy his powers of recuperation may not be very good.

There are signs of an impending quarrel between the P.M. and Eden about the Regency in Greece.

Friday, December 22nd

After the P.M. had lunched (having Mervyn Haigh, Bishop of Winchester, to be vetted for the Archbishopric of Canterbury; afterwards he told me he liked Haigh but thought Fisher, the Bishop of London, the tougher of the two), he again had interminable discussions with the King of Greece and Eden. Eden says the King keeps on telling lies.

Then the P.M. sent for P. J. Grigg and rammed down his throat an announcement about additional manpower for the army. This was subsequently rammed down the throat of others (including Bevin, who was snatched from the stalls of the Coliseum) and given to the press and the B.B.C., the idea being that at this moment when the German thrust has broken through Eisenhower's too dispersed strength, an announcement of our determination to raise a further 250,000 men would arouse the country from its present victory-complex and stimulate the Americans, who always want to go one better, to call up another million.

The P.M. dilly-dallied so much in the Defence Map Room that it was too late to go to Chequers and he dined at the Annexe. He talked to John Martin and me interminably after dinner about his differences of opinion over Greece with Eden, his intention of flying to Athens to settle the matter, and the fact that the English people throughout their history always turned on those whom they thought had served them well in hard times (e.g. Marlborough, Wellington, Lloyd George). So long did he talk that he became too tired, and it became too late, to go down to Chequers at all, and so, in spite of Sawyers and the luggage having gone ahead, we remained at the Annexe.

Saturday, December 23rd

The P.M. spent most of the day in bed at the Annexe and had lunch in his room. At 5.00 we left for Chequers, where we found Mrs Romilly, Jack, Clarissa and the Sandyses. After dinner the P.M. spoke of flying to Athens tomorrow, but though I made the preliminary arrangements I did not think seriously that he would.

Sunday, December 24th

The Cranbornes, Prof. and Horatia Seymour came to lunch. I sat between Lady Cranborne, who is one of the world's most attractive conversationalists, and Horatia Seymour. After lunch it seemed that Lord Cranborne and others had dissuaded the P.M. from his proposed venture and those whom I had warned by telephone were in a state of miserable uncertainty. However at 5.30 the P.M. agreed with Eden by telephone that both should go tonight though neither were at all clear what they should find in Athens when they got there. A chaotic evening ensued, with the P.M. telling the King, Attlee, Bevin, Beaverbrook on one telephone and me warning the C.A.S., Admiralty, Tommy, etc., etc. on the other. Mrs C. was greatly distressed but resigned herself to the inevitable. I had had my uniform sent down from London and at 11.30 p.m. we were all dressed and ready to depart, though it was difficult to drag the P.M. from the sofa in the Great Hall where he was reading telegrams, dictating manuscript comments, and carrying on a conversation with Mrs Romilly (who was most outrageously reading the telegrams too) all at the same time.

Christmas Day, Monday, December 25th

We took off from Northolt, seen off by the C.A.S., Duncan Sandys and the Prof., at 1.00 a.m. It was the first journey of the P.M.'s new C.54, a beautifully appointed aircraft provided by General Arnold.[1] The party consisted of the P.M., Anthony Eden, Bob Dixon, myself, Tommy Thompson, Miss Layton

[1] U.S. Army Air Force Chief of Staff.

and Miss Holmes (the P.M.'s two most attractive typists), a detective and Sawyers, the P.M.'s servant. Also Lord Moran.

The best record I can give of the next two days is contained in the following letter I wrote to John Martin on Boxing Day and in a description I wrote of the meeting at the Greek Ministry of Foreign Affairs:

Athens,
December 26th, 1944

Dear John,

I think you will be interested to have some sort of background to the official telegrams about our activities which will be reaching you.

Our journey went without a hitch. The C.54 is remarkably comfortable and very quiet. We had to climb to 13,500 feet over France and as no one but the P.M. was awoken for oxygen we all arose with splitting headaches. However these passed off very quickly. At Pomigliano we did not go more than 100 yards from the aircraft, having breakfast in a rather bare building which had only slightly recovered from the many bombardments it had had to withstand. We wasted but little time there but at breakfast the Prime Minister had a talk with the C. in C., Mediterranean, Slessor and Harding.[1] We found that the C.54 would be able to get into Athens, so did not change aircraft. We flew over Taranto, where I took over the controls without in any way endangering the passengers and thence across the Adriatic, past Cythera and Ithaca (which was "cloud-capped" in the best Homeric tradition) and flew up the Gulf of Corinth past Patras. We lunched in the air.

At the aerodrome Alexander, Macmillan and Leeper[2] came on board. We had a conference lasting two hours in the aircraft itself. At this conference the plan of campaign was worked

---

[1] Chief of Staff to Alexander. After the war he was appointed C.I.G.S. and was Governor of Cyprus during the E.O.K.A. troubles. Made a Field Marshal in 1953 and a peer in 1958.

[2] An Australian who joined the British Diplomatic Service in 1918. Ambassador in Athens, 1944–46, and afterwards in Buenos Aires. Subsequently a most effective Chairman of the British Council.

out and just before dark we set off on a long drive in armoured cars to the quay. The driver of my armoured car encouraged me greatly by beginning the conversation with "The last man who sat where you are sitting died yesterday morning." However nobody sniped at us on the way, although at one point we passed a place which E.L.A.S. had been mortaring during the morning.

We boarded *Ajax* just after sunset and were received with astonishing hospitality. Shortly afterwards Leeper, Macmillan and Scobie arrived bringing with them Papandreou[1] and the Archbishop. While the Prime Minister and the rest saw Papandreou, we entertained the Archbishop, who is a magnificent figure and obviously has a great sense of humour. The Admiral cleverly produced a bottle of ouzo, a nauseating Greek liqueur tasting like a cheap cough mixture. It is the colour of water, and Tommy, thinking it was water, obligingly filled up a glass of whisky with it and handed the contents to me. I have never felt nearer death.

The Archbishop impressed the Prime Minister as much as he had the rest of us and we are now in the curious topsy-turvy position of the Prime Minister feeling strongly pro-Damaskinos (he even thinks he would make a good Regent) while the S. of S. is inclined the other way.

Ajax is temporarily the Flagship of Admiral Mansfield, who is a man of great charm. The Captain, Cuthbert, was in the Cabinet Office early in the war and greeted me as an old friend. One or two of the complement of *K.G.V.*, who brought us home last January, are also on board. The ship's company celebrated Christmas in a big way and the Archbishop's arrival coincided with a deafening rendering of "The First Noel" by the ship's carol party. This seemed very appropriate. Parties in the various messes continued until a very late hour.

This morning the sun is shining brightly and I have just persuaded the P.M. to get up and go out on the quarter-deck. From the bridge one can see the smoke of battle in the street

[1] Prime Minister of King George's Greek Government and father of the republican Andreas Papandreou who came to power in the 1980s.

fighting west of the Piraeus, and there is a constant noise
of shell-fire and machine-guns. We had a splendid view of
Beaufighters strafing an E.L.A.S. stronghold on the side of
one of the hills surrounding Athens. Four of them went round
and round, diving with all their cannons blazing and then joining
in behind the tail of the preceding aircraft to continue the
process. As E.L.A.S. seem to be deficient of flak, however
well provided they may be with other weapons, the Beaufighters seem to be having a very pleasant time.

There is no nonsense about fraternising among the troops
here, who, to a man, consider E.L.A.S. and all their works
utterly loathsome. I have spoken to several and I gather that
there is a general sense of anger at the attitude of the British
press and certain elements of the Labour Party. Nobody here
has any illusions about the real character of the rebels. On
the other hand E.L.A.S., in spite of their diabolical activities,
have a strangely obliging side to them. For instance, the
telephone exchange is in the hands of E.L.A.S. but they
have never yet made any difficulties about our telephoning
messages from the aerodrome to G.H.Q., even though these,
in the form sent, provide them with no useful information.
Macmillan says that they possess many of the qualities and
defects of the Irish.

The above was written after lunch and it is now 11.45 p.m.
with the bag almost closing. This afternoon's events were the
purest melodrama. Just before we left the ship we were
straddled by shells and another fell quite close as we landed.
The meeting with the Greeks was preceded by long sessions
at the Embassy, in which the Archbishop figured prominently.
There were photographs in the garden and the Prime Minister
made a stirring speech to the staff of the Embassy thanking
them for their excellent work in arduous conditions. This gave
enormous pleasure both to Leeper and to the staff. It looked
as if E.L.A.S. would not turn up for the meeting and the
Archbishop had made his opening speech and the P.M. was
halfway through his, when there were noises off and three
shabby desperadoes, who had been searched and almost
stripped before being allowed to enter, came into the dimly-lit

conference room. All the British delegation, the American, the Russian and the Frenchman, rose to their feet, but the Greek Government remained firmly seated. The P.M. was only prevented from rushing to shake the E.L.A.S. people by the hand by Field Marshal Alexander's bodily intervention.

The proceedings then began all over again and, with the sound of rocket-firing Beaufighters, and bursting mortar shells without, the light of a few Hurricane lamps within and the spectacle of what was surely the oddest galaxy of stars ever assembled in one place, one had continually to rub one's eyes to be sure one was not dreaming. Osbert Lancaster,[1] who sat near me, has promised to send me a second carbon of his first cartoon on the subject.

Since the meeting broke up life has been pretty hectic. Miss Holmes[2] and I, who stayed behind at the Embassy to clear some things up, had a most harrowing return journey. First we fell into the hands of some Greek Home Guards, who viewed my blue uniform with deep suspicion which was, alas, confirmed when I tried to speak to them in German; then as no boat was waiting for us from *Ajax*, and as we were both going the way of Captain Oates, we finally begged a lift from the launch of a Greek destroyer. This was a precarious undertaking and I began to regret it when for the fifth time we failed to come alongside the ship properly and appeared in imminent danger of capsizing. There is no time for more now, but even Lord Moran admits that this is an unusual expedition and it is certainly not one which will be forgotten in a hurry.

We are all tired and bewildered but generally speaking happy, and the Prime Minister is in the best of health and spirits, which is the most important thing of all.

Yours ever,
Jock.

---

[1] Writer of books on architecture, which he illustrated, and producer of hilarious "Pocket Cartoons" for the *Daily Express*. At this time press attaché at the Embassy in Athens.

[2] One of the most attractive shorthand-typists at 10 Downing Street whom Churchill sometimes annexed to help with his personal work.

On the way home, three days later, I wrote the following as an official record:

DESCRIPTION OF THE CONFERENCE OF GREEK PARTIES CONVENED BY THE PRIME MINISTER ON TUESDAY, DECEMBER 26th, 1944

The Conference was due to start at 4.00 p.m., but there was doubt whether the E.L.A.S. representatives, who had been offered a safe conduct through the British lines, would come and several postponements had to be made. Shortly after five o'clock, in the gathering darkness, the Prime Minister, Mr Eden and the remainder of the British party left the Embassy in armoured cars and drove a few hundred yards down the street to the Ministry of Foreign Affairs. The security officials had had a field day: tanks patrolled the streets, an armed cordon surrounded the building, and the passes of everybody approaching the Ministry were closely scrutinised.

The Ministry of Foreign Affairs must at best be a gloomy building, and with the electricity cut off its dinginess was accentuated. Followed by the rest of the party, the Prime Minister was ushered through a seething mob of Greek politicians, of all ages and parties, of security officials and of heavily-armed soldiers, into a large rectangular room devoid of all furniture except an immense table about which some thirty chairs had been placed. The room was lit by hurricane lamps, of varying degrees of brightness, placed on the table, and was heated by evil-smelling oil stoves. Apart from a yellow glow thrown by the lamps on the faces of those seated round the table, darkness prevailed. It was a scene such as would normally be associated with the meeting of some hunted band of conspirators and this no doubt helped the E.L.A.S. delegates, when they finally arrived, to feel at ease and at home.

No seating arrangements had been made, but the Archbishop, who was Chairman of the Conference, sat down in the centre of the table on the right-hand side of the door. Mr Churchill sat on his right with Mr Eden next to him, and on the left of the Archbishop sat Field Marshal Alexander. The other British representatives spread themselves on either side facing members of the Greek Government. Monsieur Papandreou sat opposite Mr Churchill and next to him was General Plastiras,[1] whose fierce mien and waxed moustaches were the cynosure of all eyes. At the end of the table facing the door were the American Ambassador, Mr MacVeagh, the French Minister, Monsieur Beynet, and the Soviet Military representative, Colonel Popoff.

Room was left at the other end of the table, near the door, for the representatives of E.L.A.S., should they decide to come. But as time passed and they made no appearance, it was decided to begin the Conference. The Archbishop rose to his feet, a tall and impressive figure in his black robes and high black hat. His speech welcoming the Prime Minister and Mr Eden was admirably interpreted, sentence by sentence, by Major Matthews and when he sat down Mr Churchill, who was also interpreted with great fluency, began his address.

He had not, however, been speaking for more than four or five minutes when noises without heralded the belated arrival of the E.L.A.S. delegates. They were first well searched, and General Mandakas, who had brought with him a Mauser rifle and large quantities of ammunition, was required to lay them aside. He refused on principle to hand his weapons over to British troops but eventually a compromise was reached whereby the arms were placed in an empty room, the door locked and a guard placed outside. The Conference waited patiently while all this took place, and then the three E.L.A.S. leaders, dressed shabbily in khaki battledress and glancing furtively around as if they expected a trap, shuffled into the room. Following the Prime Minister's example, the British representatives and the Allied observers rose to their feet with one accord and bowed to the new arrivals. The Archbishop followed suit, but the members of the Greek Government remained firmly seated and did not so much as turn their heads to the door. The E.L.A.S. delegates

[1] The Prime Minister would insist on referring to him as General Plaster-arse.

sat down, Monsieur Partsalides on the right, Monsieur Siantos, the Secretary and brains of the rebel committee, in the middle and General Mandakas on the left.

It was decided to begin the proceedings again. The Archbishop repeated his speech and Mr Churchill then spoke for half an hour addressing his remarks largely in the direction of the E.L.A.S. delegates. Gradually, as Mr Churchill proceeded, the three rebel leaders lost their look of intimidation and seemed to abandon their suspicion of an intended *"coup de main"*. Perhaps it was wholesome that whenever they raised their eyes from the table they looked straight into the glittering spectacles, spotless uniform and impeccable bearing of Colonel Popoff, whose appearance was every inch that of an officer and a gentleman.

While the Prime Minister was speaking, the sound of gun-fire went on ceaselessly without, and at one moment the roar of descending rockets, launched by Beaufighters at some nearby enemy position, almost drowned his words. Field Marshal Alexander followed with a short but powerfully-reasoned speech which clearly left its effect on his audience. When he had finished, the Archbishop enquired whether any of the Greek representatives had questions to ask. There was an awkward pause and it was evident that a difference of opinion existed in the E.L.A.S. ranks. However just as the Prime Minister was suggesting that the British representatives should depart and leave the Greeks to their own deliberations, an aged Royalist, Monsieur Maximos, rose to his feet and, instead of asking a question, made a short and highly-coloured speech of welcome. He was followed by Monsieur Papandreou, whose speech was equally ponderous but a great deal longer, and who spoke with evident shyness and embarrassment. Then Monsieur Partsalides of E.L.A.S. arose and, beginning with the utmost diffidence, his eyes bent downwards, paid a glowing tribute to Mr Churchill. However as he warmed to his subject, his excitement got the better of him, he raised his eyes which flashed in the lamp-light and spoke with such speed and vehemence that the interpreter was unable to get a word in edgeways and was obliged to give up the unequal task. As it was clear that his speech was largely based on a misunderstanding of the intention of the Conference Mr Eden said a few words of explanation.

The time had now come to leave the Greeks to their own devices and so, headed by the Prime Minister, the British representatives walked out of the room, shaking hands as they left with members of the Greek Government and lastly with the delegates of E.L.A.S., whose bows could not have been lower, handshakes warmer nor protestations more friendly had they been ambassadors of a party under the deepest obligation to Great Britain.

On the steps of the Ministry of Foreign Affairs, while Mr Churchill was entering his armoured car, there was a further alarum, and indeed excursion, as various Greeks, headed by the eighty-four-year-old Liberal leader, Monsieur Sophoulis, made a desperate effort to flee from the Conference chamber. They were however firmly held and persuaded to return to their places at the council table.

So ended the opening session of what must surely be the strangest conference which a British Prime Minister and Foreign Secretary have ever attended.

Wednesday, December 27th
They treated us with great kindness and hospitality on board H.M.S. *Ajax* but what with the depth charges exploding by way of precaution all night and bluejackets continually bringing telegrams into my cabin I had very little sleep.

Today it was colder on the quarter-deck and the clouds obscured the sun. We lay in Phaleron Bay, with a fine view of Athens, the Piraeus, Mount Hymettus and, on the other side, Aegina and Salamis.

Eden and Dixon went ashore early to see the Archbishop and hear the result of last night's inter-Greek discussions. The P.M., Lord Moran, Tommy and I followed at noon. The rest of the party drove to the Embassy in an enclosed armoured car, but I followed behind in a smaller one with an open turret and, clutching a Tommy gun in my hands, was able to look out upon the crowds in the streets, the Acropolis, the Temple of Zeus, etc. I had last seen Athens in 1934.

There was excitement before lunch when, as the P.M. was

about to set off with General Scobie for a review of our military dispositions, a burst of machine-gun fire, coming from well over a mile away, struck the wall of a house some thirty feet over his head. Several bursts were fired and a woman in the street was killed. I was amused by our troops whose first reaction was to fix bayonets. We lunched at the Embassy. I sat between Mrs Leeper and Osbert Lancaster, now press attaché to the Embassy.

After lunch the P.M. saw MacVeagh, the American Ambassador, and gave him a piece of his mind about the very inadequate support the U.S.A. have given us in this affair. He then held a press conference, speaking to the dirtiest and most unreliable collection of "news hawks" ever assembled. The P.M. was not at his best, but the conference was not unsuccessful and the press, so I gathered from Osbert Lancaster, were pleased. It was bitterly cold in the Embassy, there being no coal for heating, and we all felt rather worried about the P.M. The Chancery, in which Osbert L. and I spent hours correcting Miss Layton's shorthand report of the P.M.'s speech to the press, was warmer; but we were all chilled to the marrow when, at about 7.30 p.m. we left to return to the ship. The Embassy is not a gay place and I thought the Ambassador, Leeper, rather grim.

On board all was light, warmth and comfort again. F. M. Alexander and Macmillan were there. The P.M. said he regretted having refused to see the E.L.A.S. delegates, but the Archbishop as well as his own colleagues had been against it.

Thursday, December 28th
There was a last-minute possibility of our staying for another session of the conference, but finally it was decided against and we went ashore at lunch-time, after the P.M. had addressed the ship's company on the quarter-deck.

We flew away from Kalamaki airfield at 2.00 and lunched as we flew westwards down the Gulf of Corinth. Attica and the islands, Parnassus and the Peloponnese crowned with snow, were glorious in the sun and the unbroken visibility.

Alexander and Macmillan flew back with us. When we reached Pomigliano, just before dusk, we got into cars and drove through

Naples to the Field Marshal's guest villa. I drove with Air Marshal Slessor who is a charming companion.

We dined at the villa as Alexander's guests. Sir John Cunningham, C. in C., Mediterranean, was there and so were Slessor and General Harding, Alexander's Chief of Staff. I sat next to the latter and had an amusing three-cornered conversation, largely about Parliament, with him and Eden. After dinner we sat about in the drawing-room and the C. in C.'s A.D.C.s joined us.

Friday, December 29th
Rising at 6.00 a.m. we flew away from Pomigliano at 8.00 a.m. The weather, as throughout the expedition, was glorious. We saw Rome and Ostia below us to starboard, with the Tiber winding its way inland, and then it was Corsica, crowned with snow, the Mediterranean, deep blue, Toulon, Narbonne, and the Pyrenees on our left. There was no cloud, as we flew northwards at between six and eight thousand feet, until we had crossed the Loire. We lunched aboard and when I saw Mt St Michel I started a hare by pointing out that the Channel Isles were still in German hands; but we were assured that our course went far eastwards of them. In the air I dictated a description of the conference at Athens.

It was fine over England and one could see the ground white with frost, but there was thick fog over London itself and so we landed on an American aerodrome at Bovingdon near Watford. Mrs C., Jack, John Martin, John Peck and Lady Moran were there to greet us. Lord M. had, incidentally, shamelessly unfolded to me during the morning his plan for becoming Provost of Eton, an appointment for which he would in every way be unsuitable. It is a Crown appointment so he wanted my advice whether he should go straight to the P.M. and ask for it. I said, very definitely, no. All this was wrapped round with protestations of having no ambitions but of this being forced on him by friends, etc.

Sunday, December 31st
At Ardley. A long and undisturbed sleep, the first for some days, was very refreshing. Went to church with Joan and the

children. Clear blue skies and a hard frost under foot – weather which has lasted since before Christmas.

Listened to the B.B.C. broadcast ushering the New Year in (very ineffective) and then to the opening of a broadcast by Hitler, who seemed in low spirits.

TWELVE

BUILD-UP TO YALTA
JANUARY 1945

Monday, January 1st
Sunshine and frost at Ardley. Bicycled to Middleton with Ann[1]
and drank rum with Diane Maxwell.
 Returned to No. 10 in the evening to find the P.M. ice-bound
at Chequers and a pile of work awaiting me.

Tuesday, January 2nd
Admiral Sir Bertram Ramsay was killed in an air crash. The
P.M. composed a crushing letter to Barrington-Ward[2] about
The Times' attitude on the Greek question, but after consultation
with Eden, Brendan, etc., decided not to send it. Meanwhile
letters, etc., from British troops in Greece show them 100 per
cent behind the Government.

Wednesday, January 3rd
The P.M. went off to Versailles to visit S.H.A.E.F.[3] and sub-
sequently Monty. He spurned the company both of the Defence
Office and the Private Office and took with him a strange trio,
Commander Thompson, Kinna[4] and Sawyers.

---

[1] Ann Elliot, formerly Child-Villiers.
[2] Geoffrey Dawson's successor as Editor of *The Times*.
[3] Somewhat over-staffed Supreme Headquarters of the Allied Expeditionary
 Force under Eisenhower.
[4] One of the clerks at No. 10 next in seniority to Charles Barker. Bright,
 intelligent and alert, he could take shorthand and sometimes, when Churchill
 was going somewhere where he judged "the young ladies" might be in
 danger, Pat Kinna accompanied him on his journeys.

Thursday, January 4th

It transpires that Archbishop Damaskinos' name is also Papandreou. As Regent he has now appointed General Plastiras Prime Minister. Leeper says in a telegram: *"Papandreou est mort; vive Papandreou."*

I heard with sorrow that Derek Dickson, Joe Stubbs and Gibbons, all of 168 Squadron, together with several others, have been killed in the last few days. The R.A.F. had a rough time on New Year's morning, the Luftwaffe coming over in strength at 0 feet and destroying many aircraft on the ground.

Friday, January 5th

The P.M. returned from France, confident about the position on the northern flank of the German breakthrough, where Monty is in command, but less sure of the southern sector.

Things are in something of a trough; Stalin has recognised the Lublin Poles, in face of our and U.S. requests that he should not; de Gaulle is throwing his weight about in military affairs; Drew Pearson, the most venomous of American columnists, has published another of our secret documents (about Italy this time) which he has procured from the State Department somehow or other; and V.2 rockets are falling like autumnal leaves.

Stole away after lunch to Hendon and flew an elegant M.38[1] put at my disposal by Commander Brabner, Under S. of S. for Air.

The P.M. says that sending Tedder to Moscow to talk about purely military affairs is like asking a man who has learned to ride a bicycle to paint a picture.

He is also incensed with Stafford Cripps for making a speech about brotherly feelings for the Germans. He says he might agree with such sentiments when victory is won, but not with a great battle raging and the Huns shooting captured soldiers in cold blood. (Eisenhower tells him they have shot 130 prisoners of war.) To bed at 2.45 a.m.

---

[1] Single-engined two-seater aircraft.

Sunday, January 7th
Went to the early service at Westminster Abbey which looks very romantic by candlelight on a dark morning.

Spent the evening and the night with Tommy Lascelles and his family at their house in Windsor Castle.

Monday, January 8th
A cold and very frosty morning. Windsor looked magnificent. Returned to London where rockets are becoming much too frequent and where the Mean Point of Impact seems to be moving westwards.

The P.M. returned from Chequers rather depressed, in spite of reassuring news from Monty. His prevalent feelings were shown in a letter to someone to whom he sent best wishes for this "new, disgusting year". John Peck thinks the prospect of the end of the war and the problems it will bring with it are depressing the P.M.; but John's view is that that is a cheap price to pay for the end of the war. Dictated myriads of letters, some harsh, some sloppy, but all dull. Jasper Ridley,[1] intelligent, experienced and wise, dined in the mess. Snow falling and lying deep.

Tuesday, January 9th
The P.M. has a cold which, he says, is attacking on a broad front. So he saw the King of Yugoslavia in bed and told him in terms of no uncertainty how his only hope lay in consenting to the agreement reached between Subasic[2] and Tito and in agreeing to a Regency. After the King had gone, the P.M. and Eden said that if they were him they would do just the opposite to what they had been advising him and snap their fingers at Tito.

It would be hard to find two worse advertisements for hereditary monarchy than George of Greece and Peter of Yugoslavia.

---

[1] The Hon. Sir Jasper Ridley, erudite trustee of the British Museum and Chairman of the Tate Gallery. For many years executive Chairman of Coutts and Co.
[2] Dr Subasic, the Ban (Governor) of Croatia, was envisaged as new head of the Royal Yugoslav Government who might be found acceptable to Marshal Tito, himself a Croat.

About midnight, while Lord Beaverbrook and Brendan were closeted in the P.M.'s bedroom, having come no doubt on some nefarious intrigue (anti-Bevin, whom the P. M. cherishes above all Labour Ministers, I suspect), Anthony Eden rang up in a storm of rage. It was about a minute from Lord Cherwell, forwarded by the P.M. to the F.O., in which Eden's assertions about the starvation confronting Europe were flatly denied. Eden told me he would resign if inexpert, academic opinions were sought on subjects to which he had given so much thought. I put him through to the P.M., to whom he ranted in a way in which neither the P.M. nor I (who was listening in) had ever heard him before. The P.M. handled the storm in a very adept and paternal way, said he would take the Prof.'s paper back and go into it himself, protested at Anthony vexing himself with such matters at the end of a long, weary day, and said there was only one thing he could and would not allow: the feeding of Europe at the expense of an already hard-rationed England.

Monty's triumphant, jingoistic and exceedingly self-satisfied talk to the press on Sunday has given wide offence. Now that he is in command of the northern part of the salient, where things are going well, he has won his point – or part of it – over Eisenhower and is indecently exultant. The P.M. has countered, to soothe the Americans (who are also rather worked up by an outspoken attack on American complacency and superiority in the *Economist*, written by Geoffrey Crowther) by means of a published telegram of congratulations to Omar Bradley.

At 1.00 a.m. came telegrams from Athens to the effect that E.L.A.S. were asking for a truce, good news which caused the P.M. to expatiate on the wisdom of holding firm. To bed at 2.00.

Wednesday, January 10th
Snow deep on the ground and bright sun. The P.M. remained in bed. He is disgusted that the President should want to spend only five or six days at the coming meeting between "the Big Three" and says that even the Almighty required seven to settle the world. (An inaccuracy which was quickly pointed out to him. Viz. Genesis I.)

Lunched at the Reform with Nicko Henderson who says that

H.M.G. are assuming the role of Metternich in the concert of Europe, a demonstrably unfair historical parallel.

Thursday, January 11th

It looks as if our policy in Greece is going to triumph, to the discomfiture of critics here and in the U.S.A. The Greek Socialist Party and Trade Unions have passed powerful resolutions in support of H.M.G. and denouncing E.L.A.S.; E.L.A.S. at Salonica have surrendered; General Scobie's new and enlarged terms in Attica look like being accepted. The P.M. therefore thinks he will have a debate next week instead of the following week so as to strike in the House of Commons while the iron is hot.

King Peter of Yugoslavia has rejected the P.M.'s and Foreign Secretary's advice and has issued an announcement refusing to accept certain parts of the Tito-Subasic agreement and the establishment of a Regency (unless he chooses the Regents). He has acted against the advice of his Prime Minister, but on that of Princess Aspasia[1] of Greece and probably of Derek Mond (Melchett's son). So H.M.G. are going to drop his cause.

Archie Sinclair is in a tangle about scandals concerning the R.A.F. pig farm at Regent's Park and the administration of B.O.A.C. General Critchley[2] is at the bottom of both. Archie is despondent.

The P.M., who was angry because I carried no revolver when we were in Athens, reverted to the subject tonight and said if I did not procure one he wouldn't take me on any further trips. So I shall.

Friday, January 12th

Minor Greek crisis owing to the fact that Scobie has signed a truce with E.L.A.S. without first stipulating the release of the hostages.

[1] Widow of King George's brother Alexander who had been King for a short time but had been poisoned by the bite of a pet monkey. Her daughter married King Peter of Yugoslavia.
[2] Brigadier A. C. Critchley, M.P. A soldier in the First World War who joined the R.A.F. in the Second World War and was much engaged in business deals.

To Stansted for the week-end. Lord and Lady Bessborough, Moyra and George were there. There were two other guests, Oswald Normanby,[1] for three years a prisoner of war and now P.P.S. to Lord Cranborne, and a Canadian soldier called Maxwell Bruce.

Saturday, January 13th
Shot in the morning, walking round clumps of trees and a duck pond with Normanby and George Ponsonby.[2] We killed five cock pheasants, three duck, a partridge, three rabbits, two grey squirrels and a green woodpecker (for which I was guilty – it flew like a teal). Among the duck was a Golden Eye, which I shot.

Monday, January 15th
The P.M. received, very formally, a Labour Deputation about Greece. He insisted on my having them all seated in the Cabinet Room before he came up from luncheon so that he might avoid shaking hands with Aneurin Bevan.

Tuesday, January 16th
The P.M. has something of a sore throat and so, after taking Questions (the House reassembled today), he retired to bed and spent the day there, composing his speech on the war for next Thursday and emptying his box.

Looking at the messages and letters that go out from this office under the P.M.'s signature, I often think how difficult it will be for future historians to know what is "genuine Churchill"

[1] Oswald, 4th Marquess of Normanby, K.G. Wounded and taken prisoner when serving with the Green Howards in 1940, he organised a school for blinded British prisoners in Germany. For this purpose he taught himself braille from a Larousse dictionary. When the Germans allowed the blind to be repatriated, they also authorised Normanby to accompany them home. Married Lord Moyne's daughter, Grania Guinness, and became Chairman of King's College Hospital and the National Art Collection Fund. Lord Lieutenant of North Yorkshire.

[2] Youngest son of Lord and Lady Bessborough, accidentally killed shortly after joining the 9th Lancers. Another of the Bessboroughs' sons had been killed many years before in a riding accident.

and what is "school of". We are all fairly good imitators of his epistolary style now, and though his speeches are of course all original, as are most of his minutes, only a few of his letters and messages are. But I defy anyone to trace a bar sinister in my message to Papandreou signed today or in recent letters I have composed for the P.M.'s signature to M. Lebrun, Mrs Philip Guedalla, Mrs Wendell Willkie, Mrs Denys Reitz, etc.

Wednesday, January 17th
The Russian offensive, which began last week, proceeds with great éclat. Today Warsaw was taken and spirits, depressed by the German success against the Americans, are again soaring in the belief the war may yet end in a comparatively short time.

I lunched with the P.M. and Mrs C. at the Annexe to meet the new South African High Commissioner, Mr Heaton Nicholls, and his wife. Others present were Brendan, Lady Ismay, cousin Nellie Graham, Edward Bridges and Mary, who is off to Antwerp shortly in command of the A.T.S. in her battery. I sat between Mary, looking very pretty, and cousin Nellie. When the Heaton Nichollses were leaving, the P.M. said to him, "Smuts and I are like two old love-birds moulting together on a perch but still able to peck."

Attended a meeting at the F.O., with Alec Cadogan, Edward Bridges and Gilbert Laithwaite about the publication of Keith Feiling's biography of Neville Chamberlain. Agreed that Feiling should be pressed to postpone publication; the matter, much of it based on official papers, is too controversial and Neville's comments, especially on the Americans and the Russians, too caustic.

Thursday, January 18th
In spite of a cold and sore throat, which had kept him in bed some days, the P.M. gaily opened the debate on the war situation in the House. He spoke for over two hours, dividing his speech for luncheon. He was in great form, both witty and combative. Before lunch he spoke of foreign politics and particularly Greece, trouncing Gallacher, Aneurin Bevan and other interruptors. His allusion to *The Times'* deplorable attitude

to the Greek crisis – he referred to a "time-honoured" news-paper – evoked a roar of laughter and applause such as I have seldom heard. In the afternoon his speech was less pugnacious, but very eloquent. Indeed, rhetorically, it was the best effort I have heard him make since 1941 or even 1940.

Friday, January 19th

The P.M. stayed in bed, but rushed down to the House at 4.00 to hear Eden wind up the debate and to vote in the division (which was brought about by that ass, Sir R. Acland, leader of the new Commonwealth Party).[1]

Saturday, January 20th

Snow again. The P.M. is spending the weekend in London, because of his cold. So as it is my "Chequers weekend", I am in attendance. The Annexe is gloomy and one has all the hard work of Chequers, and the late hours, without any of the perquisites.

Attlee has written a very blunt letter to the P.M., protesting (i) against the P.M.'s lengthy disquisitions in Cabinet on papers which he has not read and on subjects which he has not taken the trouble to master; (ii) against the P.M.'s undue attentiveness to Brendan and Lord Beaverbrook, whose views, often entirely ignorant, are apt to be thrown into the scale against the con-sidered opinion of a Cabinet Committee when that Committee brings its views to the War Cabinet. This has happened several times recently. Greatly as I love and admire the P.M. I am afraid there is much in what Attlee says, and I rather admire his courage in saying it. Many Conservatives, and officials such as Cadogan and Bridges, feel the same. However, the P.M. exploded over Attlee's letter, drafted and redrafted a sarcastic reply, said it was a socialist conspiracy, harped on nothing but the inadequate representation of the Tories in the Cabinet, in spite of their numerical weight in the House (which is beside

---

[1] A short-lived experiment to found a new left-wing party. It won by-elections at Gravesend and Chelmsford, presumably a rebellion by the local electorate against the "Party Truce"; but it received only temporary support.

the point), and worst of all, finally read Attlee's very personal letter – poorly typed by his own hand so that none of his staff should see it – to Beaverbrook on the telephone, having first of all discussed it with Mrs Churchill. As John Martin said, "that is the part of the P.M. which I do not like."

However, what of it? The Russians sweep gaily on, past Lodz, past Cracow, over the Silesian border. The war, once again, enters a fast-moving, thrilling phase and hopes rise high.

After dinner there was a film in an air-ministry room on the ground floor in King Charles Street. The P.M. bid us all cast care aside and "not bother about Atler or Hitlee", and so all the typists, drivers, servants, etc., saw first of all a first-class newsreel of the Luftwaffe attack on our airfields in Holland on New Year's Day and then Bette Davis in *Dark Victory*, a brilliantly acted film and one of the few I have seen end as a tragedy.

Sunday, January 21st
Snow lying deep, but a bright sun. The P.M. having worked till 2.30 a.m. did not wake till 11.30, when he said he felt recovered and that life had returned.

Walked in St James's Park with Mrs Churchill, who says that she thinks Attlee's letter of yesterday both true and wholesome. The last straw – to the P.M. – was when Lord Beaverbrook, against whom it was partly aimed, said he thought it a very good letter after seeing it at luncheon today. Finally the P.M., still sorely piqued but probably in his heart of hearts not unmoved by the arguments, sent Attlee a short, polite acknowledgment.

Another film after dinner, a very good thriller about blackmail, Edward G. Robinson in *The Woman in the Window*. The P.M. said that Robinson "is just like Max".

Monday, January 22nd
Things have slackened off a little, at any rate in comparison with the frenetic rush before Christmas.

The Russians are within 165 miles of Berlin and still advancing. King Peter, in the hands of his mother-in-law, has dismissed his Government and burnt his boats. We proceed without him.

Tuesday, January 23rd
The snow is still lying and more seems to be on the way. The P.M. sat up late with Harry Hopkins, who arrived yesterday from Washington. Brendan, who in 1941 said Hopkins was the finest of men, said tonight he was weak, useless and only courted because of his probably illusory influence with the President.[1]

When going to bed the P.M. said to me, "Make no mistake, all the Balkans, except Greece, are going to be Bolshevised; and there is nothing I can do to prevent it. There is nothing I can do for poor Poland either."

It seems that on the Eastern Front the Russians, whose spectacular advance continues, have a superiority of: 12–1 in tanks, 12–1 in aircraft and 7–1 in men.

Wednesday, January 24th
The P.M. told me that today was the fiftieth anniversary of his father's death. It is a strange descent, Lord Randolph, Winston, Randolph, with many characteristics in common, such as a capacity for being utterly unreasonable, but great differences of personality.

Thursday, January 25th
With snow lying and persistent hard frosts it looks as if there is to be a recurrence of the 1940 conditions.

Went to the House with the P.M. who lost his temper with Lord Winterton over the question of an enquiry about alleged irregularities in the administration of B.O.A.C. He then couldn't open his box, so we had to force it in an ante-room. Finally he made quite a good impromptu speech about the rebuilding of the House of Commons.

Friday, January 26th – Sunday, January 28th
Went to Ardley with mother. David was on leave and I celebrated my birthday delightfully in the bosom of my family. All the same I don't feel thirty.

[1] Cf Brendan Bracken's comments to me on January 10th, 1941 (Volume One, p. 393).

The weather was bitterly cold. Snow covered the fields and roads and the temperature remained doggedly below freezing point. But the January sun shone every day and the trees, white with snow, glistened entrancingly. On Saturday night David and I shot pigeon. In my R.A.F. "escape-boots" the cold was of no significance and the scene was like fairyland. In church, on Sunday, the pale sunlight streamed on to a scanty congregation and overhead, ceaselessly, we heard the drone of many Fortresses on their way to the battle line.

Meanwhile, in this unusually bitter month, the Germans are fleeing from their homes in East Germany and themselves experiencing the miseries which, albeit in summer, others suffered at their hands in 1940.

Monday, January 29th
After a two-hour wait on Bicester platform I returned to London, feeling myself like a refugee from Breslau.

In the evening the P.M., accompanied by John Martin (Leslie Rowan will follow; he has flu), left for Malta, whither Eden and the Chiefs of Staff have preceded him, en route for Yalta in the Crimea where ARGONAUT, the conference between Stalin, Roosevelt and the P.M., will take place. The conditions there sound ghastly and I am glad not to be going.[1]

Wednesday, January 31st
All very dreary and wet. Moreover Guy Millard at the F.O. being quite unable to draft a telegram to Turkey to warn the Turks that the P.M. would be flying over Turkish territory, I had to send for the F.O. file and do it myself which was annoying.

The Russians took Landsberg, the key point in what is thought to be the last line of defences before Berlin. *Sieg Heil!* Last

---

[1] Churchill invited me to go, but it would have upset office arrangements in London and John Martin (to my disappointment) dissuaded him. This saved my life, for there was no more room in the Prime Minister's C.54 and I should have been in the York which crashed off Pantellearia, having lost the way to Naples, killing all but one of the passengers.

night I listened in to the Führer, broadcasting on the twelfth anniversary of his accession to power. He was gloomy but more eloquent than of late.

THIRTEEN

APPEASING STALIN
FEBRUARY 1945

Thursday, February 1st
I went to see Ralph Assheton, Chairman of the Conservative Party, about my adoption as a candidate at the next election. He seemed to favour the idea, but the difficulty is bread and butter. If I resign from the F.O. I must find some alternative means of subsistence. Journalism seems a possibility, and the kind offices of Lords Kemsley or Camrose might be solicited. The Beaver would, I think, be very ready to help, but nothing would induce me to put myself under such an obligation.

Dined at the Reform with Nicko Henderson and Frank Pakenham.[1] We discussed foreign policy. Frank P., who is standing for Oxford against Quintin Hogg[2] at the next Election, is full of theories, the main one being the importance of directing policy by principles rather than *"raison d'état"*. His admiration for De Valera is profound.

Friday, February 2nd
A York, containing some of the ARGONAUT party, crashed in the sea off Lampedusa. Several members of the Foreign Office,

---

[1] Afterwards 7th Earl of Longford. As a Labour Minister, he later held many offices including the Admiralty and the leadership of the House of Lords. Also Chairman of the National Bank and of Sidgwick and Jackson (publishers).
[2] Learned lawyer, Fellow of All Souls and Q.C. First Lord of the Admiralty at the time of the Suez affair in 1956 and twice Lord Chancellor. Witty, explosive and a genuinely devout Christian who combined ambition with good nature, kindness and scrupulous honesty.

including Peter Loxley, were killed and also one of the officers, Newy by name, from the Defence Map Room.

Rosemary Hinchingbrooke took me to dine with Miss Joan Haslip[1] in a flat in Carrington House. The other guests were the Archduke Robert of Austria, Mrs Simon Harcourt Smith[2] (gay, attractive, *bas bleu* and a shade Rodd-ish) and Baron Gondalfieri, a courteous man with polished manners and half closed eyes who represents the Italian Government in Dublin. The Baron said that whether or not Italy went Communist was a question of food. The Archduke said that Berchtesgaden should be given to Austria as an attraction for tourists (all Germans being forbidden entry) and a source of income to the Austrian State. Mrs Harcourt Smith told diplomatic stories in a drawl and waxed eloquent about the art of cooking. Miss Haslip attacked the left-wing prejudices of the B.B.C. staff, among whom she works. Rosemary, who expects a child any moment, looked delightful but said little.

Tuesday, February 13th

The Prof., who is very much of a Jeremiah these days, tells me that nobody realises the horror of our financial prospects. We are facing an Economic Dunkirk. It is no use Amery, etc., talking about our having "a splendid market"; one might as well say that he, Prof., was a great asset to Claridges merely because he had a splendid appetite. We could only hope to survive if we took the German and Japanese pre-war markets, and as for Germany she must not be allowed to export but must live on an autarchic system and accept a low standard of living.

I know nothing of economics, but instinctively I feel the Prof.'s views to be both immoral and unsound.

Wednesday, February 14th

Ash Wednesday and St Valentine's day, an inharmonious combination. Blue skies and sunshine which enabled the air forces to

[1] Well-known author and broadcaster.
[2] Daughter of the former Ambassador to Rome, Sir Rennell Rodd (1st Lord Rennell).

destroy Dresden. The P.M. stopped in Athens to receive an ovation from the populace, freed from fear if not from want.

Everybody is furious that the British offensive near Cleves is being called Canadian and British troops are getting hardly any kudos. This is because the 1st Canadian Army is the unit, but practically all the divisions taking part are British. Such self-effacement, which has characterised our publicity throughout the war, gives great offence and makes many people adopt a very jingoistic attitude in conversation.

I saw a V.2 airburst – a loud explosion and a cloud of white smoke – in the blue sky to the north-west. It seemed to be over Sloane Street but was in fact over Finchley.

Thursday, February 15th
Read the full and interesting records of the Plenary Conferences at the Crimea. We seem to have won most of our points and the P.M. has won another great personal success. He was tireless in pressing for this conference, in spite of Roosevelt's apathy, and deserves most of the credit for what has been achieved.

Before going to bed in the C.W.R., Brendan waxed eloquent on the solid, unshakeable qualities of old Sir Dudley Pound[1], and Johnny Bevan gave a vivid description of F. M. Alexander when he first saw him: last man in for Harrow at Lords in 1910, a dramatic occasion on which Alex's defiant attitude was very impressive.

Sunday, February 18th
For dinner in the mess, being short of food, we had to borrow and devour the whole of the P.M.'s and Mrs C.'s meat ration for next week.

Monday, February 19th
The ARGONAUT party was due to return. At the last moment a landing at Northolt was found to be impossible and so they put

---

[1] Originator of the Directorate of Plans at the Admiralty, former Chief of Staff to Sir Roger Keyes and finally C. in C., Mediterranean, he was recalled to London to be First Sea Lord only six weeks before the outbreak of war.

down at Lyneham. Having myself been all the way to Northolt in vain I then set off for Reading with Mrs C. and found the P.M., Eden and Sarah awaiting us in a hotel (where the management were very startled) while the rest of the retinue were bumping crossly towards London in a Green Line bus.

I drove to London wedged between Eden and Sarah and heard a good deal about the Conference. Eden said that he thought the Tories had no right to complain about Poland. The P.M. had not sold the pass. On the contrary the Curzon line was a boundary proposed as fair by H.M.G. after the last war; we had not committed ourselves to accepting any specific western frontier for Poland; and finally we had only undertaken to recognise a new Polish Government in Poland if and when we were satisfied with its composition.

The P.M. had been very persuasive about the Dumbarton Oaks compromise (voting in the Security Council) and the Russians would have been quite happy to agree to none of their constituent states belonging to the Assembly, had not the Americans foolishly acquiesced. Finally the Americans had been very weak. The President looked old and ill, had lost his powers of concentration and had been a hopelessly incompetent chairman.

It is often forgotten that a primary objective of the British and Americans at Yalta, in days when the successful development of an atomic bomb was still far from certain, was to induce the Russians to join in the war against Japan. It was feared this might last another eighteen months or two years and cost half a million Anglo-American casualties when the main Japanese Islands were assaulted. Stalin's agreement to declare war at the appropriate time (which in the event was only a few days before the Japanese surrender) was regarded as an important achievement. So was the apparent willingness of the Russians to co-operate with the projected United Nations' Organisation and to agree to a "free and unfettered" election in Poland.

Athens had been inspiring and at Corinth, which Eden visited, he had been impressed by the keen interest taken by the British soldiers in the comments of Parliament and the press – a great contrast to the last war. In Cairo Ibn Saud had been magnificent, Shukri Quwaitli (the President of Syria) a shrewd advocate for his case, and the Emperor of Abyssinia had demanded Eritrea and several other territories but had had to be content with a couple of aeroplanes.

When we reached No. 10 the whole Cabinet was waiting to receive the P.M. in the hall and they followed him into the Cabinet Room to hear an account of his Odyssey.

After dinner James Stuart came in. The P.M. said he was very sorry to hear that William Sidney was likely to oppose the Government over Poland as he was one of those to whom office would be likely to be given. We wanted to put V.C.s in power. Though I like William, I do not agree with this principle – nor, emphatically, does James Stuart. Incidentally I have told Ralph Assheton, with whom I have been discussing my possible parliamentary future, that I would like to be considered for Chelsea when William succeeds to the peerage.

Tuesday, February 20th
Accompanied the P.M. to the House for Questions. He was received with cheers.

Lunched at the St James's Club with the Archduke Robert and Count Seilen and listened to a diatribe against the Czechs.

Wednesday, February 21st
After lunching with Zara at the 500 Club in Albemarle Street, I returned to the Annexe to receive General Anders[1] who has come from his Polish Corps in Italy, black with gloom about the Crimea Conference decision like most of his fighting compatriots. After he had arrived I went to fetch the P.M. from the dining-room where I found Lady Diana Cooper and Venetia Montagu arrayed in the magnificent robes presented to the P.M. by Ibn Saud in Cairo, Lady Diana in purple and striking a dramatic pose.

---

[1] Gallant Commander in Chief of the Polish divisions fighting under Alexander's command in Italy.

Thursday, February 22nd
Lunched with John Cairncross, who is less of a bore than he
used to be and talked with sense about the barrenness of German
philosophy – an imposing façade of a building which had no
interior decoration or furnishings.

   Went with Betty Montagu to see Flanagan and Allen, etc., at
the Victoria Palace and afterwards to dine at Boulestins. It was
a beautiful night and we walked back along the Embankment by
the misty river.

Friday, February 23rd
The P.M. accepted the draft message which I composed to
Stalin on Red Army Day, which is today.

   To Chequers. The P.M. dictated his speech for next Tuesday
on the way down. As he got out of the car at our journey's end
he was still dictating. He paused on the steps of the house and
said "whose-whose-whose history has been" (looking up at the
house) "chequered and intermingled".

   Edward Bridges came to dine and sleep and also Sir Arthur
Harris,* C. in C., Bomber Command. The P.M. was rather
depressed, thinking of the possibilities of Russia one day turning
against us, saying that Chamberlain had trusted Hitler as he was
now trusting Stalin (though he thought in different circumstances), but taking comfort, as far as Russia went, in the
proverb about the trees not growing up to the sky.

   *Before dinner, while waiting in the Great Hall for the P.M. to
   come down, I asked Sir Arthur Harris what the effect of the
   raid on Dresden had been.*
      "Dresden?" he said. "There is no such place as Dresden."
   *Though the obliteration of Dresden later became a topic which
   aroused widespread indignation, it was not at the time regarded
   as different from previous "saturation" bombing attacks on
   Hamburg, Cologne and, above all, Berlin. A principal reason
   for the Dresden raid was the intelligence report, received from
   thc Russians, that one or possibly two German armoured
   divisions had arrived there from Italy on their way to reinforce
   the defence of the eastern front. Churchill was on his way back*

*from Yalta when the raid took place and since it was in accord
with the general policy of bombing German towns massively, so
as to shatter civilian morale, I do not think he was consulted
about the raid. He never mentioned it in my presence, and I
am reasonably sure he would have done so if it had been regarded
as anything at all special.*

With regard to Spaatz,[1] the American air C. in C., the P.M.
said, "He is a man of limited intelligence." Harris replied, "You
pay him too high a compliment."

At dinner I asked the P.M. if he had read Beverley Nichols'
Verdict on India which I had urged him to take to Yalta. He said
he had, with great interest. He had been struck by the action
of the Government of India in not removing a "Quit India" sign
which had been placed in a prominent place in Delhi and which
Nichols had seen on arrival and on departure a year later. He
seemed half to admire and half to resent this attitude. The P.M.
said the Hindus were a foul race "protected by their mere
pullulation from the doom that is their due" and he wished Bert
Harris could send some of his surplus bombers to destroy them.
As for Lord Wavell, and his Anthology of Poetry,[2] he thought
him "mediocrity in excelsis".

After dinner we saw an amusing film: Bob Hope in *The
Princess and the Pirate*. Then we sat in the Great Hall and
listened to *The Mikado* played, much too slowly, on the gramophone. The P.M. said it brought back "the Victorian era, eighty
years which will rank in our island history with the Antonine
age". Now, however, "the shadows of victory" were upon us.
In 1940 the issue was clear and he could see distinctly what was
to be done. But when Harris had finished his destruction of
Germany, "What will lie between the white snows of Russia and

---

[1] General Spaatz was asked to dine by the Prime Minister at Carthage in
December 1943. Churchill told John Martin to find out how his name was
pronounced. "Like S.P.O.T.S.," said the General's A.D.C. So Martin, failing
to make allowance for the American pronunciation, was responsible for us
all, including the Prime Minister, calling him General Spots throughout the
evening.

[2] *Other Men's Flowers.*

the white cliffs of Dover?" Perhaps, however, the Russians would not want to sweep on to the Atlantic or something might stop them as the accident of Ghenghis Khan's death had stopped the horsed archers of the Mongols, who retired and never came back.

Bert Harris: "You mean now they will come back?"

W.S.C.: "Who can say? They may not want to. But there is an unspoken fear in many people's hearts."

After this war, continued the P.M., we should be weak, we should have no money and no strength and we should lie between the two great powers of the U.S.A. and the U.S.S.R. If he lived, he should concentrate on one thing: the air. Harris replied that it would have to be rockets: "The bomber is a passing phase and, like the battleship, it has nearly passed." "Then," said the P.M., "you mean we must make our island into a volcano."

Finale: The P.M. quoted "Ye Mariners of England" at length.

Bert Harris: "That was written before the invention of the 12,000 lb. bomb."

The P.M.: "Ye Doodle Bugs of England . . ."

Saturday, February 24th

President Beneš, who returns to Czechoslovakia to set up his Government next week, came to lunch and was received by a Guard of Honour. Masaryk, the Czech Foreign Secretary, also came, and Phil Nicholls, our Ambassador to the Czechs. Beneš said he had learned much during his six years in England, not least the truth of what President Masaryk had said to him in the last war, that America might be materially far more powerful than England but that England's cultural dominance was supreme and unchallenged. The P.M. said that a small lion was talking between a huge Russian bear and a great American elephant, but perhaps it would prove to be the lion which knew the way.

Duncan and Diana Sandys arrived for dinner, Duncan being in disgrace over a statement he made about housing without first consulting the P.M. or the Cabinet.

Sunday, February 25th

Winant and Prof. came to lunch. After lunch the P.M. said that he would like to make many bitter remarks about the

Government if he were not head of it. "There never has been a Prime Minister who has kept up such a steady stream of corrective sneering and jibing against the Government departments" (this apropos of an Air Ministry proposal to employ 1,000 men in an analysis of our bombing results in Germany).

Dinner was very gay and cheerful, the P.M. being at the top of his form. Sarah was there and Diana was at her best. Duncan was cheerful and Winant benevolent though sickening for flu and consequently rather dull.

Monday, February 26th
Returned to London at breakneck speed so that the P.M., who always starts late, should not keep M. Bidault[1] waiting for lunch. Spent the evening and night with the Greigs at Richmond.

Tuesday, February 27th
Galloped round Richmond Park. The going was good and the weather fine. Sorely in need of air and exercise.

The P.M. made a speech in the House about the Crimea Conference and in particular about Poland. I did not listen. He is trying to persuade himself that all is well, but in his heart I think he is worried about Poland and not convinced of the strength of our moral position.

Wednesday, February 28th
Moley Sargent tells me that the Polish Government's propaganda against the Crimea Agreement has been both extensive and effective. In fact they have been driving home the lesson which Goebbels has sought to instil: Russia is the danger, Russia will seize Poland, Russia wants to dominate Europe; Germany is the only bastion.

I went to the House with the P.M. after lunch. The debate was in full swing on a Conservative amendment in favour of Poland. The level was high. Harold Nicolson's voice was croaky

[1] Foreign affairs representative of the French National Committee and later, for many years, Foreign Minister. Some fifteen years earlier he had, as an inconspicuous professor, taught Sarah Churchill when she was at Mademoiselle Ozanne's finishing school for young ladies in Paris.

but his delivery good; Manningham Buller was staid and states-manlike; Willoughby de Eresby a bit like Bertie Wooster; Raikes sincere and eloquent. Eden wound up very well, putting the Government's case most effectively. 396 voted for the Government and twenty-five Tories against. A number abstained. One of them, William Sidney, dined with me afterwards.

In the evening came sinister telegrams from Roumania showing that the Russians are intimidating the King and Government and setting about the establishment of a Communist minority government with all the technique familiar to students of the Comintern. The P.M. was dining at Buckingham Palace, but Eden rang me up and said he viewed these events with great concern because Vyshinski, who was their executor, had come fresh from the understanding and undertakings of Yalta. When the P.M. came back, I spoke to him of the position and he said he feared he could do nothing. Russia had let us go our way in Greece; she would insist on imposing her will in Roumania and Bulgaria. But as regards Poland we would have our say. As we went to bed, after 2.00 a.m., the P.M. said to me, "I have not the slightest intention of being cheated over Poland, not even if we go to the verge of war with Russia."

FOURTEEN

ACROSS THE RHINE
MARCH 1945

Thursday, March 1st
A quiet day, the P.M. spending the afternoon at the House where
the three-day debate ended in a thumping vote of confidence in
spite of some Tory abstentions.

Friday, March 2nd
The P.M., accompanied by the C.I.G.S., Pug Ismay, Tommy
and John Peck left for a tour of the front, and Mrs Churchill and
I accompanied them to Brussels. We left from Northolt in the
C.54 at 11.00, a glorious day, and flew over Dungeness, St
Omer and Lille (seeing some of the flying bomb sites en route).
At Brussels "Mary" Coningham and Mary Churchill met us and
we all lunched at Coningham's sumptuous villa, where massed
flowers, expensive furniture and rare foods combine to create
an effect too luxurious for the H.Q. of an operational commander.
Monty's Chief of Staff, Sir Frederick de Guingand, was there
and I sat next to him – not a very striking man.

After lunch the P.M. and his party left for Monty's H.Q. at
the front and Mrs C. and I, whose visit is to Brussels, went to
the Embassy with Mary to greet the Knatchbull-Hugessens. He
is delightful but seems weak;[1] she is called "Lady Frigid" in

---

[1] Sir Hughe Knatchbull-Hugessen was, when Ambassador in Turkey, the
unfortunate victim of his valet, code-named CICERO, who was in the pay of
the Germans and was in the habit of removing secret papers from the
Ambassador's official box when he was in his bath.

Brussels, but beneath a forbidding exterior I found her "*sympa-thique*" and easy to talk to. There was a large cocktail party at the Embassy.

Mrs C. and Mary dined quietly together at the Embassy. I went back to the Air Marshal's palazzo, where I was staying, and dined with his S.A.S.O. (A.V.M. Victor Groom) and his P.A., S/Ldr. Fielding Johnson, who has been operational, and decorated, in both wars and who in this war had a son on ops. in the same Group as himself. The son, whom I remember in 170 Squadron at Sawbridgeworth, was missing in a Mosquito last week. We dined well and saw a film (Laurence Olivier and Penelope Dudley Ward in *Demi Paradise*, about a Soviet engineer who came to England).

Saturday, March 3rd

A day spent touring the Y.W.C.A.s, Y.M.C.A.s and service clubs of Brussels. Never can the welfare of the troops have been so lavishly and painstakingly cared for. We saw the magnificent Montgomery Club, in the palace of the Princesse de Ligne, and Mrs C. could not have done her job better or spoken more effectively when called upon to do so. She looked ravishing, was always interested and never condescending.

We lunched at the Embassy and in the afternoon, when the last function was over, Mary and I walked through Brussels, fighting our way through the throng of soldiers on forty-eight hours' leave, walking into shops and visiting the great church of St Gudule with its rugged gothic façade and its grey pillars within. Then we went to have a drink at 2nd T.A.F. H.Q. with Fielding Johnson and some of the crew of the C.54. Mary was, as ever, a great success. She told me of her passion for a French parachutist, de Ganay by name, and her thoughts of becoming a R.C. if she were going to marry him when he returns from the Far East.

There was a dinner party at the Embassy at which was present the new Belgian P.M., Van Acker and his wife, the Foreign Minister and Mme Spaak, the Canadian Ambassador, Aveling (the Counsellor), and la Baronne Boël, a remarkable old lady who spent most of the last war in a German cell and had a pretty hard time in this one. She told me that when she heard of Brest Litovsk[1] from her prison she had despaired and thought that all was lost; remembering this she had never despaired in 1940. After dinner I had a talk with the Ambassador who could not have been more affable. It was strange to see footmen in livery again.

Sunday, March 4th
In the large Daimler which the Air Marshal had put at my disposal I picked up Mary at the Embassy and went with her to the early service at the Garrison Church, where, amongst others, was Jean Greig.

During the morning I went for a walk with Mrs C. and we visited the beautiful Grande Place with its Hôtel de Ville and old houses with gilded fronts.

Mrs C. and Mary and the Knatchbull-Hugessens lunched with the Queen Mother at Laeken. I lunched with the Air Marshal who let himself go about Monty who, he said, was the most egotistic man he had ever met. Moreover he was indiscriminate in his ruthlessness and in Normandy had made demands for the elimination of French towns and villages which were unnecessary and many of which Coningham had refused. He aped the Americans who loathed him. Finally his handling of the recent operations, Operations VERITABLE and GRENADE, to clear the west bank of the Rhine, had been slow and, considering the paucity of the opposition, very inadequately executed. After the war Coningham understood that Monty proposed to settle down and write his history of the war and C. had little doubt what sort of bombastic and highly coloured account that would be. Further, Coningham told me he was in favour of dismembering Germany as a means of incapacitating her. Personally I am doubtful and inclined to the view that dismemberment would neither pay nor be permanent.

After lunch Mrs Churchill and I flew back to England in a

[1] Treaty of peace between Imperial Germany and Bolshevik Russia in March 1918. It was a black day for the Western Allies as the Germans were able to move to the Western Front most of their divisions which had been fighting the Russians.

Dakota. The visibility was poor and the passage bumpy.
Returned to find that flying bombs had begun again, from fixed
bases in the Netherlands, and that German bombers, for the
first time since last spring, had been over England. On the other
hand Monty's operations, if they have been slow, are now
showing great success and we have reached the Rhine in many
places. Everybody is worried about the fate of our prisoners.

Tuesday, March 6th
The P.M. and party returned from General Eisenhower's H.Q.
at Rheims in the C.54. I met them at Northolt and drove back
with the P.M. who told me he had had a great reception in
Holland, at Hertogenbosch, and had spent a good deal of time
in Germany itself. He also launched an invective against General
Plastiras, P.M. of Greece, who has surrounded himself with an
authoritarian and anti-British clique in Athens. He must go.

Wednesday, March 7th
In the evening I accompanied the P.M. to the House to hear
him answer Lord Winterton's motion on the adjournment about
the right of Members to demand a Select Committee and to
obtain it from the Government. The question at issue was Austin
Hopkinson's allegation about irregularities at the Air Ministry
(the "Pig Farm") at Regent's Park and B.O.A.C. (in both of
which General Critchley is involved). We had to wait till 8.40
p.m. before the debate on the Naval Estimates was finished. I
went to the bar to have a drink with Harvie-Watt and talked to
Lionel Berry and Johnny Gretton[1] then listened to Pilkington[2]
winding up for the Admiralty, an inexpert performance no doubt
made more embarrassing for him by the presence of the P.M.
since he had deliberately abstained from voting for the Government over the Yalta Conference (Poland) and has offered his

[1] M.P. for the Burton division of Staffordshire. His father, Chairman of Bass,
Ratcliffe and Gretton, owned three yachts including the magnificent ketch,
Cariad, which won the King's Cup at Cowes six times. He several times
lent her to my father.
[2] Having served in the Coldstream Guards and won the M.C. in the Dunkirk
campaign, he was appointed Civil Lord of the Admiralty in 1942.

resignation as Civil Lord of the Admiralty. Eventually Winterton spoke, convincingly I thought, and then the P.M. made a slashing reply which won applause and laughter too, though I did not think he quite answered Winterton's point.

During dinner I showed the P.M. a telegram from Roumania reporting that the new Russian-sponsored Roumanian Government may forcibly remove Radescu, the late Prime Minister, from the sanctuary which has been given him by the British Military mission. This inflamed the P.M. who saw that our honour was at stake. He subsequently spoke to Eden on the telephone. It seems that we may be heading for a show-down with the Russians who are showing every sign of going back on the Yalta agreement over Poland and of enforcing aggressive Communism on an unwilling Roumania. The P.M. and Eden both fear that our willingness to trust our Russian ally may have been vain and they look with despondency to the future. The P.M. is prepared to put the issue to the House and the Country with confidence in their support, but Eden, though nauseated, still hopes the Russians will not face an open breach with ourselves and the Americans. It looks as if Dr Goebbels' disciples may still be able to say "I told you so"; but, God knows, we have tried hard to march in step with Russia towards the broad and sunlit uplands. If a cloud obscures the sun when we reach them, the responsibility is with Moscow and the bitter, though for the Germans empty, triumph is with Berlin.

Thursday, March 8th
Went to the House with the P.M. who made a statement about war gratuities and saw various ministers in his room at the House. The war goes better and better: the Americans are over the Rhine north of Coblenz and both we and the Americans are rapidly clearing the west bank of the river. ? The end in April.

Saturday, March 10th
After a heavy day, in the lighter parts of which I devoted myself to writing a memorandum on the acquisition of English pictures and furniture for our Embassies and Government Houses during the inevitable sales of private collections after the war, I went

down to Mentmore. Talked to grandfather before dinner. Though very old, blind and in constant pain, he keeps up a gay demeanour and talks with grasp, wisdom and concentration of the present as of the past. He says he thinks the continuation of a coalition Government after this war will prove to be essential in some form. He told me Lord Randolph Churchill had more charm than Winston but, if that were possible, worse manners.

Sunday, March 11th

Spent the morning reading some of Lord Rosebery's essays and walking round Mentmore. A long talk with grandfather before lunch. After lunch Helen Smith[1] came in for a little, then Peggy showed me some of the treasures stowed at Mentmore (including the vast gold lamps from the *Bucentaur*, used when Venice wed the sea and now suspended in the hall). In the house are effigies from Westminster Abbey and pictures from public galleries; in the garden is Le Sueur's Charles I, better visible there than on his pedestal in Trafalgar Square. It really is a magnificent statue, showing so well Charles's obstinate forehead, the strained muscles of his horse's arched neck and even the veins on the animal's left fore-leg. The general effect does not suffer from the wealth of detail. I take pride in having instigated Winston to order its removal from Trafalgar Square. Shortly afterwards a bomb fell a few yards away.

In the riding school is the Speaker's gilded coach, together with more effigies from St Paul's and Westminster and carved choir stalls. A veritable treasure house.

Returned to London in time to dine quietly at the Travellers, where I sat with Nigel Ronald[2] who thinks (i) we shall be able to work with the Russians provided we do not expect them to use Western methods of thought and codes of behaviour; (ii) the Roumanians do not expect anything other than what they

---

[1] Daughter of Lord Rosebery and niece of Lady Crewe.

[2] Sir Nigel Ronald, after the war British Ambassador in Lisbon, where I was his Head of Chancery. Seriously wounded in World War I and thereafter always frail, he was immensely well-read and had an encyclopaedic knowledge of music. He was also an expert gardener who delighted in rare and by no means always colourful shrubs.

are at present experiencing from their Soviet conquerors. The Balkan mind does not work like ours.

Monday, March 12th
The P.M. and Mrs C. want me to accompany the latter on her coming tour of Red Cross centres in Russia, but it would upset the working of the office and also my plans for moving into Mulberry Walk[1] and so I am contracting out, even though six weeks' travel in Russia, in conditions of great comfort and with no work to do, is an attractive idea.

Lunched with Sir David[2] and Lady Kelly at the Ritz. Others present were the Italian representative (Carandini), Chips Channon, Mrs Corrigan,[3] Derek Hoyer Millar,[4] Mrs Leo Lonsdale, the new Dutch Ambassador in Paris (Witz?) and his very pretty wife. I sat between Mrs Lonsdale and Carandini. The latter, an enlightened man, said that Grandi[5] (who has recently been publishing his apologia in the *Daily Express*) was a black-hearted fascist and a double-crossing blackguard. He had said he thought it a distinction to have been condemned to death by Mussolini; he would soon have the double distinction of being condemned to death by the present Italian Government also.

Tuesday, March 13th
Brilliant summer sunshine of the last few days makes one long to be over the hills and far away.

The P.M. was largely occupied with writing his speech for next Thursday's Conservative Party Conference.

The feeding of liberated Europe looms up as one of the most serious problems to be faced. S.H.A.E.F. seem to have made a mess of things and the liberated peoples will soon be saying

[1] A house my mother had just bought in Chelsea.
[2] Ambassador to the Argentine in the war and subsequently to Turkey and the Soviet Union. His wife, Marie Noele, was a Belgian.
[3] Rich and socially ambitious American who entertained lavishly in London.
[4] Afterwards Lord Inchyra and Permanent Under Secretary at the Foreign Office. Invariably wise and charming.
[5] Italian Ambassador in London before the war. Too much trusted by those holding office and also by Churchill.

openly that they were materially better off under the Germans. The reason, apart from S.H.A.E.F.'s incompetence, is partly due to the great diversion of shipping resulting from MacArthur's and Nimitz's unexpected progress against the Japanese in the Pacific.

Thursday, March 15th

The Cabinet talked lengthily about the now serious food supply prospects. After the Cabinet, which is held in the C.W.R. nowadays because of V.2s, the P.M. sits in a chair and is carried upstairs backwards by three stalwart marines. The Cabinet trail behind and the general effect of the procession is utterly ludicrous.

Aunt Addy[1] rang me up during dinner to say that Alick[2] had been killed in a flying accident. I gathered from the Admiralty that it happened yesterday on take-off at the airfield in the Azores. He was a simple, honest and lovable character, genuinely good and in many ways gifted. He was gauche and very shy, but he could be amusing and his gentle, unassuming character made him beloved by the small circle who knew him.

Tuesday, March 20th

Cocktail party given by Harvie-Watt – chiefly politicians and Lobby correspondents, Eddy Marsh[3] dined in the mess, also an officer in the Welsh Guards, called Hardy, whom I met in the train last Sunday.

---

[1] Lady Adelaide Colville, daughter of Admiral of the Fleet the Earl of Clanwilliam, sister of Admiral Meade-Fetherstonhaugh and widow of my father's brother, Admiral Sir Stanley Colville.

[2] Viscount Colville of Culross, my first cousin and godfather. He had been a career naval officer in his youth and fought at the battle of Jutland. In 1939 he rejoined and as a Captain R.N.V.R. commanded the naval station in the Azores. He married late in life and had three sons.

[3] Churchill's Private Secretary almost continuously from 1905 to 1929 and his intimate friend. An aesthete, with a prodigious memory, he spoke in a high-pitched squeaky voice and was popular in intellectual circles, not least with "The Souls". A close friend of the poet Rupert Brooke.

The P.M. corrected very considerably the text of a speech Anthony Eden is to make at Glasgow tomorrow, grumbling much about it and saying that Eden was only half educated and had not added to it by subsequent reading. He evidently thought very poorly of the speech. He corrected it at the dining-room table (when he dines alone with Mrs C. at the Annexe they use a small circular table in the drawing-room) while I sat opposite him, assented silently to his comments, which were penetrating and to the point, and sipped brandy. Most of the rest of the evening was devoted to Under Secretarial appointments, caused by recent resignations over Poland. The Chief Whip came and Brendan arrived in time to upset the whole apple cart just as everything had been settled. At one moment, in order to check Brendan, the P.M. proceeded to give me a vivid description of the German attack on March 21st, 1918 as he had seen it from 10,000 yards behind the 5th Army front.

The more I contemplate the present trend of opinion and of events, the more sadly I reflect how much easier it will be to forgive our present enemies in their future misery, starvation and weakness than to reconcile ourselves to the past claims and future demands of our two great Allies. The Americans have become very unpopular in England; the Russians are losing their glamour and a few publicised examples of their incorrigibly bad manners and brutal methods of getting their own way will awaken that dread of their future intentions which twenty-five years of Red Bogy propaganda (preceded by a century of the Eastern Question) has left close to the surface in most Englishmen's minds. So far only a few, stirred by the wrongs of Poland and the Baltic States, have given vent to their uneasiness. It is, as grandfather would say, all very "vexatious".

Mainz and Worms were captured.

Leslie Rowan thinks the P.M. is losing interest in the war, because he no longer has control of military affairs. Up till OVERLORD he saw himself as Marlborough, the supreme authority to whom all military decisions were referred. Now, in all but questions of wide- and long-term strategy, he is by force of circumstances little more than a spectator. Thus he turns his energies to politics and the coming General Election, varying the diet with occasional violent excursions into the field of foreign politics.

Friday, March 23rd[1]

After a quick lunch with Zara at the Churchill Club I accompanied the P.M., C.I.G.S. and Tommy to Northolt, boarded a Dakota and flew slowly (so slowly that the accompanying fighter escort were reduced to going around in circles) over Dungeness, Gris Nez and Brussels to Venlo, where we landed on a heavily bomb-scarred aerodrome. The others in the party were Colonel Charrington (successor to Barney Charlesworth as A.D.C. to Sir Alan Brooke[2]), Kinna and the inevitable, egregious Sawyers (the valet).

In a few miles we were over the German frontier, whence we could see Monty's great smokescreen over the Rhine. Most of the houses, except for solitary farms, were wrecked. Slogans such as *"Sieg od. Siberien"* were written on the walls.

Charrington and I went to 2nd Army H.Q. at Walbeck, where we sleep in the Visitors' Mess, a *"Gasthaus der Drei Kronen"* renamed "The Savoy". The P.M., C.I.G.S. and Tommy are at Monty's Tac H.Q. some six miles away, living in caravans. Monty's camp surrounds a rectangular clearing (formerly a riding school) in the middle of a pine forest. The P.M. has two caravans, one for work and one for sleep. Monty has several of various nationalities and designs: one, in which he works, belonged to General Berganzoli (Electric Whiskers), another in which he sleeps belonged to General Messe, a third, filled with canaries, is fitted up as a map room. All are replete with photographs, mostly of Monty himself, but three large ones of Rommel are included and one of Rundstedt.

The 6th Guards' Tank Brigade are not far from 2nd Army, at a place called Pont. I dined there, not wisely but very well, at

---

[1] The entries for this and the next three days are written on paper headed "21st Army Group Headquarters". I had thought it wiser not to take my diary too near the front line.

[2] Viscount Alanbrooke.*

the H.Q. of the 4th Grenadiers and sat between Charlie Tryon[1] and Philip at a long table in a German mill-house, laden with fine china and glass. Filled with champagne and brandy, I went by jeep to Monty's camp after dinner and took the P.M. some important telegrams, including a venomous one from Molotov who, on the eve of what may well be our war-winning operation, had the impudence to say that the Russians were bearing the main brunt of the war. Germany's internal structure and economic position have in fact been brought to the verge of collapse as much by Bomber Command and the U.S. Army Air Corps as by the Russian advances – perhaps more so.

Saturday, March 24th
Today is D-day for Operation PLUNDER – the crossing of the Rhine. It was clear, cloudless and sunny, conditions for which we had prayed. Together with Colonel Charrington and two young liaison officers called Bullit (an American) and Gill (English) I set out by jeep from 2nd Army H.Q. at 7.00 a.m. and drove to a high wooded hill (the Staatsforst) S.S.W. of Xanten and about 1½ miles from the town. We took up our position so that we could see a great expanse of country, the Hochwald to our left, Xanten, in ruins and with one of its church spires missing, before us, and the Upper Rhine and Wesel to our right. We were there before eight and we had a long time to wait. The rising sun began to disperse the mists over the Rhine, fighters flew ceaselessly backwards and forwards above our heads; and nearly 2,000 guns, of which we could see many batteries below and to the left of us, thundered away in a gigantic barrage, which sometimes alternated with minutes of complete silence. Suddenly, far away to the north-east, a trail of white smoke or condensation began climbing skywards. It seemed to travel very slowly, but I watched its vertical path up to 30,000 or more and realised that it was a V.2, presumably en route for Antwerp or perhaps even London.

[1] Brigadier Lord Tryon, commanding the 4th Battalion Grenadiers, son of the Conservative Minister who died in 1940. After the war he was Keeper of the Privy Purse and responsible in addition for the Queen's racing establishment.

At 9.50 – the guns had been silent for twenty minutes and the dust on the other side of the Rhine was settling – we saw what we were awaiting. A host of Dakotas, flying low and in close formation, the doors in the fuselage open and a parachutist standing ready in the aperture, came over the hills behind and passed before us, right over Xanten. A solitary Flying Fortress accompanied them. To our left appeared another fleet and behind yet another. They vanished in the haze across the Rhine and, dimly, I saw parachutes beginning to open. More and more fleets of Dakotas came on, while the first lots streamed back empty overhead. The Flying Fortress reappeared, on fire, and the occupants baled out one by one as the aircraft flew steadily on, the flames spreading towards the tail. The endless stream continued and soon there were fleets of gliders too. We could see many of the gliders released while their tugs turned steeply away for home. There seemed to be but little flak, and very few failed to return. However a few returning Dakotas were in trouble and several crashed before our eyes, bursting into flames as they struck the ground. One, struggling low over Xanten, lost height irrecoverably and there was a great flash and explosion as it crashed just below us, apparently on top of one of our heavy gun positions. For two and a half hours the Armada came, but Gill and I, having seen much of it, left our hill which was now shared by many officers, press correspondents and photographers, re-entered our jeep and pushed on into Xanten itself and thence to the banks of the Rhine.

It seemed a very peaceful river and we quickly yielded to the temptation to cross to the other bank. We found room in a small launch and shortly after 11.00, long before the airborne operation was complete, we stood on the eastern bank. There were mines everywhere and we watched the sappers exploding them. Prisoners, newly taken, came marching towards us, their hands clasped behind their heads, their faces a mixture of relief and despair. We walked up a road towards the little village of Marwick, where on a bluff above the river stood a *Gasthaus* in process of being turned into a first-aid post. It was full of German prisoners keeping a strained and rather depressed *Wacht am Rhein*.

I was talking to Gill in front of the house. The Colonel of an Airborne Regiment arrived, in claret-coloured beret, with jeep and driver. I stared through the windows at the prisoners. They stared back, one young man with his cap aslant, very defiantly. Suddenly a shell exploded in the river, then another, another and another. A fifth hit the bank eighty yards from us. A sixth struck the opposite shore. Gill said it would be fun to talk to the prisoners and find out their impressions. I agreed. We moved towards the front door to ask the officer in charge if he had any objection. As we reached the door an 88 mm shell landed just where we had been standing and about ten yards from where we then were. The airborne Colonel's driver, standing beside me, was hit. An artery was cut and I was drenched in blood. Another shell brought down a tree by the corner of the house. The Germans were by now lying flat on the floor. The wounded man and the rest of us moved to the cellar, which seemed solid, and a few minutes later another shell landed a few yards from the house, wounding a second soldier. We waited for things to quieten down and then crawled out from among the debris, making our way northwards to the village of Bisslich.

We joined up with some tank officers, who gave us eggs they had just collected from a trans-Rhenanian farm and told us that the enemy were less than a mile away, not five or six as we had supposed. Then we all re-crossed the river in a Buffalo, which failed, the first time, to negotiate the steep western bank and flung us all in a heap, including the poor man with the severed artery, who, since it was in his arm, could nevertheless walk.

Back we went through devastated Xanten, where the children seemed well-fed and the population curious rather than resentful, while the sun beat down as it should in July and the dust was nearly as thick as in Normandy. We had a picnic lunch by the side of a quiet lane near Geldern.

The P.M. was thrilled by our adventures and, while pretending to disapprove, was in fact rather pleased, though Monty was not. I took Bullit to dine with the 4th Grenadiers, where we both enjoyed ourselves, and then returned to the P.M.'s caravan at Monty's H.Q. where he was working. "Sleep soundly," he said to me. "You might have slept more soundly still."

Sunday, March 25th

Still bright and clear though not quite yesterday's imitation of mid-summer.

Attended the P.M., C.I.G.S. and Monty to church parade, at which a Clydeside Church of Scotland padre preached a moving and rarely eloquent sermon. I think it is the first time I have known the P.M. go to church. After the Blessing and the National Anthem he presented some Good Conduct Certificates and then more or less preached a sermon himself, on his theme, which he often expounds, of an Influence, supreme and watchful, which guides our affairs and of the Almighty's Great Design into which all our human actions fit if we do our duty.

After church the P.M., in his 4th Hussars uniform which he has worn throughout the visit, set off to visit Eisenhower. I let Kinna go off sight-seeing with a liaison officer and myself spent the day sitting in the sun outside the P.M.'s caravan or writing all this disjointed description. I lunched in Monty's mess with some of his staff.

De Guingand (Chief of Staff) told me yesterday that he thought the Western Front should crumble in three weeks. Mathematically it seemed certain. He also described the immense planning necessitated by Operation PLUNDER and the great pains taken to neutralise the German defences before the airborne landing. First they had bombed, with the maximum weight available, all the German fighter airfields; then they had put every gun they possessed, including ack-ack, on to the flak positions; finally, in the last half-hour, when the guns stopped to let the dust settle, all the fighter bombers had been turned on to prevent the flak positions from recovering.

Dined again in the Grenadiers' mess, which is wonderfully luxurious for a combatant one, with Dresden china, white table-cloths and candles.

Returned to Tac H.Q. where the P.M. worked till after 1.00 a.m. on the Russian situation, which is murky. Molotov is playing a foul game. The P.M. said he hardly liked to consider dismembering Germany until his doubts about Russia's intentions had been cleared away.

Monday, March 26th

The P.M. set out with Monty for another tour across the Rhine. When he had gone I went with Gill, my bear-leader and a charming fellow, to Monty's air strip nearby and flew in an Auster. First of all we prospected, at low level, a new site for Monty's H.Q. near Xanten. Then we flew over the wreckage of Xanten, northwards along the Rhine, over fields pitted with thousands of shell holes and large bomb craters (sometimes filled with the carcasses of dead cows), past tented camps near Calcar where homeless German civilians were congregated, in sight of the smoke of battle beyond Rees and Emmerich, over devastated Cleves, the great Reichswald, Goch and so on. Germany has indeed paid dearly and except for a few isolated farms I scarcely saw a single house unscathed by war.

Gill and I called on Philip's battalion to say goodbye (they go into battle tomorrow) and stayed to lunch. Motoring back I noticed one or two flags hung out – the red, black and gold of the Weimar Republic. Some of the leopards will no doubt be quick to change their spots. The children looked well-fed and healthy, but the P.M. told me this afternoon that he thought their faces very strained and that for his part what he had seen of the German civilian population had moved and upset him. I think this is his reaction to the apparently sinister designs of Russia who – in addition to obvious moves against the spirit of the Yalta agreement – have now decided not to send Molotov to San Francisco but to send three subordinate officials. And yet they complained bitterly when we only sent William Strang and some military delegates to Russia in the summer of 1939, subsequently alleging that to be one of the causes of the breakdown of Anglo-Soviet talks and of their August alliance with Germany.

We said goodbye to Monty and his staff at 4.15 p.m. (Winston giving him a fine edition of Marlborough, a long inscription for his autograph book and a heap of compliments) and took off from much bombed Venlo in a Dakota escorted by twelve Spitfires. The P.M. worked in the plane, which was alternately too hot and too cold, and we landed at Northolt after an exciting week-end in glorious weather, much the better in health and temper.

Tuesday, March 27th

The newspapers have won the war already, but it certainly seems that the map of Germany is being rolled up. The 6th Guards' Tank Brigade are in the van. I am glad not to be accompanying Mrs Churchill who left for Russia in the C.54 tonight. It is better to miss the Kremlin than the victory celebrations. Mrs C. gave a small party, for the office and a few personal friends, such as Archie Sinclair, the Beaver and C.A.S., before her departure.

Wednesday, March 28th

Accompanied the P.M. to the House. Jimmy Rothschild, answering his first questions since his recent appointment as Under Secretary, was jeered and hooted. It was in deplorable taste but he took it very well. The P.M. says that if the House treats him like that again he will make him a Privy Councillor!

After Questions the P.M. announced the sad loss of Rupert Brabner, one of the most attractive younger Tories, who is missing on a flight to Canada where he was to represent H.M.G. at the winding up of the Empire Air Training Scheme.

Then the P.M. paid his tribute to Lloyd George,[1] eloquent in parts and well delivered but not, I thought, as good as that he paid to Neville Chamberlain in 1940. He was followed by Greenwood, Percy Harris (who is always effective in emptying the House), Geoffrey Shakespeare, old George Lambert (elected only a year after L.G. in 1890), Aneurin Bevan (who was generous to the P.M.'s qualities for once), W. J. Brown, Lady Astor, Thelma Cazalet and Gallacher, who said that Lenin had advised him to study L.G., as the greatest statesman England ever had.

Thursday, March 29th

The British and American armour is racing deep into Germany. The P.M. went off to Chequers for Easter.

[1] He died on March 26th.

Good Friday, March 30th
Went to Westminster Abbey at 10.00. Ante-Communion and
the Litany.

Spent Easter at Stansted, where March went out like a lion,
a strong gale and fine rain making outdoor exercise unpalatable.
Besides the Bessboroughs, Moyra and George, Arthur[1] and
Pat Ponsonby were there. Played much bezique and backgam-
mon and read a little Creevey. As our headlong advance into
Germany continues, the 6th Guards' Tank Brigade, leading into
Munster, are much in the news.

---

[1] Lord Bessborough's nephew. Served in the Welsh Guards. His first wife,
Pat, who died suddenly when still young, was an American with an exceptionally attractive personality.

IV

HEADQUARTERS:

21 ARMY GROUP.

I was talking to Gill in front of the house. The Colonel of an Airborne Regiment arrived in claret coloured beret with Jeep and driver. I stared through the windows at the prisoners. They stared back, one young man, with his cap aslant, very defiantly. Suddenly a shell exploded in the river, then another another and another. a Fifth hit the bank 80 yards from us. A Sixth struck the opposite shore. Gill said it would be fun to talk to the prisoners and find out their intentions. I agreed. We moved towards the front door to ask the officer in charge if he had any objection. As we reached the door an 88 mm shell landed just where we had been standing and about six yards from where we then were. The Airborne Colonel's driver, standing beside me, was hit. An artery was cut and I was drenched in blood. Another shell brought down a tile by the corner of the house. The Germans were by now lying flat on the floor. The wounded men and the rest of us moved to the cellar, which seemed solid, and a few minutes later another shell landed a few yards from the house, wounding a second soldier. We waited for things to quieten down and then moved out from among the debris, making our way northwards to

Individual page from Sir John's diary, Saturday, March 24th 1945.

The author on the wing of a Mustang with Flying Officer John Low R.A.A.F.,
Odiham, Hampshire, June 1944.

The Prime Minister away from 10 Downing Street.
a) A picnic among the prickly pears. Marrackech, January 1944.
b) Inspecting the Guards Armoured Division, Yorkshire, March 31st 1944.

The Quebec Conference.
Above left: Arrival at Quebec. Mr Mackenzie King stands behind the Prime Minister
Above right: Arrival at Greenock from Quebec, September 25th 1944.
Below: The Chiefs of Staff at the Citadel, Quebec. *(L to r):* Field-Marshal Sir John Dill, Admiral of the Fleet Sir Andrew Cunningham, General Sir Alan Brooke, Air Chief Marshal Sir Charles Portal, General Ismay.

Goodbye to 10 Downing Street, July 1945. Mr and Mrs Churchill, the author and Mary Churchill.

a) Lady Margaret Egerton in 1948. Before her marriage to the author, she was a Lady-in-Waiting to Princess Elizabeth.

b) The Churchills at St Margaret's, Westminster, after the author's wedding, October 20th 1948.

a) 'This is interesting. It will suit Meg no doubt to get home' – King George VI's comment on a note from Sir Alan Lascelles with the news that the author would be joint principal private secretary (with David Pitblado) to the Prime Minister following the Conservative victory in the General Election, October 1951.

b) Lady Margaret Colville with the godparents outside St Peter's, Eton Square, after the christening of her daughter Harriet in February 1953. *(L to r):* The Queen, Mrs William Whitelaw, Lady Margaret, Lord Home, the Prime Minister.

On June 23rd 1953, the day he had his stroke, Churchill greets the Italian Prime
Minister, de Gasperi.

FIFTEEN

VICTORY AND CHAOS
APRIL 1945

Monday, April 2nd
Returned to London, where the Dominions' representatives are
assembling for a preliminary canter over the Dumbarton Oaks
ground prior to the San Francisco Conference. However the
Russians are being so objectionable diplomatically, and so utterly
unco-operative about Poland, that hopes are low.

Tuesday, April 3rd
The P.M. spent the day at No. 10 – since V bombs are apparently
finished[1] – for the first time since Christmas. It is a great deal
pleasanter to work there than at the musty Annexe.

Dined with Will Codrington[2] to meet Ivone Kirkpatrick,* head
of the political section of the German Control Commission.
Kirkpatrick is a man about whom opinions differ. I found him
strikingly agreeable and his wits are certainly quick. He gave a
damning account of the inefficacy of both S.O.E. and P.W.E.,[3]
both of which have been loud in self-advertisement during the

---

[1] The last V.2 rocket to fall on England was on March 27th.
[2] Son of General Sir Alfred Codrington, Colonel of the Coldstream Guards.
Won the M.C. in the First World War and was for six years in the Foreign
Office before going into business. From 1940 he was made responsible for
Foreign Office security and was invited to be a member of the No. 10 mess.
[3] Political Warfare Executive, responsible for anti-Nazi propaganda. Richard
Crossman was one of its leading lights. It was not considered a very effective
organisation.

war. As regards S.O.E., he said that they had not even been able to organise their own communications with the French on D-day and had had to rely upon code messages from the B.B.C. The more he saw of them, the more convinced a parliamentarian he became: the open investigation of such organisations by Parliament was invaluable. He also condemned loudly, as does the P.M. very frequently, the Foreign Office addiction to the principle of "Buggins' turn" which made the selection of the best men for important posts quite impossible.

Wednesday, April 4th

The P.M. spent most of the afternoon with the King at the Houses of Parliament discussing the plans for a State Opening of Parliament. The P.M. seems to visualise the end of the German War before this month is out. He gave a dinner to Bernard Baruch* at No. 10 and then worked in the Cabinet Room while I sat beside him and acted as a salvage dump.

Thursday, April 5th

The P.M. has put in writing a very apt comment on the State Department who suggested our consulting the Soviet Government about the rearming of the Greeks: "This is the usual way in which the State Department, without taking the least responsibility for the outcome, make comments of an entirely unhelpful character in a spirit of complete detachment."

In the middle of the morning came a bombshell – a telegram from the President containing one from Stalin which accused us and the Americans of making a deal with the Germans at Berne for the purpose of holding the Eastern Front while the West was thrown open. There is no atom of truth in this, though we did inform the Soviet of certain approaches for a purely military surrender in Italy which had been made to Alexander. These in any case came to nothing but it looks as if the Germans had succeeded in persuading the Russians that something sinister was afoot. Herein may lie an explanation of the very unsatisfactory attitude adopted in recent weeks by Stalin and Molotov and, in their simplicity, no doubt they really have been taken in by the Germans. Nevertheless their accusations are entirely unjust and, to us, unthinkable. I am glad to see that the President has reacted violently; and the P.M. spent all the rest of the day – with Cabinets and Chiefs of Staff meetings – doing the same. He was even half an hour too late for lunch with the King of Norway[1] as nothing would move him from his bed until he had finished dictating the first draft of a counterblast to Stalin.

Dined at the Dorchester to meet some of the lesser Dominions' luminaries (the major ones were dining at No. 10 with the P.M.) at the expense of H.M.G. Paul Emrys Evans presided. I sat next to an Australian, Professor Bailey (personal assistant to Evatt[2]) who is an expert on constitutional law and gave me an interesting exposition of Australian federalism. I then talked to General Cawthorne[3] of the Indian Army (now Director of Military Intelligence in India) who says that we are too frightened of loosening our grip on India and of showing the Indians that we trust them. We ought to prove our confidence by some great gesture such as the appointment of an Indian Viceroy.

The Japanese Cabinet resigned. I have always felt one might back worse outsiders than the possibility of Japan succumbing before, or as soon as, Germany.

Friday, April 6th
To Chequers. Field Marshal Smuts, Janny Smuts and Sarah were there. Talk was of the Americans, the P.M. saying that there was no greater exhibition of power in history than that of the American army fighting the battle of the Ardennes with its left hand and advancing from island to island towards Japan with its right. Smuts said the Americans were certainly very powerful, but immature and often crude. We dined off plovers' eggs sent by Lord Portal and the finest South African brandy brought by Smuts.

[1] Haakon VII, formerly Prince Charles of Denmark and married to a sister of King George V. Chosen and crowned King of Norway when that country separated from Sweden in 1905. His was the last Scandinavian Coronation. Spent the war in England with his exiled Government.
[2] Minister for External Affairs in Australia. Self-assertive and devoid of charm.
[3] Australian officer who transferred to the Indian Army. One of the Indian delegation to the San Francisco Conference.

After dinner we saw the Russian film *Koutusov* presented to the P.M. by Stalin. The P.M. is greatly impressed by the unprejudiced attitude shown in the film to the Tsarist régime. Smuts said that after 1815 Russia sank into the background for a generation in spite of her victories (my recollections of the Rev. F. A. Simpson's[1] lectures on the Eastern Question don't bear this out altogether) and when Stalin died the same might well happen again.

Saturday, April 7th

The old Jewish American financier, Bernard Baruch, six foot five with thick white hair and almost deaf, arrived before lunch. So did Sir Richard Hopkins[2] and Sir Robert Knox,[3] to talk about campaign stars.

At luncheon there was a heated debate on gold and its future. Smuts said gold was like the British Monarchy: it must cease to rule but must remain as a constitutional, stabilising influence. The P.M. became passionate in support of a currency based largely on commodities and only partly on gold; he also made great play with the American gold dug into the earth at Fort Knox. Baruch said gold always had been paramount and given people confidence. Anybody would take gold rather than paper. It had been so in the time of Alexander the Great and, whatever the P.M. and Smuts said, so it would remain.

Went for a brief walk with Sarah after lunch. After dinner – at which the themes were diamonds, cartels and butterflies, and in particular the Cullinan diamond – we saw various films including the Russian one of the Yalta Conference, which was very long

---

[1] Brilliant but idle historian, given a Fellowship at Trinity, Cambridge, on account of two excellent books about Napoleon III. He never finished the proposed trilogy. As a priest he was eccentric but his occasional sermons in Trinity Chapel attracted congregations from far and wide. His comment on one essay I wrote was: "Never write that something was inevitable. Only death is inevitable." Since then I have avoided the word.

[2] Permanent Secretary to the Treasury, head of the Civil Service and a Privy Councillor. Churchill had an affection for him dating from his years as Chancellor of the Exchequer, and insisted on addressing him as Sir Richard Valentine Nind Hopkins! Nind fascinated him as a Christian name.

[3] Remarkably obstinate Secretary of the Honours Committee.

and almost incredibly detailed. The P.M. worked on his box in the White Parlour till 2.30 a.m., waxing very contemptuous of the F.O. who, he said, always had to be active and never could see when it was wise to do nothing. *Mise en demeure* was a very good diplomatic phrase, but he never saw it used nowadays.

This reference to the Cullinan diamond reminds me that Churchill told us a story, which Smuts, who said he had entirely forgotten it, confirmed as true. Shortly after the treaty with South Africa in 1906, when we gave the defeated Boers back their freedom, the Cullinan diamond was discovered and was presented as a mark of loyalty and appreciation to King Edward VII. Since the King designated it part of the Crown Jewels, and not his personal property, the Government assumed responsibility for cutting it. It was so large that it had to be divided into two stones, one of which is now at the top of the sceptre and the other in one of the crowns. The Cabinet decided that it should be cut in Amsterdam, which was the traditional centre for diamond cutting. They also told the Dutch diamond cutters that they might keep the chips as payment for their work, although the diamond cutters declared with commendable honesty that the value of the chips was far greater than the cost of the work. His Majesty's Government, however, cared nothing for that, provided they did not have to foot any bill. When this became known, Generals Botha and Smuts organised a public subscription in the Union of South Africa to purchase the chips from Amsterdam and re-present them to the British Crown. Years later I repeated this story to Queen Elizabeth II who said that she often wore a brooch made from the chips of the Cullinan diamond, which Queen Mary had left to her, but that she had not had any idea of their origin.

Churchill, when he told the story, said that he thought it a shameful episode in British Cabinet history.

Sunday, April 8th
Mr Peter Fraser, the New Zealand P.M., came for luncheon and to stay the night. There was a vast luncheon party including, in addition to all those staying here, the Deputy P.M. of Australia

(Mr Forde), the Australian Minister of External Affairs and his somewhat faded, blonde Mrs Evatt, the Duchess of Marlborough, Blandford[1] (on leave from an O.C.T.U.) and Lord Cherwell. The P.M. posed the question: "What is now Hitler's best course?" and answered it by suggesting a repetition of the Hess trick on the lines of "I am responsible; wreak your vengeance on me but spare my people". The Duchess of Marlborough suggested that in such a case the only course would be to take him back and drop him by parachute over Germany. Smuts said that if he were Hitler he would fight on, to the last, in the mountain redoubt near Berchtesgaden.

After lunch I showed Forde the house. He was ill-at-ease in strange surroundings and among people with unfamiliar habits – a great contrast to Menzies. While we stood in the rain on the croquet lawn looking at the west front of Chequers, which is its best side, Mr Forde asked me what this type of architecture was called. I said it was Elizabethan. "Well," he replied, "in Melbourne we have a lot of fine residences of the same type of architecture, but out there we call them Tudor."

The Smuts family left, after the Field Marshal had inspected a Guard of Honour of Welsh Guards in front of the house, and so did the Australians. The sun was shining brilliantly and the P.M. went off to his revolver pit in the woods for a shooting match with Blandford. I took Mr Fraser for a walk up Beacon Hill and found him full of conversation, though much saddened by the loss of his wife. He fears, as do I, that San Francisco and the World Organisation may never come to much on account of the vetos of the Great Powers and the impossibility of holding the world together if the Big Three fall asunder. Personally I feel strongly that the whole subject should have been approached much more humbly, starting with regional associations at the bottom instead of a glittering World Council and Assembly at the top. However Mr Fraser was too captivated by the sight of

[1] He, Freddy, 2nd Earl of Birkenhead, Constantine, Earl of Mulgrave, Robin, 2nd Viscount Thurso, and my daughter Harriet were Winston Churchill's godchildren.

some cherry blossom against the blue sky, and by asking me about the recent Greek imbroglio, to pursue this unsettling topic further.

Before dinner I sat on a seat above the croquet lawn writing to Mary, in Brussels. Judge Rosenman, Roosevelt's representative in Europe to investigate the problem of supplies for liberated Europe, came to dine and sleep, but though he had much of the former he had little of the latter as the P.M. kept him up till 3.00 a.m. on the theme that Britain shall not starve or lower her exiguous rations still further to feed Axis satellites while the American army and civil population live on their present gigantic diet. There was also talk about housing, from which emerged the astonishing fact that we were in fact the best housed country in the world before the war. Lord Cherwell said we had three per cent slums. The U.S.A. had less than two-thirds of their population properly housed.

Monday, April 9th
During the weekend Bevin made a strong political speech attacking the Conservatives. The P.M. said to me while he was dressing at Chequers that if the Labour Party were going ahead on those lines, he thought the time had come for him to *brusquer les affaires* – i.e. to hasten the departure of the Opposition groups from the Government.

He and Sarah went off to Chartwell for lunch, to profit from the warm sun and to investigate the mysterious theft of the P.M.'s favourite goldfish from the upper pond there. I returned to London.

Brendan made a slashing reply to Bevin. The Coalition is nearing its end, though in matters of foreign and military policy it is still solid.

Tuesday, April 10th
A brisk canter in Richmond Park where I examined a large V.2 crater near White Lodge. There have been no V.1s or V.2s for over a week.

Stalin has answered the P.M. both about Poland and the accusations he made about negotiations with the Germans. He has climbed down, ungraciously, in his own way about the latter. It boils down to this: the Russians are jealous of our rapid successes in the West while, on the Oder at any rate, they are stuck. The explanations are briefly:

   i   Our weapons are better and man for man our soldiers more efficient;

   ii we have massive air superiority and they have none;

   iii the Germans view our advance with less horror than they do that of the Russians – and not without reason.

Wednesday, April 11th

There is a good deal afoot. In the military field we still race towards the Elbe, from which we are not now far. In the political field, Poland and the coming conference at San Francisco, France's place in the sun and the problem of supplying food to liberated areas are all pressing matters. Internally, the shadow of the return to party politics means constant sessions of the P.M. with James Stuart, Ralph Assheton, Brendan, Lord Beaverbrook, and the canvassing of non-party members of the Government to remain when it is re-formed.

Von Papen[1] has been captured in the Rühr, the first of the war criminals to be taken alive.

In the car, on the way back from No. 10 to the Annexe at 2.30 a.m., the P.M. told me that in July 1940 a number of Tories had tried to break up the Government and to engineer the formation of a kind of dictatorial triumvirate consisting of L. G., himself and Bevin. The instigators had been Amery, Harold Macmillan, Boothby and P. J. Grigg. The P.M. had suggested to Amery there and then that he should resign and make his explanations to Parliament. He gave me a lifelike account of the speech he would have made in reply.

The Americans have reached the Elbe.

---

[1] Franz von Papen. Adroit and slippery politician who was Hitler's predecessor as Chancellor of the Reich. Narrowly escaped death in the 1934 "Night of the Long Knives" and ended as German Ambassador to Turkey during the war.

Thursday, April 12th
President Roosevelt died in the afternoon. The news did not reach the P.M. till midnight, but I gather he was very distressed. It is a bad moment for the removal of America's one great international figure.

Friday, April 13th
The President's sudden death has caused a great stir though his appearance in recent months has been a warning to many. The P.M., after much deliberation, decided not to fly over to Washington today for the funeral tomorrow.

Went with Jock Gibb[1] to stay with him and Elizabeth at their house, Mousehall, in Sussex.

Saturday, April 14th
Sat about in the garden most of the day, reading the P.M.'s copy of Arthur Bryant's *The Years of Victory*, or sauntered through country lanes ablaze with blossom and wild flowers. It is a very early year, owing to weeks of sunshine, and the primroses are Brobdingnagian, but the cowslip, like the musk before it, seems to be losing its scent year by year. This spring only a very faint scent remains. The oak is coming out before the ash.

Today, over this part of England where the Battle of Britain raged hottest and the Flying Bombs did their worst, the sky was black with Fortresses and Liberators returning from the bombardment of the German pocket on the Gironde. Meanwhile in Germany things move at a great pace and very soon the Russian and the Western armies will have linked up. Only a hundred miles separates them and the Americans are securely over the Elbe.

Sunday, April 15th
Lunched at the Turf, with Hinch, and then proceeded to Cambridge to stay with Winstanley. After tea we went to the Fellows'

[1] Son of Sir Alexander Gibb, the celebrated engineering contractor. He was a publisher, beginning his career with the well-known firm of Methuen and Co. He was kind enough to publish a travel book I wrote when I was only nineteen.

Garden. Surely there has never been such a spring. Its earliness and its beauty have made me quite botanically minded. The cherries are weighed down with blossom. The chestnuts and the lilac are already out, as is the wistaria in Great Court, before the daffodils have faded. In the Fellows' Garden Wilderness there is a fantasia of blossom, tulips, daffodils, lilac (mauve and white) and berberis, while the tall avenue of elms wears its early coat of distinctive pale green. And all beneath a china blue sky. We walked back through the garden of John's, along the path where three and a half years ago I drilled as an A.C.2, now banked with cherry and with tulips, along the avenue of limes and cherries that leads over the Cam to Trinity, and through to the Bowling Green. Winstanley said it had been nearly as beautiful in 1940, but then it had been quite painful to enjoy the peaceful seclusion; in fact to enjoy it had been impossible. To me the memories of that spring and summer are different: excitement of a new and almost delirious kind was my predominant emotion.

Winstanley told me three stories worth recording:

i. Lord Acton, whom he had consulted about studying Luther's works, had said that he would find him difficult to comprehend because he would never understand the deep strain of brutality in the German character. Lord A. was, of course, himself half German and brought up in Germany.

ii. At Hatfield Gerald Balfour told a man he was a Philistine. The man replied, "What is a Philistine?" Old Lord Salisbury said from afar, "A Philistine is a man who is killed by the jawbone of an ass."

iii. An American, dining at Pembroke, told many long and improbable stories. After one of them had been doubted he turned to Professor Whibley and said, "Won't you bear me out, young man?" Whibley replied, "It was a young man who bore out Ananias."

Dined in Hall. Afterwards repaired to the Vice Master's rooms, with their magnificent Elizabethan ceiling, with Sir William Clark (formerly High Commissioner to South Africa and P.S. to Lloyd George), Bernard Darwin, Prince Obolensky and Dennis Robertson, now Professor of Economics in the University. We talked of Russia. Obolensky said he doubted the theory that Russia had gone wholly nationalist. He thought there were still two forces in the country, of which that of pure Communist doctrine was not much the weaker.

Monday, April 16th
Returned to London which is unnaturally sweltering in mid-summer heat. Judging from the weekend's telegrams the P.M. seems to have started famously with President Truman.

Tuesday, April 17th
After an early lunch at the Travellers, I returned to the Annexe where the P.M., just back from the memorial service for President Roosevelt at St Paul's, was feverishly composing over the luncheon table his tribute to the President. I thought it adequate but not one of his finest efforts, or in any way comparable to his epitaph on Neville Chamberlain in 1940.

I went down to the House with him. Proceedings were greatly delayed by the behaviour of the recently elected Scottish Nationalist member for Motherwell (Dr McIntyre) who insisted on making his bow to the Speaker without sponsors, thus contravening a resolution of the House dating from 1688. The Speaker sent him back behind the bar and there ensued an hour's debate on the subject, ending in a division. It all seemed very trivial when the galleries were packed to hear the P.M.'s tribute to Roosevelt, but Labour members insisted that if McIntyre did not choose to have sponsors, since no other Member agrees with his Scottish Nationalist views, then it was right on principle for him to refuse to have any.

The P.M. spoke well, his voice thrilling with emotion when he quoted Longfellow's lines "Sail on, O ship of state", which the President sent over by the hand of Wendell Willkie during one of our darkest hours.

The P.M. worked in bed, in the best of spirits and temper. He talked, most unwarily, across the open Atlantic telephone to Anthony Eden (in Washington on his way to San Francisco); he had a long session with Moley Sargent, of whom he thinks

highly, partly because I once told him of Moley's disparaging
remarks on the F.O. balcony during the hysterical scenes when
Chamberlain came back from Munich; he read the early editions
of tomorrow's newspapers (an ancient vice now only pursued
when he has made a speech); and reverting, for the fifteenth
time, to my escapade during the Rhine crossing, he said, apropos
of the airborne soldier who was wounded beside me, that one
could say everyone had been in it, "airborne and chairborne side
by side".

> *In September 1938, when I was working in the Foreign Office,
> I walked out on to the balcony overlooking Downing Street to
> watch the scenes of joy and emotion when Mr Chamberlain
> returned from Munich. The Foreign Office as a whole was
> strongly anti-Munich and nobody joined me for a long time.
> Eventually one of the French windows opened and Sir Orme
> Sargent (Deputy Under Secretary) strolled out on to the balcony.
> "You might think," he said, "that we had won a major victory
> instead of betraying a minor country. But I can bear anything
> as long as he doesn't talk about peace with honour." A few
> minutes later Mr Chamberlain appeared at a first-floor window
> in No. 10 and told the crowd that he had brought back not only
> peace, but peace with honour.*

Wednesday, April 18th
It is so hot and sunny the dog-days might be here. Nobody
seems to remember such weather in April before.

Thursday, April 19th
The P.M. is annoyed with Tito who now looks almost exclusively
to Russia, oblivious of past favours from us. He feels we should
now back Italy (from whom Tito will claim Trieste, etc.) and
thus aim at splitting the Italian Communist party.

At Mulberry Walk where the floors were filthy and we could
get no charwomen, mother spent the evening on her knees
scrubbing the kitchens and I handled a broom in the other rooms.
I then dined with Bob Coates at Pratts. Those at dinner talked
of classical education, India, the merits of respective Dominions,

and German atrocities. The papers are full of the latter, with stomach-turning photographs, consequent on the Allied armies overrunning Buchenwald and other German concentration camps. Proof is now supplied that the stories of the last ten years have not been just propaganda, as were many of the last war's atrocity stories.

Eisenhower told the P.M. the other day that when the Mayor and Mayoress of Weimar were shown Buchenwald they went home and hanged themselves.

Friday, April 20th
Before dinner the P.M. recorded, in my presence, a message which, with those of Stalin and President Truman (who seems to be showing great good sense and to be earning golden opinions), will be broadcast when the armies of Soviet Russia and the Western Allies link up. He then dined alone with Lady Lytton[1] whom, he told me, he once nearly married. At midnight he left for Bristol to present honorary degrees – in very different circumstances from when I accompanied him there in the spring of 1941 while the fires of the previous night's blitz still burned.

Saturday, April 21st
I am impressed by the weakness of American foreign policy: in Greece, as in Roumania, the State Department are petrified of associating themselves with any démarche which might be ill-received by the American press or by Congress. Fear of popular criticism hamstrings diplomacy.

Monday, April 23rd
Very busy at the office. The P.M.'s box is in a ghastly state. He does little work and talks far too long, as he did last December before his Greek adventures refreshed him. This time, I think, it is the Polish question and the unsatisfactory conversations proceeding on that subject at Washington between Eden, Stettinus[2] and Molotov that are weighing him down.

---

[1] Pamela, Countess of Lytton, born Pamela Plowden. Churchill told me he proposed to her in a punt when they were both staying at Warwick Castle. She said no; but their affection for each other survived.
[2] American Secretary of State after Cordell Hull and before James Byrnes.

Tuesday, April 24th
The P.M. is now becoming an administrative bottleneck. He persists in thinking he can be Foreign Secretary as well as P.M. and Leader of the House, and in addition to everything else proposes to take the chair at the Lord President's Committee.

Wednesday, April 25th
Lunched with Moyra Ponsonby at the Churchill Club. Returned to find a telegram from Stockholm reporting Himmler's wish to surrender to the Western Allies and the fact that Hitler is moribund with cerebral haemorrhage. This may be a last-minute attempt to separate us from the Russians but the P.M. immediately summoned a meeting of the Cabinet and the C.O.S. and sent off the whole story to Stalin. At any rate it shows that, as the P.M. said to me, "they are done".

Dined with Mrs Henley and Juliet Daniel.[1] We talked a lot about these German atrocities, as everybody in England has been talking since the publication of the photographs and accounts of Buchenwald, Belsen, etc.

Thursday, April 26th
At No. 10 there is a feeling of expectancy, based on yesterday's telegram but damped by the continued impasse over Poland (Stalin, by telegram, and Molotov in the U.S., keep on insisting that the re-organisation of the Polish Government should be on the Yugoslav model – which has in fact been a complete victory for Russia in that benighted land). We are also damped by the amount of work pouring in and the failure of the P.M. to deal with it.

After lunching with Buster Long, I went to No. 10 where the P.M. had Baldwin and the Archbishop of York[2] lunching with him. I was left with the Archbishop (whom I thought saintly, sensible and of great charm as well) while the P.M. darted off to the House. I followed him there but half missed Questions. Back at the Annexe the P.M. dictated a long and masterly

[1] Formerly Juliet Henley.
[2] Cyril Garbett, previously Bishop of Winchester.

telegram to Stalin, one of his very best efforts. He also despatched a telegram against the F.O. tendency of bullying the Hapsburgs, in which he said that if we had been a little less hasty in overthrowing the ancient dynasties after the last war, but had left a "crowned Weimar Republic" with which to co-operate, there might well have been no Hitler. He instructed me to see that this telegram was given wide distribution inside the F.O. which he accuses of republicanism.

The P.M. returned from dining with Massigli, the French Ambassador, to find a nice telegram from Stalin, indeed the most friendly U. J. has ever sent. This quite fascinated him and I sat beside him in his room at the Annexe while he talked of nothing else, first of all to Brendan for one and a half hours and then to me for another one and a half. His vanity was astonishing and I am glad U. J. does not know what effect a few kind words, after so many harsh ones, might well have on our policy towards Russia. My suggestion that this telegram – thanking the P.M. for his attitude and his frankness over the Himmler-Bernadotte[1] business – might be prompted by a certain shame over the unworthy suspicions entertained over the earlier German approach to us (operation CROSSWORD[2]) was impatiently swept aside. Further joy was caused by a generous message from de Gaulle. But no work was done and I felt both irritated and slightly disgusted by this exhibition of susceptibility to flattery. It was nearly 5.00 a.m. when I got to bed.

Friday, April 27th
The P.M. was in benign mood. I had to stand behind him in the Cabinet and show him just which telegrams were where when

---

[1] Count Bernadotte, a cousin of the King of Sweden, acted as a go-between for the Germans and the Western Allies. He had reported Himmler's willingness to arrange the surrender of all his troops in north Germany to the Anglo-Americans. Churchill not only declined, but immediately informed Stalin of the approach.

[2] Secret plan for the surrender of the German armies in Italy, instigated by Allen Dulles who had talks in Zurich with S.S. General Wolff on behalf of O.S.S. without letting the President or the State Department know he was doing so.

he read them, purring with pleasure, to a Cabinet which had already seen copies.

However after lunch the clouds descended with the announcement of a smashing Commonwealth victory over the Conservative at Chelmsford, a Conservative seat. The Beaver, Brendan, James Stuart and Ralph Assheton were at once summoned for a lengthy conclave.

Saturday, April 28th
A heavy day, moving into Mulberry Walk the second van-load of furniture from Madeley and coping, for the first time in my life, with a boiler (success limited). The house begins to look habitable and all we now need is a cook.

Sunday, April 29th
Charles Barker drove round to tell me that CROSSWORD had at last succeeded: the Germans had accepted unconditional surrender on the Italian front. He stayed to help cope with the blinds. Betty Montagu called to see the house and I then had lunch with her at the Churchill Club.

So far succeeded with the boiler as to have a hot bath.

Monday, April 30th
The newspapers are full of "Victory any minute now", and so indeed are we all. But opinion remains sober and I doubt there being the same jubilation or the same illusions as in 1918.

A hectic two hours when the P.M. returned at 6.00 from Chequers, matters being complicated by the shocking mess in which John Peck had left the box and by the endless telephone calls from the press.

SIXTEEN

PARTY POLITICS RENEWED
MAY–JUNE 1945

Tuesday, May 1st

Feverishly busy. After lunch the P.M. took Questions and told a House full to overflowing with people expecting a victory announcement that he had no statement to make about the war situation except that it was much better than it was five years ago.

On the way out we met the Duke of Norfolk. The P.M. said how glad he had been to see him at the Cabinet yesterday (when the arrangements for a State Opening of Parliament were discussed). It was such an agreeable change to see an Earl Marshal there instead of all the usual Air Marshals.

Back at the Annexe I sat in on a conference with Moley Sargent, Pug and Joe Hollis about zones of occupation in Vienna, the desirability of Alexander getting Venezia Giulia before Tito, and other kindred questions. The whole proceedings bore out a remark of Pug's, made later tonight, that the P.M. can be counted on to score a hundred in a Test Match but is no good at village cricket. The most recent example of the Test Match style is a long and masterly telegram to Stalin, a final appeal to resolve the Polish impasse.

As Lord Beaverbrook is being too high-handed about the Tory Party and the coming election, the P.M. saw him before dinner and protested. He then had a political dinner party, to discuss election propaganda to which, in addition to Lord B., Oliver Lyttelton, James Stuart and Ralph Assheton were bidden. Brendan was not included, as the P.M. is well aware that people, and particularly the Tory Party, are beginning to look askance at the Brendan–Beaver combination.

In the middle of dinner I brought in the sensational announcement, broadcast by the Nazi wireless, that Hitler had been killed today at his post at the Reichs Chancery in Berlin and that Admiral Doenitz was taking his place. Probably H. has in fact been dead several days, but the 1st May is a symbolic date in the Nazi calendar and no doubt the circumstances ("fighting with his last breath against Bolshevism") were carefully invented with an eye to the future Hitler Myth and Legend. The P.M.'s comment over the dinner table was: "Well, I must say I think he was perfectly right to die like that." Lord B.'s reply was that he obviously did not.

The party caucus stayed till 3.00 a.m. and the P.M. then dawdled over a few telegrams until after 4.00 a.m. I am writing this at that unseemly hour, cursing politics and all politicians, staring with exasperation at a box crammed with important unlooked-at papers and rather hoping that at the coming election the sovereign people follows the recent example of the electors of Chelmsford. At least socialism should not prevent one going to bed at a respectable hour.

Wednesday, May 2nd
While the last remnants of Axis power are tottering, the leaders of Germany and the Quislings engaged in flight or self-destruction, whole armies surrendering in Italy and on the Elbe, and a new era being vaporously discussed in San Francisco, the British Government machine is partly occupied by a threatened clash of arms between British Honduras and Guatemala. A cruiser is steaming westwards at full speed from Gibraltar; British bomber squadrons are bombing up; anxious glances are cast towards Washington. Then comes the news that the whole story is a mare's-nest and that fighting which had been observed from the air was really a forest fire. *Parturiunt montes et nascetur ridiculus mus.*

After last night's orgy I felt tired and irritable and overwhelmed by the gigantic heaps of paper in the box, on my table and indeed everywhere in the office. So I went home early and thereby missed the P.M.'s 7.30 p.m. dash to the House of Commons to announce unconditional surrender of the German forces in Italy to Alexander's armies. However, all is not well in that part of the world: Tito has beaten us in the race for Trieste and Venezia Giulia and, backed as he is by Russia (which has also, unilaterally, established its own puppet government in Vienna) it is hard to see how he can ever be dislodged. Still by backing Italy against Tito's claim to possess Trieste we may split the Italian Communist party and thus at least save Italy from the Russian imperialist clutches. As it is, the Soviet looks like dominating Europe east of a line drawn from the North Cape to Trieste and soon the pressure will be turned on Turkey. Our only entry on the credit side is that the Americans occupy *de facto* great parts of Germany which belong *de jure* to the Russian zone of occupation. Hamburg and Lübeck are ours.

Went home to find the married couple whom mother has engaged had arrived and also that she had since discovered that the man had just completed a three-year sentence for fraud and embezzlement. This was something of a shock, but we decided, after dining at the "Good Intent", that we ought to give him a chance to make good. Besides his wife seems honest and hardworking. All the same, an "old lag" for a butler, with several other previous convictions, is something of an experiment. Mulberry Walk now begins to look charming.

Thursday, May 3rd
The press and Parliament all on tenterhooks. They are even drawing startling deductions from the negative fact that the P.M. (who stayed in bed till 6.00 p.m.) did not go to the House to answer his Questions.

Poland and the stupid bellicosity of the French towards Syria and the Lebanon chiefly to the fore. The P.M. drafted some masterly telegrams on both subjects.

My démarche about St James's Park is bearing great fruit. Iron railings are appearing to preserve the grass and the unsightly paths trodden by the side of the lake are being dug up and resown. The Ministry of Works, in obedience to a minute which I submitted to the P.M., have taken rapid action.

The P.M. sat up till 3.30 and actually worked.

Friday, May 4th

It looks as if the Germans opposite Monty may surrender en masse, but there is a threat of the Russians trying to get to Denmark first by parachute, and thus control the Kattegat. Meanwhile it seems that Alexander did reach Trieste before Tito, but the latter announced he was there, no doubt to try and establish a prior claim. Now he is protesting vigorously.

Lunched at New Court with Tony Rothschild, arriving scandalously late owing to the Cabinet failing to rise till 1.50. Lord Bennett,[1] Sir Basil Brooke[2] and Colonel Vickers were the other guests. In conversation it was pointed out that in the former occupied countries, the underground organisations have necessarily been built up on a basis of lies and intrigue. It will be very difficult to ensure that this does not become the tradition of public life and, on the children in particular, the effect may be very noxious.

Left St Pancras by 9.15 p.m. train for St Boswells with the luxury, rare in these days, of a first-class sleeper.

Saturday, May 5th – Saturday, May 12th

At Floors, staying with Mary Roxburghe. The Border was at its best and bathed in sunshine. On Sunday, May 6th, the French Ambassador and Madame Massigli came to luncheon and also Monsieur Rocher.[3] Lord and Lady Minto came to meet them. I was much taken with Lady Minto.

The Coldstream Guards being at Hawick, we saw a good deal

---

[1] Portly, unpopular Conservative Prime Minister of Canada, 1930–35. Restored the acceptance of titles in Canada and was himself made a Viscount in 1941.

[2] Nephew of Field Marshal Lord Alanbrooke. Prime Minister of Northern Ireland for twenty years from 1943. Leader of implacable Ulster Unionists, he first promoted and then undermined his successor, Terence O'Neill. Created Lord Brookeborough in 1953.

[3] Member of the French Embassy Staff.

of them. Bob, Bill and Ronnie Dawnay came for the week-end and Hugh Norman, Andrew Cavendish and David Chetwode came to dinner. Others who dined were Elizabeth Dunglass, Lord Robert Innes Kerr and Jimmy Coats (who expected to talk of nothing but racing and fishing and was terrified when Mary and I talked enthusiastically about obscure non-conformist sects we had discovered in *Chambers Encyclopaedia*).

Tuesday, May 8th, was V.E. Day. Mary and I lunched with the Balfours at Newton Don where we played bridge and listened to the Prime Minister announcing the end of the war against Germany. In the evening, after attending a packed service in the kirk, we went into Kelso to see the great bonfire. Mary, being recognised, was clapped by the populace.

I spent the days shooting pigeon, browsing in the magnificent library (chiefly on Captain Gronow's memoirs[1]) or walking with Mary by the Tweed and through the glorious country round Floors. On Friday, May 11th, we bicycled over to lunch near Coldstream with Elizabeth Dunglass (who is vivacious, competent and agreeable) and then went with her to see Lord Home's remarkable rhododendron wood at the Hirsel. In the evening we motored over to Mellerstain, one of the Adam brothers' proudest achievements, to dine with Lord and Lady Haddington. Lady Haddington is as fascinating as her sister Lady Minto.

Returned to London by train, arriving at Mulberry Walk at 11.30 on Saturday, May 12th.

Sunday, May 13th
Went with mother to a solemn thanksgiving at St Paul's. In the afternoon Betts and I watched the King and Queen and the Princesses drive through Trafalgar Square on their way to St Paul's and then sat gossiping between the lions at the foot of the Nelson Column under a poster which said in large yellow letters "Victory in Europe – 1945".

[1] Memoirs of the Napoleonic Wars.

Monday, May 14th

At No. 10 I found everybody looking rather strained after a week of violent rejoicing and tumult. Mrs Churchill was just back from Russia where her tour has been a remarkable success.

The volume of work is if anything more pressing than when I left. Victory has brought no respite. The P.M. looks tired and has to fight for the energy to deal with the problems confronting him. These include the settlement of Europe, the last round of war in the East, an election on the way, and the dark cloud of Russian imponderability. In Venezia Giulia we stand on the brink of an armed clash with Tito, secure of Russian support, who wishes to seize Trieste, Pola, etc., from Italy without awaiting the adjudication of the Peace Conference. The Americans seem willing to stand four square with us and Truman shows great virility; but Alexander has alarmed them – and incensed the P.M. – by casting doubts on the attitude of the Anglo-American troops, should there come an armed clash with the Yugoslavs. Equally, as regards the Polish question, Russia shows no willingness to compromise and storm clouds threaten. Finally, as if we had not enough, de Gaulle sends a cruiser full of troops to Syria, where the position is delicate and the feeling against French domination strong, and there is a possible threat of a show-down, with British troops involved, in the Levant.

At 2.30 the P.M. went to bed, leaving almost untouched the voluminous weight of paper which awaits his decision. He told me that he doubted if he had the strength to carry on.

Tuesday, May 15th

Another very heavy day. I feel as if all the benefit of a week's leave has been almost sapped already.

Thursday, May 17th

The P.M. tells me he feels overpowered by the prospect of a meeting of the Big Three, which is imminent and which in view of the clash of interests over Poland, Venezia Giulia and Austria is vitally important, coinciding with a General Election which also ought not to be postponed. He is weighed down by the responsibility and the uncertainty. *Bellum in Pace.*

Friday, May 18th
The P.M. and Mrs C. set off for Chartwell and I went to
Chequers to dine and await them. Meanwhile, after a Conservative meeting at No. 10, the P.M. has written to Attlee, Sinclair
and Ernest Brown, saying that he hopes they will agree to
preserve the Coalition till the end of the war with Japan but that
he cannot agree to fixing a date for an election in the autumn
since that would mean an attempt to carry on the Government
in an atmosphere of faction and electioneering. Attlee came to
see the P.M. at the Annexe and was favourably disposed to
trying to persuade his party to continue at its Whitsun Blackpool
conference. He has Ernest Bevin with him in this.

The P.M. was so pleased with Chartwell that he stayed,
leaving me in comfortable solitude at Chequers.

Saturday, May 19th
A lovely hot day. Went for a long walk and did my best to put
the great array of papers in the box, most of which have been
unlooked at for many days, in some order.

Harold Macmillan, summoned from Italy because of the Venezia Giulia crisis, arrived at tea-time with Robert Cecil,[1] who is
acting as his A.D.C. The P.M. was still loitering with his geese
and goldfish ponds (recently plundered of their, to him, precious
occupants by a thief or an otter – it was long before anyone
dared break the news) at Chartwell and so I took Macmillan and
Robert up to Beacon Hill. I don't like the would-be ingratiating
way in which Macmillan bares his teeth.

The P.M. arrived for a late dinner and after it we saw a film.
Then a very little work was done, in the Private Secretary's
room, and a good deal of aimless discourse took place.

Sunday, May 20th
Whitsunday. The P.M. can't get the political prospect out of his
head and all day the conversation was on a coming election,
occasionally varied with fears of the Russian peril or a diatribe

---

[1] Conservative M.P. for Bournemouth, 1950–54. Only surviving son of Lord
Cranborne and himself eventually 6th Marquess of Salisbury.

against those who wish to treat all leading Germans as war criminals and to leave none with authority to administer that battered and disordered land.

General Auchinleck and his wife, whom I thought frightful and the P.M. thought attractive, came to lunch. Prof. and I devoted great energies to eradicating many of the P.M.'s papers and we did contrive to get some of the remainder dealt with.

Bert Harris, C. in C., Bomber Command, came to dinner.

Monday, May 21st

In the afternoon Randolph arrived and Harold Macmillan, who had left yesterday, returned. Just as the Prof. and I had all but reached our goal of getting "the box" dealt with, Attlee rang up from his Blackpool conference and gave his reply to the P.M.'s letter which was negative. At once all was swept aside and electioneering became the only topic, while the P.M., Macmillan and Randolph all tried their hands at drafting a reply to Attlee. They think they have manoeuvred skilfully, by placing on the Labour Party the onus of refusing to continue and of preferring faction to unity at a time when great dangers still remain. I don't think the P.M. is quite happy about this, but for all the other Tory politicians the time has now passed "when none were for the party and all were for the state". The most assiduous intriguer and hard-working electioneer is Lord Beaverbrook. Brendan, who is offended with the P.M. over a number of minor slights, is sulking in his tent.

Tuesday, May 22nd

Remained at Chequers till 5.00 p.m. when we returned to London in time for the P.M. to preside over a meeting of Tory ministers. At Chequers the P.M. stayed in bed. He wrote an admirable letter to the King, for the archives he said, and brought to fruition one to Mr Attlee, for publication. Lord Beaverbrook persuaded him to leave out the last paragraph, which had contained generous references to the help of his late Labour colleagues.

I read the letter to Attlee to him on the telephone, as the P.M. wanted it published on the 6.00 news. It took me about forty minutes to do as Attlee insisted on copying it down himself, in long hand, word by word on a very indistinct line.

So tomorrow the P.M. resigns and the Government which has won the war is at an end.

Wednesday, May 23rd
The P.M. went to the Palace at noon, as pre-arranged, and asked to resign. Then there was a pause, as the P.M. was anxious to emphasise to the public that the King has the right to decide for whom he shall send, and at 4.00 he returned to be invited to form a new, and a Conservative, Government. On the whole I think the people are on the P.M.'s side in this preliminary skirmish and it is generally supposed that many will vote for the Conservatives merely out of personal loyalty to W.S.C. Parliament will be dissolved in three weeks and the election will be on July 5th.

At No. 10 no work is being done by the P.M. We are all having to deal ourselves with many papers which ought to be submitted to him and I have persuaded the Foreign Office to send us the very minimum of minutes. I "weed" every day some sixty per cent of the Foreign Office telegrams. I suppose that three times as much paper comes to us now as in 1940 and that the P.M. sees half as much. But, of course, the problems, though more immediately grave then, were simpler in that the machinery of Government was far less elaborate and we had no Allies. Now there are boards and committees without number and two mighty Allies to be considered at every turn, apart from the host of lesser concerns such as French tactlessness in the Levant, Greek claims to the Dodecanese, internal Italian feuds, etc., etc. In 1941, when I left to join the R.A.F., I used often to be comparatively idle for days at a time and to think we were overstaffed. Now, apart from the Prof., Desmond Morton and Harvie-Watt we are six Private Secretaries (of whom Anthony Bevir, concentrating on Patronage, and Miss Watson on Parliamentary Questions, take no part in the routine of the office in current affairs), three male clerks, three eminently efficient women who look after the vast files of secret papers, and about sixteen typists, etc. Yet we seem to be understaffed.

Thursday, May 24th
The P.M. devoted the day to the formation of what the press calls a "Caretaker Government". Brendan has refused the Admiralty, though he thinks it the most attractive of offices, and is aiming for a combination of the Ministry of Production and the Board of Trade.

With politicians coming and going – glints in all their eyes – and the Chief Whip in constant attendance, no work was done, even in regard to a telegram from Stalin demanding a third of the German Navy and merchant fleet (all of which have surrendered to us).

I was interested by some of the bombing figures showing our and the American share of the bombing of Germany:

R.A.F.	678,500 tons	on Germany only.
U.S. Army Air Force	684,700	

Total for both forces everywhere in Europe: 2,170,000 tons.

Losses in Europe:	R.A.F.	10,801 aircraft
	U.S.A.A.F.	8,274 aircraft.

Friday, May 25th
More Government-making. Brendan has now taken the Admiralty and Harold Macmillan the Air Ministry. Alec Dunglass becomes an Under Secretary at the F.O. and William Sidney at the M. of Pensions.

Saturday, May 26th
Joan[1] lunched with me and we went together to a memorial service for Alick[2] at Holy Trinity, Brompton, at the unsuitable hour of 1.30. It was his birthday. There were but few people there, but the choir were good and the service adequate.

Am reading Trevelyan's *Social History of England*. Denis Speares[3] brought round after dinner his brother, just released

---

[1] My sister-in-law, Joan Colville.
[2] Lord Colville of Culross.
[3] A fellow pilot in the R.A.F.

from an *Oflag*, who gave a remarkable description of an attempted escape and his subsequent adventures at the hands of the Gestapo.

Sunday, May 27th
Went to Cherkley for the night to stay with Lord Beaverbrook. He was alone when I arrived and he took me for a long walk to see his chickens, to look at the little house he gave Mrs Norton (whose death last winter was a great blow to him), and back through the woods and valleys. He told me at length the story of Bonar Law's resignation and Lord Curzon's disappointment and then switched off to sing the praises of Brendan (whom he is backing against Eden for the Leadership of the Tory Party) and to complain that the P.M. had maltreated him in a number of ways over appointments.

When we got back to the house Harold Balfour, just returned from West Africa and about to become a peer, arrived, followed by Lord Queensberry[1] and Brendan.

Before dinner there was an incident which was indicative of the strong social chip on Lord Beaverbrook's shoulder. In the course of attacking Eden he said that the latter owed his success to his birth and education. He then turned on the assembled company and said that true men of quality, like Harold Balfour, Brendan and himself had worked their way up from nothing by sheer hard work and ability, whereas Lord Queensberry and I were like Anthony Eden and had only got where we were because of the circumstances in which we were born. Having made this attack, with flashing eyes, he then proceeded to send for the Scottish Psalter and read aloud to us several of the metrical Psalms. I think he did this as a form of grace before dinner and a possible means of making amends to the Almighty.

We had an excellent dinner with a magnum of champagne and lots of brandy, followed by a rotten film. When Balfour and Queensberry had gone, there followed a long political conver-

[1] 11th Marquess of Queensberry. Married at this time to the elegant portrait painter Cathleen Mann. Himself a dedicated clubman (he was a member of ten), he ran a successful and popular one for the armed forces during the war.

sation, with attacks on Bevin and praise of Morrison (the Beaver-brook–Bracken theme), abuse of Eden and Anderson and of the recent appointment of Dunglass[1] (who is pro-Pole while they are violently pro-Russian) as Under Secretary at the F.O. The evening was fun, with a real buccaneering, racketeering atmosphere. Of course, they are both utterly mischievous and will do the Conservative Party countless harm, at this election and afterwards.

Monday, May 28th

Awoke to a glorious view through the Dorking Gap, a bath in a fantastically over-luxurious bathroom, and a single poached egg accompanied by the *Daily Express*. Brendan had said he would be ready to leave for London at 9.30 but was not in fact ready until 11.30. Meanwhile I sat in the sun and poked about in Lord B.'s library, in the belief that books often tell one much of their owner. His were mostly dull, the lesser novelists and the standard biographies. But on a reading desk, by the side of two dictaphones, stood the Bible, open at the Psalms and in a nearby bookshelf was Wilkes's notorious *Essay on Woman*, an obscene parody of Pope's *Essay on Man*, which on publication was burned by the public hangman. Copies are therefore rare.

Lord B. came down, sat beside me in the sun, carried on some politico-journalistic intrigue by telephone, told some unknown caller that he would surely try and get him the Financial Secretaryship of the War Office (which he subsequently made no attempt to do), blackguarded James Stuart to somebody else as a Highlander, at once treacherous and loyal (James stands up against the Beaver–Brendan schemes and wields too much influence over appointments for their liking), discoursed to me cheerfully on various subjects, and finally, after a debunking description of Charles Dickens' private life, presented me with one of the maligned author's first editions.

Brendan came down and talked politics for an hour, saying that the socialist plot was to nationalise only the mines, the Bank

---

[1] Alexander Douglas-Home, subsequently 14th Earl of Home, Sir Alec Douglas-Home and Lord Home of the Hirsel.*

of England and electricity, but that if they nationalised the last they controlled industry as a whole and the second would tie finance to their apron. Eventually we left in Brendan's car and he talked the whole way up to London in an absolutely sane and sensible way.

Later in the day Lord B., who had argued with me that the Prof. had been utterly wrong about the V-weapons (the Prof. opposes him about the Bretton Woods financial project) sent me part of his dossier on the matter, each page taking one instance in which the Prof. could be shown to have been utterly wrong. He must be an uncomfortable colleague.

Lunched with Robert of Austria at the St James's Club. At 4.30 p.m. the P.M. gave a party at No. 10, to which I went, for the outgoing members of the Government and the new Cabinet. Conservative, Liberal and Labour met on most friendly terms.

More Government appointments (minor offices), the dissolution Honours List, satisfactory telegrams from Truman and Uncle Joe about a Big Three meeting in Berlin, and bed at 3.00 a.m.

Tuesday, May 29th
The House of Commons met, with the Labour Party in Opposition. I was not there, but gather there was a good deal of noise.

Opinion seems to be that in the election the forces, particularly the army, will vote left. Lord Queensberry told me that eighty per cent of the soldiers coming through his club say they will vote Labour. On the other hand it is thought the P.M. will counter-attract many votes purely on personal grounds and the Tories, apart from Brendan, are confident. Today I bet Leslie Rowan five shillings that Labour will get in, or rather that the Government (Conservative, Liberal National and Independent) will not get a majority.[1]

Wednesday, May 30th
The new Cabinet met for the first time. No. 10 is being refurbished and made ready for constant use and we may soon be

[1] I later hedged my bet by wagering Nicko Henderson ten shillings that the Tories would win. So I was down five shillings.

able to leave the dismal Annexe for good. Immersed in rather interesting problems and papers. In the Levant the threatened storm between the French and the Syrians has broken and my sympathies are not with the French. War has made people too "trigger-happy" as the Americans call it.

John Martin tells me he is leaving No. 10 at the end of June for the Colonial Office.

Thursday, May 31st
Dined at Pratts with Bob Coates. Mother returned from Badminton, for the last time, as Queen Mary is about to return to Marlborough House.

*   *   *

On Friday, June 1st, I went down to Chequers with the Prime Minister and the week-end was largely devoted to the preparation of the first political broadcast of the series which members of all parties are making before the General Election on July 5th. The P.M.'s, the first of four which he is to make, was a fighting and provocative effort, mentioning the necessity of a political police to a really socialist state. He delivered it on the evening of Monday, June 4th, in the little study, hung with small Constables, at Chequers. I sat in the room with him while he delivered the broadcast and was amused to note that his gestures to the microphone were as emphatic as those he uses in a political speech to a large audience and far more pronounced than those he employs in ordinary conversation. The speech, in which, contrary to general supposition, neither Brendan nor the Beaver had a hand, aroused widespread criticism and did not really go down well, at any rate with the educated classes. For the first time he was speaking against the clock which made him hurry unduly.

And now, a few weeks after the war in Europe is over, I bring to an end this diary which is essentially a war-time measure and which began a week after hostilities broke out. Those sunny days of September 1939 seem to belong to a past life. The whole face of Europe has changed, physically and spiritually also. For us the great problem is Russia, whose intentions we cannot with certainty fathom and whose more sinister designs seem to be crystallised in the Polish question, as far from solution as ever. "The Big Three" are to meet in Berlin on July 15th and after their conference we may see more distinctly the shape of things to come.

Elsewhere Europe is in no happy state. France is ruled by a hyper-sensitive autocrat whose foolish and impetuous actions – in the Levant, and in the Val d'Aosta where he ordered his troops to resist the orders of the Supreme Commander, Eisenhower – effectively block the close friendship with the Western Powers which all thinking Frenchmen and all their friends abroad see to be indispensable to the recovery of France and to the restoration of Europe.

In Italy six weak parties conduct their petty intrigues while Allied Military Government keeps the peace and the partisans of the north commit their counter-atrocities against fascism in the same spirit that originally produced the worst fascist excesses. In the Balkans, apart from Greece and Turkey, Russian puppets rule unhampered by free elections and the system of "rule by the Party" is established. In Spain Franco holds precarious sway, reviled by the outside world and threatened by Spanish republican concentrations behind the Pyrenees. He seems to be toying with the idea of restoring the monarchy in order to present an appearance of respectability.

Germany hangs her head, bewildered and disgraced, while the Russians vary in their zone between fraternisation, to counteract the prevailing preference for the English and Americans, and a policy of rape, murder and arson. Whether Austria is to be free is problematic and at present the Russians have set up a government, headed by an octogenarian Social Democrat (to give it respectability) but boasting Communists in the Ministries of the Interior and Education which are the Ministries that matter. Over all Europe hangs the cloud of insufficient supplies, disjointed distribution, lack of coal and a superfluity of destitute and displaced persons. The situation is no easier, nor are the prospects apparently brighter, than before the first shot was fired.

At home the first intoxication of victory is passing. The parties are creating bitterness, largely artificial, in their vote-catching hysteria. Brendan and the Beaver are firing vast salvos which mostly, I think, miss their mark. Labour propaganda is a great deal better and is launched on a rising market. Without Winston's personal prestige the Tories would not have a chance. Even with him I am not sanguine of their prospects, though most of their leaders are confident of a good majority. I think the service vote will be Left and the housing shortage has left many people disgruntled. The main Conservative advantage is the prevailing good humour of the people and the accepted point that Attlee would be a sorry successor to Winston at the meeting of the Big Three and in the counsels of the Nations.

I have written a great deal in these pages, much that I ought not to have written and much that was not worth writing. I have omitted many of the details, as indeed many of the great or significant events, which would have made it easier to recall the scenes as they passed before me. But however great or little its value may be to me in the years to come, it records one fact for which I have good reason to be thankful. I have lived as interesting and as varied a life as could be conceived, and I have experienced things which the ordinary course of events would never have brought my way, during five and a half years in which the rest of humanity has suffered the extremes of boredom and depression only alternating with those of grief, horror and fear. If I have not profited, then there is none but myself to blame.

J. R. C.
June 18th, 1945
4 Mulberry Walk.

SEVENTEEN

END OF WAR COALITION

Having written this rather sententious farewell to my diary, I nevertheless kept brief notes of my activities for the next four months from which this chapter is constructed. Early in October, I rejoined my parent department, the Foreign Office, after six years' secondment.

When William Sidney succeeded his uncle as Lord De L'Isle and Dudley I applied for the nomination in his Chelsea seat, strongly supported by both Winston Churchill and Brendan Bracken. However, a matter of hours before my application was received the Conservative Association had already selected another candidate. My strongly Liberal mother, and her equally Liberal step-mother, Peggy Crewe, showed no inclination to condole with me.

On June 20th my grandfather died at his home at West Horsley. I went straight from the funeral in the lovely red sandstone church at Barthomley on his remaining Crewe estate to join Winston Churchill's train at Leeds; for though he was on an electioneering tour in which it would have been improper for officials to take part, he was still Prime Minister, required to deal with the daily business of Government.

He addressed vast and enthusiastic crowds at Leeds, Bradford and Preston. The train moved on to Glasgow where he made about ten speeches to deafening applause. He drove to Edinburgh along roads thronged with cheering men, women and children, and when he finally returned to the train, after a reception in Edinburgh as warm and moving as in Glasgow, he said to me that nobody who had seen what he had that day could have any doubt as to the result of the coming election. I said that I would agree if it were a presidential election.

July 5th was polling-day. The Conservative Central Office and Lord Beaverbrook both forecast a majority of at least a hundred seats for the Government. Winston Churchill decided to take a fortnight's holiday, the first he had had since war began. A hospitable Canadian, Brigadier-General Brutinel, who owned the Château Margaux vineyard, offered his house, Bordaberry, near Hendaye. The General had somehow contrived to remain in France throughout the German occupation and had been a leading conspirator in arranging for escaping Allied airmen and prisoners of war to cross the Pyrenees into Spain.

So on July 7th Mr and Mrs Churchill, Mary, Lord Moran and I flew to Bordeaux. The Prime Minister devoted most of the time to painting. He was accompanied and advised on his artistic expeditions by a talented artist, Mrs Nairn, wife of the British Consul at Bordeaux, who had been at Marrakech when we were there in January 1944 and had won Churchill's esteem. The rest of us walked, visited Biarritz, St Jean de Luz and Bayonne, watched Basque dancing at Hendaye and drank the finest clarets. We were joined for a day or two by Duff Cooper.

In the mornings we bathed from a sandy beach. The Prime Minister floated, like a benevolent hippo, in the middle of a large circle of protective French policemen who had duly donned bathing suits for the purpose. His British detective had also been equipped by the thoughtful authorities at Scotland Yard for such aquatic duties. Round and round this circle swam a persistent French Countess, a notorious *collaborateuse* who hoped by speaking to Winston Churchill to escape the fate which the implacable *résistance* were probably planning for her. It reminded me of the mediaeval practice of "touching for the King's evil". The encircling gendarmes, patiently treading water, thwarted her plot, but she did entrap me on the beach. Looking at her golden locks I felt pity and hoped she would not suffer the fate of those shorn girls I had seen at Bayeux the preceding summer. I believe that in the end her good looks, and no doubt her influential connections, saved her from anything worse than a short prison sentence.

Before we left for France Churchill asked President Truman to telegraph the result of the test of the first atomic bomb shortly due to take place in the Nevada desert. "Let me know," he had signalled, "whether it is a flop or a plop." When we were about to leave Bordaberry a telegram came from the President to the Prime Minister. It read: "It's a plop. Truman." A new, glaring light was shed on the future of the war against Japan.

On July 15th Churchill left for a meeting of the Big Three at Potsdam where my colleagues Leslie Rowan and John Peck awaited him, together with the whole British delegation and, by Churchill's special invitation, the leader of the Opposition, Clement Attlee, for whom he had even been thoughtful enough to provide a valet. It was, Attlee told me afterwards, the first and last time he ever had a valet.

I returned to No. 10 with Mrs Churchill and acted as the rearlink until, ten days or so later, the Potsdam Conference adjourned so that Churchill, Eden and Attlee might fly back to London for the declaration of the polls. This had been delayed three weeks so that the service voting papers could be flown home from distant parts of the world and added to the votes cast in Britain.

Early on July 26th the Prime Minister, Beaverbrook, Brendan Bracken and David Margesson seated themselves in Churchill's own map-room, opposite the entrance to the Annexe in the Office of Works building. Special arrangements had been made for the results to be flashed on a screen as each was announced. After half an hour it was evident there was going to be a landslide to the Labour Party. Nobody was more surprised than Attlee who, driving to Chequers three weeks later, told me that in his most optimistic dreams he had reckoned that there might, with luck, be a Conservative majority of only some forty seats.

That evening Churchill resigned and the King sent for Attlee. There was world stupefaction, not least at Potsdam, where Stalin supposed that Churchill would have "fixed" the results.

It was surprising to find myself on July 27th, 1945, Private Secretary to Mr Attlee. It was still more surprising to read the letters from people, many of them in high official places and apparently devoted to Churchill, who wrote to Attlee saying how much they rejoiced in the election result. Prominent among these was General Sir Archibald Nye, Vice Chief of the Imperial General Staff, a post he owed to Churchill personally. He wrote to say how delighted he was by the election result both on political and personal grounds. Having read his letter I was astonished to travel up in the lift with him to attend a party Duncan Sandys gave that evening for the outgoing Conservative administration.

When I said to Dr Dalton[1] that he must indeed be gratified, he replied that while the Tories had left the constituencies untended, their agents being for the most part away fighting, he, like Herbert Morrison, had spent much time and effort in ensuring that the Labour electoral machinery was in good order. However, Sir Edward Bridges and Sir Alan Lascelles persuaded the King to suggest to Attlee that Bevin should be Foreign Secretary rather than Dalton who had originally been intended for the post.

Attlee and Bevin returned to Potsdam, with, to the astonishment of the Americans and Russians, exactly the same team as had ministered to Churchill and Eden. Meanwhile I was lent to Churchill to help him clear up his affairs. Chequers was placed at his disposal for the week-end after the election and I went with him. There was a large family party and we drank a rehoboam of champagne for dinner. I recorded that Churchill said it was fatal to give way to self-pity, that the new Government had a mandate which the Opposition would have no right to question, and that in matters of national as opposed to party interest, it was the duty of everybody to support them, facing as they were the most difficult task of any peace-time Government in modern times. In foreign affairs, at any rate, he stuck to that resolution.

Nevertheless internal political bickering began soon enough. It started with a severe letter from Churchill to Attlee complain-

---

[1] Old Etonian son of Canon Dalton, tutor to Edward VII's sons. Minister of Economic Warfare in the war-time coalition.

ing of an injudicious statement Professor Harold Laski had made during the election campaign. As I was spending part of my time at No. 10 and part of it at Claridges, where the Churchills were temporarily installed, I helped draft both the charges and counter-charges in the ensuing correspondence. It was a wholly Gilbertian situation, especially as neither Churchill nor Attlee saw any objection to the role I was expected to assume.

On August 2nd the new Prime Minister returned from Potsdam, with all too little settled by the Big Three, and completed the formation of his Government. He thought he should acquire a sober "Anthony Eden" black Homburg hat and asked me where to buy one. With deliberate irony I took him to Lock's in St James's Street, the most aristocratic hat-maker in London. He bought a hat that suited him well.

A few days later I made this brief diary note: *"August 6th. The first atomic bomb was dropped on Hiroshima and a new terrifying era begins. I had known of the project since 1941, but had never fully realised its implications until now. The startling news was, at Winston's express request, broken to an unprepared England by W.'s statement (drafted last weekend at Chequers) with a preface by Attlee."*

The mood was one of elation; for a long drawn-out end to the war, with hideous further casualties, now seemed certain to be avoided and few people paused to contemplate the subsequent implications.

On August 15th I saw on the tape-machine at No. 10 that Japan had surrendered. I brought the news into the Cabinet room where Attlee was closeted with Lord Louis Mountbatten who was professing Labour sympathies. Such is the fallibility of great men's memories that Mountbatten subsequently averred he had heard the news at the Admiralty and had darted across the Horse Guards Parade to tell the Prime Minister. I am quite sure my own recollection is correct. Not, of course, that it matters in the least except as a minor indication of the inaccuracies of history.

My diary note for August 15th reads: "The Japanese, conquered by the atomic bomb, accepted the Potsdam terms of surrender and, after several days of uncertainty, Mr Attlee announced the news last night at midnight. V.J. Day.

"The King and Queen opened Parliament in state. I drove to the house with Mr Attlee through exuberant crowds. Winston received the greatest ovation of all. Debate on the Address. I listened to Attlee and to Winston."

Attlee lent Churchill the Prime Ministerial C.54 aircraft to fly to the northern Italian lakes for a painting holiday; and on August 17th I went to Chequers with the Attlees for a long weekend. I was "greatly attracted by his simple charm and lack of ostentation or ambition".

The contrast with my previous weekends at Chequers was, however, notable. Mrs Churchill's superb cook had vanished and the A.T.S. replacement, though she did her best, was not in the same class. The new Labour Prime Minister was more formal in his dress and behaviour than his Conservative predecessor. At dinner a starched shirt and stiff butterfly collar was the order of the day. Mrs Attlee, distinguished looking and clearly a beauty in her youth, was welcoming and friendly, but Mrs Churchill's sometimes caustic comments and unflagging perfectionism were missing.

Attlee asked me what I thought of Geoffrey de Freitas who was there to be vetted as a candidate for Parliamentary Private Secretary. Charming, I said, and highly intelligent. "Yes," replied Attlee, "and what is more he was at Haileybury, my old school." Churchill, though he sometimes said nice things about me, never included in his recommendations that we were both Old Harrovians. I concluded that the old school tie counted even more in Labour than in Conservative circles.

None of this detracted from Attlee's virtues of total honesty, quickness, efficiency and common sense. He was an outstanding manager of an often difficult team; and he was the only Prime Minister of the United Kingdom in the twentieth century, apart from Sir Alec Douglas-Home, who had no shred of either conceit or vanity. In the mornings he tended to be a little astringent: after luncheon he was invariably mellow and most approachable.

On August 21st, the day after we left Chequers, Ernest Bevin, Anthony Eden's replacement as Foreign Secretary, made

a speech on foreign affairs which caused dudgeon in left-wing
continental circles and caused Oliver Stanley to comment on
"The Importance of being Anthony". As for me, the time soon
came to go to a farewell luncheon which the Attlees gave for
my mother and myself, to say goodbye and to leave 10 Downing
Street, as I wrote in my diary, "for the third and presumably
the last time".

PART THREE

OCTOBER 1945–
OCTOBER 1951

EIGHTEEN

PASTURES NEW
OCTOBER 1945–OCTOBER 1951

In the Southern Department of the Foreign Office, where I arrived in October 1945, the country allotted to my care was Yugoslavia, about which I already knew a certain amount owing to Winston Churchill's frequent preoccupation with Tito, King Peter and the Ban of Croatia (Dr Subasic).

My predecessor at this desk was John Addis, who now succeeded me at No. 10, thus continuing a policy which began with my own appointment in 1939, and has persisted ever since, that there should be a member of the Foreign Service among the Prime Minister's secretaries. However, John Addis had been on leave for three weeks before I took his chair so that I was faced with a gargantuan pile of papers awaiting attention, was obliged to take bags full home at night and found myself working fifteen to sixteen hours a day.

I was not amused when a few days after establishing myself in the Southern Department I received a sharp note from Addis enquiring why a question from the Prime Minister about Yugoslavia had not been answered. On searching through the heap of papers in my in-tray I found that the question was contained in a letter *I* had written weeks before we changed places. I hope he showed Mr Attlee my caustic reply.

Relations with Tito were no longer what they had been a few months earlier. He was now, and for four years to come, firmly in the Stalinist camp; he had tried to seize the Italian territories of Trieste and Venezia Giulia; and he had even contemplated occupying Austrian Carinthia. Part of my job was to compose in flowery prose indignant despatches to our Ambassador in Belgrade instructing him to complain, in the name of His Majesty's Government, of the tyrant's behaviour. As exercises in composition they were enjoyable; as protests they were ineffective. Another of my duties was to pronounce whether Yugoslavs captured by our forces in Italy and demanded by Tito should or should not be returned to Yugoslavia for probable execution. As a rough and ready rule it was agreed that no Chetniks, loyal supporters of King Peter but at one time prone to collaborate with the Italians, should be sent back to Tito-land. On the other hand, the leaders, though only the leaders, of the Croat terrorist Ustasi, who were guilty of many atrocities, should be surrendered. Few of them were caught. This policy, especially as it related to the Chetniks, infuriated Tito; but Ernest Bevin stood no nonsense from the Yugoslav Ambassador when he called to protest. Bevin never did stand any nonsense, from Members of Parliament, Trade Unionists, foreigners or his own colleagues.

In due course I was promoted assistant head of the department, which meant that the misdeeds of the new Communist régimes in Hungary, Roumania, Bulgaria and Albania were added to my Yugoslav responsibilities, as was the shilly-shallying of the recently elected Greek Government and their increasingly vociferous claim to Cyprus.

All this meant hard labour, and most of it was depressing because not only did Molotov persistently say No on behalf of the Soviet Union to every proposal we made for some semblance of democracy in the Balkans, but also because Britain was subjected to an economic stringency still grimmer than in the war. It was galling to watch living conditions improve month by month in France and Italy while we, the victors, languished in bleak monotony. Gloom reigned in the bomb-devastated streets of London and the provincial cities. The winter of 1946–47 was the worst for fifty years. The Thames froze at Westminster Bridge and in Chelsea I often had to dig thick snow from round the wheels of my car after a stationary hour or two. There was a fuel crisis and domestic coal supplies were severely rationed.

All my girl-friends were platonic; London was grey; life was grey.

A change of occupation, and an unexpected one, came my way in the spring of 1947. Sir Alan Lascelles invited me, in the King's name, to become Private Secretary to the twenty-one-year-old Heiress Apparent, Princess Elizabeth. I did not want to abandon my diplomatic career for too long, but I said yes with alacrity on the basis of a two-year secondment, spurred on by Winston Churchill who pronounced: "It is your duty to accept." It was in the event a greater pleasure than a duty, for I served a young lady as wise as she was attractive. She already had three hard-working ladies-in-waiting, who dealt with her heavy load of correspondence from the general public; but I was the first male member of her Household. They were for me two wholly enjoyable years beginning, four months after my appointment, with Princess Elizabeth's marriage to Lieutenant Philip Mountbatten, an event which with nationwide rejoicing, splendid decorations and the re-emergence of State carriages and the Household Cavalry in full-dress uniform, helped to lift the encircling gloom.

Food parcels from the United States and the Dominions, which were doing so much to alleviate the austerity in thousands of British homes, had been matched by hundreds of tons of tinned food of every variety, given by British communities abroad as wedding presents for Princess Elizabeth to distribute as she saw fit.

How to distribute them was a problem. I consulted Stella, Lady Reading. She had been secretary to Lord Reading, who rose from cabin-boy to Viceroy of India, and when his first wife died he married her. Realising that there were many tasks for women to perform which were not the responsibility of established organisations such as the Red Cross, St John of Jerusalem or the women's uniformed services, she had brought her natural organising gifts to fruition by founding the Women's Voluntary Service, with its headquarters in Tothill Street and its activities projected throughout the country. She and her devoted volunteers found no challenge unacceptable in war or peace.

Up till then those whom I consulted had said with one accord: "Hand it all over to the Ministry of Food." Princess Elizabeth was far from content with this unimaginative proposal, well knowing how unlikely the donors were to be gratified; and that was why I suggested confiding in Lady Reading.

She mobilised a hundred or so willing members of the W.V.S. They, with the King's permission, took over the large kitchens at Buckingham Palace during the Royal Family's holiday at Balmoral the following year. By the end of September 1948, thousands of beautifully packed and well assorted food parcels had been despatched to widows and old-age pensioners throughout the kingdom, each containing a message from Princess Elizabeth personally. Thanks to Lady Reading and the agreement of the Post Office to send the parcels free of charge, the whole operation cost almost nothing.

This is but one example of the drive, the willingness to leap any hurdle, which Lady Reading inspired in a body of selfless women volunteers who worked so hard and whose praises have not been adequately sung.

One of Princess Elizabeth's ladies-in-waiting, Lady Margaret Egerton, endowed with a beautiful voice, had been wont to sing a metrical psalm, "The Lord's my Shepherd" (Crimond), in the heather at Balmoral and had taught the two princesses a little-known descant. Princess Elizabeth decided to have this at her wedding, but nobody could find the score of the descant. Lady Margaret, tunefully accompanied by the two princesses, therefore sang it to the Organist and Precentor of Westminster Abbey who took down the notes in musical shorthand and taught it to the Abbey Choir. On the wedding day nobody was more surprised than the composer of the descant who, far away in Stirling, listened to the service on his radio. Since then both the metrical psalm to the tune Crimond and the descant have been consistently popular in churches throughout the British Isles and the Commonwealth.

Before the wedding there was a magnificent evening party at Buckingham Palace for which sparkling tiaras and orders emerged from long years of storage. The guests were as various as half a dozen foreign Kings and Queens on the one hand and

Beatrice Lillie and Noël Coward on the other. The Roumanian Government took advantage of King Michael's presence in London to declare a republic, something they had not dared to do while he was still in Bucharest because of his popularity with his people. An Indian Rajah became uncontrollably drunk and assaulted the Duke of Devonshire (who was sober), but otherwise there were no untoward events. However, Queen Mary, scintillating as ever in a huge display of jewellery, without giving the least impression of vulgarity or ostentation, was somewhat taken aback when Field Marshal Smuts said to her, "You are the big potato; the other Queens are all small potatoes."

Apart from the colour and national jubilation which marked the royal wedding, the outlook was black as the country stumbled through a rough economic blizzard. After talking to Winston Churchill at his birthday dinner party on November 30th, 1947, at 28 Hyde Park Gate, I made this gloomy entry in my diary:

Winston is in sombre mood, convinced that this country is destined to suffer the most agonising economic distress. He says that the anxiety he suffered during the Battle of the Atlantic was "a mere pup" in comparison. We could only get through if we had the power of the spirit, the unity and the absence of envy, malice and hatred which are now so conspicuously lacking. Never in his life had he felt such despair and he blamed it on the Government whose "insatiable lust for power is only equalled by their incurable impotence in exercising it". The phrases and epigrams rolled out in the old way, but I missed that indomitable hope and conviction which characterised the Prime Minister of 1940–41.

While the Princess and the Duke of Edinburgh were away on their honeymoon the King gave a party for the Foreign Ministers of Britain, the United States and Russia who abandoned their squabbles at Lancaster House to come to Buckingham Palace and drink champagne cocktails. Winston and Molotov talked like old friends and Princess Margaret engaged Vyshinski[1] in a

---

[1] Andrei Vyshinski, hard-line Soviet prosecutor of Stalin's victims, with special responsibility for the imposition of Communist régimes on the Balkan countries.

twenty minutes' argument which much impressed him. He said to me that if only she had not been a Princess she would assuredly have made a most formidable advocate. The Foreign Secretary, Ernest Bevin, who for all his virtues liked to take personal credit for most things, told me – when I said at the end that the party had done more good than any number of meetings at Lancaster House – that he was glad I thought *he* had organised it well. Hector McNeil,[1] Minister of State at the Foreign Office, asserted that photographs of Molotov's earnest conversations with the King and Winston Churchill would have been powerful diplomatic weapons.

My duties as a courtier did not hinder excursions into other circles. Once or twice, with Peter Townsend,[2] Meg Egerton and my Communist friend Janet Margesson (beginning to lose her faith in the Kremlin), I spent an evening at the Dockland Settlement and, as the following extracts from my diary show, I sometimes strayed into more rarefied atmospheres:

Friday, December 19th
Dined at the French Embassy to see Elizabeth Chavchavadze,[3] who is staying there. Lady Cunard, Lulu de Vilmorin,[4] Peter Quennell, Garrett Moore, Violet Trefusis, Hugh Ross and Gérard André[5] were the other guests. A wonderful dinner, and conversation ranging from gossip to Baudelaire. Lady Cunard, who is always original, said that Lord Louis Mountbatten was

---

[1] At one time journalist on the *Daily Express*. Labour M.P. for Greenock. Able and faithful supporter of Ernest Bevin who much preferred him to his predecessor, Philip Noel-Baker.
[2] Group Captain Peter Townsend, D.S.O., D.F.C. and bar. Gallant Battle of Britain pilot. Equerry to the King and Deputy Master of the Household.
[3] Heiress to an American Loyalist family settled in France after American Independence. First married the Comte de Breteuil and then the talented and charming Russian pianist Prince George Chavchavadze. She had a fine *hôtel* in Paris and rented the Palazza Polignac in Venice where I stayed with her for three idyllic weeks in the hot summer of 1947. Her figure was deplorable, but her wit and culture enchanting.
[4] Much admired French novelist. Intimate friend of the Duff Coopers in Paris.
[5] Popular member of the French Embassy in London for many years. Eventually French Ambassador in Finland and Thailand.

one of the most tedious men she knew; he thought a mask of superficial charm could compensate for never having read a book.

Nineteen forty-eight began with dark prospects internationally and serious economic prospects at home. Luckily it was a singularly warm winter so that there was no repetition of the previous year's desperate coal crisis. Food parcels poured into many homes from generous people in the Dominions and the U.S.A., horrified that the British, who had given so much in lives and treasure, should still be victims of shortages and drab austerity.

Friday, February 6th, 1948
Queen Mary took Lord Cambridge,[1] Lady Helena Gibbs and me to see *Annie Get Your Gun*. It was my fourth time. H.M. revelled in it, and in addition she received an overwhelming and most touching ovation from the actors and the audience. After the song "I'm an Indian too, a Sioux", she turned to me and asked, "Is *that* one of the songs Margaret sings?" I said it was, to which she remarked, "What a pity!" I thought I had said the wrong thing and done Princess Margaret ill-service, but a minute or two later her grandmother reverted to the subject and said, "What a pity I have never heard her!"

Saturday, February 7th
Stayed the week-end with Tony and Yvonne Rothschild at Ascott.[2] Tony has a magnificent library and some admirable pictures. The house is certainly as comfortable as could be wished, but overheated bedrooms always give me restless nights.

Sunday, February 8th
After Tony, Ann and I had been for a seven-mile walk (very hard going on the high road) we returned to tea where we found that agile conversationalist Princess Marthe Bibesco[3] whom I had

[1] Queen Mary's nephew.
[2] At Wing in Buckinghamshire.
[3] French writer who married a Roumanian. An internationally known "blue-stocking".

met dining with David[1] and Jean Lloyd. We discoursed till dinner. Speaking of the institution of monarchy she said that when the King is no more *"les termites se désinterressent de la termitière"* – a fact to which she ascribes the political maladies of France.

We spent most of the evening after dinner trying to persuade Madame Laffon, an attractive French friend of Yvonne, who has three children at school in England, that English schools were not riddled with homosexuality and that incessant and brutal corporal punishment was not an invariable feature of the curriculum. Such are the curious conceptions which one race forms of another.

Thursday, February 19th
Sorine, the Russian artist who is painting Princess Elizabeth and being given innumerable sittings, told me I had a very interesting head. I should have been more flattered had he not told Jean Elphinstone precisely the same last week!

> *Meanwhile I had fallen head over heels in love with one of Princess Elizabeth's ladies-in-waiting, Meg Egerton. As she was strikingly good-looking, and no less strikingly vivacious, she had many suitors. I had an unfair advantage because my office, on the second floor of Buckingham Palace, was next to the lady-in-waiting's suite of rooms. So she found it hard to escape.*

Saturday, May 1st
I arrived last night at Chartwell Farm to stay with Mary and Christopher Soames.* Tonight we dined with Winston at Chartwell. Sarah and Bill Deakin[2] made up the party. Dinner began badly, with reading of the newspapers and monosyllabic

---

[1] Son of George Lloyd, distinguished proconsul and Secretary of State for the Colonies. Himself Under Secretary of State at the Home Office and then the Colonial Office, 1952–57. Married Lady Jean Ogilvy.

[2] A distinguished historian who helped Churchill on his life of Marlborough and *History of the Second World War*. The first British liaison officer with Marshal Tito in Yugoslavia and after the war Master of St Anthony's College, Oxford.

answers; but when the champagne had done its work, Mr C. brightened up and became his brilliant, gay and epigrammatic best. He gave me the proofs of Volume II of his book, May 1940 to the end of that year, to read and comment on.

Sunday, May 2nd
Six weeks of warmth and sunshine have given way to cold and rain. Christopher had tummy trouble; Mary a vile carbuncle which gave her great pain. In the evening we went to Winston's private cinema, saw an exceptionally good film called *To Be Or Not To Be*, and dined most agreeably. Winston, who had been busy all day painting a red lily against the background of a black buddha, switched from art to Operation TIGER,[1] and rather to my embarrassment told in great detail the story of my trouble with Monty when he took me out to Germany for the crossing of the Rhine in March 1945. He was scathing about Monty's self-advertising stunts and said he presumed British soldiers would soon have to be called "Monties" instead of "Tommies". Speaking of the Anglo-American disputes over the question of a Second Front in the Cotentin in 1942, Winston said, "No lover ever studied every whim of his mistress as I did those of President Roosevelt."

Monday, May 10th
Princess Elizabeth and Prince Philip, attended by Meg and myself, dined at the French Embassy. After dinner I talked to Hector McNeil who said that if the Russians were sly enough to make some conciliatory gesture, with the object of appeasing popular sentiment in the democracies, the F.O. would not know how to deal with the situation. But he said it would not be in accordance with the way their minds worked to do so.

*   *   *

Early in 1948 I had suggested to the Foreign Office that it would be good for Anglo-French relations if Princess Elizabeth and

[1] Transport of tanks for Wavell's army through the Mediterranean in 1941.

Prince Philip, whose wedding had been romanticised and enthusiastically covered in every country outside the Soviet bloc, were to visit Paris. I approached Ernest Bevin who said he wholeheartedly applauded the suggestion provided it was not in March. "Lent?" I queried. "No," he replied, "because I expect a Communist drive in Paris then and because the Government's ban on foreign travel won't be raised till May 1st." The King approved, and so the first royal visit to France for nine years took place in May during probably the hottest Whitsun weekend ever known.

It was exhilarating, if exhausting. The Princess won Parisian hearts on the very first day, because the quality of her French accent and the contents of a speech broadcast from the steps of the Musée Gallièra were an astonishment to those who had been expecting a dull oration and a heavy English accent. Nothing enchants the French so much as foreigners with a fluency in their language, especially if the speaker is a pretty girl and a Princess into the bargain. With a calmness which has always been one of her characteristics, she refused to be disconcerted by the constant clicking of cameras and the loud ringing of nearby church bells while she was speaking.

We drove to Versailles. All the fountains, including those in the woods, were playing in shimmering heat, and we lunched at the Grand Trianon. The tablecloths and napkins, with delicately embroidered E's, P's, and roses, had been specially woven for the occasion. We made a triumphal journey down the Seine, all the banks lined by enthusiastic crowds, to the Hôtel de Lauzun where de Gaulle's brother, Pierre, President of the Paris Municipal Council, gave a greatly overcrowded reception in dripping heat. There was a dinner-party of sixty-four at the Embassy, followed by a still larger reception, at which the Princess glittered in the diamond tiara and necklace the Nizam of Hyderabad had given her as a wedding present. On Whit Sunday we all walked to a special early service at the Embassy church, followed by Mattins at 10.30. Nobody could say that the future Supreme Governor of the Church of England was neglecting her duties. Prince Philip looked and felt ill, but with characteristic determination he insisted on going through with the heavy programme.

Indeed he made a major contribution to the successful fulfilment of more than usually arduous duties during the whole time we were in Paris.

We went to Fontainebleau, lunched at Barbizon and visited Vaux-le-Vicomte. Princess Elizabeth said she thought it the most perfect house she had ever seen. Everywhere, at Fontainebleau, at Barbizon, at Vaux, there were cheering crowds on the roads and in the streets, and as we re-entered Paris the throng was so great that the cars had difficulty in moving. That night, after a visit to the Opéra, it was the same story as the Prince and Princess stood floodlit at the top of the steps. In four hectic days Princess Elizabeth had conquered Paris.

I was gratified when President Vincent Auriol kissed me on both cheeks and made me an Officer of the Légion d'Honneur, but I was brought down to earth by my mother when I returned home. "That," she said, "is what used in my youth to be called a dinner medal."

The crowds were as dense and the plaudits just as loud in Britain as Princess Elizabeth, accompanied by Prince Philip whenever his naval duties allowed, travelled far and wide throughout the kingdom. Her speeches were usually reported on the front pages of the national newspapers. Quite mysteriously, a visit by a young princess with beautiful blue eyes and a superb natural complexion brought gleams of radiant sunshine into the dingiest streets of the dreariest cities. Princes who do their duty are respected; beautiful Princesses have an in-built advantage over their male counterparts.

Falling in love coincided with a relaxation from travel, for the Princess was expecting her first child and had cancelled her engagements. It was also a distraction from unsavoury world events. I had no inclination to brood on the international situation which was dominated by the dangerous crisis arising from the refusal of the Russians to allow the Western powers to feed the people in their zones of Berlin. I wrote: "We have taken a very firm line and cannot go back on it. The Russians may find it difficult to climb down without losing face, especially as they have a serious problem with Marshal Tito who has deviated from the Party line. The question of 'face' has caused so many wars." In the event the Russians were forced to climb down as a result of the brilliantly executed Berlin air-lift. Interference with that would have meant war; and at that time the Russians had no atom bomb.

> Whatever happens we have got
> The Maxim Gun and they have not.

For another year or two that late Victorian verse was still quotable.

At the end of July Meg Egerton and I became engaged and for me everything, even Berlin air-lifts and Molotovian intransigence, was bathed in the rosiest of hues. We were married at St Margaret's, Westminster, on October 20th, 1948, causing a traffic jam in Parliament Square of major inconvenience to the public.

In September 1949 my two years of secondment from the Foreign Office expired and after a farewell visit to the King and Queen at Balmoral, we sailed for Lisbon where I had been appointed Head of Chancery in the Embassy. If I had been thrilled by my time as a courtier, it was not just on account of the glamour, considerable though that was. A lasting impression was the dedication and total honesty of those for whom and with whom I worked, qualities I have not seen excelled.

We were two years at the Embassy in Portugal, during the course of which I spent a month in the beautiful but scantily developed colony of Angola, then firmly controlled from Lisbon. I also had an unexpected two hours with Doctor Salazar. He seemed to me an idealist of genuine personal humility. Many, though probably not at that time a majority, of the citizens of Portugal would have disagreed with me sharply; but if he ruled his fellow-countrymen severely, he did on the whole rule them well, at least until he became obsessed with the preservation of the Portuguese Colonies in total contradiction to the new spirit of the times. The two Iberian dictators, Franco and Salazar, used methods that were sometimes harsh; but they were cast in a finer mould than their contemporary tyrants in Germany,

Italy and Russia, and their government was a great deal more beneficent. The ordinary citizen in Spain and Portugal had no need to lower his voice or look anxiously over his shoulder when talking politics in a café.

The time, however, was approaching for me to regard foreign policy from a less parochial viewpoint.

PART FOUR

OCTOBER 1951–
APRIL 1955

NINETEEN

"CHURCHILL IS BACK"

We went home from Lisbon on leave in October 1951, just before the General Election. Mr Attlee, having won a majority of only six seats at the election held eighteen months before, concluded that he must try again. We were invited to an election night party given by Lord Camrose* at the Savoy. In days when television sets were still comparatively rare, there was no quicker or pleasanter way of hearing the results. Those at the Savoy included Sir Norman Brook,[1] successor to Sir Edward Bridges as Secretary to the Cabinet. "Hello," he said. "Back on leave?" It was an innocent enough question.

The Conservatives had a majority of sixteen, marginally better than that of the outgoing administration. Having absorbed the fact, we set off on the following day to stay, en route for a holiday in Scotland, with my mother-in-law near Newmarket. It was the Cesarewich meeting. As I watched the races and contemplated my losses (endemic, as far as I am concerned, on a race-course) an agitated official emerged from the Jockey Club Stand and asked if I was Mr Colville. When I assented, he said, "It's the Prime Minister wants you on the telephone." "Whatever he asks you to do," advised my innately cautious wife, "say No."

I heard a familiar voice: "Norman Brook tells me you are home on leave. Would you, if it is not inconvenient (but do pray

[1] Later Lord Normanbrook.*

say if it is), take a train to London and come to see me?"

"Tomorrow morning?"

"No, this afternoon."

Of course I did, and was invited to be the new Prime Minister's Principal Private Secretary. I was, by Whitehall standards, some ten years too young for such an appointment. There were two more potent objections. The first was that although I knew a certain amount about foreign affairs and could doubtless get by on Commonwealth, Colonial and Defence matters, and perhaps with luck on Education and Trade, I was abysmally ignorant of the Treasury, of economics generally, of Housing, Local Government, Transport, Pensions, Industry and Agriculture. Secondly, Mr Attlee had appointed to the job, only a month or so previously, David Pitblado,[1] a competent and knowledgeable Treasury official. If Pitblado were now required to make way for me, it would smack of favouritism and those who mattered in Whitehall would resent the imposition of a largely unqualified incumbent to replace a highly qualified one. Moreover, it would be grossly unfair to David Pitblado.

I made these points to Churchill and said that although deeply gratified by the invitation, I felt I must decline. "Rubbish," he replied. "Pitblado is doubtless an excellent man, but I must have somebody I know. Go and talk to Edward Bridges."

Bridges said that if this was what the Prime Minister required, I must do as I was told. I argued and said it would not be regarded as a good start for the new Prime Minister. So he eventually proposed a solution whereby David Pitblado and I should be Joint Principal Private Secretaries. It should have been a recipe for ill-will and mismanagement, but in the event it worked well. I was close to the Prime Minister personally, despite an age gap of forty years, for one of Churchill's endearing

---

[1] Had been a delegate to the San Francisco Conference in 1945. In 1949 he was an Under Secretary in the Treasury whereas I was only a First Secretary in the Foreign Service (who saw no reason whatever to promote me to equal status). Afterwards he was economic Minister at the Embassy in Washington, Permanent Secretary at the Ministry of Power and thereafter at the Ministry of Technology and the Civil Service Department. A civil servant of high ability and unfailing efficiency.

and enduring characteristics was to treat young men as if they were his contemporaries. I became a frequent channel of his communication with other Ministers, many of whom I already knew well. Pitblado for his part handled with exemplary skill the Treasury, the Civil Service and economic affairs.

There were many, including his wife, who did not think Churchill should return to office a month short of his seventy-seventh birthday. At first he himself, as he told me when I rejoined him, intended to remain Prime Minister for one year only, and then hand over to his invariably loyal lieutenant, Anthony Eden, whose courage, energy and integrity, though not always his judgment, Churchill consistently respected. He just wanted, he said, to have time to re-establish the intimate relationship with the United States, which had been a keynote of his policy in the war, and to restore at home the liberties which had been eroded by war-time restrictions and post-war socialist measures.

Circumstances in 1951 were totally different from those existing in 1945, but Churchill began by trying to re-create the situation as he had left it six years before. His faithful associates, General Ismay and Lord Cherwell, were brought into the Cabinet against their own better judgment. Lords Woolton and Leathers were recalled for an unsuccessful experiment as Overlords of clutches of government departments. For a few months Churchill combined, as he had in the war, the office of Minister of Defence with that of Prime Minister; but then it occurred to him that Field Marshal Alexander, of whom he had the highest opinion, would be excellent for the post, oblivious of the fact that Alexander, while a soldier of indisputable gallantry and an excellent emollient as Supreme Allied Commander in Italy, had no experience of Whitehall or of Parliament. So the poor Field Marshal was withdrawn from the Governor Generalship of Canada, in which he was both happy and successful, to become an unhappy and unsuccessful Minister of Defence. General Sir Ian Jacob,* by then Director of Overseas Services at the B.B.C., was conscripted to be Alexander's Chief Staff Officer. When Winston Churchill wanted something and chose to exercise his persuasive gift, there were few who found it possible to refuse.

Thus Auld Lang Syne was ringing out along the Whitehall corridors and I suppose that I myself was a small part of the refrain.

Yet if some were disturbed by this attempt to revert to the past, others were not. In Britain, and perhaps still more in other countries of the free world, the signal "Churchill is back" carried some of the nostalgic appeal that it had for the Royal Navy on September 3rd, 1939. His name was a household word far beyond the shores of the British Isles. Roosevelt was dead; Stalin was now recognised to be an ogre; Churchill alone of the world's political leaders was placed by millions of people on a pedestal wearing a halo. His return to power seemed to many to presage the recovery of hopes tarnished by the dismal aftermath of the war.

If those hopes, like almost all human hopes, fell short of complete fulfilment, it is nevertheless true that in the three and a half years of Churchill's last administration, there was a shedding of austerity, a return to comparative prosperity and a temporary restoration of peace on earth. This was not so in the first year when, as my diary illustrates, the financial situation remained bleak and rationing was as severe as ever. However, late in 1952 the clouds began to lift and by the time of Queen Elizabeth II's Coronation in June 1953, the prospects were brighter than they had been for many years past.

The tones of Auld Lang Syne were gradually muted and in due course the Overlords, Field Marshal Alexander and Lord Cherwell, thankfully departed. General Ismay became Secretary General of N.A.T.O. Sir Ian Jacob, to his great relief, returned to run the B.B.C. Lords Beaverbrook and Bracken, by this time inseparable allies, seldom crossed the threshold of 10 Downing Street, though Bracken's devotion to Churchill did not waver. The Korean war ended; the Coronation was an occasion for even greater national enthusiasm than the royal wedding six years before; Mount Everest was conquered by a British expedition; rationing was a misery soon forgotten; larger foreign travel allowances were granted; and though Churchill's last ambition, to bring the Cold War to an end after Stalin's death, was frustrated, the early 1950s do in retrospect seem like a golden summer.

All this is the more remarkable in that the new administration inherited both a war in the Pacific and an alarming economic crisis at home. It may not be altogether extravagant to suggest that the figure of Winston Churchill brooding benevolently over the scene and, as his eightieth birthday approached, as much cherished by the Labour Party and the Liberals as by his own side, made a significant contribution to the sense of well-being which briefly filled the hearts of men in the United Kingdom and far afield.

With the strain of war-time leadership relaxed, he was now less irascible and impatient than of old and readier to be convinced by argument, provided the right moment was chosen for the exercise. The charm and the lovable qualities were undiminished and at Chartwell, now a more frequent weekend resort than Chequers, he was a solicitous host.

At least until the midsummer of 1953 his mind was as clear and his reactions almost as prompt as in former days. He still dictated incisive minutes, though the menacing red labels, ACTION THIS DAY (carefully hoarded by the messengers at No. 10 and placed on the Cabinet Room table the very day of his return) were no longer in use. His speeches were heard with attention in the House of Commons, reported at length by the press and seldom interrupted except by cheers. He still dominated the Cabinet, now more like Buddha than Achilles, but not with the long monologues, product of weariness, which had irritated his colleagues during the last year of the war.

Like most elderly people, he was bad at remembering names. It had not been one of his more notable gifts ten years previously. When Sir Norman Brook brought Sir Thomas Padmore on to the scene as probationary Deputy Secretary to the Cabinet, Churchill persisted in referring to him as Potsdam; and he said to me one morning, "I don't think much of that fellow Shorthorn." It required ingenuity to discover that the object of his temporary dissatisfaction was General Sir Nevil Brownjohn.

If his memory had lost some of its sharpness, that was only

by contrast with its unusual, indeed phenomenal, strength in former days. In lighter moments he could, and did, still quote verses of poetry, sing the music-hall songs of the 1890s and discourse learnedly on the American Civil War or the campaigns of Marlborough and Prince Eugene. He abandoned his war-time practices of an hour's sleep in the afternoon and perusing the first editions of the following day's newspapers before going to bed; but the number of cigars he smoked remained constant and, although he was never inebriated (or, indeed, drank between meals anything but soda-water faintly flavoured with whisky), he would still consume, without the smallest ill-effect, enough champagne and brandy at luncheon or dinner to incapacitate any lesser man.

As far as current affairs were concerned, he was as attentive to Parliament as ever, but in the ordinary day's business he concentrated his thought on those issues, mainly in the foreign field, that interested him. From time to time this led to clashes with the Foreign Secretary, Anthony Eden, who objected to Prime Ministerial interference in his diocese. Churchill was content to leave much of the rest, except where housing, food and labour relations were concerned, to Ministers and officials whom he no longer pursued on points of detail. He made greater use of his Private Office to handle relationships with his colleagues; he was influenced by the sensible and usually moderating opinions of his new son-in-law and Parliamentary Private Secretary, Christopher Soames; and he listened to the advice of the Secretary to the Cabinet, Sir Norman Brook, whose wisdom and diligence he esteemed and whose company he found so agreeable that he elected him to the Other Club. That was the highest personal honour he could confer, and not one offered to either of Norman Brook's predecessors.

The diary I kept during Churchill's second administration was spasmodic, and latterly confined largely to foreign journeys; for though marriage is an honourable estate, it is seldom a tonic for diarists unless they behave like Pepys.

On November 25th, 1951, I made the following note of a dinner-party conversation at Chequers. There was present

Richard Casey, Australian Minister of Foreign Affairs, at one stage of the war a much praised Minister of State in Cairo and a future Governor General of Australia.

The Prime Minister said that he did not believe total war was likely. If it came, it would be on one of two accounts. Either the Americans, unable or unwilling any longer to pay for the maintenance of Europe, would say to the Russians you must by certain dates withdraw from certain points and meet us on certain requirements: otherwise we shall attack you. Or, the Russians, realising that safety did not come from being strong, but only from being the strongest, might for carefully calculated and not for emotional reasons, decide that they must attack before it was too late. If they did so their first target would be the British Isles, which is the aircraft carrier. It was for that reason that Mr Churchill was anxious to convert this country from its present status of a rabbit into that of a hedgehog.

Mr Casey said that there was an ancient Lebanese proverb to the effect that one did not cut a man's throat when one had already poisoned his soup. Mr Churchill said he agreed: it was a matter of supererogation. Mr Casey thought that until the sores in Malaya, Indo-China and the Middle East had been cured, the Russians might consider that the soup was poisoned.

Churchill wasted no time in setting forth for America. There were defence matters to discuss and the progress of the Korean War. The Americans were bearing the brunt of the fighting, but there was also a sizeable British contingent, including the gallant Gloucestershire Regiment, and representative forces from other members of the United Nations. At the Potsdam Conference Churchill thought well of Truman who had assumed Roosevelt's mantle with shrewdness and determination. Since then there had been the Truman Doctrine, relieving Britain of her burden in liberated Greece; and the two men had established an immediate friendship in 1946, travelling together by train to Fulton,

Missouri, where Churchill roused the world with the eloquent warning he gave in his Iron Curtain speech.

On returning home in January 1952, I wrote this account of our journey to North America:

On Boxing Day I went with John[1] to shoot at Lennoxlove and caught the night train to London in order to prepare for departure to America with Mr Churchill. We boarded the *Queen Mary* on New Year's Eve, a party of thirty in all which included Eden, Ismay, Cherwell, Slim[2] (C.I.G.S.), McGrigor[3] (First Sea Lord), Roger Makins,[4] Norman Brook and David Pitblado. The *Queen Mary*'s anchor was found to be fouled and so we had to spend the night on board, alongside the quay at Southampton. Lord Mountbatten came from Broadlands to dine and talked arrant political nonsense: he might have learned by heart a leader from the *New Statesman*. The P.M. laughed at him but did not, so Pug Ismay thought, snub him sufficiently. He caused much irritation to the Chiefs of Staff. I escorted Mountbatten off the ship. As we walked down the corridor he put his arm on my shoulder and said: "Without you, Jock, I should feel no confidence, but as you are back I know all will be well." It was, of course, intended as a friendly remark, but flattery, especially when so exaggerated, makes one wonder why one should be thought so naive.

During the crossing we worked on our briefs: oh, the amount of paper that even a small conference evokes! It was very difficult to get the P.M. to read any of it. He said he was going to America to re-establish relations, not to transact business. Fellow passengers included Hector McNeil, Ruth Draper[5] and

---

[1] My brother-in-law, John, Earl of Ellesmere, later 6th Duke of Sutherland.

[2] Field Marshal Viscount Slim, Commander of the 14th Army and hero of the campaign in Burma. C.I.G.S., 1948–52. Governor General of Australia, 1953–60.

[3] Admiral of the Fleet Sir Rhoderick McGrigor, C. in C., Home Fleet, 1948–50. First Sea Lord, 1951–55.

[4] Lord Sherfield.*

[5] Celebrated American whose impersonations held audiences sometimes in helpless laughter and sometimes close to tears.

Priscilla Tweedsmuir[1] – of all of whom we saw a good deal.

On January 3rd we steamed into New York and our party was taken ashore by special arrangement on the Brooklyn shore. The reception was on a huge scale but ill-organised and Pug Ismay and I got separated and all but lost. There followed a flight to Washington and four nights in that city, with conferences at the White House, two of which I attended. Churchill stayed at the British Embassy with the Ambassador, Sir Oliver Franks.* President Truman was affable but not impressive and I did not think Acheson[2] or Lovett[3] anything out of the way.

There was an embarrassing incident at the first White House meeting. The President and the Prime Minister sat facing each other, flanked by their respective Chiefs of Staff, and one of the main topics for discussion was naval command of the N.A.T.O. forces, to which we laid claim since the Americans were in command on land. It fell to the First Sea Lord, the diminutive but intelligent Sir Rhoderick McGrigor, to present our case. He went red in the face, large drops of perspiration appeared on his brow and he was too overawed to do more than stutter a few disjointed words. The C.I.G.S., General Slim, stepped into the breach and presented the naval case coolly and calmly. It was a magnificent *tour de force* by the representative of another service and it was evident that the Americans were as impressed as we were. They agreed to the British proposal.

On January 9th we listened to the President address Congress on the State of the Union and then went by train to New York. Before we left the Embassy the Prime Minister, at Sir Oliver Franks' request, agreed to address the staff assembled in the garden. When he walked out on to the terrace for this purpose,

[1] Priscilla Thomson by birth. Her second husband was John Buchan's eldest son. She was the slim, attractive and quick-witted Conservative M.P. for South Aberdeen. Minister of State in the Scottish Office and then in the Foreign Office in Edward Heath's 1970 Conservative Government.

[2] Dean Acheson served in Roosevelt's administration and was Secretary of State in Truman's. Respected and liked by Anthony Eden. It was he who said, "Britain has lost an Empire and has not found a rôle."

[3] Robert A. Lovett, a partner in Brown Brothers Harriman. Influential member of Roosevelt's war-time Government and Secretary for Defense in Truman's Cabinet from 1951 to 1953.

he gasped with astonishment. In front of him, filling the entire garden, was a crowd not, as he had expected, of some fifty or sixty people, but, including the wives and children, the best part of a thousand. The service departments in particular were grossly overmanned. He addressed the huge gathering most affably, but he instructed me to procure a detailed list of the officers attached to the Embassy. I did so when we returned to London and discovered that there were, amongst many others, forty-seven lieutenant-colonels and forty-three wing commanders. Evidently nobody had given thought to reducing the vast staffs established in a war which had ended six and a half years previously. The Prime Minister then issued a peremptory order, in his capacity as Minister of Defence, and a drastic reduction was effected.

The P.M. stayed with Bernie Baruch at his flat in E. 66th Street and I with the Henry Hydes[1] in their house on E. 70th Street. On Thursday, January 10th, the Hydes took me to dine with Mrs George Widener and on to the Metropolitan Opera where, in the interval, I met the Duke and Duchess of Windsor and the latter's friend, Mr Donoghue.

Late that night we entrained for Ottawa, where the P.M. had a great reception. We stayed with the Alexanders at Rideau Hall, Christopher Soames having meanwhile joined the P.M.'s party in New York. We were exceedingly comfortable at Government House, and nobody could have been more charming than the Alexanders. Moreover I was pleased because I wrote a speech for the P.M. to use at a banquet for both houses of Parliament, in respect of which he said: "This is very good; too good. I may feel bound to use it in which case it will be the first time in my career I have ever used somebody else's speech." In the event he did not; but I was flattered.

While we were at Rideau Hall, Churchill discussed with Alexander the unsatisfactory situation in Malaya where Chinese

---

[1] Henry Hyde, brought up in France and educated in England, was my greatest friend at Cambridge. In the war he joined General Donovan's O.S.S. and was responsible for its successful operations in France. He became a successful international lawyer in New York. At this time he was married to an extremely pretty French wife, Mimi de la Grange.

Communist guerillas were attacking troops and British-owned plantations. A new, energetic and resourceful Commander in Chief was required, and Churchill ordered Sir Gerald Templer[1] to be flown out to Ottawa for inspection and interrogation by himself and Alexander. The latter's high esteem of Templer, who was then unknown to Churchill, carried weight, but on arrival at Ottawa Templer himself so impressed Churchill that he offered him the command right away.

On the 15th we left by train for Washington and on the 17th the P.M. made a great speech to Congress, which I attended on the floor of the House. Lord Knollys,[2] Bill Elliot[3] and other Embassy people present thought it had had a chilly reception; but we were quite wrong. Congress reacted slowly, but the subsequent praise was generous – except at home where the Labour Party asserted that the P.M. had committed us to a more active part against China.

Churchill had been still in bed putting the finishing touches to his speech when Sir Roger Makins came into the room to say the cars were at the door and we ought already to be leaving for the Capitol. In the Prime Minister's speech it was essential to refer to Britain's contribution in the Korean War, which had been raging since 1950. "If the Chinese cross the Yalu River, our reply will be – what?" "Prompt, resolute and effective," suggested Roger Makins on the spur of the moment. "Excellent," said Churchill. He wrote these words in the text of his speech, got up, dressed and reached the Capitol with two minutes to spare.

It was these words with no special significance except to declare that the Allies would react strongly to such an attack, which the Labour Opposition interpreted to mean that an atomic

[1] Field Marshal Sir Gerald Templer. Brought the Malayan operations to an entirely successful conclusion.
[2] 2nd Viscount Knollys. Won a D.F.C. in the First World War. Was Governor of Bermuda, 1941–43, Chairman of Vickers Ltd, and of several insurance companies. Public spirited and a delightful personality.
[3] Air Chief Marshal Sir William Elliot, Chairman of the British Joint Services Commission in Washington.

bomb would be used. Such a thought had not crossed Churchill's mind nor, I believe, President Truman's.

We returned to New York on the 19th and though the P.M. caught a cold which prevented a triumphal drive down Broadway, we had a gay time. Then on January 23rd we sailed in the *Queen Mary* and reached Southampton on my thirty-seventh birthday, January 28th. Meg had come down with Mrs Churchill, Mary, Lady Brook, Lady Moran and Mrs Pitblado to greet us and they all had luncheon with us on board.

A few weeks later I wrote this further narrative:

On February 5th there began a foreign affairs debate in the House. I heard Anthony Eden make a somewhat insipid speech and then the Opposition put down a vote of censure on the P.M. personally. He prepared to answer it on the following day by a fighting speech revealing the dramatic fact that the Labour Government had gone further in committing us to bomb China in certain circumstances than anyone supposed and that he had entered into no new commitments.

On the morning of February 6th I arrived at No. 10 early and asked the Private Secretary on duty for the text of the speech. He said that there was no need to think of it further: Edward Ford[1] had just been round from Buckingham Palace to announce that the King was dead.

When I went to the Prime Minister's bedroom he was sitting alone with tears in his eyes, looking straight in front of him and reading neither his official papers nor the newspapers. I had not realised how much the King meant to him. I tried to cheer him up by saying how well he would get on with the new Queen, but all he could say was that he did not know her and that she was only a child. He summoned a Cabinet that morning and he

---

[1] Served in the Grenadier Guards. Second Private Secretary to George VI and Elizabeth II. Secretary to the Pilgrim Trust, 1967–75, and Registrar of the Order of Merit. Married Virginia, the daughter of Lord Brand.

insisted on my attending it. It was, I think, the only time I attended a whole Cabinet meeting.[1]

For a week all normal business came to a standstill, while the world showed a large and genuine measure of grief, the new Queen returned from Kenya and the Government dealt with all the ceremonial and constitutional matters attendant on a Demise of the Crown. All had in fact been prepared the previous September when the King had his serious lung operation.

On Friday, February 15th, Meg and I went to the King's funeral at St George's, Windsor, on a bright, cold day, and were moved by the sound of the pipes drawing closer and closer as the funeral cortège approached the Chapel. I remembered so vividly sitting in the nave on a warm June evening in 1947 when the King and Queen took their guests there to hear Dr Harris play the organ.

During the next weeks much happened. First there was trouble over the name of the Royal House. Prince Philip wrote a strongly, but ably, worded memorandum protesting against a proposed Proclamation saying that the House remained the House of Windsor. This annoyed the P.M. and on his behalf I attended two meetings of the Lord Chancellor, Lord Privy Seal, Home Secretary and Leader of the House of Commons (Crookshank)[2] to draft a firm, negative answer. In the end I had more or less to recast it myself and the P.M. accepted it in final form on March 12th. This had all arisen because Queen Mary sent for me on February 18th to say that Prince Ernst August of Hanover had come back from Broadlands and informed her that Lord Mountbatten had said to an assembled house party of royal guests that the House of Mountbatten now reigned. The poor old lady, who had spent a sleepless night, was relieved when I said that I doubted if the Cabinet would contemplate such a change. Indeed when I told the P.M. he had at once

---

[1] It was not until after Churchill resigned that officials, apart from the Cabinet Office Secretariat, were admitted to Cabinet meetings.

[2] A Grenadier officer in the First World War. M.P. for the Gainsborough division of Lincolnshire. In February 1952 he was Minister of Health and Leader of the House of Commons.

consulted the Cabinet who said unanimously that they would tolerate no such thing.

The name of Windsor had been adopted by a decree of King George V in 1917. It was alleged, apocryphally or not, that on hearing the news the Kaiser, not usually renowned for his wit, said: "Well then, let us have tonight at the Opera a performance of the Merry Wives of Saxe-Coburg-Gotha." The name Mountbatten was also new, having replaced Battenberg at the same time as the Royal House, which had no generally accepted name after the death of Queen Victoria (the last of the Hanoverians), became Windsor and Queen Mary's family, the Tecks, became Cambridges. Prince Philip had logic on his side when he suggested that his children should be the House of Edinburgh; but the trouble was caused by Lord Mountbatten's tactless assertion which put both the Cabinet and the leaders of the Opposition up in arms.

Then came the foreign affairs debate which had been adjourned. The P.M. made a good but much interrupted speech, discrediting Attlee and Morrison and dumbfounding his attackers. He followed it up the next week with a speech in the Defence Debate, two days after handing the Ministry of Defence over to Lord Alexander. This was followed by a clever Budget, slashing the food subsidies but providing new incentives for hard work and overtime by lowering the bottom rates of income tax.

But all this had been a severe strain on the P.M. On Friday, February 22nd, Lord Moran came to me with the news that on the previous evening the P.M. had had a small arterial spasm. This might be the precursor of an immediate stroke; if not, it was at least a plain warning that if the pressure was not relaxed dire results would follow in six months or less. He wanted political advice and so we went to see Lord Salisbury and Tommy Lascelles. The former thought W. might go to the Lords, leaving Eden to manage the Commons, and thus remain P.M. till after the Coronation in May 1953. Nowadays a repetition of the

Salisbury–A. J. Balfour[1] partnership would normally be impracticable; but Winston is not an ordinary person, the country as a whole would not like to see him go, and with America as with the continent of Europe he is far our greatest asset.

We kept our counsel until the debates and the budget were over, but on March 13th Lord Moran, having first consulted Mrs Churchill, wrote him a letter – which did not, however, tell quite the whole story. He took it, so I gather, with sang-froid; but he does not know that anyone apart from Mrs C. knows of this matter.

Friday, March 14th

I was on duty this week-end. Instead of staying at Chartwell as usual, Meg and I both went to spend the week-end with Mary and Christopher Soames and were lodged in the cottage in the garden which Winston himself built.

After dinner I went up to the big house. I scored a success – for the Admiralty – in putting W. off Admiral Vian,[2] whom he was contemplating forcing the Admiralty to send as C. in C., Portsmouth instead of Edelston, by telling him the deplorable impressions Vian created at Lisbon.

Saturday, March 15th

Quite busy all day. The Mark Wyndhams came to lunch with the Soameses. They are obviously *not* on good terms with John and Pamela (whom I like very much and with whom we stayed at Petworth a few weeks ago).[3] After luncheon Winston and I saw

[1] From 1895 to 1902, while his uncle, Lord Salisbury, was Prime Minister, A. J. Balfour was First Lord of the Treasury and Leader of the House of Commons, becoming Prime Minister himself in 1902.

[2] As Captain of H.M.S. *Cossack* he had by a daring raid into a Norwegian fjord, in March 1940, rescued the British merchant seamen held prisoner on the German ship *Altmark*. However, as C. in C. of the Home Fleet in the early 1950s he was much criticised by the officers of his flagship, *Vanguard*, and he was disliked both in naval and civilian circles.

[3] John Wyndham, later Lord Egremont, was Mark Wyndham's elder brother. Much cherished private secretary to Harold Macmillan, he married the exceedingly beautiful Pamela Wyndham-Quinn and inherited Petworth and Cockermouth from his uncle.

a film on guided missiles, explained by a brilliant man called Mitchell from the Ministry of Supply. These will evidently revolutionise defence in war and may go some way to neutralise the atomic bomb.

Sunday, March 16th
At 6.00 we all went to a film (*Edward and Caroline* – French and admirable) at Chartwell, where we dined afterwards. W. liked Meg (who was petrified of him) and told me he found her charming indeed. He is worried about Egypt, where he thinks Eden is throwing the game away; irritated with the Prof. who is being tiresome about atomic matters; and disturbed by the thought that the old-age pensioners may suffer in consequence of an otherwise admirable Budget.

Saturday, March 22nd – Sunday, March 23rd
Drove to Chequers with the P.M. Meg was invited for the weekend and other guests were the Salisburys, the Alexanders and the Soameses. Lord Montgomery and the Prof. came to luncheon on Sunday – Monty, mellow and in good form but, as ever, trying to lobby the P.M. about matters in which he is but slightly interested (this time Greece and Turkey) or on which he hardly thinks Monty an expert. The P.M. is angry, almost to breaking point, with the Prof. who is digging in his toes over the control of atomic energy. In the long gallery on Sunday night, after the rest had gone to bed, he told Christopher and me that the programme of the Tory Party must be: "Houses and meat and not being scuppered." He didn't feel quite happy about the latter though he does not himself think war probable unless the Americans lose patience. As he subsequently added, perhaps "not being broke" is going to be our major difficulty and preoccupation.

Quite favourably impressed by Alex this time. He is not original or clever, but I thought he showed common sense on most things, even though he usually took the obvious line. Surprisingly he feels strongly about class distinction: he loved Canada for its absence and is alarmed by it in his own Brigade of Guards.

Friday, April 4th

Last Monday we moved into 60 Westminster Gardens and we are now in a state of chaos. This morning the results of the L.C.C. elections, which went strongly for the socialists, were published. The P.M. took them well though he found them a shock. The reason, I have no doubt, is that the country hoped a Tory Government would mean relaxations and more food: in fact it has meant controls as stringent as ever and severer rationing.

Tonight Meg and I dined with Joey[1] and Sarah Legh to meet the Queen. Jamie Leveson[2] was the sixth. It was the first time I had seen her since her Accession, though I had lunched with her at Clarence House just before Christmas. She looked handsome in black with two strings of huge pearls, seemed animated and gave us both the impression that she was at ease and self-possessed.

Saturday, April 5th

Meg has been feeling more than usually unwell of late. She had a pregnancy test this morning and it was positive.

Monday, April 7th

A tedious Honours Committee this morning. Some of the P.M.'s wishes cause consternation – especially baronetcies for "Bomber Harris" and Louis Spears.

Tuesday, April 8th

Trouble with the Ministry of Transport which has been brewing for long came to something of a head. The P.M. wants to denationalise road haulage as quickly as possible. Personally I think that undoing what the last government did, in the certain knowledge that they will re-do it when next they come into power, is folly; and this applies more to iron and steel than to road transport.

---

[1] Hon. Sir Piers Legh, Master of the Queen's Household. He had an apartment in St James's Palace.

[2] Later 5th Earl Granville, M.C. A first cousin of the Queen.

There is also trouble with Eden over the Egyptian situation, the P.M. wishing to take a much stronger line with the Egyptians than Eden does. The latter is rather discredited in the P.M.'s eyes at present. I don't myself quite see how he can prove a very good successor to Winston when he has no knowledge or experience of anything except foreign affairs.

Wednesday, April 9th
This afternoon Queen Mary, who had been ill, asked me to come and see her and received me in bed (looking very regal all the same in a vast bed, with a monogrammed back, an embroidered quilt of extraordinary beauty and a huge canopy). She kept her eyes closed throughout the conversation but in spite of feeling wretched, and constantly complaining how tiresome it was to be old, she was very determined in what she said and more than usually downright on the subject of her relations.

Lunched today at the French Embassy, a party in honour of Pug Ismay who is going – strongly against his original wishes – as Secretary General of N.A.T.O.

Saturday, April 19th
W.S.C. has been at Chartwell over Easter with a heavy cold and I have been moving things in and out of Westminster Gardens, Meg being not allowed to do anything strenuous. I went down to Chartwell for the night and was alone with the P.M. who is greatly exercised over the position of nationalised transport which is now in the home fore-front, the real problem being how to denationalise the road transport, open it to free competition and yet prevent the railways from becoming insolvent. The position as far as I am concerned is getting a little difficult: W. complains he sees very little of me, but I can't push myself more to the front without hurting my colleagues' feelings. But W. says he has nothing in common with any of them (they haven't the same friends and don't play Oklahoma![1]) and won't have them to Chartwell if he can avoid it.

---

[1] A two-handed card game popular at the time.

Am in correspondence with George Trevelyan, the Lord Chancellor and Tommy Lascelles about a book called *The Daughter of Time*[1] which seeks to prove that the Princes in the Tower were murdered not by Richard III but by Henry VII.

Saturday, April 26th – Sunday, April 27th
Went to Chartwell for the weekend. The P.M. plans to sack Lord Woolton and make "Mr Cube" (Lord Lyle) Chairman of the Tory Party.[2] He also revealed to me a private project for getting the Queen Mother made Governor General of Australia. We went through the Honours List during the weekend and I was pleasantly surprised to find the P.M. amenable to my views on most points.

On Sunday evening Lord and Lady Donegall[3] came bringing a Russian film called *The Fall of Berlin*. Russia, it seems, won the war single-handed and now breathes nothing but peace.

I gave Christopher Soames a lecture on not appearing to have too much of the P.M.'s ear. It is dangerous for his future. I like him increasingly, though his manners can be coarse. Brendan Bracken, with whom I had a drink the other day, says that Eden is violent against Christopher.

Tuesday, May 6th
Tonight I went with the P.M. to dine with the Massiglis[4] at the French Embassy. The others at dinner were Eden, Alexander, General Juin[5] and Gérard André, also Madame M. who couldn't

---

[1] A book by Josephine Tey (Elizabeth Mackintosh) who also wrote (as Gordon Daviot) the play *Richard of Bordeaux*. She argued for the theory that Henry VII, not Richard III, murdered the Princes in the Tower. This fascinated Sir Alan Lascelles, the Lord Chancellor (Lord Simonds) and me. I persuaded Churchill to read the book: he said he still thought Richard III was the villain.

[2] He afterwards preferred the idea of Malcolm McCorquodale.

[3] 6th Marquess. Born when his alleged father, the 5th Marquess, was eighty-one. His heir and cousin (b. 1861) was probably in fact his father, but had to be content with remaining the heir for as long as he lived. Donegall wrote articles for the *Sunday Despatch*.

[4] One of de Gaulle's right-hand men and a powerful force for moderation. A successful French Ambassador in London after the war.

[5] Marshal of France. Joined the Allies in 1942 and commanded Free French troops in North Africa and in Italy.

bear to be out of it but left us at the end of dinner. General Juin
was inhibited by his bad English. The P.M. said Germany must
be given fair play: if France would not co-operate we, America
and Germany must go forward without her. He wanted to see
British, American, German and French contingents march past
him at Strasbourg, each to their own national songs: in creating
international unity, national marching songs could play a great
part.

When Juin said that General Koenig had now gone into politics
the P.M., looking at Alexander, said far be it from him to run
down soldiers turned politician. Look, he said, at Napoleon.
Wellington, too, I ventured. No, he replied, Wellington was a
politician turned soldier. A totally invalid statement.

Alexander, next to whom I sat, said to me that war was a
tradition among men. As Clausewitz had put it, it was a way of
pursuing national policy "by other means". But he thought the
atomic bomb might well put a stop to all that: it might be the
end of war by making war impossible. He thought, too, that now
was the time to show an imaginative policy to Germany: we
should lose all if we niggled.

Massigli said that Pinay, the new French P.M., had come to
stay. He believed a new political stability was dawning in France.

Thursday, May 15th
Tonight the P.M. and Mrs C. gave a farewell dinner for the
Eisenhowers at No. 10, on the eve of his departure from
S.H.A.P.E. to become a candidate in the Presidential Election.
There were thirty-two to dinner, including most of the war-time
Chiefs and the present Service Ministers – Alexanders, Tedders, Alanbrookes, Portals, Jumbo Wilson, Attlees, etc. Both
the P.M. and Ike made admirable speeches. When Ike left he
said that if he were elected he would pay just one visit outside
the U.S.A. – to the U.K. – in order to show our special
relationship. The atmosphere could not have been more cordial
– though things almost started badly with neither the P.M. nor
Mrs C. knowing that it was white tie and decorations.

Friday, May 16th
Went to Chartwell this evening. Alone with the P.M. who is
low. Of course the Government is in a trough, but his periods
of lowness grow more frequent and his concentration less good.
The bright and sparkling intervals still come, and they are still
unequalled, but age is beginning to show. Tonight he spoke of
coalition. The country needed it he said, and it must come. He
would retire in order to make it possible; he might even make
the demand for it an excuse for retiring. Four-fifths of the people
of this country were agreed on four-fifths of the things to be
done.

Saturday, May 17th
A heatwave. I lunched alone with W. who recited a great deal
of poetry. While he slept in the afternoon I bathed in the
swimming pool, and then we drove for two hours to Chequers.
On the way he dictated notes for a speech to wind up the
transport debate next Wednesday. He says he can only dictate
in a car nowadays. His theme seems a good one: the nationalisation by the socialists of only 41,000 vehicles was for doctrinaire, not practical motives, and they need 80,000 people,
including 12,000 clerks, to run them. Private owners [of transport for hire] to a total of 800,000 have been driven to the most
uneconomic measures to survive. When he had finished he said
to me: "It is a great mistake to be too mechanically minded in
affairs of State."
   At Chequers were Lord Montgomery, Duchess of Devonshire
(Moucha), Antony and Dot Head, Marques and Marquesa de
Casa Valdes and their pretty daughter Maria.
   The men sat up till 2.30 gossiping about strategy and Generals
in a lively manner.

Sunday, May 18th
Heatwave intensified. Worked with W. all the morning; sat on
the lawn and gossiped most of the afternoon: walked on the
monument hill (the whole party went, notwithstanding all the
picnickers) after tea. Monty in role of grand inquisitor: how did
the P.M. define a great man? Was Hitler great? (P.M. said No

– he made too many mistakes). How could P.M. maintain that
Napoleon was great when he was the Hitler of the nineteenth
century? And surely the great religious leaders were the real
great men? The P.M. said their greatness was indisputable but
it was of a different kind. Christ's story was unequalled and his
death to save sinners unsurpassed; moreover the Sermon on
the Mount was the last word in ethics.

Monty has become a mellow, lovable exhibitionist; tamed but
lonely and pathetic. He is not afraid of saying anything to
anybody. But Maria de Casa Valdes scored (to Monty's great
delight) when she asked him: "But you tell me you don't drink,
and you don't smoke: what *do* you do that is wrong? Bite your
nails?"

Monday, May 19th
Drove to London in shimmering heat with Antony Head.
Attended the first meeting of the Coronation Joint Executive
Committee at St James's Palace, Bernard Norfolk presiding over
a large mixed Commonwealth gathering most competently.[1]

Tuesday, May 20th
This evening Brendan, with whom I had a drink, was very
gloomy about the Government's prospect, doubtful about W.'s
ability to go on and highly critical of R. A. Butler* whose financial
policy he has been attacking vigorously in the *Financial Times*.

Wednesday, May 21st
Transport debate in House of Commons. W. who spoke fifth
made a good impression, but I cannot help feeling it is both
wrong and foolish to denationalise transport and steel, however
doctrinaire may have been the motives of the late Government
in nationalising them. When the Labour Government get back
they will be renationalised and this political game is not only
unsettling for the economic life of the country but a blow to the

---

[1] The Duke of Norfolk, Earl Marshal, was in overall charge. At this and
subsequent meetings the Committee recommended that the Coronation
should not be televised. The Cabinet accepted this recommendation, but
the Queen did not.

constitutional "Gentleman's Agreement" that one Government did not normally set about undoing the work of its predecessor. It is clear that a large element in the Tory party feel the same.

Friday, May 23rd
W., who had been at Chartwell all day, came up to speak at a Tax Inspectors' dinner with a speech almost entirely written by me. This is indeed a sign of advancing senility – and it wasn't nearly as good as the one I wrote for him in Ottawa.

Friday, May 30th
The country is in a bad way. It is difficult to see how our economic ills can be cured and at the moment nothing that is done seems to be more than a short-term palliative. The remedy for 50 million people living in an island which can maintain 30 million and no longer leads the world in industrial exports or in capital assets invested abroad is hard to find. Harold Macmillan said to me at the Turf yesterday that he thought development of the Empire into an economic unit as powerful as the U.S.A. and the U.S.S.R. was the only possibility. At present this seems to be neither pursued nor envisaged.

The Government is in a bad way too. Their popularity has fallen owing to bad publicity, rising prices and a silly policy of denationalisation. Winston is, I fear, personally blamed both in the country and by his own party in the House. Mrs Churchill does not think he will last long as Prime Minister.

Saturday, May 31st
Went to Milton[1] to stay with Tom Fitzwilliam[2] for Whitsun.

There was a Conservative Fête on the Monday, addressed by Miss Patricia Hornsby Smith[3] who was staying in the house.

The Duke of Rutland, Elizabeth Ann Naylor-Leyland and I judged a beauty competition.

[1] The Fitzwilliams' house near Peterborough.
[2] 10th and last Earl Fitzwilliam, owner of Wentworth and Milton. He married Joyce, widow of Lord Fitzalan of Derwent, was renowned as a judge of fox-hounds, and was a kind and generous host.
[3] Conservative M.P. for Chislehurst. Under Secretary at the Ministry of Health and later at the Home Office. Made a peeress in 1977.

Friday, June 13th – Sunday, June 15th

I spent the weekend at Chartwell. Last Friday and Saturday I went racing with the P.M. at Lingfield. On Saturday evening Lord Cherwell and Bill Deakin came to stay. We did little work, but W. was in better form than of late, though still depressed. He told me that if Eisenhower were elected President, he would have another shot at making peace by means of a meeting of the Big Three. For that alone it would perhaps be worth remaining in office. He thought that while Stalin lived we were safer from attack than if he died and his lieutenants started scrambling for the succession.

He also elaborated his theme of "the commodity sterling dollar" – an international medium of exchange based on the world price of, say, fifteen commodities over a period of three years. This year, for instance, the years chosen would be 1948, 1949, 1950; next year 1949, 1950, 1951; and so on. The Prof. said that such a scheme had possibilities if the Americans would lend it their support and their material backing.

Feeling wearied by the prospects of the future I wrote the following in the early hours of the morning:

It is foolish to continue living with illusions. One may bury one's head in the past, reading James Boswell or the privately printed letters of Labouchère to Lord Rosebery; or one may talk of forcing reality on the people by a slump with the accompaniment of hunger and unemployment and the consequent acceptance of a lower standard of living. But the facts are stark. At the moment we are just paying our way. A trade recession in America will break us; the competition of German metallurgical industries and the industrialisation of countries which were once the market for our industrial products will ruin our trade sooner or later and sap the remaining capital on which our high standard of living is based.

It costs too much to live as we do. The price of keeping a man in hospital is more than £700 a year. To send an individual to settle in the Commonwealth costs £1,000 a head.

What can we do? Increasing productivity is only a palliative in the face of foreign competition. We cannot till sufficient soil to feed 50 million people. We cannot emigrate fast enough to meet the danger, even if we were willing to face the consequent abdication of our position as a great power and even if there were places for two-fifths of our population to go.

The British people will face war or the threat of invasion with courage. It yet remains to be seen if they will accept a lower standard of living.

Lord Cherwell sees hope in the union of the English Speaking World, economically and politically. He thinks that just as the Scots complained of Union with England but ended by dominating Great Britain, so we in the end should dominate America. He thinks that Roosevelt, had he lived, and Winston, had he remained in power in 1945, might have led us far along the road to common citizenship. They often spoke of it. But now England, and Europe, distrust, dislike and despise the United States.

Some pin their faith in the development of the Empire as a great economic unit, equal in power to Russia and the U.S.A. We have left it late. Ambitious efforts, such as the groundnuts scheme, have failed.

It is easier for the old. Their day is almost over. Meg and I hope for a child in November. It should be easier for him or her if neither hunger nor nuclear fission cut life short, because the child will grow into a new world. We are the transitional generation, who have climbed to the watershed and will soon look down the other side, on a new world. It will be wiser neither to think nor to speak too much of the past.

The Prime Minister is depressed and bewildered. He said to me this evening: "The zest is diminished." I think it is more that he cannot see the light at the end of the tunnel.

Nor can I. But it is 1.30 a.m., approaching the hour when courage and life are at their lowest ebb.

Friday, June 20th
I again went to Chartwell. Alone with the P.M. but joined by Norman Brook in the evening.

After we had fed the fish – indoors and out[1] – and driven away the horses which were eating the water lilies in the lake, we had lunch together. W. greatly exercised by the economic prospects. He said: "I can assure you it is the most horrible landscape on which I have ever looked in my unequalled experience." But when champagne and brandy had done their work he talked of the Chamberlain family – Joe the greatest of the three; Austen, generous and gallant but whose whole work came to nothing; Neville who was not above scheming to ruin Baldwin at the time of the Duff Cooper–Petter[2] election in the St George's Division of Westminster so that Neville might profit by his fall.

After the usual film, Christopher and Mary dined and Norman, who wanted to talk confidentially about the weak position of sterling and suggest changes in the Government, was irked because Christopher would not leave us. However he did tell the P.M. that Woolton should give up the Home Affairs Committee and that Eden should take it over, relinquishing the F.O. The P.M. also thinks Eden should have a change but says he is "Foreign Officissimus" and doesn't want to go.

Saturday, June 21st
A somewhat wasted morning (much more fish-feeding); luncheon with W. and Norman devoted to desultory discussion of the Treasury, of Defence and of the economic position; and returned to London with Norman, leaving the P.M. to go to Chequers.

Monday, June 23rd
This afternoon Sir Oliver Franks came in, like a breath of fresh air from the U.S.A. He thought everybody too gloomy. We must edge our way out of this crisis: the balance of payments had begun to improve, as he had said it would, in May; time was

---

[1] Apart from his outdoor ponds, full of large golden orfe, Churchill established in his working library at Chartwell tanks full of brightly-coloured small tropical fish, each tank supplied with an elaborate oxygen apparatus. Feeding the fish was a frequent diversion from serious work.

[2] Sir Ernest Petter was put up by Lords Beaverbrook and Rothermere as an anti-Baldwin candidate.

needed for remedial measures to take effect. People talked a lot of the popular insensitiveness to our plight; but as four-fifths of the population had known seven years of prosperity and a standard of living higher than ever before, it was not surprising they paid little attention to cries of economic alarm. Successive Chancellors of the Exchequer spoke as if the impoverishment felt by one-fifth of the people was an experience shared by all.

I gathered he would not consider the chairmanship of the Governors of the B.B.C. which W. had hoped he would take.

Went to see Brendan. Discussed the same theme as with Franks. He thinks the Overlords should go, especially Woolton, Leathers and the Prof. He says Eden's small coterie of advisers and friends don't want him to leave the F.O.: they think he might mar his reputation in other fields.

Monday, August 11th
Returned from Chartwell after a long weekend. I have been particularly slothful about this diary of late, partly because it has been such a hot summer.

The session ended in heated feelings, partly engendered by the Government's forecast of important decisions to announce, coupled with their failure in the event to do so – and one of the worst speeches I have ever heard W. make about defence.

Now the Churchills are at Chartwell. Just before he went (Mrs C. being at Capri) W. took Meg and me to see *The Innocents*, a stage version of Henry James' *The Turn of the Screw*. He got a great welcome but embarrassed us by being unable to hear and asking questions in a loud voice.

Philip's Dragon *Orthos* sank under him at Cowes last Saturday; King Farouk has abdicated; the Persian situation deteriorates with the return of Mossadeq[1] to power; Anthony Eden and Clarissa Churchill are engaged. Clarissa, who was at Chartwell for the weekend, is very beautiful but she is still strange and bewildering, cold if sometimes witty, arrogant at times and

---

[1] Democratic but nationalist Prime Minister of Persia, who quarrelled with the Shah, sought to nationalise the British oil installations at Abadan and invariably fainted at awkward moments.

understanding at others. Perhaps marriage will change her and will also help to calm the vain and occasionally hysterical Eden. W. feels avuncular to his orphaned niece, gave her a cheque for £500 and told me he thought she had a most unusual personality.

Friday August 15th – Monday, August 18th
Meg and I spent the weekend at Chartwell. Montgomery was the other guest, with his persistent but oddly endearing egotism (even on the croquet lawn). He and I and Sarah were godparents to Jeremy Soames, christened in Westerham Church on Sunday, 17th. On the 18th Christopher and I shot duck at Sheffield Park and lunched there; in the evening Churchills, Soameses and Colvilles went to see *The Yeomen of the Guard* at Streatham. The P.M. was received with immense acclamation by the audience.

Friday, August 22nd – Monday, August 25th
Again to Chartwell with Meg, this time alone with the Churchills except for Horatia Seymour and in glorious sunny weather. There is a slight drama. W. has persuaded Truman to join with him in sending a message, signed by them both, to Mossadeq in Teheran about the Persian oil question. W. himself did it and the F.O. and oil people agreed. It is the first time since 1945 that the Americans have joined with us in taking overt joint action against a third power. Fear of ganging up has hitherto prevented them. But Anthony Eden, completing his honeymoon in Lisbon, is furious. It is not the substance but the method which displeases him: the stealing by Winston of his personal thunder. Moreover, should Eisenhower be elected President of the U.S.A. in November – an event thought to be decreasingly probable – there will be further trouble on this score, because W. has several times revealed to me his hopes of a joint approach to Stalin, proceeding perhaps to a congress in Vienna where the Potsdam Conference would be reopened and concluded. If the Russians were unco-operative, the cold war would be intensified by us: "Our young men," W. said to me, "would as soon be killed carrying truth as death."

Meg and I spent all September at Mertoun.[1] *When I returned to London at the end of the month I accompanied the Prime Minister to Balmoral where he went in his capacity as Prime Minister at his own suggestion. The Queen and Prince Philip, who had a very young party staying with them, may have been a little reluctant, but the visit went off well and was in the event enjoyed by both sides, although Winston (aged nearly seventy-eight and not having touched a gun for years) complained to me on the way home that he thought he should have been asked to shoot!*

Sunday, November 9th

I have not written this for many weeks, partly from laziness, partly because living in flats, with a shared writing table, militates heavily against keeping a diary. I have been to Chartwell numerous weekends, but although much has been said and a few things done there is nothing especially noteworthy. However, I do record that last Wednesday evening, November 5th, after Eisenhower's victory in the American Presidential Election had been announced, Winston said to me: "For your private ear, I am greatly disturbed. I think this makes war much more probable."

He (W.) is getting tired and visibly ageing. He finds it hard work to compose a speech and ideas no longer flow. He has made two strangely simple errors in the H. of C. lately, and even when addressing the Harrow boys in Speech Room last Friday what he said dragged and lacked fire. But he has had a tiring week, with speeches, important Cabinet decisions, etc., so that I may be unduly alarmist.

On Friday, November 7th, Ashley Clarke[2] lunched with me at the Turf and offered me the post of Counsellor and head of Chancery in Washington next summer if I can escape from No. 10 then.

---

[1] My brother-in-law's house in Berwickshire.

[2] Afterwards Ambassador in Rome. His knowledge of both music and Italian was such that he was able to give a lecture to an enthralled audience of cognoscenti from the stage of the Scala in Milan. On retirement he was the prime mover in the steps taken to preserve Venice from decay and destruction.

Dreadfully tied up with the Coronation arrangements.

Meg's baby, approaching delivery, has turned the wrong way up and now the right way up again. It appears to be a most energetic child.

Sunday, November 30th

Winston's seventy-eighth birthday. Meg and I entertained him, Mrs Churchill, Mary and Jane Portal[1] to lunch in the Ladies' Annexe of the Turf Club.

We then had tea with the Lascelles at St James's Palace and when I got home I felt unnaturally cold.

Monday, December 1st

Retired to bed with a temperature of 103.

Tuesday, December 2nd

Meg, to avoid my flu, was packed off to the Nursing Home at 31 Queen's Gate.

Wednesday, December 3rd

At 2.45 a.m. Harriet Jane was born. Her mother had a disagreeable time; her father languished anxiously in bed. Visited Meg and the child briefly after luncheon. Harriet did not look beautiful.

Her Christian names were subsequently re-registered as Elizabeth Harriet, because the Queen offered to be a godparent. So did the Prime Minister, and they came to the christening. This led to a curious historic coincidence because having no christening robe we borrowed one from Lord Jersey. It had been made over a hundred years previously for the baptism of the then Lord Jersey's son, my sister-in-law's grandfather. On that occasion, in 1845, Queen Victoria and Sir Robert Peel stood sponsors in person. Thus, quite fortuitously, the same robe came to be used on the next, and probably only other, occasion that a

---

[1] One of Churchill's personal secretaries. Attractive niece of Rab Butler and Marshal of the R.A.F. Lord Portal. After her second marriage to Charles Williams she was a magistrate, a member of the Parole Board and secretary of the Other Club.

*Sovereign and her Prime Minister both attended a christening
as godparents.*

Thursday, December 4th
Harriet's looks improved. Meg says she has a will of iron.

Friday, December 5th
Harriet almost beautiful, except for abominable squint. Left for
Arundel to stay with Bernard and Lavinia Norfolk.

Saturday, December 6th
While I shot in bright sunshine, Meg, Harriet and London were
enveloped in one of the worst fogs ever.

Sunday, December 7th
Returned to London and the fog. Meg has had no less than forty
bunches of flowers sent to her.

TWENTY

NEW YORK AND WASHINGTON
JANUARY 1953

Saying farewell to the outgoing President Truman and greeting
the incoming President Eisenhower was an excellent excuse for
a further journey to the United States. Sir Roger Makins had
been appointed British Ambassador in Washington, in succession
to Sir Oliver Franks, and he and Lady Makins travelled with us.
Fortunately they knew the Embassy well, for they had but a
few days after their arrival to prepare for the reception of the
Prime Minister and for his Washington programme. I took a
Stationery Office note-book with me and wrote as follows:

Tuesday, December 30th, 1952
The Prime Minister, Mrs Churchill, Mary and Christopher
Soames and I left Waterloo at 7.30 p.m. bound for Southampton
and the *Queen Mary*. We dined on the train and talked of many
things, from the War of 1812 to the future of Pakistan. We went
on board about 9.45 and occupied a series of eminently luxurious
cabins.

Wednesday, December 31st
We sailed at 10.15 a.m. I worked with the P.M. for most of the
morning and lunched *en famille* in his dining-room, with the
usual gastronomic excellence associated with these liners. At
Cherbourg we sent off a bag. Christopher and I had a Turkish
bath.
  Sir Roger and Lady Makins to dinner. The P.M. said he

thought the recent treason trials in Prague, with so many Jews among the condemned, indicated that the Communists were looking towards the Arab States, Persia and North Africa and were deliberately antagonising Israel. He also said he would preach to Eisenhower the vital importance of a common Anglo-American front "from Korea to Kikuyu and from Kikuyu to Calais".

Saw the New Year in at a somewhat amateurish ceremony in the main lounge.

Thursday, January 1st, 1953
A quiet day on board with sunshine and smooth seas. We all lunched and dined in the Verandah Grill. During the evening Winston told me several things worth remembering. He said that if I lived my normal span I should assuredly see Eastern Europe free of Communism. He also said that Russia feared our friendship more than our enmity. Finally he lamented that owing to Eisenhower winning the presidency he must cut much out of Volume VI of his War History and could not tell the story of how the United States gave away, to please Russia, vast tracts of Europe they had occupied and how suspicious they were of his pleas for caution. The British General Election in July 1945 had occupied so much of his attention which should have been directed to stemming this fatal tide. If F.D.R. had lived, and had been in good health, he would have seen the red light in time to check the American policy: Truman, after all, had only been a novice, bewildered by the march of events and by responsibilities which he had never expected.

Friday, January 2nd
Life flows evenly on this great Cunarder and one feels detached from the speed and flurry of the world. Therefore the irruption of one or two short cypher telegrams, one of which was wholly corrupt, was irritating; but the food in the Verandah Grill, walks on the Sunshine Deck and the pleasures of a Turkish bath soothed away all irritation. We had warning of a Force 12 hurricane, but we altered course and evaded it.

Saturday, January 3rd
Sunshine and Mediterranean blue seas on the Great Newfoundland Banks. The P.M. gave a cocktail party before dinner to which, amongst others, the Munsters, Makinses, Lord Listowel, Lord Birdwood, Admiral Johnston (U.S.N.), Sir E. Hall Patch, Lord Iliffe, J. Wilson Broadbent (*Daily Mail* Diplomatic Correspondent in Washington and very charming) came.

After dinner, in the Verandah Grill, I was left alone with the P.M. and fired at him about thirty questions which he might be asked at his press conference on arrival in New York. He scintillated in his replies, e.g.:

Qn: What are your views, Mr Churchill, on the present stalemate in Korea?

Ans: Better a stalemate than a checkmate.

Qn: How do you justify such great expenditure on the Coronation of your Queen, when England is in such financial straits?

Ans: Everybody likes to wear a flower when he goes to see his girl.

Qn: Is not British policy in Persia throwing Persia into the hands of the Communists?

Ans: If Britain and America refuse to be disunited, no ill can come.

And there were many others as good or better. I wished so much I had had a microphone.

Sunday, January 4th
Last day at sea. Read briefs and papers relating to the Eisenhower talks with the P.M. The Makinses to lunch. All pleasantly quiet. P.M.'s bill for Verandah Grill and for wines, and private telephone calls – £83.10.0.

Monday, January 5th
Docked in New York at 8.15 a.m. Pandemonium let loose. Mr Baruch, high dignitaries, low officials, Embassy people, pressmen swarmed on board. The P.M. saw the press in the Verandah Grill and answered questions well; but perhaps less well than the night before last.

When we disembarked we went to Baruch's flat and thence I drove to Henry and Mimi Hyde's house on E. 70th Street, where I am staying.

General Eisenhower arrived amid the flashing of bulbs at 5.00 p.m. and greeted W. with: "Well, the one thing I have so far learnt in this damned game of yours is that you have just *got* to have a sense of humour." After a blinding photographic session, Baruch and I withdrew leaving the two to talk of many things (papers about which I deposited on a table beside W.).

Returned for dinner at which Eisenhower, Baruchs (father, son and daughter), Sarah, Christopher, Mr and Mrs C. and Miss Navarro[1] were present. Winston said that a protoplasm was sexless. Then it divided into two sexes which, in due course, united again in a different way to their common benefit and gratification. This should also be the story of England and America. Ike talked about Cleopatra's Needle (how the Egyptians raised it), the charm of the Queen, the intelligence of the Duke of Edinburgh, and a few war-time indiscretions.

After dinner I listened to the P.M. and the President Elect talking: Winston made one or two profound observations. For instance, "I think you and I are agreed that it is not only important to discover the truth but to know how to present the truth"; and (apropos of the recent treason trials in Czechoslovakia) "That they should think it good propaganda is what shows the absolutely unbridgeable gulf between us."

Bernard Baruch, next to whom I sat at dinner, told me that he thought European unity, in some striking form, was essential if America was not to tire of her efforts – and only Winston (who, he said, was deaf to his pleas on the subject) could bring it about. England now had three assets: her Queen ("the world's sweetheart"); Winston Churchill; and her glorious historical past. I said there was a fourth: her unrivalled technical ability. But his pleas for rapid action were met by the following remark of Winston's: "It may be better to bear an agonising period of

[1] Bernard Baruch's nurse and companion to whom he left quite a large part of his wealth.

unsatisfactory time . . . You may kill yourself in getting strong enough."

Tuesday, January 6th
A day of unrelenting activity. After a hideous morning, during which Mrs C. and Mary left for Jamaica, I lunched at the Knickerbocker Club with Gladwyn Jebb.

At 2.30 I went to the Commodore Hotel with a letter and Cabinet Paper for Ike from the P.M. Ike kept me twenty minutes, talking about Persia, and John Foster Dulles* was with him too, in a rather bare hotel room which is his office until he moves to the White House on January 20th. He was very genial and talked a great deal. Has a bee in his bonnet about "collusion" with us: is all in favour of it clandestinely but not overtly. Dulles said little, but what he did say was on our side. Ike struck me as forceful but a trifle naive.

At 6.00 John Foster Dulles came for a conversation with the P.M. He brought with him Winthrop Aldrich, the new American Ambassador in London. He began by saying that 1953 was a critical year: if the new administration did not get off to a good start, and the American people lost faith in it, who could say what might happen. W. said that he, for his part, thought nothing should be done for some four months: "the trees do not grow up to the sky"; we should let events in many places – Korea, Persia, Egypt – take their course and see where we found ourselves. At this point I left them. Subsequently W. told me what passed and I made a record for the F.O.

Wednesday, January 7th
Wrote a document about Anzus[1] and Anzam for the P.M. to give Ike this evening.

At 4.30 the Duke of Windsor, Duchess of Windsor, Mrs Luce[2] (a beautiful woman shortly to be appointed American Ambassador in Rome on account of Luce's support of the

[1] Establishing military co-operation between the United States, Australia and New Zealand.
[2] Clare Boothe, a beautiful actress who married Harry Luce, founder and owner of *Time* and *Life*.

Republicans in the recent Election), Mrs Philip Reid,[1] Mr Swope,[2] Sarah and another Baruch daughter came to drinks. Mrs Luce tried to cross-question W. about the *Tory* antagonism to Chiang Kai-Shek, but W. (a) thought she said *socialist* (b) wasn't playing! The Windsors would not go, and Eisenhower arrived at 5.00. So Ike and Winston went to another room. The only remark of Ike's I overheard was: "We must not make the mistake of jeopardising big things by opposition to little". This seems to be one of the bees in his bonnet.

The P.M. told me, after Ike had left, that he had felt on top of him this time: Ike had seemed to defer to his greater age and experience to a remarkable degree. I made a record of what W. told me had transpired.

Governor Dewey[3] came to dinner. The others present were Baruch, W.S.C., Christopher and myself. For a lawyer Dewey seemed to have a remarkably inaccurate memory for dates and places, but otherwise he talked well and made himself agreeable. All was quiet until towards the end of dinner John Foster Dulles arrived, by invitation. He had come, at Ike's suggestion, to say what he felt about a project of W.'s for not returning to England in the *Queen Mary* on January 23rd but remaining another fortnight in Jamaica, going to Washington for three or four days on February 1st or 2nd, being joined there by Rab (who would stay on for the economic discussions arising out of the recent Commonwealth talks) and returning home on February 7th. Dulles said he thought this would be most unfortunate, whereupon W. sat up and growled. He explained that the American public thought W. could cast a spell on all American statesmen and that if he were directly associated with the economic talks, the fears of the people and of Congress would be aroused to such an extent that the success of the talks would be endangered. W. took this very reasonable statement ill, but Christopher and I both took pains to assure Dulles afterwards that we thought he was absolutely right.

---

[1] Owner of the *Herald Tribune*.
[2] An editor and publicist who was Baruch's closest friend.
[3] Thomas Dewey, Republican candidate in the 1948 Presidential Election.

Irritated by this, W. let fly at Dewey after dinner and worked himself into a fury over certain Pacific Ocean questions. Christopher and I again applied soft soap subsequently. We told Dewey that a sharp debate was the P.M.'s idea of a pleasant evening and assured him that he would only have spoken thus to a man whom he trusted and looked upon as a friend.

But, alas, this was not so. W. was really worked up and, as he went to bed, said some very harsh things about the Republican party in general and Dulles in particular, which Christopher and I thought both unjust and dangerous. He said he would have no more to do with Dulles whose "great slab of a face" he disliked and distrusted.

For what it is worth my impression of the leading New Men is that they are well intentioned, earnest, but ill informed (which can be remedied) and not very intelligent – excepting Dulles – (which cannot). Ike in particular I suspect of being a genial and dynamic mediocrity.

Thursday, January 8th

We took off from La Guardia airport at 11.15 a.m. in President Truman's magnificently fitted aircraft "The Independence". At Washington, after a brilliant landing with a 400-foot cloud base, we were met by Dean Acheson, Roger Makins and others.

Luncheon at the Embassy, Kit Steel[1] and wife and Bernard Burrows[2] being present. Talk ranged from what has gone on in New York to the war of 1812 and the responsibility for it of slow communications.

At 4.00 the P.M. went to the White House. At 5.30 the following came for cocktails to the Embassy: Vice President Barkley, Senator Bridges, Senator Taft, Senator Johnson, Senator Wiley, Senator Millikin and Senator George; Representative Martin (Speaker of the House) and Representatives Halleck and Rayburn. I talked to Millikin, Barkley and Rayburn (whom I liked) and to Halleck (whom I thought abominable).

---

[1] Minister at the Embassy. Afterwards Ambassador in Bonn.

[2] Head of Chancery, whose successor I was invited to be. Afterwards Ambassador in the Persian Gulf and in Turkey.

My luggage had been left in New York so I had to borrow divers garments for dinner from divers people, including the P.M.'s very shabby second pair of evening shoes. It is the first time I have actually found myself standing in his shoes!

The President arrived for dinner at 9.00. Others at the dinner party were: Dean Acheson, Snyder, Averell Harriman, General Marshall, General Bradley, General Bedell Smith,[1] "Doc" Matthews,[2] the Ambassador, the P.M., Kit Steel, Sir E. Hall Patch, A.C.M. Sir William Elliot, Christopher, Dennis Rickett.

I sat between General Bradley[3] and "Doc" Matthews. We had very agreeable conversation until the P.M. and the President decided to hold the table. This happened after the P.M. had, quite wrongly, proposed the Queen's health. The President later said, quite rightly, that this was for him to do and so we had to drink it twice.

There was some talk about Stalin. Truman recalled how at Potsdam he had discovered the vodka Stalin drank for toasts was really weak white wine, and how when W.S.C. had said the Pope would dislike something, Stalin had answered "How many divisions has the Pope?" W. said he remembered replying that the fact they could not be measured in military terms did not mean they did not exist.

After dinner Truman played the piano. Nobody would listen because they were all busy with post-mortems on a diatribe in favour of Zionism and against Egypt which W. had delivered at dinner (to the disagreement of practically all the Americans present, though they admitted that the large Jewish vote would prevent them disagreeing publicly). However, on W.'s instructions, I gathered all to the piano and we had a quarter of an hour's presidential piano playing before Truman left. He played with quite a nice touch and, as he said himself, could probably

---

[1] Eisenhower's Chief of Staff during the 1944–45 campaign. After the war a power in the State Department.

[2] Influential official in the State Department, much esteemed by the British Embassy.

[3] Omar Bradley, commander of the American forces in France and Germany in 1944–45, initially under Montgomery. Appointed to command S.H.A.P.E., the peacetime successor to S.H.A.E.F. in Europe.

have made a living on the stage of the lesser music-halls.

When he had gone, the political wrangle started again, this time between W. (unsupported) and Dean Acheson (supported by Harriman, Bedell Smith and Matthews). The main bones of contention were the European Defence Community,[1] which the P.M. persists in describing as "a sludgy amalgam" infinitely less effective than a Grand Alliance of national armies, and the situation in Egypt where Acheson and Co. have far greater hopes of General Neguib[2] (our last hope, they say) than has W. The Americans, apart from Truman and Marshall, stayed till 1.00 a.m. I had an uneasy feeling that the P.M.'s remarks – about Israel, the E.D.C. and Egypt – though made to the members of an outgoing administration, had better have been left unsaid in the presence of the three, Bradley, Bedell Smith and Matthews, who are staying on with Ike and the Republicans.

Friday, January 9th
We left the Embassy at 9.30 a.m. and boarded "The Independence" for Jamaica. We had a very rough flight until we were south of Florida and both Christopher and I were a little worried about the effect of the bumps on W. However he ate a huge steak for lunch and had his usual brandy and cigar, so I concluded he must be looking worse than he felt.

We flew over Cuba, bathed in sunlight, to Montego Bay, where we landed in the presence of a guard of honour, a band and Mr Bustamente.[3] We drove through the town, W. sitting up on the back of an open car, and thence for two and a half hours in the dark to Prospect, a house near Ocho Rios lent to the P.M. by Sir Harold Mitchell.

Saturday, January 10th
Overcast, cloudy and hot. Bathed in the morning. In the afternoon the Governor's A.D.C. drove the Soameses, myself and a girl called Daphne Walthall to see local sights, including a "pub

[1] The proposed European army.
[2] Leader of the officers who deposed King Farouk and established a republic in Egypt. Later deposed and succeeded by Colonel Nasser.
[3] Prime Minister of Jamaica (which was still a British colony).

crawl" of the best known hotels (of which I thought Jamaica Inn the most fabulous).

Sunday, January 11th
Not good weather. Lord Beaverbrook to luncheon. He spoke very disparagingly of Anthony Eden. Then all drove to the Brownlows' house, Roaring River, for drinks. The P.M. (who last night said he would give £10,000 to be back at Chartwell) is cheering up a bit.

Monday, January 12th
Bathed by myself at Laughing Water Beach (a superb mixture of salt and fresh water against a background of golden sand and waving palms). A golden retriever stole my towel.

Went with Christopher and Mary to lunch with Lord Brownlow,[1] whose house is marvellous (with lovely furniture brought from Belton, wide verandahs and a spreading view of the park and the sea beyond). His daughter, Caroline Cust (vivacious and agreeable), his son Edward and a painter called Hector Whistler were there.

After dinner, *en famille* at Prospect, W. attacked Christopher and me violently for criticising one of his literary assistants. I told him, after the tirade, that I thought he had been guilty of the most unprovoked aggression since September 1939. He said of Ike that he was "a real man of limited stature" – which, I think, about sums the new President up.

Everybody very nicely says they wish I were not going home so soon and W.'s goodnight words were: "If I didn't admire Meg so much, I wouldn't allow you to go."

Tuesday, January 13th
Christopher and I got up at 5.00 a.m. to go deep-sea fishing with Ernest Hemingway's brother, but the weather was bad and the sea rough so we had to abandon the plan.

---

[1] "Perry", 6th Lord Brownlow, owner of the magnificent Belton House near Grantham and an intimate friend of the Duke of Windsor, whom he conducted to exile in December 1936.

Sarah[1] and Lady Foot arrived for luncheon and about 4.00 p.m. I drove away with Lady F. for Kingston, taking with me the last three chapters of Winston's war memoirs which he had been correcting.

Stayed the night at King's House with the Governor[2] and Lady Foot. Very agreeable dinner party at which two highly cultivated negroes were present: Mr Grantley Adams, Chief Minister of Barbados, and a man of remarkable intelligence called Springer who is attached to the University at Kingston. Sir Hugh Foot spoke of the evils of ju-ju in Africa and we had a long and learned argument about the merits of dealing with evil by the old and sharp puritanical approach or by the modern psychological method which seeks to explain and justify actions however wicked. Foot gave most interesting examples, from his own experiences as a Colonial administrator. In Palestine collective punishment, by fine, had been wholly efficacious in stopping the 1,000-year-old feuds which took the form of cutting down a neighbour's tree; in Cyprus the administration had encouraged villagers to take collective action, *by voting*, against the tough herdsmen from the hills who brought down their goats to feed on and ravage the valley pastures; in Jamaica the Government was just taking measures against predial theft by forcing the guilty to sit in their own doorways from sunset to sunrise for a period of weeks or even months – a modern version of the stocks and an attempt to use public humiliation as a deterrent.

Wednesday, January 14th
Rose at 5.15 a.m. and was taken by the A.D.C. to Palisadoes airport, whence I flew in a Viking to Montego Bay. Changed there into a Stratocruiser for Nassau and New York.

Was met at N.Y. by a representative of the U.K. Delegation

[1] Sarah Beauchamp, formerly Oliver.
[2] Hugh Foot, afterwards Lord Caradon, most of whose life was spent in the Colonial Service, holding important posts in many countries, including the Governorship of Cyprus at the start of the E.O.K.A. terrorism. Minister of State in the Foreign and Commonwealth Office and permanent British representative at U.N.O., 1964–70.

and by the Manager of B.O.A.C. Changed into a London-bound Stratocruiser which, after stopping at Gander (temperature 10°F in contrast to 80°F at Jamaica this morning), deposited me in a fog at London Airport at 12.00 noon on Thursday, January 15th, thus bringing to an end this brief American journey.

TWENTY-ONE

THE PRIME MINISTER'S STROKE

On May 11th, 1953, the Prime Minister, who was acting as Foreign Secretary in Anthony Eden's absence on protracted sick-leave, opened a foreign affairs debate with a well thought out and equally well delivered speech, partly about our relations with Egypt, but ending with the offer of an olive branch to the Soviet Union. He made this speech wholly contrary to Foreign Office advice since it was felt that a friendly approach to Russia would discourage the European powers working on the theme of Western union. However, Selwyn Lloyd,* the Minister of State, was personally enthusiastic about it, as were most of the Tories and the Opposition. I thought it a statesmanlike initiative and knew it to be one which was entirely Churchill's own.

There followed the Coronation of the Queen with all the attendant gaieties and celebrations, of which I wrote an account at the time and now attach as an appendix to this volume. For two cheerful months flags flew, bands played and party spite was muted, though the Scottish Nationalists continued to make an absurd fuss about the Queen being Elizabeth II rather than Elizabeth I. They had stolen the Stone of Scone from Westminster Abbey and blown up pillar boxes with EIIR on them. They were satisfied (at least for the time being) when the Queen and Parliament agreed that any future sovereign should take whichever was the higher number stemming from English or Scottish history. Thus a new King James would be James VIII, but a new King Henry would be Henry IX. Charles I and Charles

328 THE PRIME MINISTER'S STROKE

II were Kings of both England and Scotland; so Charles III would satisfy both.

While this peculiar royal arithmetic and other matters of scarcely greater significance were being debated, an unexpected event occurred. I wrote the following in my diary early in July 1953:

On June 23rd Meg and I dined at No. 10 for a big dinner in honour of the Italian Prime Minister, de Gasperi. Meg sat between Hector McNeil and Lord Rennell of Rodd, I next to Kenneth Clark. At the end of dinner W. made a little speech in his best and most sparkling form, mainly about the Roman Conquest of Britain! After dinner he had a stroke, which occurred while he was in the pillared room among the guests. He sat down and was almost unable to move. After the guests had left, he leant heavily on my arm but managed to walk to his bedroom.

The next day he presided at the Cabinet, but his speech was slurred and his mouth drooping.[1] It was obvious that the Bermuda Conference with Eisenhower and *a* French Prime Minister (France had been without one for a month) must be postponed. We were to have sailed in H.M.S. *Vanguard* the following Tuesday.

On Thursday, June 25th, I went to Chartwell with W. and Lady C. I stayed nearly a fortnight. To begin with he went downhill badly, losing the use of his left arm and left leg. At this stage Lord Moran told me he did not think Winston would live over the week-end. It looked as if he would have to resign and I was in constant touch with Tommy Lascelles, Lord Salisbury, Eden and Rab Butler. A Caretaker Government under Lord Salisbury for six months, until the Conservative Party could choose between Eden (now convalescing in America from a gall-bladder operation) and Butler, was mooted. But W.'s recuperative powers, both physical and mental, invariably outstrip all expectation and after a week he began rapidly to

[1] Nobody seemed to notice that he did not stand up to say goodbye to de Gasperi or any of the ladies. Equally Rab Butler later told me that nobody at the Cabinet table on June 24th noticed anything strange except that the Prime Minister was more silent than usual.

improve, though his powers of concentration appeared slight and he preferred Trollope's political novels to work. Butler presided at the Cabinet and Salisbury went to Washington to meet the Americans and the French.

Meanwhile the Princess Margaret–Peter Townsend story broke in the press when his appointment as Air Attaché in Brussels was announced. The subsequent publicity was most distasteful.

The staff at No. 10, Christopher Soames and myself in particular, were in a quandary. Two days after his stroke, when I drove down to Chartwell alone with the Prime Minister (Lady Churchill having gone on ahead to prepare the household), he gave me strict orders not to let it be known that he was temporarily incapacitated and to ensure that the administration continued to function as if he were in full control. We realised that however well we knew his policy and the way his thoughts were likely to move, we had to be careful not to allow our own judgment to be given Prime Ministerial effect. To have done so, as we could without too great difficulty, would have been a constitutional outrage. It was an extraordinary, indeed perhaps an unprecedented, situation.

I could not obey Churchill's injunction to tell nobody. The truth would undoubtedly leak to the press unless I took immediate defensive action. So I wrote urgently and in manuscript to three particular friends of Churchill, Lords Camrose, Beaverbrook and Bracken, and sent the letters to London by despatch rider. All three immediately came to Chartwell and paced the lawn in earnest conversation. They achieved the all but incredible, and in peace-time possibly unique, success of gagging Fleet Street, something they would have done for nobody but Churchill. Not a word of the Prime Minister's stroke was published until he himself casually mentioned it in a speech in the House of Commons a year later.

A second factor of great help to us was the wisdom and coolness of the Secretary of the Cabinet, Sir Norman Brook, whom I consulted as soon as the crisis occurred. My colleagues and I had to handle requests for decisions from Ministers and Government departments entirely ignorant of the Prime Minister's incapacity. Discussion of how best to handle such enquiries, whether by postponement, by consultation with the Minister or Under Secretary responsible or, in some cases, by direct reply on the Prime Minister's behalf were the subject of daily discussion with the Secretary of the Cabinet. It was the more difficult for us because Anthony Eden, the second in command, had his operation on the very day Churchill had his stroke and because, although R. A. Butler took charge of the Cabinet with tact and competence, we knew that Churchill was unwilling to delegate his powers to anybody.

This situation lasted the best part of a month. It was eased for Pitblado and me by a third factor, the sense of responsibility and the down-to-earth intelligence of Churchill's son-in-law, Christopher Soames, Member of Parliament for Bedford. He had over the previous five years won the affection and trust of his formidable and, in the first instance, somewhat doubtful father-in-law. He now held the place in Churchill's heart so long reserved for Randolph who had been incapable of filling it. As Parliamentary Private Secretary, Christopher was in a curious position. He grew closer every month to Churchill, whom he even lured into owning racehorses (and was accordingly dubbed "The Master of the Horse" by Randolph); but he was not in principle supposed to see Cabinet Papers or secret documents. That indeed had accounted for Sir Norman Brook's worries described in my entry for June 20th, 1952. However, in the unusual circumstances prevailing, it seemed to me that, whatever the rules might be, Christopher should be given access to many papers he was not supposed to see, including Cabinet papers. In the event the shrewdness of his comments, combined with his ability to differentiate between what mattered and what did not, was of invaluable help in difficult days.

Before the end of July the Prime Minister was sufficiently restored to take an intelligent interest in affairs of state and express his own decisive views. Christopher and I then returned to the fringes of power, having for a time been drawn perilously close to the centre. For the next two years the distance between the fringes and the centre was far shorter than it had once been.

Wednesday, July 15th
To Glyndebourne with the Normanbys. Went by train, a party of fourteen including Fritzy[1] and Bridget of Prussia, Howard de Walden,[2] Cyril Egerton,[3] the Dunboynes,[4] Mary Roxburghe, John Lewis. Saw *Cosi Fan Tutte* admirably performed.

Thursday, July 16th
Meg gave away prizes to the nurses of St Giles' hospital and made a short speech admirably. Then to the garden party at B.P. Pouring rain. We inadvertently got mixed up with Sherpa Tensing[5] and the Everest party.

Saturday, July 18th
To Cherkley for tea and dinner. The main object was to show Lord Beaverbrook some papers about the Duke of Windsor's activities in Spain and Portugal[6] during 1940 and to ask his opinion. He was in good form and the party, consisting of Lord B.'s granddaughter, Jean Campbell,[7] Sir Patrick Hennessy,[8] Lord B.'s French mistress and Mr Junor[9] of the *Evening Standard* was entertaining. Lord B., who has given me a good many first editions, presented me with one of *The Jungle Book*.

[1] Prince Frederick of Prussia, son of the German Crown Prince and married to a daughter of Lord Iveagh.
[2] John. Lord Howard de Walden, famous in the racing world.
[3] First cousin of my wife.
[4] Patrick, Lord Dunboyne, a contemporary of mine at Cambridge. Became a Q.C. and in due course a judge.
[5] On Coronation Day the news had broken of Edmund Hillary and Sherpa Tensing reaching the summit of Everest.
[6] The so-called Marburg papers, found in the German Government files, related in detail the German attempt in 1940 to persuade the Duke of Windsor to stay in Portugal. Ribbentrop hoped to make use of him after a successful invasion of Britain.
[7] Lady Jean Campbell, daughter of Beaverbrook's daughter Janet and the Duke of Argyll. She was a first-class journalist who wrote accounts of U.S. affairs for the *Evening Standard*. One of her husbands was Norman Mailer.
[8] Chairman of the Ford Motor Company in Britain. A long-standing friend of Beaverbrook and Bracken and of mine.
[9] Sir John Junor, afterwards Editor of the *Sunday Express*.

Sunday, July 19th

By way of contrast lunched at Stratfield Saye to look at a house which the Duke of Wellington offers to let to us. We thought it most attractive.

Went to Chartwell for dinner as R. A. Butler was to be there, with his speech for the foreign affairs debate. W. much improved in powers of concentration. He did a little work before dinner (including approval of my draft reply to a tricky P.Q. about the Regency Act – made tricky by the Pss Margaret–Townsend explosion); he sparkled at dinner; and after dinner he went carefully and meticulously through Rab's speech.

Drove back to London with Rab, who is very, very smooth, though oddly enough an agreeable companion. He says he will serve loyally under Eden and that anyhow some of the Conservative Party might not want him (Rab) as P.M. because of Munich. We discussed potential troubles when Anthony Eden returns next week fully expecting that he is shortly going to form a new administration. But there is no certainty that the P.M. intends to give up: on the contrary I surmise that he still hopes to bring off some final triumph, like Disraeli at the Congress of Berlin in 1878, and perhaps light the way to the end of the Cold War. Rab says he hopes his end will be like that or, if it cannot be so, like Chatham's[1] end.

Tuesday, July 21st

Listened to Rab open the foreign affairs debate. It was a dull speech, yet more dully delivered. He is certainly no orator. And it left the Opposition, and indeed most of his hearers, with the thought: where is Winston's great peace initiative of May 11th? It is entombed in a guarded oration inspired by Frank Roberts[2] (now a great power in the F.O. who dislikes the P.M. and all his policies and who sat smiling contentedly beside me in the official box while Rab unfolded his dismal and pedestrian story).

---

[1] Lord Chatham fell back in a fit during a fiery speech in Parliament opposing the British withdrawal from the American Colonies and died shortly after.

[2] There were few cleverer or more conscientious members of the Foreign Office. His strong inclination to the Eden rather than the Churchill theme of foreign policy accounts for my acid comment on a man I respect.

Friday, July 24th
Lunched alone with W. at Chartwell. He is now amazingly restored, but complains that his memory has suffered and says he thinks he probably will give up in October or at any rate before the Queen leaves for Australia in November. Still very wrapped up with the possibility of bringing something off with the Russians and with the idea of meeting Malenkov[1] face to face. Very disappointed in Eisenhower whom he thinks both weak and stupid. Bitterly regrets that the Democrats were not returned at the last Presidential Election.

Monday, July 27th
At Chequers. Anthony and Clarissa Eden came to luncheon, the former thin and frail after his three operations but in good spirits. He is, of course, thinking above all of when he will get the Prime Ministership, but he contrived to keep off the subject altogether today and to talk mainly of foreign affairs. He thinks the fall of Beria three weeks ago may have been a defeat for moderation. The signs, flimsy though they be, do seem to point that way.

Gave Winston *Candide* to read. He has had a surfeit of Trollope's political novels.

Today the Korean War ended – after months of infuriating haggling over the terms of the armistice.

Friday, July 31st – Tuesday, August 4th
To Chequers again. Lord Beaverbrook came on Friday night, in disgrace because of an unpleasant cartoon of Lord Salisbury in the *Daily Express*. Winston has seen more of Lord B. since his illness than at any time since he formed the present administration. Junor, of the *Evening Standard*, told me when I lunched with him last Wednesday, that the Labour Party saw in an (imaginary) split between W. and the rest of the Cabinet over four-power talks with Russia their best propaganda line for many a day. The *Daily Express*, because of Lord B.'s hatred of Lord Salisbury (and of the nobility in general), seems to be playing

---

[1] Stalin's successor who, in the event, had only a short tenure. His colleague at the top of the Politburo, Beria, was executed.

roughly the same hand. However, at Chequers Lord B.'s charm soon thawed the resentment – though Winston had the Visitors' Book removed so that Lord B.'s signature should not be visible when Lord Salisbury arrived next day!

The Edens, the Salisburys, Meg, Mary and Christopher were there for the week-end. Randolph, Sarah and Duff Cooper came over on August Bank Holiday. The underlying interest was two-fold. First of all the two invalids: Winston and Eden. The latter was burning with the big question-mark: "When do I take over?" The former had told me in private that if asked he would say that the more he was hustled, the longer he would be. However, Eden (warned by Patrick Buchan-Hepburn,[1] Brendan and, I expect, Rab – with all of whom I have discussed the problem in recent weeks) said nothing. He looked very frail and probably realises he must first prove that he will be fit to be P.M. himself.

The second drama is our attitude to Russia. Winston is firmly hoping for talks which might lead to a relaxation of the Cold War and a respite in which science could use its marvels for improving the lot of man and, as he put it, the leisured classes of his youth might give way to the leisured masses of tomorrow. Eden is set on retaining the strength of N.A.T.O. and the Western Alliance by which, he believes, Russia has already been severely weakened. W. is depressed by Eden's attitude (which reflects that of the F.O.), because he thinks it consigns us to years more of hatred and hostility. Still more depressing is that Lord S. says he found Eisenhower violently Russophobe, greatly more so than Dulles, and that he believes the President to be personally responsible for the policy of useless pinpricks and harassing tactics the U.S. is following against Russia in Europe and the Far East.

On Sunday I went with W. to Royal Lodge where he had an audience of the Queen. He said that he had told her his decision whether or not to retire would be made in a month when he saw

---

[1] Conservative Chief Whip. Created Lord Hailes. Governor General of the short-lived West Indies Federation established by Harold Macmillan. An outstandingly good amateur artist.

clearly whether he was fit to face Parliament and to make a major speech to the Conservative Annual Conference in October. He also asked, and received, permission to invite Eisenhower here on a State Visit in September or October. He has learned from Winthrop Aldrich (U.S. Ambassador) that Eisenhower would do this for him but for nobody else – after he retired there would be no question of it. It would be a great event, because U.S. Presidents seldom if ever go abroad and none has been here since Woodrow Wilson at the end of World War I.

Meg and I left Chequers on Tuesday, August 4th.

Thursday, 6th – Sunday, 9th August
At Chequers again. Meg, Nanny and Harriet came over for the day on the 9th and I drove them home. On the 8th, Lord Salisbury, Rab Butler and William Strang came for a meeting at 12.00 noon about the reply from Russia to the three-power note sent after the Washington Conference. The P.M. took the meeting in the Hawtrey room, the first time he has presided at a meeting since the Cabinet on the morrow of his stroke. The line he had proposed was accepted: namely to ask the Americans a lot of questions and leave them the burden of drafting the answer: this in spite of contrary and long-winded drafts prepared by the F.O. The old man still gets his way: usually because it is simple and clear, whereas the "mystique" of the F.O. (as Selwyn Lloyd calls it) tends to be pettifogging and over detailed. After the meeting we had a most agreeable luncheon party, the P.M. in sparkling mood. He said that all his life he had found his main contribution had been by self-expression rather than by self-denial. And he has started drinking brandy again after a month's abstinence. Apart from his unsteady walk, the appearances left by his stroke have vanished, though he still tires quickly. However Lord Moran told me he thought there might be another stroke within a year. Indeed it was probable.

On the afternoon of the 8th Monty came for the week-end. I walked up Beacon Hill with him (the weather for the last week has been gorgeous). He volunteered the opinion that Frank Roberts was a menace to the country with his "rigid constipated mentality". After dinner we talked, the P.M., Monty and I, till late about the two world wars. Monty and the P.M. said the Americans had made five capital mistakes in the military field in the last war:

i. They had prevented Alexander getting to Tunis the first time, when he could easily have done so.

ii. They had done at Anzio what Stopford did at Suvla Bay: clung to the beaches and failed to establish positions inland as they could well have done. The P.M. said he had intended it to be a wholly British expedition.

iii. They had insisted on Operation ANVIL, thereby preventing Alexander from taking Trieste and Vienna.

iv. Eisenhower had refused to let Monty, in OVERLORD, concentrate his advance on the left flank. He had insisted on a broad advance, which could not be supported, and had thus allowed Runstedt to counter-attack on the Ardennes and had prolonged the war, with dire political results, to the spring of 1945.

v. Eisenhower had let the Russians occupy Berlin, Prague and Vienna – all of which might have been entered by the Americans.

Monty told me he had got Ridgway[1] sacked from S.H.A.P.E. He had gone off to America specifically to tell Ike that this was necessary and had found Ike alive to the fact. But Ridgway, who had been made American Chief of Staff, still thought he had been promoted and not sacked!

He inclines to agree with Lord Salisbury about Ike's present political ineptitude but says he is the prisoner of Congress.

Tuesday, August 11th – Wednesday, August 12th
At Chequers again, alone with the P.M. and Norman Brook. Talk about reconstituting the Cabinet. Possibly Eden Leader of House and Lord President, Salisbury Foreign Secretary; or Harold Macmillan Foreign Secretary, Eccles Minister of Housing, Patrick Buchan-Hepburn Minister of Works. But all depends on W.'s own future and he gives himself till the end of September to decide.

---

[1] Successor to Eisenhower as Supreme Commander in Europe.

Much talk about Russia: the P.M. still inclining to think we should have another shot at an understanding. He said, "We must not go further on the path to war unless we are sure there is no other path to peace."

Wrote a Cabinet Paper, which the P.M. accepted, about the Windsor papers (relating to the Duke's activities in Spain and Portugal in 1940). The P.M. still set on suppression.

Friday, August 14th – Saturday, August 15th and Monday, August 17th
At Chartwell. P.M. coming round towards resignation in October. Says he no longer has the zest for work and finds the world in an abominable state wherever he looks. Greatly depressed by thoughts on the hydrogen bomb. He had a nightmare on Thursday, dreaming that he was making a speech in the House of Lords and that it was an appalling flop. Lord Rothermere came up to him and said, "It didn't even *sound* nice."

He made a good pun at luncheon on Monday. We were talking about a peerage for Salter, who is to be removed from the Ministry of Materials. Christopher asked whether he could not also get rid of Mackeson[1] from Overseas Trade, but said he didn't merit a peerage. "No," said W., "but perhaps a disappearage."

When the explosion of the first hydrogen bomb was announced in an after-dinner speech in the United States, the only English paper to carry the news was the Manchester Guardian. *The Prime Minister read it in bed at 10 Downing Street and immediately telephoned to the Chiefs of Staff and everybody else in Whitehall who might know about the matter. Nobody did. The account in the* Manchester Guardian *described in some detail the effect of exploding a thermo-nuclear bomb and the P.M. said to me that we were now as far from the age of the*

---

[1] M.P. for the Folkestone and Hythe division of Kent. A Conservative Whip, 1947–52, and then Secretary for Overseas Trade. He was given a baronetcy in 1954.

*atomic bomb as the atomic bomb itself from the bow and arrow.
His subsequent reaction, which he fully maintained over the
rest of his Prime Ministership, was that this ghastly invention
might perhaps present humanity with a real chance of lasting
peace, since war would now be impossible.*

Tuesday, August 18th

W. came to London to hold his first Cabinet since June. After it
he discussed Cabinet changes further. Eccles may now be given
Overseas Trade and Cabinet rank; or he might be Minister of
Education. I said to the P.M. that I shouldn't like to be educated
by Eccles. "Oh," he said, "I don't know. Good taste is not part
of the curriculum."

*   *   *

Meg and I were leaving for the South of France on Wednesday,
but the hotel at Beauvallon has closed because of the French
strikes. We have sent Harriet off by train to Ladykirk and shall
now go northwards ourselves by car.

We left on August 21st, staying at Stetchworth[1] for two or
three days and then going to Scotland until September 20th. We
stayed at Ladykirk with the Askews, at Drummond with the
Ancasters, at Douglas with the Homes, at Gartshore with the
Whitelaws and at Mertoun.

Harriet divided her stay between Ladykirk and Gartshore.

On September 24th I flew out to the South of France to be
with Winston at Cap d'Ail, near Monte Carlo, where Lord
Beaverbrook lent him his villa, La Capponcina, for a recuperative
holiday, and where Meg joined us. There were two episodes I
found entertaining.

Beaverbrook had provided his guest not only with a chef of
quality and a judiciously stocked cellar, but also with a small
black Fiat car which had known better days. It was not in much
demand, for we seldom ventured beyond the garden or the

---

[1] Near Newmarket. My mother-in-law, Violet, Lady Ellesmere, lived there
after her husband died.

rocky shore where Churchill, with his detective, Sergeant Murray (who was also an artist), spent hours painting the rocks and pine trees. However, Churchill had never been averse to casinos, and one evening he thought it would be fun to go to Monte Carlo and try his luck at the tables. I said firmly that I thought it a most unsuitable expedition for a Prime Minister shortly to preside over a Party Conference at Margate, since he was bound to be recognised, photographed and thereafter severely criticised. When I eventually succeeded in dissuading him, he insisted I should go in his place. From the recesses of his private black box he extracted several 20,000 Italian lire notes, relics of a painting holiday by Lake Como some years previously. He endowed me with them, declaring that if I won we should share the winnings, but that if I lost his lire nest-egg he would bear no grudge.

So, after dinner, while Meg and the Prime Minister settled down to play Oklahoma (still one of his favourite card-games) I drove the battered Fiat to Monte Carlo in this unusual representative capacity and entered the flamboyant, late Victorian Casino. I played Chemin de Fer with conspicuous ill-luck and quickly lost the French franc equivalent of all the Prime Ministerial lire. I was then informed that the notes I had proffered in payment for the chips received in exchange were found to be an extinct issue, no longer legal tender. I escaped, with some difficulty, on the strength of an I.O.U. and drove back, much dejected, to La Capponcina. Churchill said that somebody should have told him the Italians had changed their currency; but he did subsequently take steps to redeem my I.O.U.

A day or two later we had an outing which I have recorded in less detail elsewhere.[1] Churchill recalled something Mrs Reggie Fellowes had told him. Daisy Fellowes was a wicked but attractive lady, French by origin, who, according to Clementine, tried to seduce Winston at the Ritz Hotel in Paris shortly after the Churchills were married. It was an unsuccessful effort and she had been forgiven, even by Clementine.

This notorious lady had recently been to a restaurant in the

[1] In *The Churchillians* (Weidenfeld & Nicolson, 1981).

Italian resort of San Remo where she was shown a remark-able crustacean called a sea-cricket. The Prime Minister, always fascinated by birds, beasts and fishes, now suggested that we should dine at San Remo and examine this unusual creature.

Lord Beaverbrook's chef was given a night off and Sergeant Murray informed the French police of our intention. In pitch darkness and pouring rain we entered the two-doored Fiat, Meg and I cramped uncomfortably behind and Churchill sitting in front beside Sergeant Murray, who acted as chauffeur as well as artistic adviser and detective. When our shabby little car emerged from the drive we found two shiny black limousines and a posse of police motorcyclists waiting to escort us. We set off at speed, but had not gone far before the window next to Churchill came adrift. Meg leant forward, the rain and cold night air rushing in upon her, and held it partially closed. A few minutes later we reached the Italian frontier where guards of honour, alerted that the famous British Prime Minister would be passing by, presented arms as this strange procession tore through the open barriers.

At San Remo the alleged abode of the sea-cricket proved to be a dark and ramshackle *estaminet* by the quay-side with bare wooden tables. It was empty, and the *patron* was astonished by the arrival of a large motorised police force and a battered little Fiat from which emerged a figure whom he evidently recognised.

"Where," asked Churchill, "is the sea-cuckoo?"

"Sea-cricket," said Meg by way of explanation.

"I have come," said Churchill, quite unabashed, "to see the sea-cuckoo."

Round the *estaminet* stood glass tanks, which must normally have been replete with every kind of crustacean awaiting death for the gastronomic pleasure of customers. But an equinoctial gale had been raging for several days and even the most intrepid fisherman had declined to put to sea. So all that was visible in the tanks was one jaded langouste and a few prawns. San Remo was searched from east to west for a sea-cuckoo or cricket, and a disappointingly ugly crustacean was finally produced. We ate spaghetti and *prosciuto con melone* at the bare boards with a grumpy Prime Minister who should have learned by experience to disregard suggestions made by Mrs Reggie Fellowes.

The next day Meg had a temperature of 103 degrees. Churchill returned to Downing Street accompanied only by his valet and Sergeant Murray. One of the shiny French police cars transported him to Nice airport, and I stayed for almost a week's extra holiday with my convalescent wife, well cherished by Lord Beaverbrook's chef. Working for Churchill could be pyrotechnic; it was seldom dull.

October 1953
Winston cannot make up his mind whether or not to go on as P.M. On the whole he inclines to do so or at any rate to see what he can do. He certainly wants to, but is a little doubtful of his capacity to make long speeches. He thinks he will take the big one he has to make on October 10th, at the Conservative Conference at Margate, as the test. His conversation at Cap d'Ail was of little else, apart from the tragedy that the Bermudan Conference had not taken place and the desirability of him and Eden meeting Malenkov and Molotov face to face.

Eden, of course, longs for him to go; and Patrick Buchan-Hepburn, with whom I had a talk before going to France, thinks there will be trouble in the House and in the Conservative Party if he does not.

On October 9th I went to Margate with W. for the Conservative Conference. He made a big speech the following day and did it with complete success. He had been nervous of the ordeal: his first public appearance since his stroke and a fifty-minute speech at that; but personally I had no fears as he always rises to occasions. In the event one could see but little difference, as far as his oratory went, since before his illness.

Meanwhile a sudden scheme for a meeting with the President at the Azores next week (we going in *Vanguard*) has been turned down by Eisenhower. The blunt truth is that E. does not want to meet him as he knows he will be confronted with a demand for a conference with the Russians which he is unwilling to accept. W. was for pursuing the matter but was stopped by a chance remark of mine on Friday evening when I said to him, "What subjects are you going to discuss when you get there?" It suddenly dawned on him that everything he might say to the President would necessarily be met with a negative response and that on other topics, such as Egypt, he (W.) would have nothing to offer but criticisms and complaints of the U.S. attitude. To bring the President 1,000 miles for that seemed discourteous and unfair.

Eden, who though still thin looks a great deal better, also had his success at Margate. On the surface he seems resigned to W. remaining in power (W. told me, after his speech, that he now hoped to do so until the Queen returned from Australia in May). There are two potential causes of friction: (i) Egypt. If W. and Eden fall out over that – assuming the Egyptians agree to our terms – W. would have the support of the Conservative Party against Eden but not of the Opposition. (ii) A visit to Malenkov. Here W. would have the support of the country and the Opposition against Eden, backed by the Foreign Office and a section of the Conservatives. W. thinks a meeting, of an exploratory kind, might do good and could do no harm. The F.O. think it might lead to appeasement and would certainly discourage our European allies who would relax their defence efforts if even the shadow of a détente appeared. The Foreign Office and the U.S.A. are at one in thinking that Russia's slightly more reasonable attitude of late is due less to Stalin's death than to the success of our own constant pressure and increased strength.

On Saturday night we got back to London from Margate and I dined at No. 10 with W. and Clemmie and Duncan and Diana Sandys. W. very elated by his success, but more tired than one might have hoped.

*   *   *

At this stage I abandoned keeping a diary, in the main because living in the country, and above all moving to a new home at Stratfield Saye, absorbed such energy as might otherwise have been left to me by the end of the day. I did, however, keep detailed accounts of two more journeys to America, which were written at the time.

TWENTY-TWO

THE BERMUDA CONFERENCE

Once again I purloined a small Stationery Office note-book.

Tuesday, December 1st, 1953
Tonight we left Heathrow for Bermuda in the B.O.A.C. aircraft
Canopus, which took the Queen to Bermuda last week. Our
party included the P.M., Mr Eden, Sir N. Brook, Sir P. Dixon,
Sir F. Roberts, Denis Allen,[1] Evelyn Shuckburgh,[2] John Priest-
man,[3] Christopher Soames, David Pitblado, Lord Cherwell and
Lord Moran, with not too numerous assistants and ancillaries.

Strong headwinds obliged us to land at Shannon. Thence to
Gander, where snow was lying on the ground and so, after about
seventeen hours of journeying, to Bermuda where the Governor
(Sir A. Hood), the foremost citizens, and a Guard of Honour
of the Royal Welsh Fusiliers, complete with goat and white
"hackles", greeted us.

The main party stayed at the Mid-Ocean Golf Club and at the
Castle Harbour Hotel. I have been lent Henry Tiarks'[4] villa "Out

---

[1] An Under Secretary in the Foreign Office, subsequently Commissioner
General in S.E. Asia and Ambassador to Turkey.
[2] Principal Private Secretary to Anthony Eden. Afterwards Ambassador to
N.A.T.O. (in Paris) and to Italy.
[3] Assistant Private Secretary to Anthony Eden. Later joined the Council of
Europe and became Clerk of the European Parliament.
[4] A senior director of Schröders, the merchant bank, and a man of great
generosity.

of the Blue" and have invited Lord Cherwell, Norman Brook and Christopher Soames to share its luxurious comfort and beautiful view.

Thursday, December 3rd
This morning went to the airport with the P.M. for the ceremony of receiving the French Prime Minister, M. Laniel,[1] and the Foreign Secretary, M. Bidault. Last time this conference was proposed, the French could not form a Government and the meeting had to be postponed week after week until just as we were packing to leave the P.M. had his stroke.

Lunched in the P.M.'s dining-room at the Mid-Ocean with Eden, Cherwell, Brook, Bob Dixon and Christopher as the other guests. An undistinguished conversation. Rushed away to see the Governor and the Speaker of the Assembly, both of whom are exercised over the colour question. There was a row because when the Queen was here last week no coloured guests were invited to the banquet at Government House. The P.M. has insisted that two should be asked to the Governor's banquet tomorrow. This meant tampering with the precedence list (oh horror!) and leaving out three most important local guests. I solved the problem by dropping instead three of our delegation.

Bathed twice today in a limpid blue sea (temperature nearly 70 degrees) and dived by the rocks to look at black and yellow striped fish shaped like melons.

Dinner with the P.M., Prof., Lord Moran, Brook, Christopher and Pitblado. The P.M. got going well after dinner, but the room was too small and we were all but perishing from the heat. The P.M. said, "It may be that we are living in our generation through the great demoralisation which the scientists have caused but before the countervailing correctives have become operative."

First prize to the Prof. who began illustrating a point with the following words: "I was told by a Russian waiter at Los Angeles in 1912 . . ."

Delicious balmy night and the noise of the tree frogs is far better than that of crickets. We sat outside on the terrace at midnight with no discomfort.

[1] Short-lasting and by no means memorable French Prime Minister.

Friday, December 4th

Went to a delegation meeting with N. Brook at the Castle Harbour Hotel and escaped in time to bathe before luncheon, while the P.M., who had met Eisenhower and Dulles on their arrival at the airport, pirated the former and took him to lunch privately in his room. This greatly disturbed both Dulles and Eden who neither of them trust their chief alone. However, the P.M. seemed, from what he told me, to get a good deal out of Ike including some alarming information about tough American intentions[1] in certain circumstances.

When Ike had left, the P.M., Christopher and I walked to the beach and the P.M. sat like King Canute defying the incoming tide (and getting his feet wet in consequence) while C. and I bathed naked and I swam out to fetch Winston some distant seaweed he wished to inspect.

At 5.00 there was the first Plenary Meeting, of which I made a record. There were memories of former conferences. The Big Three first sat on the porch in wicker chairs and were photographed in a manner reminiscent of Teheran. Then, when the conference started, all the lights fused and we deliberated by the light of candles and hurricane lamps as in Athens at Christmas 1944. After a turgid if quite intelligent speech by Bidault, the P.M. (who had not prepared anything to say) launched forth into a powerful disquisition on his theory – which he calls a "double-dealing" policy – of strength towards the Soviet Union combined with holding out the hand of friendship. He spoke of contacts, trade and other means of infiltration – always provided we were united and resolute in our strength. Only by proving to our peoples that we would neglect no chances of "easement" could we persuade them to go on with the sacrifices necessary to maintain strong armed forces. This, coming after an intransigently anti-Russian speech by Bidault ("the only decent Frenchman" as Evelyn Shuckburgh called him to me), upset the Foreign Office representatives except for Denis Allen who thought the speech statesmanlike and constructive. Frank Roberts and

[1] Of an atomic nature.

Shuckburgh said it was a disaster. I gather Eden felt the same. But I think Allen was right.

Ike followed with a short, very violent statement, in the coarsest terms. He said that as regards the P.M.'s belief that there was a New Look in Soviet Policy, Russia was a woman of the streets and whether her dress was new, or just the old one patched, it was certainly the same whore underneath. America intended to drive her off her present "beat" into the back streets.

I doubt if such language has ever before been heard at an international conference. Pained looks all round.

Of course, the French gave it all away to the press. Indeed some of their leakages were verbatim.

To end on a note of dignity, when Eden asked when the next meeting should be, the President replied, "I don't know. Mine is with a whisky and soda" – and got up to leave the room.

Busy with Norman Brook doing the record of the meeting, while the P.M., Eden, Cherwell and Lord Moran went to the dinner at Government House. We all (the rest of us) dined in the P.M.'s private dining-room where we thought the food would be a good deal better than in the Grill Room.

Saturday, December 5th

To the British delegation suite at the Castle Harbour for a briefing meeting. Everybody greatly perturbed by the American attitude on (a) the prospects (b) their action, in the event of the Korean truce breaking down. This question has such deep implications that it is undoubtedly the foremost matter at the conference – though it has to be discussed behind closed doors with the Americans. No atomic matters can be talked about to the French who are very sensitive at having no atomic piles or bombs. The P.M., Ike, Lord Cherwell and Admiral Strauss[1] discussed the matter in the President's room from 11.30 till lunch-time.

This afternoon, while standing on the beach, I talked to Douglas MacArthur of the State Department. He said that the

[1] Head of the American Atomic Energy Commission. He worked closely with Lord Cherwell.

French system was hopeless, though Bidault was doing all he could. If E.D.C. [the European Defence Community: a plan for a European army] were not ratified, the American administration could ask for no appropriations from Congress and would have to re-orientate their whole policy to Europe.

I did not go to the Plenary Meeting – leaving David Pitblado to do this. Instead I went with Christopher to Government House for a quarter of an hour as the Governor was giving a cocktail party.

We gave a dinner party at "Out of the Blue" for Pug Ismay who arrived today. Meanwhile the P.M. and Eden were dining alone with Eisenhower and Dulles and were engaged in grim conversations about the future actions to be taken in the event of a breach of the truce in Korea. Eden was most particularly perturbed by this and by the effect on public opinion in England. There was also discussion of a draft speech, mainly on atomic matters, which Eisenhower wants to deliver next week at the General Assembly of the United Nations. Christopher read it aloud in the P.M.'s bedroom, while I sat in a chair and the P.M. and Eden, still fully dressed in dinner jackets, lay side by side flat on the P.M.'s bed. The Americans had of course gone to their own apartments by then.

Sunday, December 6th

This morning everybody was in rather a state. First there is the momentous matter of last night's discussion[1] which far outstrips in importance anything else at the conference. Secondly there is E.D.C. The Americans are disgusted with the French but nevertheless convinced that E.D.C. is the only alternative for them to withdrawing to the periphery of Europe. The French, wily diplomats that they are, have at least this card to play: Bidault and the Quai d'Orsay are all for E.D.C. and have done everything possible to meet the American point of view. Therefore, say the Americans, it is the British who must satisfy the

[1] The American inclination to use the atomic bomb in Korea if the Chinese came to the aid of the Communist North Koreans, a suggestion strongly resisted by Churchill and Eden.

French Chamber of Deputies by guaranteeing to leave their troops on the continent for a defined number of years or even by actually joining the E.D.C. Thus it is we who are to suffer on account of French weakness and obduracy. Of course, the obvious answer is (i) we will keep our troops on the continent as long as the Americans agree to do so, (ii) we could not possibly get our Parliament and people, or the Commonwealth, to accept our actual membership of E.D.C.

The Prime Minister, when first I went to see him this morning, was engaged in writing a letter to Ike approving, apart from one or two points, the text of his draft speech to U.N.O. I took it down to the beach to show Eden who was lying there with Dulles, engaged in a mixture of bathing and negotiation. Anthony Eden at once said that in view of what we knew from yesterday's private talks with the Americans, approval of the terms of the speech in all its aspects would make us accessories before the act. He proposed the insertion of a statement that in view of our exposed position, we had to make reservations. This the P.M. accepted and sent me down with the letter to give it to the President.

Eisenhower was in his sitting-room, cross-legged in an armchair, going through his speech. He was friendly, but I noticed that he never smiled: a change from the Ike of war days or even, indeed, of last January in New York. He said several things that were noteworthy. The first was that whereas Winston looked on the atomic weapon as something entirely new and terrible, he looked upon it as just the latest improvement in military weapons. He implied that there was in fact no distinction between "conventional weapons" and atomic weapons: all weapons in due course became conventional weapons. This of course represents a fundamental difference of opinion between public opinion in the U.S.A. and in England. However, he said that America was prepared to be generous in the sacrifice of fissionable material to an international authority that she was willing to make.

I told him that a reference to "the obsolete Colonial mould" contained in his draft speech would give offence in England. He said that was part of the American philosophy. I replied that a lot of people in England thought India had been better governed by the Viceroy and the British Government of India than at present. He said that as a matter of fact he thought so himself, but that to Americans liberty was more precious than good government.

W. saw him for half an hour before lunch and he agreed to remove the obnoxious phrase about colonialism and to substitute for the United States being "free to use the atomic bomb" a phrase about the United States "reserving the right to use the atomic bomb".

It has been a gloriously sunny day. I bathed twice and lunched out of doors.

After luncheon there was trouble because the Foreign Ministers had sent off to Adenauer the text of their proposed reply to the Soviet Government, accepting a conference at Berlin in January, without showing it to Ike or W. (Laniel retired to bed yesterday with pleurisy and a temperature of 104 degrees). W. remonstrated strongly with Eden and wanted to have left out the reference to German reunification, on the grounds that you couldn't confront the Russians at Berlin with both our determination that Western Germany should be an armed member of E.D.C. *and* a demand that Eastern Germany be united to it. Eden enlisted the support of Dulles (even heavier and more flabby now than last January) and after pointing out that German reunification had figured in all the previous notes, and that Adenauer expected it, they won their case. In the confusion Frank Roberts, who was in a state of fury with the P.M., was mistaken by the latter for one of Dulles' advisers and treated to a homily as such.

During the Plenary Conference, which centred on E.D.C. and which again Pitblado attended, Christopher and I entertained to drinks at "Out of the Blue" Alastair Buchan,[1] Wilson Broadbent (*Daily Mail*), Ed. Russell,[2] and one or two members of the delegation.

---

[1] Younger son of John Buchan, Lord Tweedsmuir. An energetic journalist and writer.

[2] American provincial newspaper owner, always friendly and forthcoming, married to the Duke of Marlborough's eldest daughter, Sarah, not to be confused with Winston Churchill's daughter.

Dined at the "Pink Beach" with Christopher, Ed. Russell, and two particularly glamorous American women called Mrs Steele and Miss Jinx Falkenburg. The latter is the sister of the Wimbledon champion and obviously a champion herself in other ways. There is no doubt that American women are supreme in the art of flattering the male ego.

Dragged self away to return to the Mid-Ocean and put a thoughtful P.M. (unconscionably bored by a dinner given in his honour by the French) to bed. He said, as I have been feeling for the past forty-eight hours, that all our problems, even those such as Egypt, shrink into insignificance by the side of the one great issue which this conference has thrown up.

A snake runs away from you because it is frightened. But if you tread on its tail it will rear up and strike you. This is to me an analogy with Soviet Russia. I put it to Eden who agreed most heartily.

Before going to bed the P.M. told me that he and Ike had agreed to treat forcing through the ratification of E.D.C. as a combined military operation. If it does not go through, the Americans do not agree with the P.M. that Germany must be invited to join N.A.T.O. On the contrary they talk of falling back on "peripheral" defence, which means the defence of their bases stretching in a crescent from Iceland via East Anglia, Spain and North Africa to Turkey. This, in the P.M.'s view, would entail France becoming Communist-dominated (and finally going the way of Czechoslovakia) while the Americans sought to rearm Germany sandwiched between the hostile powers of Russia and France. Frank Roberts thinks that we shall in the event just get over the E.D.C. hurdle. If we don't, the P.M. intends to go all out to persuade the Americans to work for the Germany-in-N.A.T.O. alternative. This is a precarious situation.

Monday, December 7th
Today there were endless Plenary Meetings, three in all. I attended two of them and recorded the talks about Egypt and about Indo-China. Most of the morning meeting was *in camera* – discussing the one thing of importance that has arisen at this conference. The last, about the Communiqué (which was bound

in any case to be colourless and uninformative) lasted till 1.30
a.m. The real mistake was having the French, with whom none
of the things we mind most about can be discussed and who, at
the Plenary Meetings, insist on making long formal statements
(e.g. on Indo-China) explaining the situation at length – as if we
didn't know the facts (rather than the remedies) already.

Eden told me that the P.M. did really well at the meeting *in
camera* and turned the minds of the Americans.

Tonight I dined in Hamilton with Mrs Steele, Ed. Russell and
Christopher but returned at 10.30 to the Mid-Ocean where
discussions on the Communiqué were in full swing – the French
being adamant about some reference to E.D.C. It was curious
that Eden, not Bidault, went up to seek agreement from the
bed-ridden Laniel.

Tuesday, December 8th
This morning I strolled down to bathe with John Foster Dulles,
who said that the presence of the French, and the constant need
for interpretation, had greatly hampered the conference. Since
it was the Americans who insisted on the French being invited,
I thought this indeed ironical. The surf was heavy on the beach
and Dulles was twice capsized.

The P.M. went to see Ike at 10.00 and told me that he said
to him that the Americans sending arms to Egypt after January
1st would have no less effect in the U.K. than the British sending
arms to China would have in the U.S.A. The President, he said,
took this seriously.

Eisenhower also told him that he was in favour of International
Conferences provided there was no agenda *and* no communiqué.
The press here (nearly 200 of them) are furious at the scanty
information they have received. Alastair Buchan had the impudence to tell me that conferences such as this should be arranged
for the convenience of the press.

The President left before lunch, and Bidault with Parodi and
de Margerie came to take leave of the P.M. before their
departure. W. said to Bidault that if he had been rough on the
French it was not because he loved them less than formerly,
but because he wanted to urge them to save themselves and

not, in consequence of refusing E.D.C., to force the Americans to fall back on a "peripheral" defence of Europe. It was not the French Government which was "bitching" (a word de Margerie found difficulty in translating!) it all but the French parliamentary system. With this Bidault heartily concurred.

This evening the Speaker (Sir John Cox) gave a dinner for the House of Assembly in the Mid-Ocean – the Conference Room having rapidly been converted for the purpose. The P.M. was the principal speaker and did it very well. The Governor, Sir Alexander Hood, was outstandingly eloquent; the Speaker outstandingly turgid.

I sat between two members of the Assembly. Bermuda has a parliamentary system in which there are no parties but each member votes according to his conscience. This is simplified by property qualifications for the franchise which means that out of 35,000 inhabitants only 5,000 can vote. One of my neighbours was gravely annoyed that the P.M. should have insisted on two coloured men being asked to the banquet which the Governor had given for the Big Three. No black men had been asked to the banquet given for the Queen a fortnight ago and there had been a fuss both in the House of Commons and in the British press which had prompted the P.M.'s action.

Wednesday, December 9th

A day of rest and glorious sunshine. Played golf in the morning with Norman Brook on the Mid-Ocean golf course which is both good and beautiful. Saw a number of strange birds – bright blue and bright red, also a long-legged white bird like a crane. The cedar trees all over the island have died of a blight and present a strangely funereal effect.

Lunched with the P.M., Eden, the Governor, the Speaker, Pug Ismay, Lord Cherwell and Christopher. Then drove with Christopher to Hamilton where the P.M. inspected the Bermuda Regiment.

Christopher and I entertained Evelyn Shuckburgh, John Priestman and Denis Allen to dinner at the villa. They went for a midnight bathe while I went to collect Mrs Steele at the Coral Beach Club and went with her to hear calypsos at the Elbow

Beach. Returned to the villa at 3.30 a.m. and found myself locked out. Prof.'s valet/secretary, the admirable Harvey, saved the situation.

Thursday, December 10th
Bathed in the morning and attended to the P.M. who was in a cantankerous frame of mind. I, too, was mentally dyspeptic.

In the afternoon drove with Norman Brook to St George's, the old capital, to see the beautiful seventeenth-century colonial style church, white without and roofed with delicious-smelling cedar beams within. The early colonial stone memorial tablets are particularly delightful. It is notable how many Governors and eminent citizens were carried off by yellow fever in comparatively early youth. Observed, with amusement, that the vain Lord Moran had contrived to have his signature, solitary on a large sheet of writing paper, inserted in the treasure chest, among seventeenth-century silver, with those of the Queen, Mr Eden and M. Bidault.

Boarded the B.O.A.C. aircraft Canopus at 8.00 p.m. with the rest of the British delegation and the now recovered M. Laniel. The P.M., who didn't want to have to talk French, contrived to have him sent straight to his bunk on Lord Moran's advice, after arranging for him to dine before we left. Heavily drugged, the unsuspecting M. Laniel went to sleep and did not disturb the dinner party on board.

The four-hour difference of time between Bermuda and London rather puts one out for eating and sleeping purposes.

John Priestman stood on his head in the main cabin saying that he wanted to be the first Englishman who had ever done so in mid-Atlantic.

Friday, December 11th
We reached London after a wonderfully smooth flight at 11.30 a.m. G.M.T. Before landing I dictated a long letter descriptive of the Bermuda Conference for the P.M. to send to the Queen, who is shortly due at Fiji in the *Gothic*.

We reached Downing Street 12½ hours after leaving the

Mid-Ocean Club. Magic carpet indeed. And so the £2.2.6. I had spent on insuring my life was fortunately wasted.

After luncheon I took the train to Woking, with mama and Violet Bonham Carter[1] as travelling companions. The latter very incensed with W.S.C. who, she says, promised her that there should be a free vote in the House on the vexed question of sponsored television. She asked me to tell him that she was affectionate but disaffected!

Met by Meg, looking very well, and found Harriet enchanting though aloof, and suffering from a whooping cough injection.

[1] Lady Violet Bonham Carter, daughter of Asquith by his first marriage. A leading Liberal protagonist and first-class public speaker. Very old friend of Churchill.

TWENTY-THREE

VISIT TO THE U.S.A. AND CANADA
JUNE 1954

Thursday, June 24th
At 7.45 p.m. we took off from Heathrow, the following party:
    The Prime Minister
    Mr Eden
    Lord Cherwell
    Lord Moran
    Sir Edwin Plowden
    Sir Harold Caccia
    Denis Allen
    Anthony Rumbold
    Christopher Soames
    Me (or perhaps it should be I) plus
    an unusually small body of ancillaries.
The journey was planned by the Prime Minister as long ago as
last April, but its purposes have varied as the weeks went
by. Primarily it was to convince the President that we must
co-operate more fruitfully in the atomic and hydrogen sphere
and that we, the Americans and British, must go and talk to the
Russians in an effort to avert war, diminish the effect of Cold
War and procure a ten years' period of "easement" during which
we can divert our riches and our scientific knowledge to ends
more fruitful than the production of catastrophic weapons.
Now, owing to Anglo-American disagreement over S.E. Asia,
reflected very noticeably at the Geneva Conference, the meeting
has become in the eyes of the world (and the Foreign Secretary)

an occasion for clearing the air and re-creating good feeling. The main topics are to be: Indo-China, Germany if E.D.C. fails, Egypt and atoms.

We had a prosperous flight in the Canopus, landing for an hour at Gander. It only became bumpy when we approached the American coast (which was, of course, the moment I chose to write this).

Friday, June 25th

On arrival at Washington we were met by Nixon, the Vice President, and Foster Dulles. Winston and Christopher are staying at the White House; I at the Embassy. I spent most of the day at the White House where, on arrival, W. at once got down to talking to the President. The first and vast surprise was when the latter at once agreed to talks with the Russians – a possibility of which W. had hoped to persuade the Americans after long talks on Indo-China, Europe, atoms; on all these the first impressions were surprisingly and immediately satisfactory while the world in general believes that there is at this moment greater Anglo-American friction than ever in history and that these talks are fraught with every possible complication and difficulty.

The White House is not attractive; it is too like a grand hotel inside. Moreover all the lights burn all the time which is extremely disagreeable at high noon – particularly as the sunshine is bright and the temperature in the 90°s.

This evening, after the official conversations – at which Eden and Dulles were present – the President gave a dinner for the P.M. to meet the American Cabinet. I was not bidden and went instead to dine with the Empsons,[1] in their garden, by the light of candles and fireflies. To bed, very tired, at 11 p.m.

Saturday, June 26th

After a comfortable night and delicious breakfast, to the White House for the morning. The P.M. was closeted with the Presi-

---

[1] Sir Charles Empson, Commercial Minister in Washington. He and his wife, Monica, had been hospitable to my wife and me on our honeymoon, when he held a similar post in Rome. He was later Ambassador to Chile.

dent, again to his great satisfaction. Christopher and I made the acquaintance of his large staff and also swam in the indoor pool (water temperature 86 degrees). The P.M. met the leaders of Congress at lunch and (according to his own account) addressed them afterwards with impromptu but admirable eloquence! I lunched at the Embassy with the Makinses. They have delicious food provided by a French chef.

At the White House all the afternoon. Good progress, this time on Egypt. The P.M. elated by success and in a state of excited good humour. In the middle of the afternoon meeting, while Christopher and I were sipping high-balls and reading telegrams in his sitting-room, he suddenly emerged and summoned us to go up to the "Solarium" with him so as to look at a great storm which was raging. I can't imagine anybody else interrupting a meeting with the President of the United States, two Secretaries of State and two Ambassadors just for this purpose. The Russian visit project has now been expanded (by the President, so the P.M. says) to a meeting in London, together with the French and West Germans, at the opening of which Ike himself would be present.

Dined with Rob Scott[1] and his wife. Interesting conversation with several State Department officials, especially Merchant and Byroade, about recognition of Communist China.[2] Their reasoning is ruled far more by sentiment than by logic. No answer to my question whether we should have been well advised to break off relations with Yugoslavia in 1947 because our feelings towards Tito's régime were so bitter.

Sunday, June 27th
All day at the White House except for luncheon at the Embassy. At 10.30 a.m. the President, in his luxurious cinema, showed us *The White Heron*, a film of the Queen's tour.

The Russian project has shrunk again as Dulles has been getting at the President. W. still determined to meet the Russians as he has now an assurance that the Americans won't object.

[1] Minister at the British Embassy.
[2] Which the British had done and Americans had not.

Invited to dinner with the President. Others there were, besides the P.M. and Eden, Dulles, Bedell Smith, Winthrop Aldrich, Roger Makins, Merchant, Christopher Soames. Very gay dinner, during which the P.M. and the President spoke highly of the Germans and in favour of their being allowed to rearm. The President called the French "a hopeless, helpless mass of protoplasm". Eden took the other line, with some support from Dulles, and ended by saying he could not be a member of any Government which acted as Ike and Winston seemed to be recommending. After dinner we adjourned to the Red Room and worked collectively and ineffectively on the draft of a Declaration – a kind of second Atlantic Charter – which the P.M. and the President propose to publish. It seems to me a very messy affair.

The P.M. went to bed at 12.00 elated and cheerful. He has been buoyed up by the reception he has had here and has not as yet had one single afternoon sleep. His sole relaxation has been a few games of bezique with me. Roger Makins said he never remembered a more riotous evening.

Monday, June 28th
Meeting in the President's office at 10.00 to discuss the Declaration (in which the P.M. had suddenly espied some Dulles-like anti-colonial sentiments) and the draft minutes on Indo-China, E.D.C. and Egypt. This was a much more orderly affair and was satisfactorily concluded.

At 12.30, having issued a separate and rather colourless communiqué on the subjects that have been discussed, we all set off for the Hotel Stattner to lunch with the Washington Press Club. A disgusting luncheon after which the P.M. answered written questions that had been handed in with his best verve and vigour. Everybody greatly impressed by the skill with which he turned some of the most awkward. Himself so pleased by his reception that when I leant over to collect his notes he shook me warmly by the hand under the impression that I was a Senator or pressman endeavouring to congratulate him.

After lunch the P.M. and Eden drove to the Embassy, whither they move their headquarters this afternoon. I played bezique with a highly contented Winston (in spite of the fact that I won 26,600 in one solitary game), but at 6.00 he was still fresh enough to address, first, the Commonwealth Ambassadors and after them the British press representatives. This was followed by a huge dinner at the Embassy, from which I mercifully escaped. I dined with Ed. and Sarah Russell at the Colony restaurant. Meanwhile at the Embassy the P.M. was holding forth about the Guatemala revolution (a current event) and, according to Tony Rumbold,[1] making the Foreign Secretary look rather small in argument (the F.S. being all for caution and the P.M. being all for supporting the U.S. in their encouragement of the rebels and their hostility to the Communist Guatemalan régime). I talked to the P.M. as he went to bed and he said that Anthony Eden was sometimes very foolish: he would quarrel with the Americans over some petty Central American issue which did not affect Great Britain and could forget about the downtrodden millions in Poland.

Tuesday, June 29th

A hectic morning for me at the Embassy mainly concerned with arrangements for the publication of the Eisenhower–Churchill Declaration of Principles, to which the Cabinet had suggested a few amendments. The P.M. went down to the White House at 11.30 to settle this and to take leave.

Luncheon party at the Embassy. The American guests were Dean Acheson, Eugene Meyer, Senator Hickenlooper, Mr Sterling Cole (Chairman of the Atomic Energy Commission), Mr Whitelaw Reid, Ed. Russell. I sat between the latter and Edwin Plowden.[2] After lunch the P.M. became jocular. He said that if he were ever chased out of England and became an American citizen, he would hope to be elected to Congress. He would then propose two amendments to the American Constitution: (i) that at least half the members of the U.S. Cabinet should have seats in Congress (ii) that the President, instead of signing

---

[1] Sir Anthony Rumbold, Bt., Evelyn Shuckburgh's successor as Principal Private Secretary to Anthony Eden.

[2] Afterwards Lord Plowden. Held numerous appointments of great importance including Chairmanship of the Atomic Energy Commission.

himself Dwight D. Eisenhower a hundred times a day, should
be authorised to sign himself "Ike".

At 3.30 we left the airfield, seen off by the Vice President
and Dulles, in a Canadian aircraft for Ottawa. Mike Pearson,[1]
Canadian Foreign Minister, travelled with us. I played bezique
with the P.M. most of the way.

We reached Ottawa at 5.45 p.m. Guards of Honour of all
three Services – the band in scarlet and bearskins – "Rule
Britannia" played as a special tribute to the P.M., a short
broadcast message (written by me), and a slow drive to the
Château Laurier Hotel.

Dinner in the P.M.'s suite: St Laurent,[2] Howe (Minister of
Defence), the Prof., Sir A. Nye (High Commissioner), Christopher and self. Dinner excellent (caviare, etc.). Nye most
interesting and agreeable, also Howe. St Laurent dumb and a
little glum – possibly even a bit shocked. A most secret subject[3]
discussed with apparent success. Left the party as soon as I
could get away in order to record this and to draft a speech for
the P.M. to broadcast tomorrow.

Wednesday, June 30th
The P.M. and Anthony Eden went to a meeting of the Canadian
Cabinet and at 12.00 noon the former addressed the press
correspondents. He did not do it as well as in Washington, but
it went down all right. Tony Rumbold and I then lunched with
Nicholas Monsarrat, author of *The Cruel Sea*, and now Information Officer in the High Commissioner's Office. A gentle
intelligent man, he prophesied that in South Africa it might
well be that when Malan[4] went, the extremists (Strydom and
Donges) would get the upper hand. A republic would be declared,
Natal would secede and out of the resulting civil war would come
a great native uprising.

The P.M. would spend most of the afternoon reading the
English newspapers so that he started his broadcast (to which

[1] Later Prime Minister of Canada.
[2] French-Canadian Liberal Prime Minister.
[3] The American threat to use the atomic bomb in Korea.
[4] Nationalist Prime Minister who had beaten Smuts in a General Election.

I contributed a few sentences) very belatedly, recorded it after we were supposed to have left for the Country Club and in consequence made everything late throughout the whole evening. Our drive to the Country Club, in huge open Cadillacs, was impressive because of the affectionate cheering crowds. The dinner there, given by St Laurent, was also impressive, partly on account of two moving speeches made by the two Prime Ministers and partly because all the Canadian Ministers, etc., present were so delightful. I sat between Campney, from Vancouver, who becomes Minister of Defence tomorrow, and Mr Beaudouin, the Speaker. The latter, a French Canadian, was voluble, sentimental and rather a bore, the former interesting and redolent of that enthusiasm tempered by modesty which distinguishes the Canadians from their southern neighbours.

After dinner we had a tumultuous ovation at the airport and flew in a Canadian aircraft to New York, I playing bezique with a somewhat tired but very triumphant P.M. Boarded the *Queen Elizabeth* at 1.00 a.m.

Thursday, July 1st
A milling crowd came on board, Baruch, Giraudier (a Cuban who keeps Winston supplied with cigars and brandy at home) to see the P.M., Roger Makins, etc., to see Eden, Henry and Mimi Hyde to see me. Bags, newspapers, letters succeeded each other at confusing speed and all in a heat and humidity which seemed, if anything, to increase as we sailed away at noon, past Manhattan and down the Hudson River.

Lunched with the P.M. in the Verandah Grill. Oh, the changes that have taken place, in order to please the great dollar-producing clientele, since last we sailed on the *Queen Mary* in January 1953! The Verandah Grill food, which formerly equalled or surpassed many famous French restaurants, has become Americanised and has sunk to a level of ordinariness, if not tastelessness, which bewilders and disappoints. The same applies in lesser degree to the service and the appearance of the ship's company.

We went on the bridge after lunch and then I played bezique with the P.M. till dinner-time. Dined in the Verandah Grill with

Lord Moran and Tony Rumbold. Afterwards we saw a series of short films – all American. It is a pity, and rather a humiliating pity, that the Cunard line must go to these lengths to de-Anglicise themselves.

Friday, July 2nd
Still very hot. Indeed today and yesterday are more oppressive than any day in Washington. The broken ice has moved further south than usual this year and we are taking the southern Gulf-Stream route.

The P.M. told me this morning he was decided on an expedition to Russia, where he would ask freedom for Austria as an earnest of better relations. Meanwhile Anthony Eden, who has only come back by sea because he wants to talk over future plans and to get a firm date for Winston to hand over to him, is feeling bashful about choosing the right moment and last night consulted me about this. I thought, and said, how strange it was that two men who knew each other so well should be hampered by shyness on this score. This morning the opportunity came and W. tentatively fixed September 21st for the hand-over and early August for the Moscow visit. Returning to his cabin he then dictated to me a long telegram to Molotov proposing talks with the Soviet leaders in which the U.S. would not, indeed, participate but could, W. thought, be counted on to do their best with their own public opinion.

We all had a gay luncheon in the P.M.'s dining-room, but after luncheon the fun began over the Molotov telegram. Eden went on deck to read; Winston retired to his sitting-room and had the telegram shortened and amended. He asked me to take it to Eden and to say he now intended to despatch it. Eden told me he disliked the whole thing anyway: he had been adding up the pros and cons and was sure the latter (danger of serious Anglo-American rift, effect on Adenauer and Western Europe, damage to the solid and uncompromising front we have built up against Russia, practical certainty that the high hopes of the public would be shattered by nothing coming of the meeting) far outweighed the pros. However, what he really disliked was Winston's intention of despatching the telegram without showing it to the Cabinet. Why couldn't he wait till we were home and let A.E. deliver the message to Molotov when he saw him at Geneva? Would I tell W. that if he insisted, he must do as he wished but that it would be against his, Eden's, strong advice.

I imparted this to W. who said it was all nonsense: this was merely an unofficial enquiry of Molotov. If it were accepted, that was the time to consult the Cabinet, before an official approach was made. I represented, as strongly as I could, that this was putting the Cabinet "on the spot", because if the Russians answered affirmatively, as was probable, it would in practice be too late for the Cabinet to express a contrary opinion. W. said he would make it a matter of confidence with the Cabinet: they would have to choose between him and his intentions. If they opposed the visit, it would give him a good occasion to go. I said this would split the country and the Conservative Party from top to bottom. Moreover if he went on this account, the new administration would start with a strong anti-Russian reputation. After a great deal of talk Eden was sent for and eventually agreed to a compromise which put *him* "on the spot". The P.M. agreed to send the telegram to the Cabinet provided he could say that Eden agreed with it in principle (which of course he does not). Eden weakly gave in. I am afraid the P.M. has been ruthless and unscrupulous in all this, because he must know that at this moment, for both internal and international reasons, Eden cannot resign – though he told me, while all this was going on and I was acting as intermediary, that he had thought of it.

Bezique with W. till dinner, which Charles Moran, Tony Rumbold and I had downstairs. Then a film, followed by drinks with Gavin[1] and Irene Astor who are travelling home on board.

Saturday, July 3rd

Cooler. Atlantic breezes instead of the Gulf Stream. Worked with W. most of the morning and composed telegrams, descriptive of the Washington talks, to Menzies and Holland[2] which

---

[1] 2nd Lord Astor of Hever, married to Field Marshal Earl Haig's daughter, Irene (Rene).

[2] Prime Minister of New Zealand.

the P.M. accepted. Drinks with the Astors before luncheon, which we had in the P.M.'s dining-room with Charles Moran, Christopher and the Prof. The latter was in his best anecdotal form. I liked his apocryphal story of Victor Cazalet and Lady Colefax[1] having a race after an electric lion. Victor won because Lady Colefax would keep on stopping to tell the public she had known the lion as a cub.

After lunch I succeeded in getting away with only one game of bezique and making Christopher take over. Saw Eden this morning. Got the impression that he was aggrieved with W. which I don't find surprising. W., on the other hand, complains to me that he was trapped into sending the telegram to the Cabinet, had forgotten it was the weekend, and now he wouldn't get a reply till Monday. So he telegraphed to Rab saying that he assumed the telegram had already gone on to Moscow.

Dined in the Verandah Grill with the Astors and Tony Rumbold. Then joined the P.M. and Eden. The former was now quite reconciled to the Cabinet having been consulted about the Molotov telegram because Rab had telegraphed suggesting only one or two small amendments and had appeared generally satisfied with the main idea. So everybody went to bed happy and W. and I played bezique, to my great financial advantage (six grands coups!) till nearly 2.00 a.m.

Sunday, July 4th
The P.M. deep in Harold Nicolson's *Public Faces* and greatly impressed by the 1932 prophecy of atomic bombs. Went to church, which was packed. Then descended to the profane and played bezique till luncheon. The Astors, Christopher and I lunched with the P.M. who was in splendid form, describing the heart trouble he developed in consequence of dancing a *pas seul* after dinner at Blenheim some fifty years ago, elaborating the desirable results which would come from re-establishing the Heptarchy in England (so as to ease the pressure on Parliament) and teaching Gavin, a non-smoker, to smoke cigars.

[1] Well-known London hostess who collected everybody of political and intellectual importance at her dining-room table, fed them well and amused them.

A Turkish bath this evening, followed by dinner with the Astors and Adrian Bailey in the Verandah Grill, a cinema and a blood row between Winston and Anthony Eden. This arose in the following way. I went down about 11.30 to see how their dinner party (W.S.C., A.E., the Prof., Moran, Christopher) was getting on. Everybody very jovial when suddenly Miss Gilliatt[1] brought me a telegram from Roger Makins about the effects in America of a speech made by Senator Knowland,[2] who has evidently implied that we have been pressing the Americans to let Red China into U.N.O. and has said that if this happens, the United States will leave the Organisation. Eden read the telegram first and said that he objected to H.M.G. saying anything in reply to Knowland: it looked as if we minded. The P.M. then read it and wanted to issue a statement from this ship to the effect, first, that the matter had not been seriously discussed during the Washington talks and secondly that there was no question of our recognising Red China while she was still in a state of war with the United Nations.

Eden said that if we made any such statement it would destroy all chance of success at Geneva: we ought to keep entry into U.N.O. as a reward for China if she were good. The P.M. looked grave: he had not realised, he said, that what Knowland said was in fact the truth – Eden *did* contemplate the admission of China into U.N.O. while a state of war still existed. Eden got red in the face with anger and there was a disagreeable scene. They both went to bed in a combination of sorrow and anger, the P.M. saying that Anthony was totally incapable of differentiating great points and small points (a criticism that has an element of truth in it).

Christopher and I then went to the Verandah Grill with Gavin and Rene, Tony Rumbold and two American girls. We danced and drank champagne till nearly 4.00 a.m.

---

[1] Elizabeth Gilliatt, daughter of the leading gynaecologist Sir William Gilliatt, was one of Churchill's personal secretaries.

[2] Right-wing Republican senator and strong supporter of Chiang Kai-Shek against the Chinese Communists.

Monday, July 5th

The P.M. looked still grave and depressed this morning and dictated to me a minute about the Knowland question. Anthony Eden did not wake up till 12.00, but he seemed to have recovered his equanimity and was cheerful when I handed the minute to him. We lunched in the P.M.'s dining-room (he staying in bed). In the afternoon I talked to Rene on deck, played bezique and at 6.30 there was a small cocktail party for fellow passengers given by the P.M. and Mr Eden.

We all dined in the P.M.'s dining-room. It was a most amicable occasion, last night's differences resolved and the P.M. saying that provided A.E. always bore in mind the importance of not quarrelling violently with the Americans over Far Eastern questions (which affected them more than us) a way ought certainly to be found of bringing Red China into the United Nations on terms tolerable to the U.S.A. This was followed by much quoting of Pope, Shakespeare and others on the P.M.'s part and a dissertation on Persian and Arabic poets and writing by Eden (who apparently got a First in Oriental Languages at Oxford). To bed at 2.00.

Tuesday, July 6th

Cherbourg at 9.00 a.m. and a swift passage homewards. We docked at Southampton just before 5.00 p.m. after a passage which scarcely a ripple had disturbed – at any rate as far as the sea was concerned. Meg met me and drove me to the Old Rectory at Stratfield Saye with the disconcerting news that the Italian cook whom we have just imported at great expense from Treviso is six months' pregnant. Up till the present a series of disasters has accompanied our "moving in".

I told Winston that I believed the cook's downfall to have been brought about by a man in a street in Verona after dark. "Obviously not one of the Two Gentlemen," he commented.

*   *   *

The following day, July 7th, there was a Cabinet in the course of which W.S.C. revealed his intention to meet the Russians and also another even more startling decision recently taken by the Defence Committee and communicated to St Laurent and Howe in Ottawa at dinner last Tuesday. In the evening I heard from Lord Swinton the reactions of the Cabinet, underlined even more forcibly by Harold Macmillan after dinner at No. 10 (an official dinner for Ismay in his capacity as Secretary General of N.A.T.O., during which I sat next to Sir W. Haley, editor of *The Times*). In consequence of all this Lord Salisbury said he must resign. I became much involved in the subsequent activities, being approached separately by Lord Swinton and the Lord Chancellor and asked by them to explain all the circumstances to Sir M. Adeane for the information and (as the Lord Chancellor thought) possible intervention of the Queen. Salisbury both dislikes the Russian project and objects to the P.M.'s action in approaching Molotov without consulting and obtaining the agreement of the Cabinet. Lord Swinton has represented to him, first that this is the "end of a voyage" with Winston and that a similar case is therefore unlikely to occur; secondly, that his resignation will do great harm to Anglo-American relations because it will be greatly played up by those who, like Senator Knowland, will cry out against the Russian talks and will be represented as a revolt by Lord Salisbury against an anti-American move on the part of Winston and Eden. Also, of course, it will be highly embarrassing to Eden.

Friday, July 16th
Things came to a head today, at any rate within 10 Downing Street. Before luncheon Harold Macmillan came to see Lady Churchill and told her that the Cabinet was in danger of breaking up on this issue. When he had gone she rang me up and asked me to come and see her. I in fact knew more about the situation than she did and since she proposed to "open" the matter to Winston at luncheon, I suggested I should stay too.

She began by putting her foot into it in saying that the Cabinet were angry with W. for mishandling the situation, instead of saying that they were trying to stop Salisbury going. He snapped back at her – which he seldom does – and afterwards complained to me that she always put the worst complexion on everything in so far as it affected him. However, he did begin to see that Salisbury's resignation would be serious on this issue, whereas two days ago when I mentioned the possibility to him he said that he didn't "give a damn". On the other hand it became clear that he had taken the steps he had, without consulting the Cabinet, quite deliberately. He admitted to me that if he had waited to consult the Cabinet after the *Queen Elizabeth* returned, they would almost certainly have raised objections and caused delays. The stakes in this matter were so high and, as he sees it, the possible benefits so crucial to our survival, that he was prepared to adopt any methods to get a meeting with the Russians arranged.

*   *   *

I wrote the following in August:

It ended thus. There was a crucial Cabinet on Friday, July 23rd, at which Lord Salisbury threatened to resign and was supported by Harry Crookshank. W. did not therefore send off the telegram he had drafted to Molotov, more especially as he had received from Eden a cold and almost minatory minute just before the Cabinet began. The matter was adjourned till Monday, with the threat of Lord S.'s resignation hanging over everybody and the still more alarming possibility that Winston, if thwarted, would resign, split the country and the party and produce a situation of real gravity.

We went to Chequers for the weekend. It was a stag-party: Lord Goddard [Lord Chief Justice], Lord Swinton, Oliver Lyttelton, Walter Monckton*, Prof., Brendan Bracken, Desmond Morton* and me, with Christopher arriving for dinner on Sunday night. There was much laughter, many anecdotes (at which Lord Goddard excels) and prodigious feats in the repetition of verse. But the air of crisis permeated it all and Oliver Lyttelton, who is in any case resigning the Colonial Office next week to go back to business, was positively alarmist. However, on Sunday a note from the Russians was published, answering one of ours dated May 7th and demanding a meeting of thirty-two powers to discuss the Russian European Security plan. "Foreign Secretaries of the world unite; you have nothing to lose but your jobs," was the P.M.'s first comment on this proposal. It was nevertheless clear that we could hardly go forward with the P.M.'s plan for bilateral talks in the face of this new Russian proposal and so the critical Cabinet on Monday morning passed off without dispute. A new telegram to Molotov was decided upon and the text of it agreed by the P.M. and Eden on Monday afternoon. Unless the Russians react strongly in favour of a meeting, the prospective visit to Russia is likely to be postponed *sine die* and the P.M., feeling that he has at least made the effort and is justified as far as his frequent policy statements over the last two years are concerned, is content – at least on the surface. Lord Salisbury is smiling again.

But the P.M., in spite of his undertaking to Eden on the *Queen Elizabeth* that he will resign about September 20th, is showing new signs of irresolution on that issue. The thought of abandoning office grows more abhorrent as the time comes nearer. I doubt if he realises what trouble is in store for him from his Cabinet colleagues if he stays on. But I think he does realise how difficult it would be for them to *turn* him out without ruining their chances at the next election.

The Cabinet went away for the recess, some of them glum, some of them bewildered. Winston retired to Chartwell where I spent much of August with him. As the days went by he became less reconciled to giving up office and adumbrated all sorts of reasons why he should not. Never had a P.M. been treated like this, that he was to be hounded from his place merely because his second-in-command wanted the job. And what was there in the argument that the new régime needed a year to take over before an election? On the contrary there was little for a new Government to offer and as an election drew near it would be a target for abuse by half the country. Eden had far better start an entirely new deal after a General Election. It looks like a terrible and painful struggle and Anthony, of course, will say: I was promised July, then

September 20th; why should I now believe he will even hand over at the next election? Meanwhile the Russian visit, not over-enthusiastically received by Molotov, seems to have sunk into the background.

TWENTY-FOUR

THE PRIME MINISTER'S RESIGNATION

[Written in two parts: the first six days before
the resignation, the second immediately after it]

March 29th, 1955

When he asked me to rejoin him, in October 1951, Winston said
it would probably be only for a year. He did not intend to remain
long in office but wished to initiate the recovery of the country
under a Conservative Government. However, although many
people, recalling Baldwin's action after the Coronation of King
George VI, predicted that Winston would make way for Anthony
Eden after the Coronation, he never had any intention of so
doing. The Margate speech, in October 1953, satisfied him that
he could still dominate the scene; but, of course, in the winter
of 1953–54 Eden's "hungry eyes", as Winston called them,
became more beseeching and more impatient.

During the spring of 1954, when Eden went to Geneva for
the Five-Power Conference, he had extracted what he thought
a promise – and what almost certainly was a half promise – that
W. would go at the end of the session. On a Sunday at Chequers
(in March or April) he had a long talk with W. in the small
sitting-room across the passage from the dining-room and
emerged with sparkling eyes to tell me that he was doubtful
whether he ought to form his Government at the beginning of
the summer recess. Ought he not to meet Parliament with it at

once and not wait for that till October? He asked me to look up the precedents. I did so and wrote to him in manuscript, when he was at Geneva, to the effect that there were no clear precedents one way or the other; but in 1905 Campbell Bannerman had certainly governed quite a time before presenting himself and his Government to Parliament. In spite of this he foolishly wrote to Winston saying that he attached importance to this point and hoped W. would go in the middle of July so that A. could form his Government before the House rose. Winston replied that he had given no promise and had in any case now decided not to resign at the end of the session.

Under pressure Winston next said that he would go on September 20th, 1954. The fact that Eden only came back with him on the *Queen Elizabeth* in order to settle the issue, had occurred to W. just before we embarked and almost induced him to fly home instead.

But in August 1954 the Prime Minister again changed his mind. Why should he resign? He wrote to Anthony, who was on holiday in Austria, a masterly letter which went through about six drafts during the week of August 10th–18th. He emphasised the folly of taking over the end of an administration and becoming the target for electoral abuse, and he said that he intended to reconstitute the Government and remain in office. He reminded him of the dismal careers enjoyed at No. 10 by Rosebery after Gladstone and by Balfour after Salisbury. Eden was dejected, but there was in fact nothing he could do about it, and the P.M. had a great personal success at the Conservative Conference in October 1954 at Blackpool.

Even the press now began to be tired of speculating on W.'s resignation, except for the *Daily Mirror* which had a personal vendetta against him. But Winston himself, seeing the hopes of a Top Level meeting deferred owing to Eisenhower's unwillingness to meet the Russians, began to tire of his position. During the winter months, alone with him at the bezique table or in the dining-room, I listened to many disquisitions of which the burden was: "I have lost interest; I am tired of it all." So he finally decided to go at the beginning of the 1955 Easter recess and, after he had ruminated on this for some weeks, he told A.E.

and Rab Butler. He also invited the Queen to dine on April 4th, 1955, the eve of his resignation. The secret was closely guarded.

On Friday, March 11th, I set off with Winston for Chequers in a Rolls Royce he contemplated buying. On the way we went to the Zoo to see his lion, Rota, and his leopard, Sheba. Shortly after we had reached Chequers, and had settled down to bezique, there arrived a minute from Anthony Eden covering a telegram from Makins in Washington which described various manoeuvres suggested by the Americans for inducing the French to ratify the London–Paris Agreements which have taken the place of the European Defence Committee as the basis of Western European Defence. These included a suggestion that Eisenhower should go to Paris on May 8th, 1955, the tenth anniversary of V.E. Day, and solemnly ratify the agreements in company with President Coty, Adenauer and Sir Winston Churchill. W. did not take in the implications at once. Lord Beaverbrook came to dinner (the first time for many months) and it was not until he had gone that W. re-read the telegram and the somewhat discouraging and disparaging minute which accompanied it. Of course, he said to me, this meant all bets were off: he would stay and, with Eisenhower, meet the Russians. I pointed out that no suggestion of meeting the Russians was made, but he brushed this aside because he saw a chance of escape from his increasingly unpalatable timetable.

The next morning he had not changed his mind and wrote to A.E., who was at Dorneywood, to tell him. Not surprisingly this produced an infuriated reply and there was every sign of trouble. It happened on Monday in the Cabinet. Anthony had been warned by Norman Brook and by me (I had given the P.M. and Norman dinner at the Turf on Sunday night) to stick entirely to the merits of the American proposal. But at the end of the Cabinet he raised the personal issue, and W., in the face of silent and embarrassed colleagues, said coldly that this was not a matter on which he required guidance or on which Cabinet discussion was usual. Eventually, when it was established that Eisenhower did not contemplate a meeting with the Russians (and to this end there were quiet talks between the American

Ambassador, Aldrich, and Sir Ivone Kirkpatrick – of which the
P.M. knew nothing and of which I only heard by accident),
Winston gave way and announced he would still go as
planned.

The ensuing days were painful. W. began to form a cold hatred
of Eden who, he repeatedly said, had done more to thwart him
and prevent him pursuing the policy he thought right than
anybody else. But he also admitted to me on several occasions
that the prospect of giving everything up, after nearly sixty
years in public life, was a terrible wrench. He saw no reason
why he should go: he was only doing it for Anthony. He sought
to persuade his intimate friends, and himself, that he was being
hounded from office.

The truth was this. He could still make a great speech, as
was proved in the defence debate on March 1st. Indeed none
could rival his oratory or his ability to inspire. But he was ageing
month by month and was reluctant to read any papers except
the newspapers or to give his mind to anything that he did not
find diverting. More and more time was given to bezique and
ever less to public business. The preparation of a Parliamentary
Question might consume a whole morning; facts would be
demanded from Government departments and not arouse any
interest when they arrived (they would be marked "R" and left
to moulder in his black box); it was becoming an effort even to
sign letters and a positive condescension to read Foreign Office
telegrams. And yet on some days the old gleam would be there,
wit and good humour would bubble and sparkle, wisdom would
roll out in telling sentences and still, occasionally, the sparkle of
genius could be seen in a decision, a letter or a phrase. But was
he the man to negotiate with the Russians and moderate the
Americans? The Foreign Office thought not; the British public
would, I am sure, have said yes. And I, who have been as
intimate with him as anybody during these last years, simply do
not know.

Like the fish which is almost landed, he made the last struggle
to escape from the net when the day of his resignation was only
a week off. At least I *think* it is the last struggle, because at the
time of writing it is not over. On Sunday, March 27th, he learned

that Bulganin [Soviet leader] in spite of the fact that the French Senate had ratified the agreements, had spoken favourably of Four-Power talks. On the evening of March 28th, after W. had dined with Rab and discussed the forthcoming Budget, he told me that there was a crisis: two serious strikes (newspapers and docks); an important Budget; the date of the General Election to be decided; the Bulganin offer. He could not possibly go at such a moment just to satisfy Anthony's personal hunger for power. If necessary he would call a party meeting and let the party decide. This latter threat was one he had made during the March 11th–15th crisis and I had said that it would indeed make an unhappy last chapter to his biography if it told how he had destroyed the party of which he was the leader. However, I took all this to be late-night fantasy, a rather pathetic indication of the grief with which he contemplated the approach of his political abdication.

It was not. In the morning he was coldly determined not to go. He sent for Butler and despatched him as an emissary to Eden to say that the proposed timetable must be changed. As for me I preached to Tony Rumbold that for Eden "Amiability must be the watch-word". The Prime Minister thrived on opposition and showdowns; but amiability he could never resist.

Tonight he and Lady C. dine with the Edens who are giving a supposedly farewell dinner in their honour. During the day A. E. has at least had the good sense not to say or write anything.

Written shortly afterwards, but not dated:

On the morning of the 30th W. told me that the dinner-party had been agreeable, but that previously, at his audience, he had told the Queen he thought of putting off his resignation. He had asked her if she minded and she had said no! However he had had a very good night and felt peacefully inclined: he did not really think there was much chance of a top-level conference and that alone would be a valid reason for staying. At 6.30 p.m. he saw A.E. and Rab to tell them his decision. Before the meeting he said to me, "I have been altered and affected by

Anthony's amiable manner." This proved to me that the advice I had given was right and I am sure that the result, though pathetic, is in the best interests of all.

When the meeting was over, W. was a sad old man. He asked me to dine with him, but I could not on account of Sheran Cazalet's[1] twenty-first birthday party. All he said was: "What an extraordinary game of bezique we had this afternoon. I got a thousand aces the very first trick and yet in the end you rubied me."

On April 4th the Queen and Prince Philip dined at No. 10. It was a splendid occasion. The party consisted partly of the Senior Cabinet Ministers, partly of grandees like the Norfolks and partly of officials and family friends – some fifty in all. Lady Churchill took special pains about the food and 10 Downing Street can seldom if ever have looked so gay or its floorboards (soon due to be demolished)[2] have groaned under such a weight of jewels and decorations. There were incidents: the Edens, whose official precedence was low, tried to jump the queue advancing to shake hands with the Queen and the Duchess of Westminster put her foot through Clarissa's train ("That's torn it, in more than one sense," said the Duke of Edinburgh); Randolph got drunk and insisted on pursuing Clarissa with a derogatory article about Anthony Eden he had written for *Punch*; Mrs Herbert Morrison became much elated and could scarcely be made to leave the Queen's side; and I had a blazing row at dinner with Patrick Buchan-Hepburn because I had persuaded Lady Churchill to ask Alec and Elizabeth Home (he being Minister of State for Scotland) while James Stuart, the Secretary of State, had not been invited.

When they had all gone, I went up with Winston to his bedroom. He sat on his bed, still wearing his Garter, Order of Merit and knee-breeches. For several minutes he did not speak and I, imagining that he was sadly contemplating that this was his last night at Downing Street, was silent. Then suddenly he

---

[1] Daughter of Peter Cazalet by his first wife. Later married Simon Hornby, Chairman of W. H. Smith.
[2] The decision had been taken to pull down Nos. 10, 11 and 12 Downing Street and rebuild them.

stared at me and said with vehemence: "I don't believe Anthony can do it." His prophecies have often tended to be borne out by events.

The next evening Winston put on his top hat and frock coat, which he always wore for audiences, and went to Buckingham Palace to resign. Having ascertained from him some days before that if he were offered a Dukedom he would refuse, I pressed Michael Adeane to persuade the Queen to make the offer. Michael asked if I was absolutely sure it would be declined and I said that I was. Nevertheless I had qualms while the audience lasted and was relieved when Winston told me, on his return from the Palace, that the Queen had said she would be happy to make him a Duke and that though he had been tempted for a moment, he felt he would prefer to remain in the Commons till he died. Besides, he said, what good would a Dukedom be to Randolph; and it might ruin his and little Winston's political careers.

The following day we left in a special plane for Syracuse: Winston and Lady Churchill, Lord Cherwell and I. Meg was invited but she was soon to have another baby and did not feel up to it. In Syracuse it rained almost solidly for a fortnight. Winston painted one of the caves and we entertained Harry and Clare Luce who descended on us from Rome. The Prof. talked much of the crying need for higher technological education and I volunteered to try to raise the money for a new institute or college, to be inspired and promoted by Winston. [It was thus that Churchill College had its origins.]

Our visit, intended for three weeks, was cut short because of the cold and wet and we came home about April 20th. I had decided to leave the Foreign Service, in spite of flattering offers to be Head of Chancery in Washington, Paris and Bonn from Roger Makins, Gladwyn Jebb and Derick Hoyer Millar, the respective Ambassadors in those posts, and I had done so because I had been so long out of that world. Indeed out of eighteen years in the Diplomatic Service I had only served six directly under the Foreign Office, two abroad and four at home. So I had accepted an invitation to join Philip Hill,[1] instigated by

[1] Philip, Hill, Higginson, merchant bankers; subsequently Hill Samuel and Co.

my cousin Bill Cavendish-Bentinck. Accordingly there I went, at the beginning of June 1955, about a fortnight after my elder son, Sandy, was born.

APPENDICES

THE CORONATION OF QUEEN ELIZABETH II

Sunday, May 31st, 1953

The newspapers are saying that the lavishness, the popularity and the magnificence of the Coronation are due to the inspiration of Sir W. Churchill. Some Labour supporters doubtless think he will have an election on the emotional proceeds. All this is far from the case. Indeed he thinks it is being overdone, particularly by the newspapers, and he has had little or nothing to do with the preparations. But it is certainly a gay time and the country has gone wild with delight, showing its enthusiasm by decorations which are far more elaborate than those of 1937.

Meg and I, living temporarily at Chobham, have neither the energy nor indeed the strength to go to all the parties and the celebrations to which we have been invited. We went to the Coronation Ball at the Albert Hall on Wednesday last, May 27th, after a dinner-party of sixteen at 10 Downing Street (W.S.C. resplendent in his Garter, with the diamond star that belonged to Castlereagh); and on Friday (after I had spent an agreeable but exhausting twenty-four hours alone with W. at Chartwell) we went to the Household Brigade's Ball at Hampton Court. That was a splendid affair. The whole Palace was floodlit and the fountains were surrounded by massed flowers. Every man wore a tailcoat and decorations, the Knights of the Garter in knee-breeches. Almost every woman wore a tiara and a dress worthy of the occasion. We danced in the Great Hall and supped in the orangery. A world that vanished in 1939 lived again for the night, which obliged by being a fine and balmy one. The Queen, dancing with the Duke of Edinburgh and looking as beautiful as the people imagine her to be, stopped to ask us how her goddaughter did and whether she was yet out of control. She must, I thought, have wished she lived at Hampton Court rather than Windsor.

On Saturday and Sunday we recovered, with the help of some strenuous gardening, and eschewed the garden party at Hatfield with the prospect of so much before us in the coming week. Meanwhile in London Coronation fever grew, the crowds milling through the streets to see the banners and the arches, to catch a glimpse of the arriving celebrities among whom the most famous, such as Nehru and General Marshall, pass for nothing among so many. Practically all traffic was stopped and the police were near to being overwhelmed. Never has there been such excitement, never has a Monarch received such adulation, never has so much depended on the weather being kind for the great day.

Thursday, June 4th

But the weather on June 2nd was certainly not kind. Meg and I left at 7.15 a.m. for Westminster Abbey under skies cold, grey and threatening. I wore the full-dress uniform of the Diplomatic Service, with white knee-breeches; Meg her wedding dress with tiara. We sat in the Queen's box, to which she had kindly invited us, immediately above the Queen Mother and the Princesses. We were seated next to the Count and Countess of Barcelona[1] and to Porchy.[2] Though we saw little of the procession entering the Abbey, we saw every movement of the Queen, including the anointing, better than ninety-five per cent of the people in the Abbey, and looked straight at the massed peeresses whose robes and jewels sparkled with unique magnificence and whose movement as, with white gloved hands, they put their coronets on was aptly compared to the corps de

---

[1] Parents of King Juan Carlos of Spain.
[2] Lord Porchester, son of the Earl of Carnarvon, and a close friend of the Queen, whose racing manager he became.

ballet in *Lac des Cygnes*. Before the service began I walked out into the road between the Abbey and Westminster Hall and there, with some fifty peers in their crimson robes and others in pre-war full dress uniforms, I watched the Prime Ministers in their clarences and the Queen Mother's procession drive past towards the entrance of the Annexe. The skies were grey but the downpour did not come until well after the Coronation service had begun.

We lunched, rather poorly, in Westminster Hall. My mother, also in the Queen's Box, rushed home, took off her tiara and set off by underground to some evening festivity in Shoreditch. Meg and I, members of a less stalwart generation, went to bed till dinner. Then, with Owen[1] and Ruth Gwynedd, we joined the Prime Minister in a room in the Ministry of Materials from which to see the great fireworks display on the Thames. We returned with difficulty through the crowds to No. 10 and thence to the Soames' house in Eaton Place for a delicious midnight feast with them, the Westmorlands, the Rupert Nevills, Sarah Beauchamp and a couple of totally fish-out-of-water American actors.

Written later in June

On Friday, June 5th, we went, again in full dress uniform, to the Foreign Secretary's banquet to the Queen, given by Sir W. Churchill in the absence through illness of Anthony Eden. It was at Lancaster House, just restored to its ancient glories at phenomenal expense, and while the tables were bright with the Duke of Wellington's famous "Ambassador's" Service of gilt plate, the walls and the rooms were decorated by Constance Spry with flowers. Over 150 people sat down to dinner. Meg was between Prince Jean of Luxembourg and the Sheikh of Kuwait (the richest man in the world, but apparently a very grumpy magnate) and I between the representative of San Marino (in a magnificent uniform) and the soberly clad Icelander. W.S.C. was in his full dress of Lord Warden of the Cinque

---

[1] Grandson of Lloyd George, married to Ruth Coit with whose parents we were staying.

Ports, the Duke of Edinburgh in naval fulldress which had been temporarily revived for the Coronation, and almost everybody resplendent in seldom-seen uniforms and jewels. After it was over we drove down the illuminated Mall – an unforgettable sight – to a reception at Buckingham Palace where again unwonted brilliance reigned.

On June 6th we went to the Derby, driving behind Winston's car at breakneck speed on the wrong side of the Kingston by-pass. We saw Gordon Richards win his first Derby on Pinza, beating the Queen's Aureole, from Sybil Grant's[1] box and afterwards dined at the Durdans.[2]

On Monday, June 8th, we went to Covent Garden to see the gala performance, before the Queen, of Benjamin Britten's opera *Gloriana* written for the occasion. Oliver Messel's decor was superb, and the audience – well dressed at Covent Garden for a change – matched it. But the music was above our heads and the episode depicted by the opera, Elizabeth's squalid romance with Essex, totally unsuited to the occasion.

On Tuesday, June 9th, there was a vast Commonwealth dinner at No. 10 for the visiting Prime Ministers, followed by a reception which, thanks to lavish supplies of good champagne, was far superior to normal occasions of this kind. The Queen of Tonga stole the show.

On Friday, 12th, I escaped the Banquet to the Queen at the Guildhall and went to Chartwell. On the following day Tommy Lascelles drove down to tell the P.M. and me of Princess Margaret's wish to marry the recently divorced Peter Townsend – a pretty kettle of fish.

The Prime Minister's first reaction after Lascelles had left was to say that the course of true love must always be allowed to run smooth and that nothing must stand in the way of this handsome pair. However, Lady Churchill said that if he followed

---

[1] Wife of General Sir Charles Grant and sister of Lord Rosebery and Lady Crewe. Extraordinary to behold, but the wittiest and most entertaining woman I have ever known.

[2] House at Epsom bought by Lord Rosebery, the Liberal Prime Minister (1892–1895), and bequeathed to his daughter, Lady Sybil Grant.

this line he would be making the same mistake that he made at the abdication.

This gave me an opportunity of asking him what he had really intended at the abdication. Had he contemplated the possibility of Mrs Simpson as Queen of England? He said that he had certainly not. He was, however, loyal to his King whom he wrongly believed to be suffering from a temporary passion. His scheme, and that of Lord Beaverbrook, had been to frighten Mrs Simpson away from England. When she was gone he hoped the King would retire to Windsor and "pull up the drawbridge, post Lord Dawson of Penn[1] at the front gate and Lord Horder at the back gate", and let it be announced that he was too ill to undertake public business.

Winston said that great measures were taken to frighten Mrs Simpson away. Bricks were thrown through her windows and letters written threatening her with vitriol. "Do you mean that you did that?" I said, aghast. "No," he replied, "but Max did."

Years afterwards I told this story to Lord Beaverbrook who said that he certainly did not, but it was possible somebody from the Daily Express *might have! He also said that whereas it was probably true that Winston's principal motive had been loyalty to the King, his had been that it was all a lot of fun.*

I omit accounts of the lavish balls and other festivities which followed the Coronation – the Naval Review, magnificent fireworks at a great Windsor Castle ball, visits to Sutton to stay with the Sutherlands and many other purely social activities, all of them in sparkling contrast to the constraints of the previous years and seeming to usher in a period of prosperity and relaxation. They may have been, for a privileged few, the bubbles on the surface; but the surface itself was for the next ten years much less troubled than would have seemed credible twelve months previously.

One of the last emblems of austerity to vanish was sugar and sweet rationing. Churchill had, against the advice of the

[1] Lord Dawson and Lord Horder were the best-known London doctors.

Minister of Food, insisted that this be abolished before the crowds assembled, from home and abroad, for the Coronation. He was warned that such action might lead to a chaotic shortage. In fact, by the autumn of 1953, there was a glut of sugar.

APPENDIX TWO

THE SUEZ CRISIS
1956–57

On Friday, October 26th, 1956, Meg and I went to a cocktail party given by the Duchess of Kent at Kensington Palace. The Edens came and I had a long talk with Anthony. The Hungarian revolt had just begun and he was elated by the apparent split in the Communist empire. I found him cheerful and apparently exhilarated.

The following week Britain and France intervened against Nasser and landed troops at Suez. Most people were a bit doubtful of the morality, but assumed that at least we were sure of success. What they criticised subsequently (apart from the Labour Party which persisted in mouthing pious but unconvincing platitudes about the United Nations) was our failure to finish the job and the slowness of our military action. The Americans, at the climax of a Presidential Election, took immediate umbrage and voted at U.N.O. with Russia against us. Anglo-American relations sank to a level unknown in recent history.

On Tuesday, November 20th, I dined with Winston and urged that as he was the only Englishman to whom Eisenhower would listen he should write to him and ask him to put events in their proper perspective. He was reluctant, but finally agreed that I should prepare a draft of what I suggested he might say. This I accordingly did and he despatched it, almost unaltered, through the U.S. Embassy, showing it to nobody in H.M.G., but sending a copy to the Queen.

Draft letter for W.S.C.   November 22nd, 1956
to send Eisenhower

There is not much left for me to do in this world and I have
neither the wish nor the strength to involve myself in the
present political stress and turmoil. But I do believe, with
unfaltering conviction, that the theme of the Anglo-American
alliance is more important today than at any time since the
war. You and I had some part in raising it to the plane on
which it has stood. Whatever the arguments adduced here
and in the United States for or against Anthony's action in
Egypt, it will now be an act of folly, on which our whole
civilisation may founder, to let events in the Middle East come
between us.

There seems to be growing misunderstanding and frus-
tration on both sides of the Atlantic. If they be allowed to
develop, the skies will indeed darken and it is the Soviet Union
that will ride the storm. We should leave it to the historians
to argue the rights and wrongs of all that has happened during
the past years. What we must face is that at present these
events have left a situation in the Middle East in which spite,
envy and malice prevail on the one hand and our friends are
beset by bewilderment and uncertainty for the future. The
Soviet Union is attempting to move into this dangerous vac-
uum, for you must have no doubt that a triumph for Nasser
would be an even greater triumph for them.

The very survival of all we believe in may depend on our
setting our minds to forestalling them. If we do not take
immediate action in harmony, it is no exaggeration to say that
we must expect to see the Middle East and the North African
coastline under Soviet control and Western Europe placed at
the mercy of the Russians. If at this juncture we fail in our
responsibility to act positively and fearlessly we shall no longer
be worthy of the leadership with which we are entrusted.

I write this letter because I know where your heart lies.
You are now the only one who can so influence events both
in U.N.O. and the free world as to ensure that the great

essentials are not lost in bickerings and pettiness among the nations. Yours is indeed a heavy responsibility and there is no greater believer in your capacity to bear it or well-wisher in your task than your old friend Winston S. Churchill.

Ike's immediate reaction on receiving this letter was to make public a friendly reference to this country and to say that he would see we did not suffer as far as oil supplies were concerned. He sent W. a long answer (obviously written by himself because expressed in so woolly and unscholarly a way). He admitted that Anglo-American solidarity in the face of Soviet Russia was far more important than any of the present issues, but he made it plain that he had been deeply offended by Anthony Eden's failure even to inform him of what we proposed to do. The reply showed at once his sincerity and his smallness of mind. I think it also showed that W.'s letter had taken effect.

In Egypt things went from bad to worse, and together with many others I formed the view that Eden ought to go and that, however indisputable both his courage and his integrity, one could never again feel confidence in his judgment. The senior members of the Foreign and Civil Services were outspokenly hostile to the whole performance. Conservative Members of Parliament with whom one talked were very lame in the defence of their Chief. Nigel Birch (S. of S. for Air) and Christopher Soames (Under S. of S. for Air) were frankly hostile to Eden in their private comments to me and accused him of having decided insanely on war against Nasser as soon as he heard the news, at the end of July, of the nationalisation of the Suez Canal. They also maintained that we had intervened when we did, rather than let the Israelis themselves carry their attack as far as the Canal, because (albeit indirectly, through the French) we were committed in advance to help Israel by destroying the Egyptian Air Force.

About this time John Junor, Editor of the *Sunday Express*, and I formed a luncheon club. It had nine argumentative members and five rules. The former were:

John Junor and me.

Sir Walter Monckton, Chancellor of the Duchy and Member of the Cabinet.

Lord Hailsham, First Lord, but not in the Cabinet.
Mark Bonham Carter.
Edgar Lustgarten.
Ian Gilmour (owner of the *Spectator*).
Woodrow Wyatt (former Labour Secretary of State for War)
Roy Jenkins (Labour M.P.).
The latter were:
1. The laws of libel and slander shall not apply.
2. The Official Secrets Act shall be treated with contempt.
3. Physical violence shall as far as possible be avoided.
4. There shall be no sneaking.
5. Mr Randolph Churchill shall not in any circumstances be admitted.

We had our first luncheon on December 11th and it was clear to me that Walter Monckton had been opposed to the whole Suez venture. He ought no doubt to have had the courage to resign, but I suppose he did not want to give the Labour Party an important handle to their propaganda (which seemed, in these weeks, to be directed far more to the interests of the party than the welfare of the nation).

On Thursday, November 29th, Winston had told me in reply to a direct question that he thought the whole operation the most ill-conceived and ill-executed imaginable. It was at luncheon at 28 Hyde Park Gate. I had begun by asking him if he would have acted as Eden had if he had still been Prime Minister. He replied, "I would never have dared; and if I had dared, I would certainly never have dared stop." He also said that if Eden resigned he thought Harold Macmillan would be a better successor than R. A. Butler.

The departure of Eden, taken suddenly ill, to Jamaica seemed to many people a disastrous decision from the point of view of his own political future. It was an island much patronised by tax evaders and affluent idlers, and with petrol and oil rationed again in England, the retreat of the Prime Minister to a parasite's paradise seemed to rank prominently in the annals of ministerial follies.

After Christmas with the children at Ladykirk,[1] Meg and I went to stay at Sandringham for the New Year. We travelled to Wolferton on the afternoon of December 31st with the Salisburys, and in the train we discussed the whole Suez affair in great detail. Lord Salisbury said he was still convinced that some action had been necessary and that to do nothing would have led to still greater disaster. There was a bubble, or a boil, which had to be pricked or else we should have had a far greater explosion in the Middle East at a later stage. It might, however, be that mistakes had been made in the way we carried out our plan. It might indeed have been better not to proclaim that our objective was to divide the two combatants (which meant we had to stop when we did) but to say frankly that we were driven to take action against the Egyptian dictator. I gathered that he himself had been ill when the fateful decision was taken, and it was while in bed at Hatfield, with more time than usual to read Intelligence Reports, that the magnitude of the Soviet aid to Egypt and Syria had become clear to him. Immediately he recovered he made a speech in the House of Lords on this subject (and I must say it was the first statement on the Government side, albeit made several days after our ultimatum, which made me feel there might be some real justification for what they had done). In reply to a question he said he had no idea why this aspect of the affair had been allowed to go by default in the initial stages. He did *not* contradict me when I said I suspected Eden's personal pique against Nasser had had a lot to do with our precipitate action. The reason for this pique is not hard to find if one remembers Eden's passionate defence, against Winston's obstinate distaste, of the 1954 treaty with Egypt – to which I have referred earlier in this diary [page 342].

I told Lord S. frankly that like many others I could never again have confidence in Eden's judgment or handling of affairs, however much I might admire his courage and integrity. He seemed a little ill at ease when he said that he could see nobody to take his place. Why not Macmillan, I asked? His reply was,

[1] Home of Major John and Lady Susan Askew, my wife's sister.

both Meg and I thought, evasive: he said something about Macmillan being a very tired man.

Incidentally, on the way up to Ladykirk on December 20th, I had put the same point to Alec Home (S. of S. for Commonwealth Relations). He, too, had not demurred at my suggestion that Eden must go, and had rather grudgingly agreed that Harold Macmillan would be the preferable successor. He also said he had never been through such a period: Munich had been nothing to it.

On January 9th the news broke that the Queen was returning to London and Eden was going to resign. The world seemed to think that Rab Butler would succeed. Personally I felt sure Macmillan was the man and I was confident that both Winston and Bobbety Salisbury would be asked and would recommend Harold M.

Randolph "scooped" the situation by an article in the *Evening Standard* on the night Eden resigned. He was guilty of a "chronological inexactitude" in saying that Lord Salisbury had been with the Queen at Sandringham on the night of Monday, January 7th. From this inaccurate statement a lot of rumour grew about Lord S. paving the way with the Queen, etc.; and the Labour Party impudently questioned the accepted constitutional convention that the sovereign chooses the Prime Minister. They overlooked similar occasions in 1931 and 1940.

APPENDIX THREE

POSTSCRIPT TO SUEZ

On April 7th, 1957, I flew home from New York after a week in America in connection with Winston's and my technological scheme, which was the basis for the establishment of Churchill College, Cambridge.

Air Chief Marshal Sir William Dickson,[1] formerly C.A.S. and now Chairman of the C.O.S. Committee, was on board. We talked for hours, and after he had told me how much he and his military colleagues disapproved of Alanbrooke's diaries, recently published, and after we had both consumed several whiskies and sodas, he dilated with considerable frankness on Suez. The following points emerged:

1. Anthony Eden's personal rage and animosity against Nasser. This made him beside himself on many occasions, and Dickson had never been spoken to in his life in the way the P.M. several times spoke to him during those tempestuous days. (Freddy Bishop, Eden's Principal Private Secretary, had previously told me the same, adding that he had finally given up making allowances for A.E. or feeling sorry for him.)
2. The French were convinced that nothing but Nasser's fall could save Algiers for them. Eden thought highly of Mollet and Pineau[2] and considered that no other French Government could be as good. When they came to London they

---

[1] Later Marshal of the Royal Air Force.
[2] French Prime Minister and Foreign Minister.

made an impassioned plea for common action and said that otherwise they must resign. They said that in 1940 W.S.C. had offered France union with England. Now, on behalf of France, they would like to repeat the offer. Eden and Selwyn Lloyd said this was impossible at present, but they evidently felt still more beholden to the French on account of this offer.

3. The French had definitely "colluded" with Israel, and all parties to the attack were agreed that it had to be before the U.S. Presidential Election. If it were left till afterwards, Eisenhower would checkmate it. The U.S. were not told of our intentions because Eden and Eisenhower had had a long exchange of letters on the subject and the latter had refused to be moved by any of Eden's arguments, some of which (e.g. the reactions of the Arab world) were shown by subsequent events to be fallacious. Eden was convinced, by much past experience, that American thought and policy over the Middle East was both ill-informed and impractical.

4. Eden during the final days was like a prophet inspired, and he swept the Cabinet and Chiefs of Staff along with him, brushing aside any counter-arguments and carrying all by his exaltation.

5. Monty and Winston (influenced, I think, by Monty) had thrown spanners into the military wheel by pressing for a landing at Mersa Matruh and an armoured sweep on Cairo. This, in Dickson's view, was absurd. Monty himself had told me this would have been the right course when he lunched with us at Stratfield Saye in December. The Chiefs of Staff, however, intended to hold the Canal with three divisions, plus some troops along the Mediterranean coast as far as Tel el Kebir. Apparently they and the Cabinet thought they would not have to stay there long before Nasser fell from loss of face. In my opinion this showed a most improvident assessment of Egyptian and Arab nationalist feeling.

6. We gave way on economic grounds alone. At a 10 p.m. Cabinet in the P.M.'s room at the House, it being clear that the U.N. Assembly was going to vote for sanctions against us and probable that the U.S. would vote with the majority, the Chancellor of the Exchequer (H. Macmillan) said that

although he had been greatly in favour of the action we took, he must tell the Cabinet that if sanctions were imposed on us, the country was finished. There was therefore nothing for it but to climb down. The Russian threats had not been taken into serious consideration.

And in New York, Wall Street financiers and taxi-drivers alike had said to me: you were right to go in, but why on earth didn't you finish the job? They did seem to admit a certain U.S. responsibility and it was evident that in the space of a few months Eisenhower's vast domestic prestige had sunk far. Of Dulles I did not hear one good word.

Postscript: April 6th, 1966
At lunch today at Windsor Lord Caccia[1] told me he had been present in Washington shortly after Suez when Dulles asked Selwyn Lloyd why on earth we did not go through with the operation!

---

[1] Harold Caccia, British Ambassador in Washington, 1956–61, and Permanent Under Secretary of State at the Foreign Office, 1962–65.

BIOGRAPHICAL NOTES

BIOGRAPHICAL NOTES
(Indicated by * in the text)

Alanbrooke, Field Marshal, 1st Viscount, K.G., G.C.B., O.M., G.C.V.O., D.S.O. (1883–1963) Uncle of Sir Basil Brooke, Prime Minister of Northern Ireland, he was educated mainly in France and distinguished himself as a gunner in World War I. He went from being G.O.C., Southern Command, in 1939 to lead the 2nd Corps in Lord Gort's British Expeditionary Force, and he fought a successful holding action against the advancing Germans on the eastern flank in May 1940. He was briefly in command of the troops sent to northern France after Dunkirk, but returned home to be once again in charge of Southern Command and, thereafter, of Home Forces. From the end of 1941 he was C.I.G.S. for five years, at once spellbound and exasperated by Churchill and gravely disappointed not to be given command of Operation OVERLORD. He was an admirer and faithful supporter of Montgomery. After the war he was appointed Lord Lieutenant of London, the Master Gunner of St James's Park, Chancellor of Queen's University, Belfast and Constable of the Tower. He was a keen naturalist with a passion for bird-watching.

Alexander of Tunis, Field Marshal, 1st Earl, K.G., G.C.B., G.C.M.G., C.S.I., D.S.O., M.C. (1891–1969) Harrovian cricket hero, wounded three times in World War I and noted for his courage under fire, he was engaged in operations in Russia (1919) and on the Indian North-West Frontier. By 1930 he had already been mentioned in despatches for gallantry seven times and had commanded his regiment, the Irish Guards. He was given the 1st Division in the British Expeditionary Force, 1939–40, and Lord Gort having been ordered to hand over command to him to avoid capture, he was put in charge at the end of the evacuation and was among the last to leave the Dunkirk beaches. After holding Southern Command in the invasion-threatened summer of 1940, he commanded the British forces in Burma in 1942 and presided coolly and competently over the retreat before the numerically superior Japanese. At the end of 1942 he was made Commander in Chief in North Africa, with Montgomery commanding the 8th Army, and thence he went to Sicily and Italy as Supreme Allied Commander. After the war he was Governor General of Canada, 1946–52, to the entire satisfaction of both the Canadians and himself, until Churchill hauled him back to Britain in 1952 to be an inadequate and far from happy Minister of Defence. He was Churchill's *beau idéal* of a soldier and the admiration was mutual.

Amery, the Right Hon. Leopold, C.H. (1873–1955)

Harrow, Balliol and All Souls between them produced this prodigy of energy, mental and physical, minute in height but vast in intellect. He professed to speak seventeen languages, but was never put to the test. He worked for ten years at *The Times*, and became a Birmingham M.P. in 1911. For part of World War I he was assistant secretary to the War Cabinet and made such an impression on the leading politicians that he was soon, in succession, First Lord of the Admiralty, Secretary of State for the Colonies, for the Dominions and finally, from 1940 to 1945, for India. There were those who thought he was *too* clever and

there were others who objected to his casting his net a little far outside his own waters. He was, however, certainly one of the best-known political figures in the first half of the twentieth century.

His elder son Jack, who was at school with me and had considerable charm, unfortunately became a fascist, broadcast enemy propaganda from Italy during the war and was hanged for treason after it. So excessive a retribution would surely not have been his fate had his father not been eminent. His other son, Julian, who strove valiantly to save his brother, went into politics early, married Harold Macmillan's daughter and held several ministerial offices.

Avon, Anthony Eden, 1st Earl of, K.G., M.C. (1897–1977)

From Eton and Christ Church, Oxford (where he won a First in Oriental Languages), and after three years' active service with the King's Royal Rifle Corps, he went into Parliament at the age of twenty-six as Conservative Member for Warwick and Leamington. He became Parliamentary Private Secretary to Sir Austen Chamberlain at the Foreign Office and then, cherished by Stanley Baldwin, he rose quickly in the ministerial hierarchy. He was Lord Privy Seal with responsibility for League of Nations affairs and, in 1935, Foreign Secretary. Objecting to Neville Chamberlain's interference, and to the general belief that Sir Robert Vansittart was *de facto* Foreign Secretary, he shunted the latter sideways and resigned from the former's administration in January 1938. When war broke out he returned to office as Secretary of State for the Dominions, was given the War Office by Churchill in May 1940, and was back at the Foreign Office the following December. Despite frequent efforts to provide him with experience in home departments, he remained firmly attached to the Foreign Office until he became Prime Minister in 1955. He and Winston Churchill sometimes squabbled, but until Churchill's last year in office they were good friends and faithful colleagues. Indeed Eden, who was a man of the highest integrity, was never anything but faithful. By his first wife, Beatrice Beckett, he had two sons, one of whom was killed in Burma, flying in the R.A.F. His second wife was Clarissa Churchill.

Baruch, Bernard (1870–1965)

This veteran Jewish financier rose from humble origins by his financial acumen, persistence and capacity for impressing prominent American politicians. Churchill first met him in 1919 at the Paris Peace Conference where he had acquired from President Wilson a post in the American delegation.

On Churchill's visits to America he gave him useful financial advice and after the Wall Street Crash of 1929, when Churchill, who loved a gamble, was most ill-advisedly playing the market, Baruch saved him from disaster by quietly selling every time Churchill bought and vice versa. He was adviser to numerous American Presidents and wrote frequently to Churchill on political matters for which he had no flair at all. His financial flair occasionally deserted him too, as when in 1955 he advised me to put all I had into South America, the El Dorado of the future. Luckily I had nothing to put there. Churchill, though grateful to him and often his guest in New York, found endless letters containing his views on political and strategic matters a burden. He usually answered five or six together.

Beaverbrook, Maxwell Aitken, 1st Lord (1879–1964)

Many people thought he was evil. He was, in fact, impish and he was capable of great kindness. Born a son of the Manse (all influential Canadians seem to have been sons of the Manse), he made a fortune at an early age by deals which, whether or not actually dishonest, were certainly "borderline". He came to England in 1910, basking in the friendship of the Conservative leader Bonar Law, himself a Canadian, and within six months was Conservative M.P. for Ashton-under-Lyne of which he had never heard a few months before. He bought the derelict *Daily Express* in order to provide an organ for the Conservative Party and he bought and sold, at a profit, the Rolls Royce Company. Between the wars he became a highly successful press lord, circulation being his prime objective. He had a genuine enthusiasm for the British Empire, but he was an arch-appeaser of the dictators. Yet when he was made Minister of Aircraft Production in May 1940, he performed miracles of production and made a major contribution to winning the Battle of Britain. Later in the war he was markedly unhelpful, upsetting any apple-cart in sight, becoming infatuated by Stalin and urging a Second Front in totally unsuitable conditions. He opposed the planning of a Welfare State, and as the end of the war drew near he was more excited by the prospect of a return to party strife than by possible methods of winning the peace. After 1945 his influence on politics was muted, and his relationship with Churchill became distant though always amiable. In 1953, when Churchill had his stroke, nobody rallied more whole-heartedly to his help.

Bevin, Rt. Hon. Ernest (1881–1951)
This unwieldy, unlettered Trade

Unionist, formerly General Secretary of the Transport and General Workers' Union, Chairman of the General Council of the Trade Union Congress and a leader of the 1926 General Strike, was a splendid Minister of Labour during the war, an undaunted tower of strength both to Churchill and to Attlee. In 1945 he became Foreign Secretary, in preference to Hugh Dalton whom Attlee had originally intended for the post, and it fell to him to confront Molotov and the intransigent Soviet delegations, when they threw heavy spanners into the works at every conference assembled to negotiate peace treaties. The Foreign Service, whose members all came from backgrounds totally different from his, were devoted to him. Indeed, it may be doubted if there was ever a more loved and respected Foreign Secretary.

Bracken, Brendan, 1st and last Viscount (1901–1958)
His rise in the world was astonishing. An unruly, truant boyhood in Ireland, adolescent years spent with an uncle in Australia, education sought and obtained from an imaginative headmaster of Sedbergh when he pretended to be three years younger than he was: all this was the prelude to being Member of Parliament for Paddington at the age of twenty-nine, having in the meantime forced himself on Winston Churchill as

a disciple, founded *The Banker*, bought *The Economist* and become Chairman of *The Financial News*. Underneath a mop of wiry, uncontrolled red hair, behind thick glasses and a pretended ruthlessness, lay a heart of gold; and he had a memory so remarkable, for people, events and the architecture of houses, that when Brendan was available no books of reference were required. In the years immediately before the war, and during the war itself, he was a bright comet sweeping across the skies, afraid of nobody, jolting Churchill out of melancholy or intemperate moods, and proving a strikingly successful Minister of Information, in contrast to his three predecessors in the post. Yet he was a lonely man, disguising the fact with incessant and, latterly, repetitive conversation, but genuinely loved by all who dug beneath the physically unattractive façade.

Bridges, Edward, 1st Lord, G.C.B., G.C.V.O., M.C., F.R.S. (1892–1969)
Son of the Poet Laureate, Robert Bridges, he was educated at Eton and Magdalen College, Oxford. He won the M.C. in World War I and then served in the Treasury until in 1938 he was appointed Secretary to the Cabinet in succession to Sir Maurice Hankey, the first holder of the office.

Throughout the war he and General Ismay, on the military side, were the twin pillars on which the Prime Minister rested for they were first rate administrators. From 1945 till his retirement in 1956 he was Permanent Secretary of the Treasury and a great power in the land. Friendly, apt to give one a playful punch in the tummy on meeting, he was a forceful and outspoken man with a high sense of public service and propriety.

Butler of Saffron Walden, Lord, K.G., C.H. (1902–1982)
Son of a distinguished Indian civil servant who became Master of Pembroke College, Cambridge, R. A. Butler, always known as "Rab", was President of the Cambridge Union in 1924 and went on to be one of the most eminent British statesmen of the mid-twentieth century. A staunch supporter of Munich, appeasement and Neville Chamberlain, he became in due course a loyal colleague and admirer of Churchill, though to some extent a rival of both Anthony Eden and Harold Macmillan, with neither of whom he was on anything more than polite terms. He was the leading influence in reviving the fortunes of the Conservative Party after its defeat in 1945 and the policies he advocated, not far different from those of the Labour leader Hugh Gaitskell, were known as "Butskellism". He held

every senior ministerial post, including the Home Office, Foreign Office and Exchequer, and as Minister of Education in 1944 he gave his name to an Education Act of lasting importance; but twice, in 1957 and 1963, he failed to be chosen Prime Minister. He ended his career, happily, as Master of Trinity College, Cambridge.

Cadogan, Right Hon. Sir Alexander, O.M., G.C.M.G., K.C.B. (1884–1968)

A younger son of the 5th Earl Cadogan, he was at Eton and Balliol and passed top into the Diplomatic Service in 1908. He was Ambassador to China, 1933–36, and when Anthony Eden managed to dispose of Sir Robert Vansittart in 1936, he was appointed Permanent Under Secretary. Calm, sage in counsel and the very reverse of "flashy", his diaries, published after his death, caused astonishment by their outspoken and sometimes vituperative comments. From 1946 to 1950 he represented Britain at the Security Council of the United Nations and in 1952 Churchill appointed him Chairman of the B.B.C., an office he fulfilled admirably in spite of knowing nothing about radio or television. His wife, Lady Theodosia, daughter of the 4th Earl of Gosford, had rather too forceful a character and an idiosyncratic personality.

Camrose, William Berry, 1st Viscount (1879–1954)

The prime builder, with his brother Lord Kemsley and Lord Iliffe, of a great newspaper empire, of which the brightest stars in the constellation were the *Daily Telegraph* and the *Sunday Times*. Good-tempered, wise and strictly honourable in all his dealings, he was much liked by Churchill to whom he gave great financial assistance by combining with others to buy Chartwell and present it to the National Trust (on condition that Churchill should have it for his life-time), and still more by buying the Churchill papers, with which the *History of the Second World War* was composed and, after publication, giving them back to Churchill. He felt that Parliament should have shown the nation's gratitude by a substantial grant, such as was made to Lloyd George after 1918, and he did his generous best to remedy its failure to offer one.

Chandos, Oliver Lyttelton, 1st Viscount, D.S.O., M.C. (1893–1972)

An engaging buccaneer, son of a Cabinet Minister and educated at Eton and Trinity, Cambridge, he had an excellent record as a Grenadier in World War I and then made large profits in tin. Brought into the Government in 1940 as President of the Board of Trade, partly by the influence of Brendan

Bracken, he was prominent in governmental deliberations but a surprisingly poor performer in the House of Commons. He was Minister of State in Cairo in 1941, with a seat in the War Cabinet, and dealt patiently with the explosive tantrums of General de Gaulle. Minister of Production, 1942–45, he was Secretary of State for the Colonies in the 1951 Government, but retired in 1954 to be Chairman of Associated Electrical Industries. Married to Lady Moyra Osborne, a daughter of the Duke of Leeds, he had two sons and a daughter. He was a rumbustiously agreeable companion, primed with entertaining political and commercial gossip, and he wrote two books in faultless English prose.

Cherwell, Frederick Lindemann, 1st and last Viscount, C.H. (1886–1957)

To those he liked the Prof., as he was called, was generous, helpful and entertaining. Against those who had displeased him he waged a vendetta. He inherited a fortune arising from waterworks in Germany, studied physics in Berlin under the great Professor Nernst and became a friend of Einstein. He was a keen tennis-player (tennis champion of Sweden), he was always immaculately dressed and had a liking for high society. Two of his claims to enduring fame are that he revived the moribund

Clarendon Laboratory at Oxford, which under his direction became the foremost centre of low-temperature research in physics; and that throughout the war he was Churchill's interpreter in all technical matters, whether scientific or economic. He had the capacity to explain the most difficult problems in clear, simple, well-expressed English. He detested Germans (despite his successful years of study in Berlin) and ruthlessly, though unavailingly, plotted the destruction of their trade and industry. He looked with contempt on Jews and coloured people: he was arrogant and impervious to argument when his mind was made up. Yet he was good company when in the mood, never boastful of his achievements, and a loyal friend to Churchill and to many others. He was an acquired taste, but a pleasing one, despite his obvious faults, to those whom he found acceptable.

Churchill, Hon. Randolph (1911–1968)

Born with numerous golden spoons in his mouth: outstandingly handsome in his youth, a natural orator, an original wit, showing a mastery of language and the son of an already famous father. Most of these gifts he dissipated, disappointed in his political ambitions, making friends easily but losing them more easily still. His father, determined that his only son should be more cherished than he had been, eagerly introduced him, when he was still a boy, to the stimulating company of such men as Lloyd George and Lord Birkenhead. As a result he was unnaturally precocious and found most of his contemporaries dull. He was imaginative and original in his ideas, but he became self-indulgent, excessively addicted to drink and, when he felt like it, inexcusably abusive. Yet when he exerted his charm, those who had vowed never to let him over their threshold again almost invariably relented. He was a talented journalist, and some of the books he wrote won acclaim; but his early promise came to little, both his wives were tried too hard, and the efforts of his mother to counteract her husband's excessive indulgence of their son won Randolph's seldom relenting hostility. Latterly, too, he squabbled with his father, devoted though he was to him. He grew up in the shade of a giant of the forest, and that may have inhibited his own development. Perhaps Winston Churchill himself would have been a less bright meteor in the sky if his own father, Lord Randolph Churchill, had not died young.

Colville, Lady Cynthia,
D.C.V.O., D.B.E., F.R.C.M.
(1884–1968)
Twin daughter, with Lady Celia Coates, of the Marquess of Crewe, by his first marriage to Sibyl Graham of Netherby, and granddaughter of Richard Monckton-Milnes. Married in January 1908, the Hon. George Colville. From her early married days she became deeply involved in the affairs of the desperately poor borough of Shoreditch, where she started a school for mothers, a home for babies and other welfare schemes. She was a staunch Liberal, with a large number of socialist friends, Chairman of a Juvenile Court and President or Chairman of numerous charitable organisations. She was a dedicated Anglo-Catholic, a long-serving member of the Church Assembly, an outstandingly good public speaker and a woman who took endless pains for others without ever thinking of herself. From 1923 till 1953 she was a lady-in-waiting to Queen Mary on whom she had great influence. Despite her sometimes radical views George V was fond of her and used to ask her to race on his famous cutter *Britannia*.

Colville, David (1909–1986)
Eldest son of the Hon. George and Lady Cynthia Colville. Educated at Harrow and Trinity College, Cambridge; joined Lloyds Bank in 1931 and was Treasurer of the Bank when war was declared. Married, 1933, Lady

Joan Child-Villiers, daughter of the 8th Earl of Jersey, with magnificent Titian-red hair. After five years' service in the R.N.V.R. he was invited by Mr Anthony de Rothschild to join the Rothschild bank, of which he became the first non-member of the family, and the first Christian, to be a partner. He had a high reputation in the City.

Colville, Philip (b. 1910)

Second son of the Hon. George and Lady Cynthia Colville. Educated at Harrow and Trinity College, Cambridge. Joined Cazenove and Ackroyd, stock-brokers, but accepted a partnership in R. Nivison and Co. shortly before the war. He enlisted in the Grenadiers, fought in France in May/June 1940, became adjutant of the 4th battalion and served with the 6th Guards' Tank Brigade from the summer of 1944 to the final defeat of Germany. A keen yachtsman, owning a *Dragon* class boat for over thirty years, he was at one time Rear-Commodore of the Royal Yacht Squadron. Also a first-class bridge player and an unconscionably lucky card-holder. He is Treasurer and financial adviser to King's College Hospital and a member of the Council of the Royal National Lifeboat Institution.

Crewe, Robert Crewe-Milnes, 1st and last Marquess of Crewe, K.G. (1858–1945)

Son of the celebrated man of letters, Richard Monckton-Milnes, Lord Houghton, and Annabel, sister and heiress of the last Lord Crewe, whose great estates in Cheshire and Staffordshire he inherited as well as his father's house and land at Fryston, near Ferrybridge, with a famous library.

After Harrow, while still at Trinity College, Cambridge, he became engaged to Sibyl Graham, daughter of Sir Frederick and Lady Hermione Graham of Netherby. She died suddenly after seven years of marriage, a sorrow he described poignantly in verse (for he wrote good poetry), leaving him disconsolate with four children under six. A Liberal follower of Mr Gladstone, in 1892 he was appointed Viceroy of Ireland at the early age of thirty-four. In 1895 he inherited the Crewe estates, was created Earl of Crewe and three years later married Lady Margaret Primrose, aged eighteen, younger daughter of the former Prime Minister, Lord Rosebery. He was tall, handsome and a well-informed, attractive talker: she fell in love with him across the dining-room table at Mentmore.

When the Liberal Government of 1905 was formed, he was given high Cabinet office, being Secretary of State for the Colonies, and later for India, Lord President, and Leader of the House of Lords, with the unenviable task of taking the Parliament Bill, limiting the Lords' powers, to the Upper Chamber. Mr Asquith is on record as saying that there was no member of his Cabinet on whom he relied so much. His speeches read well, but were poorly and hesitantly delivered, reflecting the caution with which he chose his words. In 1911 he was given the Garter and created a Marquess.

He was briefly President of the Board of Education and, surprisingly enough, Chairman of the L.C.C.; but although he was for six years Ambassador in Paris (1922–28), Lord Lieutenant of London, leader of the Liberals in the Lords and Secretary of State for War in the 1931 National Government, his political career effectively ended when Lloyd George succeeded Asquith as Prime Minister in 1916.

His tastes were catholic, though his religion was Anglican. Of scholarly inclination, well-read in all branches of literature, a good historian and a competent classicist, he was at the same time devoted to the Turf, a breeder of racehorses, and a lavish host, perhaps the last of the Whig grandees. There was no better company when he was in expansive mood, but he nevertheless seemed detached from human beings, except for his wife, and was dutiful rather than affectionate to his daughters. He lost both his sons, one by each marriage, when they were still young and this heart-breaking experience probably accounted for his apparent lack of interest in other people, masked though it was by unwavering courtesy.

Cripps, Hon. Sir Stafford, C.H., F.R.S., K.C. (1889–1952)
Product of Winchester College and University College, London, he was a son of the 1st Lord Parmoor. His wife, Dame Isabel, was an intelligent Eno's Fruitsalts heiress. He did well at the Bar, became steadily more radical in politics and was elected Labour M.P. for Bristol East in 1931, standing on the far left of the party. He was a devout Christian, a vegetarian and a foe to alcohol. He moderated his political views considerably after being Ambassador in Moscow, 1940–42, and returned to London to a seat in the War Cabinet and the leadership of a House of Commons which had a vast Conservative majority. From 1942 to the end of the war he was Minister of Aircraft Production.

In the post-war Labour Government he was, first, President of the Board of Trade and from 1947 Chancellor of the Exchequer, the very emblem of austerity. Austere he may have been, but he was honest through and through and nobody had a more kindly smile. He was clever, but not always sensible.

De L'Isle, Viscount, V.C., K.G., G.C.M.G., G.C.V.O. (b. 1909)
Educated at Eton and Magdalene College, Cambridge, he was a chartered accountant and worked in Barclay's Bank. Having joined the supplementary reserve of the Grenadier Guards, he fought with the regiment in the war, won the V.C. by a feat of gallantry at Anzio and married Jacqueline, daughter of Field Marshal Viscount Gort, V.C. He was elected M.P. for Chelsea in 1944 and deplored the Yalta agreement on Poland. Succeeding his uncle as Lord de L'Isle and Dudley, he inherited the mediaeval Penshurst Place with its fourteenth-century hall and cherished it with the utmost care all his days. In 1951 he was Secretary of State for Air, a task he performed efficiently till Churchill resigned, and from 1961 to 1965 he was Governor General of Australia. A right-wing Tory, dedicated to duty, his kindliness and generosity won him many friends. Apart from Lord Roberts, also a winner of the V.C., he was the only Knight of the Garter ever able to put any letters in front of K.G. after his name.

Dodds, Lady Annabel (1881–1948)
Eldest daughter of the Marquess

of Crewe and Sibyl Graham of Netherby. In 1902 she married the Hon. Arthur O'Neill, M.P. for Mid-Antrim, who was the elder son and heir of Lord O'Neill. He died at Ypres, while serving with the 2nd Life Guards, the first M.P. to be killed in World War I. She had five O'Neill children. In 1922 she married Major Hugh Dodds and had two more sons. She had the capacity of making her companions feel more intelligent and amusing than they really were, and she was a "great lady" without being at all arrogant or ostentatious. When her father died in 1945 she changed her name to Dodds-Crewe.

Dulles, John Foster (1888–1959)
He was a successful lawyer, but personal charm was not among his attributes. Eisenhower appointed him Secretary of State in 1952. His grasp of foreign affairs was slight and he directed American foreign policy insensitively. During the run-up to the 1956 Suez operation, he was guilty of inconsistencies and changes of mind which infuriated both the French and the British and had a significant bearing on the whole unfortunate episode. It would have been better if he had stuck to the law. He was an intelligent man of high moral character and deeply serious intent. His fate was to be the wrong man in the wrong place at the wrong time. His brother,

Allen, of the Office of Strategic Services under General Donovan, and later head of the C.I.A., was a more cosmopolitan and sophisticated operator.

Duncan-Sandys, Lord, C.H. (b. 1908)

Son of a Conservative M.P. with a New Zealand wife, he was educated at Eton and Magdalen, Oxford, before passing into the Diplomatic Service in 1930. He served at the Embassy in Berlin in the last days of the Weimar Republic and was elected Conservative M.P. for Norwood in 1935, the year in which he married Winston Churchill's eldest daughter, Diana. In 1936, having learned from a brother territorial officer details of the shortage of anti-aircraft guns, he raised the matter in the House of Commons. Hore-Belisha, Secretary of State for War, sought to court-martial him, but parliamentary privilege as well as family loyalty were at stake and his father-in-law came powerfully to his rescue in debate. "The Sandys Case" was headline news.

From 1941 onwards his political career blossomed. He held at different times the portfolios of Works, Supply, Housing and Local Government, Defence, Aviation, the Colonies and Commonwealth Relations. Hardworking, imaginative, humorous and, as far as I was concerned,

pleasant company, he was almost always at odds with the civil servants in his various departments, disliking some and distrusting most.

He was, in the years after the war, a leading proponent of European Unity and instigated Winston Churchill to make the United Europe movement a crusade.

He was made a peer in 1974, and became president of the Civic Trust, which he had founded, and Chairman of Lonrho Ltd.

Eisenhower, General Dwight D. (1890–1969)

Although his military career had not progressed far when he was promoted to dizzy heights, and although he had little experience of tactics and strategy, there can be no doubt that Eisenhower's generosity of character, constant good nature and keen sensitivity in handling people were major factors in the Allied victories of 1943–45. His headquarters, containing an equal number of British and American officers, may not always have been efficient, but it was a model of Anglo-American co-operation, and his personality radiated optimism and goodwill. In that sense he was a good politician, but when it came to international politics he was less sure-footed, indeed disastrous in 1945 at the time of the German surrender. He could have taken Berlin and Prague: he deliberately let the Russians occupy them, despite Churchill's protests, and so ensured that the Iron Curtain clamped down with greater ease than was necessary.

After the war he converted S.H.A.E.F. into S.H.A.P.E. with the same goodwill as in war-time. Then he became a politician and the slogan "I like Ike" captivated America. Elected Republican President in 1952, he was not as amenable as Churchill could have wished, and he developed a passionate dislike of the Russians, to whom he had been so helpful in 1945. Despite a heart-attack he stood for the Presidency again in 1956 and was re-elected. He was a man with real goodness of heart and totally honest; but he was a better Supreme Allied Commander than President of the United States.

Franks, Oliver, 1st Lord, O.M., G.C.M.G., K.C.B., C.B.E. (b. 1905)
If ever there was a man for all seasons it was Oliver Franks. When he came back from the Embassy in Washington in 1952, he was pursued with earnest invitations to be Secretary General of N.A.T.O. and Editor of *The Times*, Chairman of the B.B.C., Headmaster of Harrow and numerous other offers which he politely declined. He was first and foremost a University man, a Fellow, and eventually Provost, of Queen's College Oxford, a lecturer in philosophy and finally, at the end of his career, Provost of Worcester College. In the war he shone so brightly as a temporary civil servant that he finished his Whitehall stint as Permanent Secretary, Ministry of Supply. He became, after four critical years in Washington (which included the Berlin air-lift and the Korean War), Chairman of Lloyds Bank and an obvious candidate for the Governorship of the Bank of England. Every Royal Commission wanted him to be Chairman and his last appointment of this kind was the Review Committee set up after the Falklands War. Despite the eagerness with which his patronage was sought, by government departments and industrial companies, his lasting preference was to sit smoking his pipe in philosophic contemplation and conversation.

Gaulle, General Charles de (1890–1970)
Few men in history have risen to the pinnacle of power so fortuitously. An unknown brigadier who had made a profound study of tank warfare and been taken up, right at the end of the day, by Paul Reynaud, he came to London without expecting to lead a Free French movement. Nor would he have done so if any leading French politician had been available. However, Winston Churchill saw

in him the very reverse of the defeatism which he had found in France and, once he had made his choice, he did not go back on it, though he was often tempted to do so by de Gaulle's arrogance, suspicions and ingratitude. De Gaulle was a patriot; but he was also a nationalist, and to him the erasure of the 1940 shame and the recovery of French greatness were all that mattered. Churchill protected him from the dislike and distrust of the Americans, but he was exasperated when de Gaulle took steps, often not in the general Allied interest, without consultation; nor could he stomach the General's absurd conviction that the British wished to seize the French colonies, notably Syria and the Lebanon (which the British would have paid any price *not* to possess). All the same, even when de Gaulle, as President of the Republic, was giving rein to his Anglophobe instincts by blocking British entry to the Common Market, he did on several occasions make it clear that he recognised the debt he owed Churchill.

George II, King of Greece (1890–1947)

Son of King Constantine I, he succeeded to the throne when his pro-German father abdicated in 1922 after the Greek defeat by the Turks in Asia Minor. He was deposed by the republicans two years later. However, the Greek parliamentarians were so undisciplined and the state of the country so chaotic that sentiment began to flow in the ex-king's favour. A strong man, General Metaxas, seized power and the king was restored to the throne in 1934. He had to retire to London when the Germans occupied Greece in 1941, but he never again ceased to be King and, despite the E.L.A.S. revolt and the wrangles over the appointment of Archbishop Damaskinos as Regent, his reign was endorsed by an overwhelmingly favourable plebiscite in 1945. He married a most unsatisfactory Roumanian princess and had no children, being succeeded by his brother, Paul.

Grigg, Sir Percy James, K.C.B., K.C.S.I. (1890–1964)

Educated at Bournemouth School and St John's, Cambridge, he was Private Secretary to Churchill at the Exchequer (1924–29). He was always known as P. J. After being Chairman of the Board of Inland Revenue, he went to India as financial member of the Viceroy's Executive Council. Thence, in 1939, he arrived in Whitehall, like an explosive rocket, as Permanent Under Secretary at the War Office. He had no opinion of Hore-Belisha, his Secretary of State, or of most other people's Secretaries of State. He said exactly what he thought and did not care a fig for those superior to him except, on occasions, the Prime Minister. Clever and hardworking, though holding truthfulness to be a cardinal virtue, he thought tact a social affectation.

To everybody's surprise, including his own, Churchill found him a parliamentary seat at Cardiff and in 1942 made him Secretary of State for War to replace David Margesson who was sacrificed as a scapegoat after the fall of Singapore.

He left politics when the war ended, became Deputy Chairman of the National Provincial Bank, a director of I.C.I. and other leading companies and Chairman of Bass.

Harlech, William, 4th Lord, K.G., G.C.M.G. (1885–1964)
Educated at Eton and New College, Oxford, Billy Ormsby-Gore, as he was known till he succeeded his father in 1938, became a Conservative M.P. at the age of 25 and had a distinguished political career. He was in the Cabinet as First Commissioner of Works and then as Secretary of State for the Colonies. A convinced Zionist, who nevertheless backed the proposed partition of Palestine between Jews and Arabs, he also visited more British Colonies than any other Colonial Secretary. His strong opposition to the dictators led him to fall out with Neville Chamberlain in 1938 and leave the Cabinet. He went to South Africa

as High Commissioner in 1941 and remained there till 1944, later becoming Chairman of the Midland Bank.

He knew all about Florentine sculpture and English ancient monuments. His knowledge of other subjects was encyclopaedic too, and his memory apparently infallible. On several occasions, having listened to him switch authoritatively from one subject to a totally unrelated one, I went sneakily to the *Encyclopaedia Britannica* to check his statements. They were invariably correct.

His sense of humour was not as notable as his intellect, but that want was supplied by his entrancing wife who had been Lady Beatrice Cecil, a daughter of the 4th Marquess of Salisbury. She was quick on the uptake, sincerely religious, kind-hearted, the very reverse of pretentious and a source of joy and laughter to a host of friends.

Both Lord and Lady Harlech were Conservatives, but they held liberal views and they were totally unspoilt either by success or by the esteem in which they were justly held.

Harriman, Hon. W. Averell (1891–1986)
Son of the fabulously rich American railway king, E. F. Harriman, Averell struck out on his own at an early age, founding the successful banking enterprise Brown

Brothers Harriman, and excelling at everything, from polo to croquet, to which he set his hand. In 1941 he came to Britain, as President Roosevelt's special envoy, to organise the supply of equipment. He became a friend of the Churchills and a frequent visitor to Chequers until, in 1943, he was sent as Ambassador to Moscow and formed an amiable personal relationship with Stalin. After the war he was Governor of New York and adviser to successive Democrat Presidents. When Mrs Harriman died, he married Randolph Churchill's first wife, Pamela, who became in her own right a significant feature in the Democrat Party in Washington. As late as 1983, when he was over ninety, the Harrimans visited the Kremlin and had an interview with Brezhnev in the hope of improving Soviet-American relations. By 1985 Averell Harriman and Molotov were the last survivors of the men of power in World War II.

Harris, Marshal of the R.A.F. Sir Arthur, Bt., G.C.B., A.F.C., O.B.E. (1892–1984)
Having joined the Royal Flying Corps in 1915 and served in India, Iraq and the Middle East, he was promoted from the command of a bomber group in 1940 to be deputy Chief of the Air Staff and head of the R.A.F. delegation in nominally neutral Washington. In 1942 he became A.O.C. in C.

Bomber Command and held that vital post till the end of the war. He was a controversial figure in R.A.F. circles where some thought him too ruthless, though he did not lose the respect of his sorely tried bomber crews in the costly strategic bombing raids he directed. In OVERLORD he resented the insistent demands of the army for area bombing, thus deflecting him from his principal objective of flattening German factories and towns. After the war Attlee did not recommend him for a peerage. Feeling slighted he went to live in South Africa and was managing director of the South Africa Marine Corporation. On returning to office in 1951 Churchill made him a baronet and was only deterred from recommending him for a peerage by the vehement opposition of the Air Ministry. He went back to England and lived to a great age, possessed of many more foreign than British decorations, and most carefully cherished by his second wife.

Head, Antony, 1st Viscount, G.C.M.G., C.B.E., M.C. (1906–1983)
Behind a humorous, almost "Bertie Wooster", exterior lurked a keen intelligence, administrative competence and innate common sense. After Eton and Sandhurst, he joined the Life Guards but found time for adventurous activities, including a

voyage to Australia before the mast in a wind-jammer. Having won a Military Cross in France in 1940, he joined General Ismay's staff and worked for "the Joint Planners" while his bosom friend and companion in adventure, Robert Laycock, became Chief of Combined Operations. Elected Conservative M.P. for Carshalton in 1945, he did so well in opposition that he was chosen as Secretary of State for War in 1951 and appointed Minister of Defence a few days before the Suez operation in 1956. In 1960 he was the first British High Commissioner in the newly independent Nigeria (sensibly making his acceptance dependent on the provision of a swimming pool, a tennis court and a launch with a uniformed crew). He was subsequently High Commissioner in Malaysia, and was appointed in 1968 Colonel Commandant of the S.A.S. He married a skilled portrait painter, Lady Dorothea Ashley-Cooper, daughter of the 9th Earl of Shaftesbury, K.P., and they were both honest, outspoken and the best possible company.

Henderson, Sir Nicholas,
G.C.M.G. (b. 1919)
Son of a well-known economist, he was educated at Stowe and at Hertford College, Oxford, where he belonged to a set of fashionably pink Fabians, such as Anthony Crosland, and became a friend of Hugh Gaitskell, Roy Jenkins and Frank Pakenham (Longford). Prevented by a tubercular infection from joining the armed forces, he was a temporary Private Secretary to Anthony Eden, after serving in the Minister of State's office in Cairo. He quickly made his name in the Foreign Office and was established as a full member of the service after the war. He was Private Secretary to five Secretaries of State, establishing a specially close friendship with Ernest Bevin, and went on to be British Ambassador in Warsaw, Bonn and Paris where he was much esteemed for his sartorial eccentricity as well as for his diplomatic skill. After his retirement in 1979, on reaching the age of sixty, Lord Carrington offered him the Embassy in Washington. He was notably successful in stating the British case, orally and on television, during the Falklands campaign of 1982. He married Mary Cawardias, daughter of a Greek doctor with a high reputation in London. She had two claims to fame. She was an intrepid leader of Greek guerillas during the war, and she was such a superb mistress of the culinary art that in all their posts the British Embassy dining-room was a centre of attraction.

Hollis, General Sir Leslie,
K.C.B., K.B.E. (1899–1963)
The son of a clergyman, he was

educated at St Lawrence College, Ramsgate, and joined the Marines in 1915. He was on the foretop of H.M.S. *Edinburgh*, the sole ship of the 1st Cruiser Squadron not to be sunk at the Battle of Jutland. A man of notable charm, if not as clever as Sir Ian Jacob, he became an Assistant Secretary of the Committee of Imperial Defence in 1936 and thence passed on to General Ismay's staff as his senior assistant. He remained in the office of the Minister of Defence throughout the war, liked by all and often accompanying Churchill on his travels. He remained at his post till 1948 and was then promoted to full General and appointed Commandant General of the Royal Marines.

Home of the Hirsel, Alexander Douglas-Home, Lord, K.T. (b. 1903)

Eldest son of the 13th Earl of Home and Lady Lilian Lambton, daughter of the 4th Earl of Durham. Educated at Eton and Christ Church, Oxford, he was elected, as Lord Dunglass, M.P. for South Lanark in 1931 and became Parliamentary Private Secretary to Neville Chamberlain in 1937, accompanying him to the Munich meeting with Hitler in 1938. He married Elizabeth, daughter of the Headmaster of Eton and Dean of Durham, the Very Revd C. A. Alington. He was incapacitated during the war by spinal tubercu-

losis, but in 1951 he became Minister of State at the Scottish Office and succeeded his father as Earl of Home. He was soon promoted to be Secretary of State for Commonwealth Relations, Leader of the House of Lords, Lord President and, from 1960–63, Foreign Secretary. In 1963, on Harold Macmillan's retirement, he renounced his peerage and became Prime Minister. He lost the 1964 General Election by four seats and the Conservative Party, in their folly, replaced him as leader by Edward Heath whom he nevertheless served faithfully as Foreign Secretary, 1970–74. A man universally loved and admired, by political opponents as well as supporters, he was devoid of vanity and did not know the meaning of rancour or jealousy. A lover of the countryside, he was happiest watching birds, catching salmon at his home on the Tweed or shooting grouse at his other home, Douglas in Lanarkshire.

Ismay, General Lord, K.G., G.C.B., C.H., D.S.O. (1887–1965)

Son of a senior Indian civil servant, he was educated at Charterhouse and Sandhurst, joining the army in 1905 and winning his D.S.O. in a campaign against the Mad Mullah who dominated Somaliland for more than twenty years. He had long service in India, on the North-West Frontier as a young officer and at head-quarters later, being Military Secretary to the Viceroy, 1931–33. He transferred to the Committee of Imperial Defence in London in 1936 and became its Secretary, in succession to Sir Maurice Hankey, in 1938. He was thus the natural choice to be Chief of Staff to Churchill, as Minister of Defence, in 1940. He was the main channel of communication between Churchill and the Chiefs of Staff, of whose committee he was a full member, and he was equally trusted by both. Nobody did more to oil the wheels on the sometimes bumpy road between the service chiefs and the politicians and it was due to him more than anyone else that the confrontations between the two in World War I were avoided in World War II. His ability and dedication to hard work was matched by his personal charm. He was universally known as Pug, for he looked like one and when he was pleased one could almost imagine he was wagging his tail.

He had married a well-endowed wife and after the war he looked forward to a peaceful life, caring for his herd of Jersey cows. It was not to be. In 1951 Churchill inveigled him, against his wishes, into becoming Secretary of State for Commonwealth Relations and in 1952 he was elected, for five years, Secretary General of N.A.T.O. Honours and director-ships were heaped on him, but he remained what he had always been, a straightforward, hard-working and totally honourable army officer.

Jacob, Lieutenant General Sir Ian, G.B.E., C.B. (b. 1899)
Son of Field Marshal Sir Claud Jacob, educated at Wellington, the Royal Military Academy, Woolwich, and King's College, Cambridge. A man of tireless industry (nicknamed "Iron Pants" by Antony Head), he was far above the average in both intelligence and common sense. As one of General Ismay's two principal lieutenants in the Office of the Minister of Defence, he was liked and respected by Churchill as a true professional and accompanied him on several of his foreign tours and visits. After the war he was Director of Overseas Services at the B.B.C. until summoned by Churchill in 1952 to be Chief Staff Officer to Field Marshal Alexander as Minister of Defence. He was released after a brief interval and was Director General of the B.B.C., 1952–60. Invariably public-spirited and obedient to duty, and a sharp observer of people and events.

Kirkpatrick, Sir Ivone, G.C.B., G.C.M.G. (1897–1964)
This forthright Roman Catholic from Downside and Balliol fought throughout World War I with the

Inniskillings and entered the Diplomatic Service in 1919. As First Secretary at the Embassy in Berlin, 1933–38, he was convinced that the Nazis intended war and he wholeheartedly disliked the policy of his appeasing chief, Sir Nevile Henderson, and of the Munich Settlement. Returning to Whitehall, he was made director of the foreign division of the Ministry of Information, where he was contemptuous of Duff Cooper's activities, and then controller of the European Services of the B.B.C., a function he performed with energy and fruitful results. In 1949 he was permanent Under Secretary of the German Section of the Foreign Office, from 1950 to 1953 British High Commissioner in Germany and finally, from 1953 to 1957, Permanent Under Secretary of State. On retirement he was appointed Chairman of the Independent Television Authority.

Leathers, Frederick, 1st Viscount, C.H. (1883–1965)
Chairman of William Cory and Son Ltd, and a man of power and influence in the shipping world, he was selected by Churchill (who had sat on one of his boards and been impressed by his qualities) to be Minister of War Transport in 1941. He performed his task, an onerous one during the Battle of the Atlantic, with such quiet effici-

ency that he won the admiration of all his Cabinet colleagues. He was liked and respected even though he was not given to sparkle in company. Churchill thought so well of him that he insisted on recalling him in 1951 to be Secretary of State for the Co-ordination of Transport, an office of Overlord which served no useful purpose and was abolished in 1953. He had been created a Baron in 1941, so as not to need a seat in the House of Commons, and was made a Viscount in 1954.

Maclean, Sir Fitzroy, Bt., C.B.E. (b. 1911–87)
A man of action who is also a master of the English language. Joining the Diplomatic Service in 1933, he wrote a highly acclaimed account of an adventurous journey through little visited southern provinces of the Soviet Union made when he was on the Embassy staff in Moscow. Transferred back to London in 1939, he decided to take an active part in the war. He escaped from his reserved occupation in 1941 by declaring himself a parliamentary candidate, joined the Cameron Highlanders as a private (and, in 1942, the S.A.S.) after being elected Conservative M.P. for Lancaster, a seat he held till 1959. In 1943 he was promoted to Brigadier and chosen to lead the British mission to Tito, with

whom he worked closely for two years of guerilla warfare, establishing a most friendly personal relationship. He was from 1954 to 1957 Financial Secretary at the War Office and he wrote a series of excellent books of which the best-known is *Eastern Approaches*. He married the delightful and intelligent daughter of the 16th Lord Lovat, widow of Sir Eric Phipps' younger son, Alan, a naval officer killed in the war.

Margesson, David, 1st Viscount, M.C. (1890–1965)

After Harrow and Magdalene College, Cambridge, he joined the 11th Hussars and won the Military Cross in World War I. Entering the House of Commons in 1922, he became a Whip in 1926 and Chief Whip in 1931. He controlled the Government majority in the House with exemplary skill, employing a mixture of charm (with which he was exceptionally endowed), disciplinary threat and organising ability. Loyal to Baldwin and Chamberlain, he was equally so to Churchill when circumstances changed, and no member of the 1940 Coalition Government, Conservative, Liberal or Labour, thought ill of him. Churchill made him Secretary of State for War in December 1940. He gave every satisfaction, being on most amicable terms with the C.I.G.S., Sir John Dill; but in 1942, after the fall of Singapore,

he was thrown to the wolves as a scapegoat, albeit an entirely unblemished one. In 1916 he married an American heiress, Frances Leggett, by whom he had three intelligent children; but he and his wife lived separate lives.

Martin, Sir John, K.C.M.G., C. B., C.V.O. (b. 1904)

A first-class classical product of the Edinburgh Academy and Corpus Christi, Oxford, he had a shy and retiring disposition combined with a ready wit, a delectable sense of humour and a conscientious devotion to the public service. Coming to No. 10 from the Colonial Service, with the secretaryship of the Palestine Royal Commission and the admiration of Chaim Weizmann behind him, he quickly won favour, went with the Prime Minister to the Atlantic Charter Meeting, the Casablanca, Teheran, Cairo and Quebec conferences and on several visits to Washington and Moscow; but he was too law-abiding to keep a diary. That is a pity as his writing is as agreeable as his conversation. After the war he was deputy Under Secretary of State in the Colonial Office and High Commissioner in Malta, 1965–67. His wife, Rosalind, is a daughter of a former Provost of Oriel, Sir David Ross.

Mary, Her Majesty Queen (1867–1953)

Tall and regal, with a magnificent

presence. Her mother, Princess Mary of Cambridge, immensely fat and adored by the populace, was a granddaughter of King George III; her father, the Duke of Teck, was the morganatic child of Duke Alexander of Württemberg and Countess Rhédey. The Tecks were poor, and the Duchess extravagant, so that Princess Mary of Teck seldom had new clothes and lived in strained circumstances at the White Lodge in Richmond Park, placed at the family's disposal by Queen Victoria. She was selected, doubtless with little enthusiasm on her part, to marry the heir to the throne, the Duke of Clarence. He died while they were engaged and her tryst was, with Queen Victoria's approval, transferred to George, Duke of York, whom she much preferred, though when he became King George V she held him in awe and was unsuccessful in mitigating his authoritarian treatment of their children. Queen Alexandra, her not very intelligent but strikingly beautiful mother-in-law, never liked her; but Queen Victoria, conscious of the fact, went out of her way to provide affectionate compensation. As Queen Mother she was an immensely popular figure. She had a sense of humour, a social conscience and an unswervingly rigid sense of duty. She was a discriminating collector of jade and objets d'art and catalogued, with minute attention to detail, many of the royal possessions.

Molotov, Vyacheslav M. (1890–1986)

His face was not his fortune, for it portrayed intransigence and the conviction that there was only one side to every case, namely that which represented Soviet policy. He was Chairman of the Council of People's Commissars and effectively Foreign Minister. One of the few high-ranking officials who lasted the course with Stalin into whose disfavour he never seemed to fall and whose moods he reflected faithfully. His name is for ever attached to the infamous Molotov–Ribbentrop Pact of August 1939 which allied Nazi Germany to Soviet Russia and provided for the partition of Poland as well as the seizure by Russia of the democratic Baltic States, Latvia, Lithuania and Estonia. After the war his consistently negative attitude destroyed all hope of a harmonious settlement with the Western Allies and of a generally acceptable German peace treaty. He died in 1986, a nonagenarian relic of past misdeeds.

Monckton of Brenchley, Walter, 1st Viscount, K.C.M.G., K.C.V.O., M.C., K.C. (1891–1965)

He may not have been a strong man, but he was most intelligent and never anything but well-liked, whether by the Duke of Windsor, whose intimate adviser he was, by Arthur Deakin, Secretary of the Transport and General Workers' Union, or by Winston Churchill. He played for Harrow, in company with Field Marshal Alexander, in the famous "Fowler's Match" against Eton, and his sporting activities included a Mastership of Fox Hounds. After going to Balliol, he served in the army throughout World War I, winning the Military Cross, and then became a barrister at the Inner Temple. His charm and his ability brought him important clients. He was a member of the Bar Council as well as standing Counsel to Oxford University. In 1940 he was Director General of the Ministry of Information and thereafter went to Cairo as Oliver Lyttelton's head of propaganda. In 1951 he was elected M.P. for Bristol West and joined the Cabinet as Minister of Labour, basking continuously in Churchill's favour. He declined the Home Office in 1954, but Eden made him Minister of Defence a year later. Disapproving of the Suez venture he resigned shortly before the operation started. After retirement from politics he was Chairman of the Midland Bank and the Iraq Petroleum Company, and President of the M.C.C.

Montgomery of Alamein, Field Marshal, 1st Viscount, K.G., G.C.B., D.S.O. (1887–1976)
Inspired trainer of men though he was, and much applauded for his handling of the 3rd Division in 1940, it was purely by the accident of General Gott's death in an aeroplane crash that in 1942 he was given command of the 8th Army in North Africa. With remarkable flair he restored the wilting morale of the troops and after winning the battle of El Alamein he became a national hero. In command of all the Allied ground forces in the Normandy invasion (June 1944), he moved slowly but surely, but too slowly to hamper the build-up of the German defence. However, once his armies had broken through, he led the British 21st Army Group the whole way across the Rhine to the German surrender at Luneberg Heath. On the way he quarrelled persistently with the American Generals Eisenhower and Bradley, resented having the American troops removed from his command in August, objected to being denied the concentration of stronger forces under his command on the left wing and formed the unattractive habit, then and after the war, of denigrating all the American commanders. He was undoubtedly a great General, if a cautious one, and although egocentric, and indeed vainglorious, he developed in his old age a mellowness and charm, occasionally marred by deplorable tactlessness. He was C.I.G.S., 1946–48, causing Mr Attlee much irritation,

and deputy Supreme Commander at the Supreme Headquarters, Allied Powers in Europe (S.H.A.P.E.), 1951–58. In retirement. he lived benignly in Hampshire, his war-time caravans open to inspection, his garden planted in military order and rice-pudding offered to his guests.

Moran, Charles Wilson, 1st Lord, M.C. (1882–1977)

He had a distinguished medical career, during which he was Dean of St Mary's Hospital Medical School for twenty-five years and President of the Royal College of Physicians from 1941 to 1950. He was recommended to Winston Churchill by Lord Beaverbrook in 1940, but did not see much of the Prime Minister until at Christmas, 1941, after America had entered the war, Churchill had a minor heart disturbance in Washington. Thereafter, Wilson, whom Churchill recommended for a peerage in 1943, accompanied the Prime Minister on most of his foreign travels and made notes of the views expressed by the galaxy of stars whose acquaintance he in consequence made. Highly intelligent though hyper-critical, he was usually a pleasant companion and he wrote extremely well. He seldom treated Churchill's ailments himself but always knew the right specialist to summon. *The Anatomy of Courage*, which he published in 1945, shows depth of insight and an understanding of fear; but after Churchill's death he infuriated his family and was severely criticised by the medical profession for writing *Winston Churchill, The Struggle for Survival*, excusing himself on the fallacious grounds that Churchill's health affected the outcome of the war. It was President Roosevelt whose powers were failing, not Churchill. In reviewing this book, I wrote unkindly but truthfully: 'Lord Moran was never present when history was made, though he was quite often invited to luncheon afterwards.'

Morton, Major Sir Desmond, K.C.B., C.M.G., M.C. (1891–1971)

A devout Roman Catholic, educated at Eton and Woolwich, he was shot through the heart in World War I but miraculously survived, though he always looked pale and ill. He ended that war as A.D.C. to Field Marshal Haig.

He lived at Edenbridge and was thus a neighbour of the Churchills at Chartwell. He had become head of the Industrial Intelligence Centre and, whether with or without authority is uncertain, he supplied Churchill with much information valuable to him in the 1930s when he was trying to warn the government and the country of the danger ahead.

In May 1940 Churchill brought

him to 10 Downing Street and sought to use him as his liaison with the Foreign Office, an experiment much resented in that quarter. He was at an early stage involved with de Gaulle and the Free French and later became the Prime Minister's contact with the Allied governments in London and some branches of the Secret Service. However, his usefulness declined and the Prime Minister, though certainly not wishing to be unkind, made less and less use of his services. He resented this the more because he had given the impression in many quarters that he was the Prime Minister's right-hand man. Churchill did procure a K.C.B. for him and in 1946 persuaded Attlee to appoint him U.K. delegate to the Inter-Allied Reparations Agency; but because he had been over-ambitious he died a sad and embittered man.

Mountbatten of Burma, Admiral of the Fleet, 1st Earl, K.G., G.C.B., O.M., G.C.S.I., G.C.I.E., G.C.V.O., D.S.O. (1900–1979)
Younger son of Admiral of the Fleet Prince Louis of Battenberg (1st Marquess of Milford Haven) and Princess Victoria of Hesse, a great-grandson of Queen Victoria and godson of both Queen Victoria and the Tsar Nicholas II. He had an illustrious naval career, including the command of H.M.S. *Kelly* in the battle of Crete, and he married Sir Ernest Cassell's energetic heiress, Edwina Ashley. He was Chief of Combined Operations, 1941–43, Supreme Allied Commander in South East Asia, 1943–46, Viceroy and Governor General of India, 1947–48, C. in C., Mediterranean, 1952–54, First Sea Lord, 1955–59, and Chief of the Defence Staff, 1959–65. Churchill admired his courage, but mistrusted his judgment and deplored his outspoken support, while still a serving officer, of the Labour Party. He therefore declined to agree to his being First Sea Lord until a week before his own resignation. His was the unique case in modern times of a member of the Royal Family actively involved in major political and operational affairs. He was murdered by the I.R.A. while on holiday in Ireland.

Normanbrook, Norman Brook 1st Lord, G.C.B. (1902–1967)
From Wolverhampton School and Wadham College, Oxford, he entered the Home Office in 1925. After being Principal Private Secretary and personal assistant to Sir John Anderson, he was a Deputy Secretary to the War Cabinet in 1942. Five years later he succeeded Sir Edward Bridges as Secretary to the Cabinet, the third man to hold that key post. Prime Ministers – Attlee, Churchill, Eden, Macmillan – had implicit trust in him and his rec-

ommendations were seldom turned down. Indeed, whether on appointments or on matters of home policy his influence was all but paramount, and he was the very model of a good administrator. He advised and acted with discretion, for he was by temperament reserved and entirely unostentatious. He never put a foot wrong. When Churchill decided to show his appreciation for the man he considered the most meritorious of civil servants by making him a Privy Councillor, I objected that such discrimination would be unfair to Sir Edward Bridges. So he put forward both their names. In 1956 he was appointed joint Permanent Secretary to the Treasury and Head of the Civil Service; in 1963 he was made a peer; and although he became ill from sheer overwork he accepted the Chairmanship of the B.B.C. in 1964.

Norwich, Alfred Duff Cooper, 1st Viscount, G.C.M.G., D.S.O. (1890–1954)
His claim to fame stemmed at least in part from being married to the beautiful Lady Diana Manners. In the Foreign Office before the First World War, a brave Grenadier officer during it and a Tory M.P. after it, he was a witty speaker, an interesting conversationalist and the owner of an excellent prose style; but he was idle as a Minister. As Secretary of State for War, and then First Lord of the Admiralty in the 1930s, he was regarded as a light-weight, but he did have the courage of his anti-Nazi convictions when he resigned at the time of Munich.

He could scarcely have been worse as Minister of Information (though, as successor to Lord Reith, he did wear a temporary halo), and when sent to Singapore at the end of 1941 to report on the defences he suggested no useful palliatives. However, as Ambassador to the Free French, first in Algiers, and then in Paris at the end of the war and for two years after it, he helped to restore Anglo-French relations and his letters and despatches home often brimmed over with useful analysis and intelligent anticipation.

O'Neill of the Maine, Terence, Lord (b. 1914)
Youngest son of the Hon. Arthur and Lady Annabel O'Neill. Educated at Eton. After war service with the Irish Guards, he entered Northern Irish politics as a Unionist, was Deputy Speaker of the Stormont Parliament, 1953–56, then Minister of Home Affairs, Minister of Finance and finally, from 1963 to 1969, Prime Minister. He came nearer than anybody before or since to creating an understanding between Protestants and Catholics in Ulster

and actually dared visit the Irish Prime Minister in Dublin and receive him on a return visit to Belfast. His liberalism was distasteful to the leaders of the Unionist Party, including his predecessor Lord Brookeborough. He was defeated in his constituency by the rampant Paisley and stabbed in the back by his own party. Mr Harold Wilson recommended him for a peerage in 1970. He married Miss Jean Whitaker.

Peck, Sir John, K.C.M.G. (b. 1913)

Educated at Wellington and Corpus Christi College, Oxford, he had a brilliant academic career and has, amongst other attributes, a masterly gift for entertaining and often agreeably scurrilous light verse. He was assistant Private Secretary to the First Lord when Churchill went to the Admiralty in 1939. In May 1940 he moved to 10 Downing Street as one of the Private Secretaries, remaining there with Churchill till the end of the war and staying on for a further year as Private Secretary to Clement Attlee.

Transferring to the Foreign Service in 1946, he was amongst other things Director General of British Information Services in New York, Ambassador to Senegal and finally Ambassador in Dublin, where his Embassy was burned down over his head by nationalist hooligans. He nevertheless loved Ireland and settled there in retirement.

Always witty, with a taste for the unexpected, he was at one and the same time a highly competent and amusing companion with whom to serve. He had an intelligent and hospitable Hungarian wife, Manska.

Peter II, King of Yugoslavia (1923–1970)

Son of King Alexander, assassinated during a state visit to France when Peter was only eleven. His father's first cousin, the Regent Prince Paul, who was married to the Duchess of Kent's beautiful sister and much preferred collecting pictures to governing Yugoslavia, was overthrown by General Simovic when the Germans invaded the country in March 1941, and King Peter, aged seventeen, was proclaimed ruler. He only ruled a few days before having to flee to London with his government, while General Mihailovic did his best to maintain the royalist cause in the forests and mountains. George VI was his "Koum", or godfather, and Churchill saw that the only way for Peter to retain his throne was by an agreement with Tito and the victorious partisans. To that end he tried to persuade Peter to reconstitute his royal government in London under Dr

Subasic, the Ban (Governor) of Croatia. Under the influence of his mother-in-law, Princess Aspasia of Greece, Peter insisted on maintaining an uncompromising attitude, but it is clear that Tito would not in any case have agreed to preserve the monarchy.

Portal of Laverstoke, Wyndham, 1st and last Viscount, G.C.M.G., D.S.O. (1885–1949)
Son of Sir William Portal, whose family, of Huguenot descent, made paper for £5 notes at the Laverstoke mill. Wyndham struck out from the family mould and was Chairman not only of Portals, but of Wiggins Teape and the Great Western Railway. Most agreeable in conversation and an affable host, he was ruthless to those who worked for him. After success as a war-time Regional Commissioner, he developed political ambitions and, with the help of Brendan Bracken and Oliver Lyttelton (Viscount Chandos), he obtained a ministerial post as Minister of Housing. He won incidental Prime Ministerial favour by sending both Churchill and Attlee (to whom he sucked up shamelessly, despite his Conservative affiliations) baskets of plovers' eggs from Laverstoke every spring.

Rowan, Sir Leslie, K.C.B., C.V.O. (1903–1972)
He came to No. 10 from the Colo-nial Office, via the Treasury, and was one of the ablest and most endearing men I have known. He had played hockey for England, had been well grounded in the classics at Tonbridge and had shone at Queen's College, Cambridge. Of the brightest intelligence, he was serious of purpose but possessed a rollicking sense of fun. In due course he was Principal Private Secretary, first to Churchill and then to Attlee, ministering to them both at the Potsdam Conference. He returned to the Treasury to be Second Secretary and worked with Sir Stafford Cripps as Chancellor. Why he was not promoted to be head of the Treasury is one of Whitehall's unsolved mysteries. He left to become Managing Director, and in due course Chairman, of Vickers Ltd and died too soon.

Salisbury, Robert Cecil, 5th Marquess of, K.G. (1893–1972)
Grandson of a Prime Minister, descendant of Queen Elizabeth I's all-powerful minister, Lord Burleigh, and owner of Hatfield House, he was a political figure of major importance for some twenty years. Having fought as a Grenadier in the First World War, he was, as Lord Cranborne, elected Conservative M.P. for South Dorset in 1929. Representing, with Anthony Eden, the younger element in the Tory Party, he was Parliamentary

Under Secretary at the Foreign Office, 1935–38, but resigned with Eden in protest against Neville Chamberlain's interference in foreign affairs. Back in office in 1940, he was soon Secretary of State for the Dominions, and at one stage for the Colonies, Lord Privy Seal and Leader of the House of Lords. On two occasions Churchill had his name on the list to be Foreign Secretary. His influence in the Conservative Party, in and out of office, was dominant and he held a series of high offices between 1951 and 1957 when he resigned on the Cyprus issue. He and his wife Betty, daughter of Lord Richard and Lady Moyra Cavendish, were on the closest terms of friendship with both the King and Queen and the Churchills; but "Bobbety" Salisbury was interested in everybody and was as ready to listen to the views of unimportant people as to those of Kings and Cabinet Ministers.

Selwyn-Lloyd, Lord, C.H., C.B.E., Q.C. (1904–1978)
Elected to Parliament for the Wirral division of Cheshire in 1945, he held all the important portfolios – Defence, Foreign Affairs (at the time of the Suez episode), the Exchequer (from which he was unceremoniously ejected by Harold Macmillan in 1962) and the leadership of the House of Commons. He was not, however, adequately respected and applauded until he became Speaker of the House of Commons (1971–76). He could be biting; he could appear supercilious; but often his least appreciated remarks were induced by a deadpan sense of humour which, like claret, improved as the years went by and made him an increasingly pleasant companion.

Sherfield, Roger Makins, 1st Lord, G.C.B., G.C.M.G. (b. 1904)
There have not been many diplomats or civil servants to rival Roger Makins in distinction and intelligence. From Winchester he went to Christ Church, Oxford, won a First and was elected a Fellow of All Souls. Years later his elder son did the same, so that, perhaps uniquely, father and son were Fellows of All Souls at the same time.

Rising rapidly in the Diplomatic Service, which he entered in 1928, he married Alice, daughter of Dwight D. Davis of Davis Cup fame. Anthony Eden was greatly impressed by his abilities; and so was Harold Macmillan, after he had served as his No. 2 in North Africa. So, too, was Winston Churchill in his dealings with him at the British Embassy in Washington.

He had already served twice on the staff at the Washington Embassy when, in 1953, he was appointed Ambassador. Thence he was wafted by Harold Macmillan in 1956 to be Joint Permanent Secretary of the Treasury, which was not a post for which his experience, wide though it had been, qualified him; but from 1960 to 1964 he was a successful Chairman of the Atomic Energy Commission. In so-called retirement he was amongst much else Chairman of Hill Samuel, of the Industrial and Commercial Finance Company (I.C.F.C.), of A. C. Cossor, of Raytheon International and of Wells Fargo Ltd. He was also Chancellor of Reading University, a superb ballroom dancer and the owner of one of the loudest and most totally sincere laughs in the United Kingdom.

Soames, Christopher, Lord, G.C.M.G., G.C.V.O., C.H., C.B.E. (b. 1920)
From Eton and Sandhurst, he joined the Coldstream Guards in 1939 and when the war ended became assistant military attaché at the Embassy in Paris. There he met Mary Churchill and after a short, whirlwind romance they were married in 1947. His parents-in-law knew nothing about him, but he quickly established an excellent relationship with Winston Churchill who delighted in his company. He was elected Conservative M.P. for Bedford in 1950, was Parliamentary Private Secretary to

Churchill 1951–55, and thereafter, beginning as Under Secretary at the Air Ministry, he was Financial Secretary at the Admiralty, Secretary of State for War and Minister of Agriculture in Macmillan's and Douglas Home's Cabinets. In 1968 Harold Wilson sent him as Ambassador to Paris for four years, when his impeccable knowledge of French was invaluable, but "the Soames affair" with General de Gaulle, due to leakages in London, caused him embarrassment. From 1973 to 1977 he was the senior British E.E.C. Commissioner in Brussels, and in 1979 Lord Carrington gave him the task, as Governor of Rhodesia, of presiding over the transfer of power to a black government. He got on well with Mr Mugabe. He returned to London to be Lord President and Leader of the House of Lords for two years, but left after disagreement over a settlement of a Civil Service strike. He and Mrs Thatcher were not birds of a feather.

Stanley, Col. Right Hon. Oliver, M.C. (1896–1950)
Second son of the 17th Earl of Derby. A master of epigram inside and outside the House of Commons and much sought after as a wit. He fought throughout the First World War, married Lord Londonderry's daughter and was elected Conservative M.P. for

Westmorland in 1924. He held many portfolios, Transport, Labour, the Board of Trade and, from January to May 1940, the War Office. However, he was more impressive in debate than in administration, and Churchill did not offer him an office he thought acceptable when the 1940 Government was formed. He did, however, return to the Government in 1942 as Secretary of State for the Colonies. In opposition, after the war, his rapier thrusts in debate were of value to the Conservative Party.

Stockton, Harold Macmillan, 1st Earl of, O.M. (1894–1986)
Educated at Eton and Balliol, he fought with distinction as a Grenadier officer in World War I, married the Duke of Devonshire's daughter, Lady Dorothy Cavendish, in 1920 and became Conservative M.P. for Stockton-on-Tees in 1924. Being a consistent critic of the Baldwin and Chamberlain Governments, he was not given office till 1940; but he made his reputation as British Minister-Resident in North Africa where, although removed from the mainstream of political and military policy at home, he dealt imaginatively with the vagaries of the Free French and the imbroglios in Italy after the Allied landings. He was prominent in opposition from 1945 to 1951 and then won great acclaim, as Minis-

ter of Housing and Local Government, by fulfilling the Tory promise to build 300,000 houses in a year. Thereafter he was in rapid succession Minister of Defence, Foreign Secretary and Chancellor of the Exchequer until, in January 1957, he succeeded Sir Anthony Eden as Prime Minister. The Macmillan years, following on the 1956 Suez fiasco, were years of prosperity and in the 1959 General Election he increased his parliamentary majority. He also inaugurated the Wind of Change, which led to the dismantling of the British Empire. Retiring in 1963 because of ill-health, he resumed the chairmanship of his family publishing firm, Macmillan and Co., and remained for over twenty years a much sought-after elder statesman. In 1960 he was chosen to be Chancellor of Oxford University.

Stuart of Findhorn, James Stuart, 1st Viscount, C.H., M.C. and bar (1897–1971)
Third son of the 17th Earl of Moray, married Lady Rachel Cavendish and was Harold Macmillan's brother-in-law and M.P. for Moray and Nairn, 1923–59. Outstandingly handsome and no less outstandingly downright, he was Deputy to Captain David Margesson whom he succeeded as Chief Conservative Whip in 1940. He was respected, though not particularly liked, by Winston Churchill to whom he had once

been most abusive before the war. He was one of Lord Beaverbrook's pet aversions, but Churchill always listened to his sound political advice. Secretary of State for Scotland, 1951–57.

Swinton, Philip Cunliffe-Lister, 1st Earl of, G.B.E., C.H., M.C. (1884–1972)

He was born Philip Lloyd-Greame, but changed his name on marrying an heiress. After fighting bravely in World War I, he became M.P. for Hendon and held minor office as early as 1918. Thereafter he figured, sometimes largely, in every post-war Coalition or Conservative Government, his shrewdness and drive making him indispensable. He became Secretary of State for the Colonies in 1931, but perhaps his most notable achievement was, as Secretary of State for Air from 1935 to 1938, to preside with enthusiasm over the development of the two great war winners, the Hurricane and the Spitfire. Having been closely associated with Baldwin and Chamberlain, he did not receive high office in Churchill's war-time Coalition Government, but was sent to administer West Africa. He came into his own again in 1951, winning Churchill's confidence, though mistrusted and disliked by Anthony Eden. As Secretary of State for Commonwealth Relations he was frequently consulted on matters having nothing to do with the Commonwealth, and he was made an earl in 1955. Imperious, intolerant of lesser men and with a keen eye to the main chance, he was nevertheless a man who made a mark on the history of his times.

Syers, Sir Cecil, K.C.M.G., C.V.O. (1903–1981)

A Dominions Office official who was Private Secretary briefly to Stanley Baldwin as Prime Minister and then, from 1937 to 1940, to Neville Chamberlain. He went on to be Deputy High Commissioner in South Africa under Lord Harlech and High Commissioner in Ceylon, 1951–57, ending his career as Secretary of the University Grants Committee. Intelligent, efficient, a trifle jaunty, but an admirable colleague with a well-developed sense of the ridiculous.

Tedder, Marshal of the R.A.F., Arthur, Lord, G.C.B. (1890–1967)

Educated at Whitgift School and Magdalene, Cambridge, he joined the Colonial Service but switched to the Dorsetshire Regiment in 1914 and a year later to the Royal Flying Corps. In the 1930s he played an important part in the vital modernisation of the Royal Air Force. As Air Officer C. in C. of the Desert Air Force in 1943 he was justly praised for his tactics and success; but as Deputy Supreme Commander of OVER-

LORD under Eisenhower, he was given a task less suited to his talents and he did not get on well with some of the army commanders, notably Field Marshal Montgomery. After the war he was Chief of the Air Staff and in 1950–51 Chairman of the British Joint Services Mission in Washington. Good-natured, quick in his reactions, with an unusual, occasionally twisted, sense of humour, he divided his retirement between the assorted occupations of Chancellor of Cambridge University and Chairman of the Standard Motor Company. He was made a peer in 1946.

A month before Churchill's illness at Carthage in 1943, Tedder married Mrs Black, his first, Australian, wife having recently been killed in an air accident. He thereby unwittingly caused consternation to the British representative in Tunisia, Mr Consul General Moneypenny, into whose idyllic garden he had asked leave to have his caravan towed for the wedding night. Unfortunately Mrs Black's estranged naval husband, believing the divorce not to be absolute, arrived at Mr Moneypenny's Consular palace in the middle of the night in search of his wife and sought refuge from a storm. "Go away, go away," cried the distraught Moneypenny, who had put on his dressing-gown to answer the insistent ringing of the doorbell. "You cannot stay here: try the Desert Air Force Headquarters up the road."

Thurso, Archibald Sinclair, 1st Viscount, K.T., C.M.G. (1890–1970)
Head of the Caithness Sinclair clan, he went to Eton and Sandhurst and, although an officer in the Life Guards, became Winston Churchill's second in command of the 6th Royal Scots Fusiliers in 1916. He stayed with Churchill, whom he worshipped, as Personal Secretary at the War Office, 1919–21, and then at the Colonial Office. However, in 1922 he was elected Liberal M.P. for Caithness and Sutherland. When the National Government was formed in 1931, he did not join those Liberals who, under Sir John Simon, remained loyal to Ramsay MacDonald and Stanley Baldwin. After a brief tenure of the Scottish Office, he and his chief, Sir Herbert Samuel, left the National Government on the issue of Free Trade. In 1935 he succeeded Samuel as Leader of the Opposition Liberals, vigorously opposed Chamberlain, Munich and appeasement, declined to bring his party into the Government in September 1939, but became, to his great satisfaction, Churchill's choice as Secretary of State for Air in 1940. He retained that office, in constant controversy with Lord Beaverbrook, till the end of the war. His wife, Mari-

gold, daughter of the notoriously flighty Lady Angela Forbes, had a stronger character than her husband and was a pleasant, if alarmingly determined, woman.

Winant, Hon. John Gilbert (1889–1947)

A gentle, dreamy idealist, whom most men and all women loved, he had been Governor of New Hampshire and looked like Abraham Lincoln. He came to England, with President Roosevelt's full confidence, as a welcome contrast to his defeatist predecessor, Joseph P. Kennedy. He was soon a personal friend of the Churchill family and there was seldom a week-end when he did not go to Chequers. He fell in love with Sarah Churchill, though the relationship was an innocent one. He was an introspective man, unhappily married. In 1947, no longer employed, but renting a house in South Street where he was only happy talking about old times, he suddenly returned to America and committed suicide.

Woolton, Frederick Marquis, 1st Earl of, C.H. (1883–1964)

The successful import of non-politicians into the War Coalition included Sir Andrew Duncan, Lord Leathers, Oliver Lyttelton and P. J. Grigg. As successful as any of them was Lord Woolton, who kept the nation wholesomely fed in spite of the devastation of merchant shipping by U-boats. A man with a strong social conscience, he began his adult life with energetic efforts to lessen the impact of poverty and was warden of a settlement in Liverpool dockland. Unfit for military service, he worked as an economist in the War Office during World War I and was involved in commercial and industrial matters. Almost by accident he joined the Liverpool, Manchester and Birmingham retail chain called Lewis, becoming Managing Director in 1928 and later Chairman. He was by then an important industrialist.

He made a favourable impression on Sir Horace Wilson who persuaded Chamberlain to withdraw him from the job of providing clothing for the army and to make him, in April 1940, Minister of Food. He worked miracles of organisation and became a national figure. In 1943 he was brought into the War Cabinet as Minister of Reconstruction. When Churchill was defeated in 1945, Woolton, who had once been a Fabian, was so angry with the electorate that he joined the Conservative Party, and in 1946 Churchill asked him to be Party Chairman. He so remained until 1955 and was in addition made Lord President in 1951. Though an endearing man, he was vain and inclined to be pompous, as well as sometimes indiscreet; but few served their country better.

GLOSSARY

A.A. = Anti-Aircraft
A.C.2 = Aircraftsman 2nd Class
A.D.C. = Aide de Camp
A.E. = Anthony Eden
A.E.U. = Amalgamated Engineering Union
A.F.H.Q. = Allied Forces Headquarters
A.M. = Air Ministry
A.O.C. = Air Officer Commanding
A.O.C. in C. = Air Officer Commanding in Chief
A.R.P. = Air Raid Precautions
A.T.S. = Auxiliary Territorial Service
A.T.W. = Advanced Training Wing
A.V.M. = Air Vice Marshal

B. 17 = Flying Fortress Aircraft
B. 24 = Liberator Aircraft
B.G.S. = Brigadier, General Staff
B.O.A.C. = British Overseas Airways Corporation

"C" = Brigadier Menzies, head of the Secret Service
C.A.S. = Chief of Air Staff
C.I.G.S. = Chief of Imperial General Staff
C. of E. = Church of England
C.O.S. = Chiefs of Staff
C.W.R. = Central War Room

E-boat = German torpedo boat
E.D.C. = European Defence Community
E.A.M. = Political organisation of Greek Communists
E.F.T.S. = Elementary Flying Training School

E.L.A.S. = Combatant organisation of Greek Communists

F.O. = Foreign Office
F.F.I. = Free From Infection
F.W. 190 = Focke Wulf 190 German aircraft

G.H.Q. = General Headquarters
G.O.C. = General Officer Commanding

H.E. = His Excellency
H.E. bomb = High-Explosive bomb
H.M. = His Majesty
H.M.G. = His Majesty's Government
H.M.S. = His Majesty's Ship
H. of C. = House of Commons

I.C.I. = Imperial Chemical Industries
I.O.U. = I owe you
I.T.W. = Initial Training Wing

JU. 88 = Junkers 88 German aircraft

K.G. = Knight of the Garter
K.T. = Knight of the Thistle

L.A.C. = Leading Aircraftsman
L.C.C. = London County Council

M. and B. = antibiotic drug
M.A. = Master of Arts
M.A.P. = Ministry of Aircraft Production
ME. 109 = Messerschmitt 109 German aircraft
M.F.A. = Minister for Foreign Affairs
M.I.5 = Internal Security Service

M.I.6 = Overseas Intelligence Service
M. of I. = Ministry of Information
M.P. = Member of Parliament

NAAFI = Navy, Army and Air-Force Institutes, an organisation for providing canteens for servicemen
N.C.O. = Non-Commissioned Officer
N.Z. = New Zealand

O.C.T.U. = Officer Cadet Training Unit
O.S.S. = Office of Strategic Services

P.A. = Personal Assistant
P.G. = Paying Guest
P.M. = Prime Minister
P. of W. = Prisoner of War
P.P.S. = Parliamentary Private Secretary
P.Q. = Parliamentary Questions
P.S. = Private Secretary
P.T. = Physical Training
P.W.E. = Political Warfare Executive

R.A.C. = Royal Automobile Club
R.A.F. = Royal Air Force
R.A.F.V.R. = Royal Air Force Volunteer Reserve
R.A.S.C. = Royal Army Service Corps
R.C. = Roman Catholic
R.C.A.F. = Royal Canadian Air Force
R.D.F. = Radio Direction Finding (Radar)
R.M.S. = Royal Mail Steamer
R.N. = Royal Navy
R.N.V.R. = Royal Naval Volunteer Reserve
R.S. class = *Royal Sovereign* class

S.A. = Sturmabteilung
S.A.A.F. = South African Air Force
S.A.S. = Special Air Service
S.A.S.O. = Senior Air Staff Officer

S.F.T.S. = Service Flying Training School
S.H.A.E.F. = Supreme Headquarters Allied Expeditionary Force
S.H.A.P.E. = Supreme Headquarters Allied Powers Europe
S.O.E. = Special Operations Executive
S. of S. = Secretary of State
S.P. = Service Police
S.S. = Schutzstaffel
s.s. = steam ship

T.A.B. = Typhoid anti-bacillus
Tube Alloys = code name for atomic research
T.U.C. = Trades Union Congress
T.R.H. = Their Royal Highnesses

U-boat = Untersee-boot (German submarine)
U.J. = Uncle Joe (Stalin)
U.N.O. = United Nations Organisation
U.N.R.R.A. = United Nations Relief and Rehabilitation Administration
U.X.B. = unexploded bomb

V. 1 = Vergeltungswaffe (German flying bomb)
V. 2 = German rocket
V.C. = Victoria Cross
V.C.I.G.S. = Vice Chief of Imperial General Staff
V.D. = Venereal Disease
V.E. = Victory in Europe
V.R.I. = Victoria Regina et Imperatrix

W.A.A.F. = Women's Auxiliary Air Force
W.O. = War Office
W.V.S. = Women's Voluntary Service

Y.M.C.A. = Young Men's Christian Association

INDEX

(Names marked with an asterisk* are included in the biographical notes. Married names of women mentioned in the text are placed in brackets after the entry, as are titles subsequently conferred when they differ from the original surname. The title Right Honourable for Privy Councillor has been omitted.)

Acheson, Dean, 291, 321–23, 361

Adams, Mr Grantley, 325

Addis, Sir John, 267

Adeane, Michael Lord, 369, 379

Aitken, Hon. Sir Max, 77

Ajax, H.M.S., 175, 177, 181

Alanbrooke, F. M., Viscount (*see* Brooke)

Aldrich, Winthrop, 319, 335, 360, 376

Alexander of Tunis, F. M. Earl*, 58, 75, 82, 89, 133, 174, 177, 179, 180, 182, 199, 241, 244, 246, 285–86, 292–93, 296, 298, 302

Allen, Sir Denis, 345, 347, 354, 357

Altmark, 26

Amery, Leopold*, 97, 165, 232

Ampthill, Margaret, Lady, 98, 153

Anders, General W., 201

André, Gérard, 272, 301

Anzio (Operation SHINGLE), 75, 76, 81, 82, 85, 87, 89, 93, 96, 336

ANVIL, Operation (DRAGOON), 130, 336

Ardennes Offensive, 171, 188, 227

Arnold, Gen. H. H., 173

Astier de la Vigerie, Emanuel, 103

Assheton, Ralph (Lord Clitheroe), 201, 240, 241

Astor of Hever, Gavin, 2nd Lord, 365–67

Astor of Hever, Irene, Lady, 365–67, 368

Athlone, Earl of, and Princess Alice, 142, 145–46

Attlee, Clement, 1st Earl, 60, 73, 103, 104, 130, 141, 192–93, 246, 248–49, 259–62, 296

Attlee, Countess, 103, 262

Auchinleck, F. M. Sir Claude, 248

Audley, Lady (*see* Sarah Oliver)

Avon, 1st Earl of (*see* Anthony Eden)

Avon, Countess of (*see* Clarissa Churchill)

Badminton, 136
Badoglio, Marshal, 99
Baldwin of Bewdley, Stanley, 1st
    Earl, 78, 238
Balfour of Inchrye, Harold, Lord,
    166, 251
Barker, Charles, 134, 142, 240
Baruch, Bernard*, 226, 228,
    292, 317–18, 363
Bean, Miss Lucy, 58
Beaudouin, Louis-René, 363
Beaufort, Duke of, 136
Beaufort, Mary, Duchess of, 136
Beaverbrook, Max, 1st Lord*,
    49, 56, 77–83, 91, 97, 104,
    110, 162, 193, 241, 242,
    248, 251–3, 258, 259, 286,
    324, 329, 330, 333–34, 338,
    375, 386
Bedell Smith, Gen., 81, 322, 360
Bell, Rt. Rev. G., 151
Beneš, Eduard, 80–81, 204
Berlin, Irving, 91
Berlin, Professor Isaiah, 91
Bessborough, Roberte,
    Countess of, 71, 190
Bessborough, Vere, 9th Earl of,
    158, 190
Bevan, Aneurin, 56, 155, 167,
    190, 191, 222
Bevan, Col. John, 156–7, 199
Bevin, Ernest*, 138, 154, 172,
    231, 232, 246, 252, 260,
    262, 268, 272, 276
Bevir, Sir Anthony, 48, 249
Bidault, Georges, 205, 346–47,
    353–54
Blackburne, Very Rev. H. W.,
    135
Bock, F/OR, 86
Boël, Baronne, 208–9

Bonham Carter, Lady Violet, 356
Boothby, Lord, 232
Boyd, Air Vice Marshal, 75
Brabner, Cdr. R., 161, 186, 222
Bracken, Brendan, Viscount*,
    90, 91, 93, 97, 98, 100, 102,
    104, 110, 112, 156, 157,
    159, 191, 215, 231, 242,
    248, 250, 251–52, 259, 286,
    301, 304, 309, 329, 370
Bradley, Gen. Omar, 135, 188,
    322–23
Bridges, Edward, 1st Lord*,
    104, 156–57, 191, 202, 260,
    284
Brook, Sir Norman (Lord
    Normanbrook)*, 283, 287,
    288, 307–8, 329–30, 336,
    345–48, 354, 355, 375
Brooke, Gen. Sir Alan (Viscount
    Alanbrooke)*, 91, 110, 216,
    220
Brown, Ernest, 246
Brownlow, Peregrine, 6th Lord,
    324
Brutinel, Brig. Gen., 258
Buchan, Hon. Alastair, 351, 353
Buchan-Hepburn, Patrick (Lord
    Hailes), 334, 341, 378
Bullit, Captain, 217, 219
Butler of Saffron Walden, Lord
    (Rab)*, 304, 328, 330, 332,
    334–35, 366, 375, 377, 392,
    394
Byroade, Henry, 359

Caccia, Harold, Lord, 357, 397
Cadogan, Hon. Sir Alexander*,
    55, 144, 171, 191
Cairncross, John, 201
Campney, Hon. R. O., 363

Camrose, 1st Viscount*, 283, 329

Caradon, Lord (*see* Sir H. Foot)

Carandini, Signor, 213

Casey, Lord, 53, 288–89

Cazalet, Zara (*see* Mainwaring)

Chamberlain, Neville, 191, 202, 236, 308

Chandos, 1st Viscount (*see* Lyttelton)

Charteris, Ann (*see* O'Neill)

Charteris, Lady (*see* Gay Margesson)

Chartwell, 247, 287, 300, 301, 303, 306, 307, 310, 328–29, 337, 371

Chavasse, Captain Noel, 78–79

Cherwell, Lord (*see* Lindemann)

Chiang Kai-Shek, 320

Churchill, Clarissa (Countess of Avon), 173, 309–10, 333, 378

Churchill, Clementine, Baroness Spencer-, 73–76, 78–79, 81, 84, 85, 96, 103, 107, 108, 111, 112, 131, 133–134, 137, 146, 150, 158, 159, 173, 193, 207–209, 213, 222, 246, 258, 294, 297, 305, 312, 315, 369–70, 379, 386

Churchill, Major John (Jack), 64, 73, 101, 108, 131, 159, 173

Churchill, Mary (Lady Soames), 73, 95, 103, 108, 112, 130, 158, 191, 207–9, 258, 274, 294, 297, 312, 315

Churchill, Lord Randolph, 194

Churchill, Randolph*, 74–76, 82–83, 248, 330, 334, 378, 394

Churchill, Hon. Mrs Randolph, 87, 97, 110

Churchill, Sarah (*see* Oliver)

Churchill, Sir Winston
  sense of humour, 60, 65
  speeches by, 106, 151, 154, 160, 170, 191–92, 194, 254, 293, 303, 309, 327
  and the French, 84, 103, 107, 148, 243, 302, 341, 353
  and Germany, 106, 220–21, 248, 302, 352, 360
  in North Africa, 73–85
  and the fall of Singapore, 46
  and the U.S.A., 162, 226, 227, 316–23
  relations with Stalin (*see under* Stalin *and the* Soviet Union)
  and Chiefs of Staff, 80, 111
  exhaustion of, 94, 95, 105, 172, 246, 303, 311
  and the Labour Party, 112, 137, 293
  confidence in democracy, 94, 137
  liking for young people, 86, 165
  methods of work, 59
  formation of 1951 Government, 285–88
  personal relationship with author, 15, 69, 84, 113, 117, 127, 143, 161, 300

Clark, Kenneth, Lord, 328

Coates, Anthony, 129

Coates, Lady Celia, 129, 163

Coates, Sir Clive, 17

Coates, Sir Robert, 236, 245, 254

Coles, L. A. C., 29, 35

Colville, Lady Adelaide, 214

Colville of Culross, 3rd Viscount, 214, 250
Colville, Lady Cynthia*, 64, 91, 169, 243, 254, 257, 277, 385
Colville, David*, 151, 194
Colville, Hon. George, 71
Colville, Harriet (Bowes Lyon), 312–13, 335, 356
Colville, Lady Joan, 183, 250
Colville, Lady Margaret, 270, 272, 274–75, 278, 283, 294, 297–99, 309, 310–13, 324, 328, 331, 335, 338–41, 356, 368, 379, 385
Colville, Philip*, 103, 105, 129, 217, 221, 309
Colville, Sandy, 380
Coningham, A. M. Sir Arthur ("Mary"), 96–97, 207–9
Cooper, Alfred Duff (1st Viscount Norwich)*, 83–84, 131, 334
Cooper, Lady Diana, 83, 85, 201
Cranborne, Viscount (5th Marquess of Salisbury)*, 100, 104, 106, 173, 296, 298, 328–29, 333, 334, 335, 369–71, 393–94
Cranborne, Elizabeth, Viscountess (Marchioness of Salisbury), 173, 298
Crewe, Marquess of*, 86–87, 112, 130–31, 212, 257
Crewe, Margaret, Marchioness of, 18, 87, 131, 212, 257
Cripps, Hon. Sir Stafford*, 49, 61, 186
Crookshank, Capt. H., 295, 370
Cullinan diamond, 228–29
Cunard, Lady, 272–73

Cunningham, Adm. of the Fleet Sir John, 76, 82, 174, 183
Cunningham of Hyndhope, Adm. of the Fleet, Andrew, Viscount, 108, 148–9
Cuthbert, Sidney, 129

Dalton, Hugh, Lord, 260
Damaskinos, Archbishop, 169, 170, 175–76, 178–180, 186
Daniel, Thomas, 50
Davis, Glenham, 44
Davis, T. B., 44
Deakin, Sir William, 274, 306
De Freitas, Sir Geoffrey, 262
De Guingand, Sir Frederick, 207, 220
De L'Isle, 1st Viscount (see William Sidney)
Derby, Countess of, 18, 19
Derby, 17th Earl of, 18, 19
Devonshire, 10th Duke of, 271
Dewey, Thomas, 320–21
Dickson, F/O Derek, 117–119, 186
Dickson, Marshal of the R.A.F. Sir William, 395–96
Dixon, Sir Pierson, 167, 173, 181, 345
Dodds, Lady Annabel*, 17, 160
Dodds, Major Hugh, 17
Donovan, General William J., 89–90
Dresden, 199, 202
Dulles, John Foster*, 319–21, 347, 350–51, 353, 358–60, 362, 397
Duncan-Sandys, Lord (see Sandys)
Dunglass, Lord (Lord Home of the Hirsel)*, 250, 252, 378, 394

Dunglass, Elizabeth, Lady (Lady Home), 245

Eastwood, Col. Sir Geoffrey, 144, 147
Eccles, 1st Viscount, 338
Eden, Sir Anthony (1st Earl of Avon)*, 19, 65, 103, 104, 107, 132, 144, 170, 172, 173, 179–81, 187, 188, 200, 206, 215, 251, 285, 288, 294, 298, 300, 308, 309, 310, 328, 330, 332, 333, 334, 341, 342, 345, 349–54, 357–62, 364–70, 371, 373–79, 389, 391, 392–94, 395–96
Edinburgh, Prince Philip, Duke of, 269, 271, 276–77, 295–96, 311, 378, 384, 386
Edward VIII (*see* Duke of Windsor)
Egerton, Lady Margaret (*see* Colville)
Eisenhower, Gen. Dwight D.*, 76, 78, 101, 134, 169, 186, 237, 302, 306, 310, 311, 316, 318–21, 324, 333, 334, 335, 336, 341, 348, 349–51, 353, 358–62, 375, 389–91, 396
Elizabeth, Princess (Queen Elizabeth II), 88, 269–72, 274–77, 294–95, 299, 311, 318, 327, 334–35, 342, 355, 377, 378, 379, 384, 385
Elizabeth, the Queen Mother, 301, 385
Ellesmere, John, 5th Earl of (6th Duke of Sutherland), 290

Elphinstone, Hon. Mrs Andrew, 274
Empson, Sir Charles, 358
European Defence Community (E.D.C.), 323, 349, 350, 351–52, 354, 360
Evatt, H. V., 230

Fellowes, Hon. Mrs Reginald, 339–40
Ferguson, Jock, 50
Fielding-Johnson, S/Ldr., 208
Fisher, Most Rev. Geoffrey, 172
Fitzgerald, G. M., 94
Fitzwilliam, 10th Earl, 305
Flaisjer, Yakov, 94, 170
Foot, Hugh (Lord Caradon), 325
Foot, Lady, 325
Forbes, Alastair, 151
Ford, Sir Edward, 294
Forde, F. M., 230
Franks, Oliver, Lord*, 291–92, 308–9
Fraser, Peter, 108–109, 229–230
Freir, Air Vice Marshal M. B., 56, 59, 65
Fulton speech, 289

Gallagher, William, 155, 168, 191, 222
Gannet, Jean-Louis, Marquis de, 208
Garbett, Most Rev. Cyril, 238
Garvin, J. L., 103
Gaselee, Sir Stephen, 16
Gasperi, Signor de, 328
Gaulle, General Charles de*, 68, 84–85, 133, 153, 186, 239, 246

George VI, King, 88, 134, 146, 226, 248, 260, 271–72, 294

George II of Greece, King*, 158, 169–72, 187

Gill, Capt., 217–221

Gilliatt, Elizabeth, 367

Gladwyn, Lord (see Jebb)

Glaoui of Marrakech, 82

Graham, Lady Helen, 191

Grant, Michael, 132

Greece, 167–172, 189, 190, 191, 289

Greenwood, Arthur, 48

Greig, Jean (Mrs Joseph Cooper), 101, 209

Greig, Group Captain Sir Louis, 58, 59

Grigg, Sir P. J.*, 19, 50, 172, 232

Gwynedd, Owen, Viscount (3rd Earl Lloyd George), 385

Haakon VII, King of Norway, 227

Hailes, Lord (see Buchan-Hepburn)

Hamblin, Grace, 73

Harding, F. M. Lord, 174, 183

Harlech, William, 4th Lord*, 48, 53, 54, 56, 57–58, 60, 65, 67

Harlech, Beatrice, Lady, 53, 54, 60

Harriman, Hon. Averell*, 109, 322–23

Harriman, Mrs Averell (see Mrs Randolph Churchill)

Harris, Marshal of the R.A.F. Sir Arthur*, 202–204, 248, 299

Harris, Sir Percy, 155, 222

Harris, William B., 74, 245

Harrow School, 86, 165, 311

Harvie-Watt, Sir George, 101, 210, 214

Haslip, Miss Joan, 198

Head, Antony, 1st Viscount*, 140, 144, 148, 303–4

Henderson, Sir Nicholas*, 151, 188

Henley, Hon. Mrs Anthony, 87, 238

Henriques, Sir Basil, 64

Hill, Mrs Kathleen, 142

Hinchingbrooke, Viscount (Victor Montagu), 99, 136, 151, 233

Hinchingbrooke, Viscountess, 99, 151, 198

Hitler, Adolf, 106, 108, 184, 195, 230, 242

Hollis, Lt. Gen. Sir Leslie*, 74, 76–77, 81, 83, 150, 160, 241

Hollond, H. A., 99

Holmes, Marian (Mrs Spicer), 174, 177

Home of the Hirsel, Lord (see Dunglass)

Home of the Hirsel, Lady (see Dunglass)

Hood, Alexander, 7th Viscount, 163

Hopkins, Harry, 194

Hore-Belisha, Leslie, Lord, 19, 155

Howe, C. D., 362

Hyde, Henry B., 292, 318, 363

Ibn Saud (King Abdul Aziz), 60, 200

Ismay, General Lord ("the Pug")*, 73, 138, 144, 162, 241, 285–86, 290–91, 300, 349, 369

Jacob, Lt. Gen. Sir Ian*, 285–86
Jebb, Gladwyn (Lord Gladwyn), 319, 379
Jowitt, Earl, 155
Junor, Sir John, 331, 333, 391

Kent, Princess Marina, Duchess of, 389
Keppel, Lady Cynthia (Postan), 92
King, W. L. Mackenzie, 146, 147
King George V, H.M.S., 85–86
Kinna, Patrick, 185, 216, 220
Kirkpatrick, Sir Ivone*, 225, 376
Knatchbull-Hugessen, Sir Hughe, 207
Knatchbull-Hugessen, Lady, 207–8
Knowland, Senator Edward, 367–369
Knowsley, 18–19
Korean War, 289, 293, 333, 348

Laithwaite, Sir Gilbert, 111, 191
Lancaster, Sir Osbert, 177, 182
Laniel, D., 346, 351, 355
Lascelles, Sir Alan, 60, 158, 187, 260, 269, 296, 301, 312, 328, 386
Laski, Harold, 260
Lawford, V. G., 146
Laycock, Lt. Gen. Sir Robert, 141, 144, 148
Layton, Elizabeth (Mrs Nel), 173, 182
Leahy, Fleet Admiral, 144, 146
Leathers, Frederick 1st Viscount*, 137, 140, 148, 150, 285
Leeper, Sir Reginald, 174, 175, 176, 182

Leisching, Sir Percival, 35
Lindemann, Professor F. A. (Lord Cherwell)*, 97–98, 107, 132, 137, 139, 140, 162, 173, 188, 198, 231, 248, 253, 285–86, 298, 307, 345, 346, 348, 357, 362, 365, 370, 379
Lisieux, 122, 131
Livingstone, Sir Richard, 151
Llewellyn, J. J., Lord, 110, 153
Lloyd, Geoffrey (Lord Geoffrey-Lloyd)*, 88, 165
Lloyd George, David, 1st Earl, 222, 232
Lloyd, Selwyn (Lord Selwyn-Lloyd)*, 327, 335, 396, 397
Long, Mrs Richard ("Buster"), 142, 149, 154, 238
Longford, 7th Earl of (see Packenham)
Luce, Claire, 319–20, 379
Luce, Harry, 319, 379
Lyttelton Camp, 44–52
Lyttelton, Oliver (1st Viscount Chandos)*, 241, 370

MacArthur, Douglas, 349–49
Macdonald, Malcolm, 141, 147
McGrigor, Adm. of the Fleet Sir Rhoderick, 290, 291
Maclean, Sir Fitzroy*, 82–83, 109
Macmillan, Harold (Earl of Stockton)*, 76, 97, 166, 174, 176, 182, 232, 247, 248, 250, 305, 369, 392, 393, 394, 396
McNeil, Hector, 272, 275, 290, 328

MacVeagh, Lincoln, 179, 182
Madeley Manor, 17, 72, 105, 129, 160
Mainwaring, Zara (Mrs Peter Cazalet), 18, 89, 201, 216
Maitland-Wilson, F. M. Sir Henry ("Jumbo"), 75–76, 82, 97, 109, 162
Makins, Sir Roger (Lord Sherfield)*, 290, 293, 315, 317, 321, 360, 363, 367, 375, 379
Malenkov, Georgi, 333
Margaret, Princess, Countess of Snowdon, 270, 271–72, 273, 328, 386
Margerie, Roland de, 353–54
Margesson, David, 1st Viscount*, 19, 49, 50, 89, 95, 155, 259
Margesson, Gay (Lady Charteris), 16, 89
Margesson, Janet (Mrs Buchanan), 272
Marlborough, Mary Duchess of, 230
Marsh, Sir Edward, 214
Marshall, Gen. of the Army, George C., 322
Martin, Sir John*, 73, 74, 81, 85, 120, 130, 150, 151, 155, 172, 174, 193, 254
Mary, Queen*, 136, 254, 271, 273, 295, 300
Massigli, René, 239, 244, 301
Massigli, Madame Odette, 244, 301
Matthews, H. Freeman, 322–23
Menzies, Sir Robert, 365
Merchant, Livingstone, 359, 360
Mihailovic, Gen. Draga, 82

Mikolajcyk, S., 90, 154
Millard, Sir Guy, 195
Mitchell, Sir Harold, 323
Mollet, Guy, 395
Molotov, V. M.*, 109, 220, 237, 268, 271, 364, 371
Monckton of Brenchley, Walter, 1st Viscount*, 370, 391–92
Montagu, Hon. Mrs (Venetia), 201
Montagu, Lady Elizabeth, 202, 240, 245
Montagu, Judy (Mrs Gendel), 90
Montgomery of Alamein, F. M. Viscount*, 78–79, 99, 105, 134, 154, 171, 187, 188, 209, 216–221, 275, 298, 303–04, 310, 335–36, 396
Moran, 1st Lord*, 74–76, 78–79, 83, 84, 134, 137, 139, 140, 144, 147, 148, 150, 174, 177, 183, 258, 296–97, 328, 335, 345, 346, 355, 357, 364, 365
Morrison of Lambeth, Herbert Lord, 252, 296
Morsehead, Sir Owen, 135–36
Morton, Sir Desmond*, 76, 105, 168, 370
Mossadeq, Muhammed, 309, 310
Mountbatten of Burma, Adm. of the Fleet Earl*, 261, 272, 290, 295–96
Moyne, 1st Lord, 160
Murray, Sergt. E., 338, 340

Nairn, Bryce, 79, 160
Nairn, Margaret, 258
Nasser, Abdel Gamal, 389, 391, 393, 395
Neame, Maj. Gen. Sir Philip, 75

Nixon, Richard, 358, 362
Norfolk, 16th Duke of, 241, 304, 313
Normanbrook, Lord (*see* Brook)
Normanby, Oswald, Marquess of, 190, 331
Norton, Hon. Mrs Richard, 110
Norwich, 1st Viscount (*see* Cooper, Alfred Duff)
Nye, Lt. Gen. Sir Archibald, 260, 362

O'Connor, Lt. Gen. Sir R., 75, 101
Officer, Keith, 55
Oliver, Sarah (Sarah Churchill), 73, 75–85, 103, 158, 159, 200, 228, 310, 318, 334, 385
O'Malley, Sir Owen, 90, 93
O'Neill, Ann, Lady (Mrs Ian Fleming), 158
O'Neill, Shane, 3rd Lord, 160
O'Neill of the Maine, Terence, Lord*, 86, 89, 125–26
Ormsby-Gore, Hon. John, 54, 56
Ossewa Brandwag, 45, 49
Other Club, 288
Otranto, S.S., 21–42
OVERLORD, Operation, 84, 93, 104, 113, 115–127, 135

Pakenham, Hon. Frank (Earl of Longford), 196
Padgate, 17–19
Papandreou, George, 175, 179, 180
Papen, Franz von, 232
Park, A. C. M. Sir Keith, 75
Partsalides, Dimitrios, 179–180
Paul-Boncour, Monsieur, 166
Pearson, Michael, 362

Peck, Sir John*, 59, 88, 187, 240, 259
Peter II, King of Yugoslavia*, 82, 100, 105, 170, 187, 193
Philip, Hill, Higginson Ltd, 379
Pim, Capt. Sir Richard, 82
Pineau, Christian, 395
Pitblado, Sir David, 284, 285, 290, 330, 345, 346, 349, 351
Plastiras, General, 186, 210
Plowden, Lord, 357, 361
Poland, 90, 100, 132–33, 136, 158, 194, 200, 205, 206, 237, 238, 243
Ponsonby, Arthur and Patricia, 223
Ponsonby, Hon. George, 190, 223
Ponsonby, Lady Moyra (Browne), 190, 223, 238
Portal, Jane (Lady Williams of Elvel), 312
Portal of Laverstoke, Viscount*, 87, 95, 157, 160, 227
Portugal, 278
Potts, Anthony, 24, 30, 34
Priestman, John, 345, 354, 355

Quebec Conference (OCTAGON), 134, 141–47
Queen Elizabeth, R.M.S., 363–68, 370, 374
Queen Mary, R.M.S., 137–141, 147–150, 290, 294
Queensberry, 16th Marquess of, 251, 253

Raczynski, Count Edward, 90, 154
Reading, Stella, Marchioness of, 269–70

Reith, John, Lord, 127
Ritchie, Charles, 98
Robert, Archduke, 110, 198, 201, 253
Roberts, Sir Frank, 332, 335, 345, 347, 351, 352
Romilly, Mrs Bertram, 87, 131, 173
Ronald, Sir Nigel, 212
Roosevelt, President Franklin D., 96, 99, 132, 141, 143, 144–146, 188, 199, 200, 227, 232–33, 235, 275
Rosenman, Judge, 231
Rothschild, Anthony de, 64, 161, 244, 273
Rothschild, James de, 222
Rothschild, Victor, 3rd Lord, 90
Roumania, 109, 132, 206, 211, 271
Rowan, Sir Leslie*, 136, 215, 253, 259
Roxburghe, Mary, Duchess of, 18, 244–45, 331
Royal Air Force, author's service in, 15–72, 92, 115–127
Rumbold, Sir Anthony, 357, 361–62, 364–67, 377
Russell, Edwin, 351–53, 361
Russell, Adm. Hon. Sir Guy, 153
Russell, Hon. Leo, 153–54, 158

Saint Laurent, Louis, 362–63, 369
Salazar, Dr Oliveira, 278–79
Salisbury, 5th Marquess of (see Cranborne)
Sandys, Duncan (Lord Duncan-Sandys)*, 103, 155, 159, 160–61, 173, 204–5, 260, 342

Sandys, Mrs Duncan (Diana), 103, 159, 204–5, 342
Sargent, Sir Orme, 205, 235–36, 241
Sawyers, Frank, 172, 174, 185, 216
Schreiner, Judge, 54, 55, 58–59
Scobie, Gen. Sir Ronald, 167, 169, 175, 182, 189
Scott, Sir Robert, 359
Selwyn Lloyd, Lord (see Lloyd)
Seymour, Horatia, 173, 310
Sforza, Count, 167
Sherfield, Lord (see Sir R. Makins)
Shinwell, Lord, 104
Shuckburgh, Sir Evelyn, 345, 347–48, 354
Sidney, Captain William (Viscount De L'Isle)*, 163, 201, 206, 250, 257
Simon, Sir John (1st Viscount), 55, 60
Sinclair, Sir Archibald (1st Viscount Thurso)*, 60, 65, 110, 156, 189, 246
Slessor, Marshal of the R.A.F. Sir John, 174, 183
Slim, F. M. Viscount, 290, 291
Smith, Bedell (see Bedell Smith)
Smuts, F. M. Jan, 50, 53, 59, 61, 68, 107–108, 227–230, 271
Smuts, Jan, 107–108, 227–230
Soames, Lady (see Mary Churchill)
Soames, Christopher, Lord*, 274–75, 288, 292, 298, 301, 308, 310, 315, 318, 320–21, 324, 329, 330, 337, 345–47, 349, 351, 354, 357–60, 366–67, 385, 391

Soames, Jeremy, 310
Somervell, Sir Donald, 104, 165
Sophoulis, Themistocles, 181
Soviet Union, 87, 97, 106, 109,
    132, 136, 156, 194, 211,
    215, 224, 277, 297, 334,
    337, 342, 348, 351
Spaatz, Gen. C., 203
Spain, 161, 255, 278
Spears, Maj.-Gen. Sir Edward,
    299
Speed, Sir Eric, 145
Springer, Professor,
Stalin, Marshal J. V., 88, 92, 96,
    100, 101, 186, 202, 226,
    231, 238, 239, 241, 250,
    306, 310, 322
Standerton, 59, 66
Stanley, Hon. Oliver*, 19, 60,
    262
Stansted Park, 71, 151, 190, 223
Stark, Miss Freya, 169
Stockton, Earl of (see Harold
    Macmillan)
Strang, William, 1st Lord, 221,
    335
Strauss, Admiral, 348
Stuart of Findhorn, James, 1st
    Viscount*, 91, 104, 155,
    171, 201, 215, 241, 252, 378
Stubbs, F/OJ., 117–119, 186
Suez, 389–97
Sutherland, 5th Duke of, 166
Swinton, 1st Earl of*, 155, 369,
    370
Syers, Sir Cecil*, 55, 60

Tedder, Marshal of the R.A.F.
    Lord*, 73–76, 169, 186
Teeling, Sir William, 94
Templer, F. M. Sir Gerald, 293

Thompson, Lt. Cdr. C. R., 73,
    80, 81, 101, 173, 175, 185,
    216
Thurso, 1st Viscount (see Sir A.
    Sinclair)
Tiarks, Henry, 345
Tito, Marshal J. Broz, 82, 109,
    187, 236, 243, 246, 267–68,
    277
Townsend, Group Captain Peter,
    272, 328, 386
Trevelyan, Prof. George, 301
Truman, President Harry S.,
    235, 246, 259, 289, 291,
    310, 316, 322

Valiant, H.M.S., 68, 149
Vander Byl, Mrs Piet, 58, 68
Vian, Adm. Sir Philip, 297
Victor Emanuel III, King of Italy,
    99
Vyshinski, Andrei, 206, 271

Waddell, Helen, 156
Warspite, H.M.S., 116, 149
Whitby, Sir Lionel, 138, 149,
    150
Wilson, Sir Horace, 50, 55
Wilson, F. M. Lord (see Maitland
    Wilson)
Winant, Gilbert*, 96, 162,
    204–5
Windsor, Duchess of, 292, 319,
    386
Windsor, Prince Edward, Duke
    of, 146, 292, 319, 331,
    337
Winstanley, Denys, 166,
    233–34
Winterton, 6th Earl, 155, 194,
    210–11

Women's Voluntary Service,
    269–70
Woodruff, Douglas, 169
Woolton, 1st Earl of*, 91,
    162–63, 285, 301, 308

Wormald, Colonel W. F., 102

Yalta Conference, 195, 199, 200,
    228